# Big Cat

# Big Cat

## & Other Stories

## 2007 - 2019

Gwyneth Jones

NewCon Press
England

First edition, published in the UK April 2019
by NewCon Press

NCP 188 (hardback)
NCP 189 (softback)

10 9 8 7 6 5 4 3 2 1



ISBN:
(hardback) 978-1-912950-15-7
(softback) 978-1-912950-16-4

Cover art and front cover design by Vincent Sammy
Back cover layout by Ian Whates

Edited by Ian Whates
Interior layout by Storm Constantine

# Contents

# Author's Dedication

For Christina Sinclair-Jones

# Big Cat

*When I was writing* Bold As Love *#1 I had a thrilling dream about Fiorinda and Sage, the teenage rock-brat with the dreadful past, and her unlikely best mate. They were in Cornwall, driving across the Moor at night, supposed to be taking Marlon (small boy) to a birthday party, & things had gone wrong, & the very dark and weird future… ahead of them, in my novels, was revealed… by some kind of fateful encounter.*

*Awake, I couldn't remember much, but I rarely, rarely dream about my fictional worlds, so I treasured the fragments, and from time to time, ever since, I've tried to write the story. This is probably the best and last attempt. The dead wolf dragged to the farmhouse door, the rotten little van; the cold & filthy palace, and the trees walking, were all in my dream. Maybe some of the rest, but that's all I'm sure of.*

## How a Message Was Strangely Delivered to the King's Minister

In the dark of dawn the farmer woke, listening for a sound that had invaded his sleep in a dream he could not remember. Was that a fox in the yard? Now he seemed to hear a body being dragged, maybe a big fat goose...? Actual loss of food these days, not just loss on a tight balance sheet, should have impelled him out of bed like a rocket. But he lay still. What about that other, sinister noise? Had it come from outside, or had it been part of his dream—?

It spoke again. A fierce, peremptory, coughing yowl. The farmer and his wife both sat up, bolt upright, as if yanked by puppet-strings.

"What the hell was *that*!" gasped Bel.

Tristan grabbed the shotgun (loaded) which he'd taken to keeping by their bed. "That's *not* a fox…!"

"Don't go down, Tris. Look out of the window!"

Bel groped for the lamp switch on her side. Nothing happened, it was Power Saving hours. Tristan opened a shutter, struggled with the catch of a cranky mullioned window, set deep in two hundred year old stone, and peered out. Damp, cold air washed in. It was early in May, but the weather wasn't very spring-like as yet.

"There's something by the gate. I'm going to see."

The yard was drenched in mist, its contours mysterious. A heap of old tyres loomed, baled straw bulged out of a Dutch barn. Tris lowered his gun. On the concrete track outside the yard gate a blurred, blunt-muzzled animal shape crouched, motionless. Round yellow eyes stared at him boldly – then the beast was gone. Bel came up beside him, holding a big wind-up torch like a club.

"There's nothing wrong with the poultry."

The henhouse birds were barely beginning to stir and cluck. The geese were quiet; the turkeys roosted calmly in their tree in the outdoor run.

"I should have grabbed a camera, not a gun," breathed Tristan. "Did you see it?"

"I didn't see a thing."

"There was a *big* animal on the track. Looking at me."

"There's something there now," said Bel. "On the ground."

Tris handed the shotgun to her and opened the gate cautiously; half afraid his vision was waiting in ambush. Mist swallowed the track, a grey smother in which birdsong glittered faintly. At his feet, slack and rumpled, lay the carcase of a full grown male wolf.

"Oh hell," muttered Tristan, a clean-spoken Cornishman who had never taken to the 'fucks' and 'shits' of the licentious modern world, which had so recently passed away. He stood looking at the body, stirred by awe, unease; and the thrill of the marvellous.

"Is it dead?" said Bel, whose first impulse was that they must protect themselves. "It looks dead. What do we do? Call the vet? Do we move it? Or cover it and leave it there, to preserve the evidence?"

The mist was already brightening. By the time they'd moved the body (the wolf was definitely dead), and decided what to do next, the lowing of impatient cows, and Bob the dairyman's cheery whistle, could be heard from the milking shed.

Later that morning, a couple of hundred miles away, Ax Preston, lead guitarist of the Chosen, and uncrowned Countercultural king of England, sat alone with his friend Sage Pender, perfect master of Techno-Immix, in the Whitehall office of the Minister for Gigs. Both were tall men, Sage remarkably so, and both, in this incongruous setting, had the slightly menacing presence of tamed but powerful animals. Sage wore black, slick dungarees over a terrible old sweatshirt, and the skeleton digital masks that covered his face and hands. The hand-masks disguised several fingers curtailed or absent, destroyed by infant meningitis. The skull, expressive as living flesh, was purely for dandy. Ax was equally, though differently, dressed for another world than this, in a dark red, shot-silk suit, a crisp white shirt and a black string tie. They were discussing Sage's involvement in a guerrilla cognition experiment, which was taking up too much of the Minister's time, and endangering his health.

"You get a warning," said Sage. "If I get mine, I quit. I'll have no option. What's wrong with that?"

"What kind of 'warning'?" his friend asked suspiciously. "Olwen Devi gives you notice?" Olwen, the Counterculture's chief scientist, was running the project.

"Nah, it's personal, an' transient the first time. Your left hand vanishes. You forget the colour words. You can't read—"

"*Fuck*—"

"Hey, calm down. I know what I'm doing."

"Famous last words... What colour's my suit?"

"Hm. Carmine. Violet highlights, interesting bit of chatoyance going on in the reflectance edges, where the sheen's almost silver-gilt. You want the hex triplets?"[1]

"Smartarse. I just don't want you swanning off to a neurological ward, is all, leaving me and Fio drowning in this shit—"

In the years of gathering chaos, as Europe fell apart and the United Kingdom ripped itself to shreds, popular music had become immensely significant – the only politics of a furious generation. Since the formal Dissolution of the Union, England had seen a government move to recruit this Rock and Roll muscle; that ended in a bloody shambles, a huge wave of extreme green violence, up and down the country, and a small Islamic separatist war in Yorkshire. Currently there were thirty thousand active Counterculturals, all ages, all genders, permanently camped like refugees at Rivermead, by the Thames. But the CCM (Countercultural Movement) routinely under-reported 'staybehind' numbers, and there were bigger camps elsewhere. Not to mention god

---

[1] "A hex triplet is a six-digit number... used in computing applications to represent colours" (Wikipedia)

knows how many of the truly lost: incapable of work or play, wandering around with no agenda, no food, no money, no hope. Normal service was not going to be resumed, and one man had taken on the thankless task of holding the land together. But what the hell was to be done?

"I won't desert you, Ax," said Sage. "I will not."

A phone on the desk buzzed, a rare sign of life from one of these Whitehall antiques. Minions in outer offices siphoned off landline calls, and patched them through to personal devices with added surveillance. Whitehall was full of spies, webs of intrigue, conspiracies sprouting like fairy-rings. The same as it ever was, of course; except now the suits had tasted blood.

"It'll be for you," said Sage.

"It's your name on the door."

Sage leaned over and tapped the speaker button. "Hi. You're through to the Minister for Gigs, how can I help?"

"Erm. Could I possibly speak to Mr Pender himself?"

"Go ahead."

"Oh. Is that you, Steve? I didn't recognise your voice."

Stephen was Sage's original name.

"This is my telephone voice. I don't recognise you, either."

"It's Tris, Tris Venning. I hope it's not inconvenient but I thought you'd want to know. It's about the wolves. A wolf is dead, and—"

"Hold on, *dead*? One of my wolves is dead? How did it happen?'

"It's hard to explain."

"Make an attempt."

"Er, well, short version, very early this morning, I found a dead wolf, on the track outside our yard gate, and…"

Sage asked questions (not adequately answered, apparently), and gave orders, with the brisk authority that was his secret weapon, so disconcerting when you've only known the monstrously successful, drug-sodden rockstar reputation. Ax remained silent, feeling disembodied; an eavesdropping ghost. He wondered what the other listeners, Whitehall spooks, were making of this tale… Take photos, analogue if possible. Chill the body, preserve the crime scene. Don't upload anything, and don't contact *Wolfwatch*, not yet.

"Okay… But I was hoping, er, you might send someone?"

"No problem. I'm on my way."

Sage replaced the receiver, the skull frowning ominously.

"You're going to Cornwall?"

"I think, maybe I better… As a gesture of goodwill. Those wolves are kind of my responsibility."

No 'kind of' about it. Sage was quite literally responsible for the Bodmin wolves. He'd forced through their release, in the halcyon days when Dissolution and its anarchies were malign good fun.

"Who's Tris Venning?" said Ax.

"Uster drink with us. Wanted to be an architect, as I remember, but he had to take over the farm. He's a right winger: Countryside Alliance type, not a rural CCM, but he deserves the personal touch. Those wolves are important to people. I should be there and back in a day or two."

"Why not see if Fiorinda wants to join you," suggested Ax. "She could do with a few days out of town."

Fiorinda was the third member of their Triumvirate. She was very young, razor sharp, horribly damaged, and fragile as tempered steel. She'd been friends with Aoxomoxoa for years, but she was now Ax's girlfriend. Sage considered this idea, the skull mask thoughtful.

"I'll ask her. It's time I looked in on Eval, an' all."

Eval Jackson was the former front man of Sage's band, *Axomoxoa and the Heads*, who'd been invalided out. He was hard work, according to the band (Ax had never met the man) but the Heads took turns to spend time with him, down in their old stamping ground.

## How The Queen and Her Knight Came To Cornwall

Smallstones farmyard might look better in summer, or if tastefully draped in snow. On a raw, sunless morning in May it breathed no romance, although the moor's ancient standing stones, hut circles, burial mounds and whatnot, were thick as dragon's teeth around its walls. The windows had fire shutters on the inside; the doorways on the outside, as recommended, but there was far too much flammable material about. Maybe the Vennings thought being friends with Aoxomoxoa was protection enough. Fiorinda Slater, teenage punk diva turned National Icon, picked her way around puddles of redolent slime, and looked in on some boy calves penned in a barn. They nudged her hands for the salt of her palms, heaved warm silage sighs and gazed sorrowfully at her red cowboy boots.

*Soup of the evening, beautiful soup…*[2]

Fiorinda was a devout omnivore, but meeting food that reproached you with big sad eyes got her down a little. The train journey had been appalling, full of cold, dreary unexplained halts that felt as if the world had ended. The weather was no better on Bodmin Moor, but at least the plot had thickened. Fiorinda and Sage had been shown phone photos, including a close up of the alleged victim's ID tattoo. They'd been introduced to the marble slab where the body had lain, and the sheet of smeary old plastic that had been used to transport it. But the body itself was gone. The dead wolf had been stolen!

She crossed the slime archipelago again to join the rest of the party.

Sage and the Vennings, plus their young daughter and a farm worker called Bob, were looking over the yard gate at a stretch of concrete track. Tris Venning held a bundle of wet sacking. The concrete showed no obvious signs of anything special, and the sodden ground on either side was useless, mashed to bits by sheep and cow feet.

"There wasn't much blood," said Tris. "I think it'd been suffocated. It's how big cats kill, I looked it up: they grab the prey's windpipe and choke it. But there were drag marks, muddy drag marks. I covered the track, I didn't think to cover the ground, and then it's rained a bit."

"There's no lock on the old dairy doors," said Tris's wife, Bel. "We didn't think it mattered… We'd told nobody, apart from Tris calling you. Why would anyone steal a dead wolf?"

Bel was older: and a beauty, with creamy white skin, wavy black hair pulled back in a ponytail, and deep, dark eyes. She looked *very* like her husband, Fiorinda noted with curiosity: except his hair was more brown than black, and his looks less classy. Their daughter had the same eyes and bones, too—

"I didn't know a thing about it," said Bob cheerfully. "It's noisy in the milking shed, and I'm on auto, half asleep. First thing I knew was this morning, and Tris saying we'd had a break in—"

No body, no evidence of foul play and no witnesses, thought Fiorinda. This begins to look like carelessness.

Bel Venning caught the National Icon's eye and smiled dubiously.

Without his masks, and with his ruined hands thrust deep into the

---

[2] See "Turtle Soup" Ch. 10 *Alice in Wonderland*, Lewis Carroll.

pockets of a scabrous fleece, Sage looked right for a farmyard, which Fiorinda knew she did not. Her drab waterproof was okay, but under it she was wearing indigo taffeta, and a fluffy orange cardigan: choices she now regretted. Why shouldn't I dress like this? she thought. It's not extravagant, it's charity shop, and I *like* party frocks. Don't judge me, Cornish person. I have wellies, I know mud.

"But we found *something*, this morning," said Bel. "It's up here."

She led the way, leaving the track where a stream came bubbling down from Small Tor, with a footpath beside it. Tris and Sage followed her to the foot of a granite outcrop, where the stream swirled around in a cup of stone, spilling over to soften the black earth. Tris crouched on his heels to remove small stones that secured a square of tarp.

"Have a look. What d'you think?"

Sage and Bel crouched beside him. The clear single print was nearly fourteen centimetres across (Tris had brought a ruler). The central pad was flared at the rear and curved in front, with four deeper, smaller marks set evenly around the forward end… Sage shook his head. "Hard to say. I mean, without calling in an expert, and playing devil's advocate, hard to say you guys didn't search 'panther tracks' an' fake that."

"The light was bad," said Tris, taking no offence. "I grant you that. But I saw what I saw. And I heard what I heard."

"Pity Bel didn't."

"I can't help what I didn't hear," said Bel. "But I saw the dead wolf, and what kills a wolf? Another wolf, maybe, but not like that, leaving hardly a mark. You should know what the moor's like. It's bigger than it looks on the map. It hides things—"

All three looked up, into a landscape transformed by their angle of vision: the stream's cleft a Himalayan gorge, the rough flank of Small Tor desert uplands. A curlew passed overhead and vanished into cloud, drawing a sickle of lonely sound behind it.

"On the phone you said '*she*', Tris. Was that a generic, rural-speak she*?* Or how did you know it was a female big cat?"

"I didn't… It was an impression. It's usually she-cats who leave gifts of mice on the doormat."

"You were expected to *eat* the wolf?"

"More like a good ratter, showing me she'd done the business."

Tristan replaced his tarp, arranging the small stones with stubborn care. "D'you mind if I ask you something, Steve. I mean, er, Sage?"

"Go ahead."

"Why are you guys so down on the numinous?"

Bel sighed.

"The *numinous?* What's that mean?"

"I don't believe in any kind of magic, so-called," said the farmer. "But what if there *are* strange forces behind what's happened to us? Does it all have to be evil and chaos? Couldn't there be a higher power at work?"

"I heard it was the blind greed of global capitalism, myself," said Sage. "Tris, if you want to be a Supernaturalist Pagan that's fine. But if someone killed a wolf, we're worried, and for good reason."

"So am I," said Tristan, avoiding the Minister's eyes.

They stood up. Tall Sage, blue-eyed and yellow-blond without his masks – as some Cornish are, where the Vikings left their mark – towered over Tris and Bel. But Steve Pender had used to be a gangling, antisocial and smack-addicted giant teen, when the Venning couple were already adults: tragic, maybe even noble. Their wary deference was disconcerting him. So were the lies.

"Well, it's a mystery. I don't know what more to say, right now."

"When we found the body was gone we tried to call you, but we couldn't get through—"

"Tha's okay… I'll get onto *Wolfwatch.* Maybe they're missing a wolf an' haven't told anyone. If not, I'll ask them to do a quiet head-count, leaving your version out of it. We'll be at Eval's for now, if you want to tell me anything more. How's he been, anyway?"

Bel shrugged. "Not too good, not too bad; Grace sees most of him. Look, forget that hired wreck. We'll drive you in the Land Rover."

"Nah, save your charge, we're fine."

Fiorinda had stayed on the track with Demzel. The breeze was very cold. Red curls escaped her hood and slapped her around the face; storm-cloud taffeta skirts buffeted her freezing knees, trying to escape into the sky. Demzel, a girl of about twelve, proffered a school notebook with hearts and guitars drawn on the cover, into which she had pasted pictures of Fiorinda. "Will you sign it?"

"Of course I will."

The van had no heating – and no *Wolfwatch* clearance, so the visitors took the long way round, with three cans of stinky highly flammable fluid sloshing at their backs (to avoid them getting stranded). Sage drove. Fiorinda buried her nose in an aged pamphlet she'd found on the bookstall at Paddington: *How Radio Really Works.*

"I saw a chest freezer in the back of their old dairy, with a padlock on it. Why didn't they stick the wolf in there?"

"Maybe they thought you'd prefer your meat fresh… Or didn't want to sacrifice their stash of well-aged supermarket ice cream. What d'you think of the Beast of Bodmin story?"

"Nothing. If there were big cat traces on the moor, even a hint of a population of *one*, I'd never have got the wolves released. I've no idea why they made that up. And why call me on the Whitehall number?"

"To be sure everything was on the record?"

He *can* drive, she thought, covertly watching the tight set of the skull's grin. He has just enough fingers. Obviously it hurts, in this damp and cold, but better say nothing. Don't treat him like a fucking toddler.

"I wondered. Are Tris and Bel brother and sister?"

Long pause. "Not e'xac'ly. Different mothers, each of whom took off years ago. When their evil old bastard dad died he'd left the farm to Tris. Didn't leave Bel a penny and she had nowhere to go. So they got married.

"By common law, I suppose. Was that about twelve years ago?"

"Yeah."

"Does their little girl know?"

The skull's blunt profile, already disapproving, switched to primly affronted. "Tha's a question I never happen to have asked."

"Huh," said Fiorinda. "These *Wuthering Heights* types think I look so weird, but really I'd fit right in… Demzel asked me did I ever see my father. I think she was cadging for his autograph."

Fiorinda's father was an evil old bastard rock god of the worst kind, and the less said about him the better.

The sunken lanes were a high-walled labyrinth, the petrol engine hideously loud. Sage expected fuel-jackers, and wondered which giving-him-hell fist he should use if it came to violence. Why was he unarmed? Because Ax hated guns? Seen enough of them in Yorkshire? Or was it idiotic, *but this is England!* denial? *I'm* the one who's supposed to be out of control around here, fuck it. Not the whole fucking world—

"Why are you reading that, my brat? You hate telecoms."

Fiorinda's phones had died like flies before anyone started sawing the masts down. She lost them, dropped them, they fell in the bath, they were left behind and stolen from dressing rooms; crushed by taxis.

"Know thine enemy."

"Wolves aren't alien. They're coming back all over Europe, of their own accord. The last wolf died in England less than three hundred years ago. Big cats haven't been native to Britain since the Pleistocene."

"Now you sound like a right Green Nazi."

"Don't forget the hygienic disposal of old barren ewes… The last time I was in Cornwall – 'cept when I took you and Ax to Tyller Pystri, and then I looked neither right nor left – I was slaughtering livestock for the cameras. There's bugger all you can do for an industrial dairy cow that hasn't been milked for days and is dying in agony, except kill her fast. And what I saw was *nothing* compared to other counties. Fucking hecatombs, foul huge pits heaving with dead battery chickens—"

"Yeah, yeah," said Fiorinda, eyes on her interesting pamphlet. "Heart of Darkness, Utopian Revolution Goes Straight To Shit As Usual. *Mistah Kurtz, he dead…* Been there. Done that, got the teeshirt. Years ago."

"'Course you have. Okay, I'll stop whinging… Except my Mistah Kurtz isn't dead yet. I'm taking you to meet him."

The little van fought its way up a steep hill in first gear, bucking as if it planned to fall off backwards. Sage stopped at the crest, and there was Bodmin Moor again. They got out into the wind to stare at an excrescence that had appeared in the cusp of the next hills, like an erstwhile London property developers' poster child.

"There it is. What d'you think?"

"Not sure… If your friends are up to something, I don't know what. If their alleged Big Cat incident was an anti-wolves protest, why'd they let the alleged cat meat disappear?"

"They couldn't really kill a wolf, they wouldn't dare. There never was a dead wolf, trust me on that. I meant, that's Eval's place."

"Good. And now I'm driving. You can ride er, shotgun."

Let 'em call me gun crazy, he thought: I'm travelling armed in future.

"I'm not arguing… Listen, d'you hear another engine?"

"Nah," said Fiorinda. "It's the baying of an enormous hound."

"That was Dartmoor."

## Of the Castle of the Stricken King, and What Befell There

Eval's place was a palace: a designer blockhouse set on high, looking south towards the Channel. The Lord of this Manor (he'd bought the title, with the land – he told Fiorinda this immediately) watched over the wastes from a Stephen Hawking-type throne, where he sprawled half-encircled by a wall of screens, including a bank dedicated to *Wolfwatch*, and many expensive satellite feeds. He wore his hair long, with a feathery brown beard; a Guernsey sweater and box-fresh dark blue jeans that drowned his stick-legs. His feet were soft and bare, his hands smooth and pale. He already knew about the big cat and the dead wolf: but refused to reveal his sources, and became incensed when Sage pressed the point—

At least it gave the former bandmates a topic of conversation. Maybe Fiorinda should slip away and interrogate the womenfolk. Since Eval didn't seem to keep any, she interrogated the hall itself. On either side of the screen array, clotted falls of silver and black velvet covered towering picture windows (she sneaked a look behind the curtains, but the rain had begun again, and the view was dismal). Two enormous Steinways stood on a dais, surrounded by keyboards of varying provenance. The inner walls were a slaughter of tropical hardwood; the floor a massacre of coloured marbles. The atmosphere, however, was cold, stale, and laced with domestic stinks. In a great hearth of serpentine stone heaps of bin-bags festered, oozing ichor of rot. More bags cluttered the music stage; fallen over and disgorging old newsprint.

Décor and housekeeping both by *Spinal Tap*, she decided, a judgement on Eval maybe not in the best of taste. Finally she settled on a low-slung leather chair designed purely to be looked at, and hid behind her Radio pamphlet. She was hungry and thirsty, but determined not to snap first. I'll get my crystal set going, and a posse of radio hams will come crackling to the rescue—

Eval was watching her, the whole time.

"Why the fuck would I have a spy camera in Smallstones yard? What d'you think I am, a Peeping Tom?"

"I never said *in* their yard, Ev—"

"But on Tris' manor, you did. *I don't fuckin trespass.*" Eval spun his wheels, turning on Fiorinda. "Hey, Rufus O'Niall's kid. The rock and roll queen of our Counterculture. *How* old are you now? Still jailbait?"

"If you don't know," said Fiorinda, "you can easily find out."

"Am I being offensive? So sorry. I'm only surprised at the boss here taking your dirty dad's leavings."

"I'm not offended. You're probably overdue your happy pills, poor man. Or your potty."

"Drop it, Ev," suggested the Minister. "You're not up to her weight."

Eval stared at the young girl: who stared back with calm grey eyes, icily compassionate, until he gave up and spun his back to her.

"I'll tell you what happened. Simple: some bugger had killed a wolf, ran it down, prob'ly. Bel and Tris took it on themselves to contact you, to ward off any trouble—"

"And then the body disappeared."

"Tris has decided to keep it for the pelt… Only kidding. Some *other* bugger found out, an' made it disappear to keep the death quiet."

The queen and her knight exchanged a glance. "That sounds stupid, but plausible," remarked Sage. "So there *was* a dead wolf? You saw it?"

Eval turned his attention to a red dot that had appeared, crossing the dusk of one of his screens. Someone was coming up the drive on an electric bicycle. "That's our dinner. I better make the tea. Don't offer to help, girlie. *He* knows. I don't let anyone help me in my kitchen." The chair whizzed away, the doors of the hall opening silently before it. Eval's cracked voice came back to them—

"*Sorry,* I don't keep alcohol in the house."

It was the local vicar who'd arrived, a youngish middle-aged woman in a dog collar; clerical black jumper and trousers under her bright red cagoule. The Green Man hung on the silver cross she wore, leaves and tendrils binding his brow, and spilling from his mouth – no surprise there. Half the Church of England seemed to have converted to some variety of Paganism recently (or else fled to the last redoubt of Rome). She'd brought pizza in a padded bag, and was setting out a meal for three in the palace kitchens. Eval sat enthroned off to the side, staring at his kitchen screen array, and sucking on a closed beaker. The vicar greeted Sage with friendly reserve, and looked on Fiorinda with great interest.

"I'm Grace," she said, "Grace Elderflower, Vicar of this parish, and as much of an able-companion as Eval will accept, apart from his bandmates. She offered her hand, which Fiorinda shook. "*Very* pleased to meet you Fiorinda. Sage and I are old friends, of course."

"I won't join you," said Eval, without looking round. "Pizza doesn't suit my digestion. I ordered it for Mr Hands-free."

The room was a temple of shiny gadgets, half the size of the great hall, and overheated instead of cold; but not so smelly. Sage, Fiorinda and the vicar ate pizza and drank tea, while Eval slurped his pap and talked at his screens, saving them from the burden of conversation.

"There's never anything to see on fucking *Wolfwatch*. The pack knows where all the cams are, they're not dumb. The techies show you a bunch of implants moving around, little green fairies on a grid, like *here they all are, everything's fine,* an' mostly that's all you get. Load of crap. But I'd like to see them take that big cat down! I've set up an alert so I won't miss it. Hope you like the pizza kiddie. Course you do, all kiddies like pizza."

"It's okay. The mozzarella's a bit strange."

"What d'you fucking expect, princess? This isn't London."

"I do my best," said the vicar. "But we have no buffalo milk, I'm afraid. I brought Coca Cola tonight though, the genuine article." She produced a two litre bottle, from another padded bag. "It's *so* exciting to meet you, Fiorinda. And I see another Aoxomoxoa teeshirt for me to read!" Grace smiled archly. "It's a hobby of mine. May I ask if you truly believe women are the better form of human beings, Sage?"

"Innately, yeah. Allowing that innate don't always mean expressed."

Sage had left his fleece in the hall. The message on his current terrible teeshirt said *there's no such thing as an alpha male*, with a large Greek letter, *β* for *beta,* centred above this pearl of wisdom.

"Very true… But why would women want to be *better?* For our own protection, I'm sure most of us would prefer to see moral equality."

I could snap your neck, he thought. This minute, with my big ugly bare hands. I happen to know that for sure, because I've done it: recently, in Yorkshire, tho' not to a woman. But the taint's in us all.

"It's just a teeshirt. Really I'm more into gender fluidity, me."

Grace smiled and shook her head. "It's not a joking matter, Sage."

Eval sniggered. "Oooh, yeah! Bring it on! Aoxomoxoa and Mr Cock-Sucking Holier Than Thou Ax Preston! I love it!"

"EVAL! There is NO EXCUSE for that language! And in front of the saviours of our country!"

The invalid subsided, blushing crimson. "Sorry, vicar."

"It's the language of hate. I know you don't mean it. But speak the words of hate, and you'll have hate in your heart!"

Eval hid his eyes. "I'm tired." He was suddenly, visibly trembling.

On the *Wolfwatch* cams, in papery infra-red twilight, the breeze stirred only shadows. "Let's clear out," suggested Fiorinda. "I'll help."

The Reverend Grace knew her way around. She rinsed the tea things, opened a cupboard that held the bins, and briskly cleaned and sorted what she found: transferring food scraps to a compost box. "Sage will put Eval to bed… they all do that when they come down, to give Eval a break from the professionals. He's a competent nurse, despite his hands, and the violence he claims is his essential nature. Please don't blame Eval for the little outburst, by the way. He tires easily, and he's often in pain. Will you help me take the recycling out? We have to carry it to the lane; he won't let the truck through his gates. He goes into fits if I try to clear the great hall, I don't know how he lives with the smell in there."

"What the fuck's gonna become of me? Eval propped his head in his hands and wept. "When the money's worth nothing an' the supplies run out? I'll be a crawling legless beggar."

"You're worn out. Let's get you into bed."

It was Eval Jackson who'd introduced young Steve Pender and his girlfriend to street-drug heroin, long ago. Now Sage was clean, Mary the ex-girlfriend (presumably) was clean, and medical morphine was Eval's inseparable best friend. You'll never be a legless beggar, Ev, he thought. You need health and strength for that life, poor bastard.

His hands had recovered from the cold driving, they were obedient again. He dealt with a sloppy bowel movement (would he have been so keen to take over the band, if he'd known he'd be literally handling the man's shit for years after—?): laid out the bedtime dose, without which Eval would have no rest, and stooped over his former colleague, using his height and muscle with intent. "By the way, say another word to Fiorinda about her dad, and you will get hurt. So help me."

"Fuck off. Why'd you bring her here? You know what I'm like."

"I've got reasons." Sage gently sponged slack, pale flesh, deftly switching warm towels around, and applied the night cream.

"Yeah. Like taking lovely kiddie-tits off our good king Axis."

"Nothen of the sort."

"Like hell. This is embarrassing, but did you know you've come in your pants, when I mentioned her tits? You're dripping all over me."

"You underestimate your own charms, Eval."

Die-hard, first generation Heads fans were convinced that Eval had long since recovered from his injuries. They'd taken the death of Luke Moy, Ev's replacement, who'd succumbed to viral pneumonia, as proof that the lost leader was about to return, and restore the true kingdom... Not so. The reality was this faintly stinking, hot-house room, and this wasted, failing body: prepared for the night, with infinite precaution.

"Yer stupid mask never fools me," gibbered the manikin. "I seen you looking! Ax better watch out, hadn't he? Because *as I should know*, what Steve Pender wants, he takes."

Arranging the supports that would keep blood-pooling and chafing at bay, Sage wondered why Ev tried so hard to annoy (it always happened) the most volatile of his big strong amateur carers. He clung so feebly and tenaciously to life, why take the risk of an inadvertent assisted suicide?

"What I want is for you to get a good night's sleep, mate. But since we're talking, d'you mind telling me where and when you saw the dead wolf? If you *haven't* had a cam installed at Tris and Bel's?"

"It's in Recluse Wood," said Eval, closing his eyes and extending his pallid arm. "I want to go, but they won't take me. Have a look."

A free gift, always suspect. Sage applied the popper gently, and Eval flew off to dreamland. Goodnight, me old hellraiser.

He went down to the great hall, found his fleece and checked the pockets. The analogue film roll was gone. Of course.

The palace guest rooms were small, cold, and expensively but meanly furnished. Fiorinda and her tapestry bag possessed a cupboard-sized fancy bathroom, a water bed with faux-fur trappings and silk sheets; a screen array she couldn't control, automated windows she couldn't open, curtains she couldn't close, and a wall of sliding door closets that she couldn't work out how to slide. The naked windows pleased her for a while – the sky was black and starry – but this entertainment palled. She could see the other occupied guest room, marked on a house plan screen, so she went to visit Sage.

He opened the door to her, skull-masked.

"Wha's up?"

"I need to ask you a couple of things, may I come in?"

"Sure."

Sage's room looked more liveable, if not by much. At least he had a cosy chair; to which he returned, filling it with knotted giant spider limbs. Fiorinda sat on the thick, cream carpet. The skull was looking gloomy.

"Will you tell me what really happened to Eval, now I've met him?"

Eval Jackson's allegations, after his near-fatal accident and the split that followed, had been lurid. The regrouped Heads had been stoical. It *amused* them to behave like perfect gentlemen. Nothing to add. Can't comment. If Ev wants to carry on like that, let him…

The skull curled its non-existent lip. "You were a pre-teen Heads fan. C'me on. What don't you know?"

"It was at the end of the Africa tour, *Mba Kayere*. You were in deepest Uganda, being driven around with an army escort, because of the unrest on the Congo border, or maybe it was Zaire, back then—"

"It was the DRC. I'm not quite old enough for the Zaire period."

"You did a show in a football stadium, then Eval went off on his own to a party with some rich kids who were following the band around. Their jeep crashed. They went off the road into a *rocky gorge,* and the driver, a university student called Archie Migereko, was killed instantly. The other kids had minor injuries, but Eval, who'd been in front with Archie, was *somehow flung clear*, onto rocks, and broke his back—"

"Correct in most details, far as I know or ever found out. And—?"

"I didn't believe the conspiracy crap, it was pathetic. But I've wondered, *why* did you guys let Eval trash you the way he did?"

"Ha. If there wasn't anything in it: yeah, I see the difficulty." The giant spider leaned back, the skull sighed, gazing upward. "It wasn't much of a stadium, we were deep in the sticks. More a football *pitch*, with wooden stands. I remember red beaten earth, forest all around; I remember that having the army with us had got Eval scared, which made him even more annoying. Cracks were opening, as you know. He'd been shit to deal with the whole tour, because he knew he was losing his grip. But the gig was amazing. I was looking out into a huge copper bowl, miles deep. We were in the suburbs of a city, but it felt endless: forest like the black walls encircling the universe, great veils and wisps of light; my Immix beings flowing through the crowd, an' it went on forever… But Eval had been jarring on me. On the way back to our villa I was taking the piss: something weird had happened with my fx, I thought maybe I'd woken actual evil? Ancient, pre-human spirits, just like we have in Cornwall, seeking some empty vessel to devour. We had two UPDF officers, that's the Ugandan army, with us in the van, backing me up enthusiastically... Eval hadn't made himself popular with our escort."

The skull froze blank for a moment: always an eerie effect.

"I think he went with those kids out of bravado, and then you know what happened. He didn't just break his back, he was a mess. He'd have died, if half our soldiers hadn't dutifully been tailing him. As it was, he had battlefield treatment on the spot and a helicopter to Fort Portal, the nearest big city, where the hospital team wanted to put him in an induced coma. Eval was scared, he insisted on an airlift to Cairo instead, and it didn't work out. He got an infection in his spinal fluid he's never been rid of. Had a ton of operations, internal damage that's never really healed. But on the plus side, he was perfectly lucid throughout, and had a project to occupy his mind. So how the fuck could we take that away from him, or crush him with the law, whatever he said—?"

"Okay," said Fiorinda, seeing the beaten copper bowl, miles deep. Black forest like the walls of the universe, and the magician, Aoxomoxoa, leaping and dancing behind his desks... Worlds I will never know.

"I'm not sorry I took his band. It's the luck of the game. But I wish I hadn't been telling him horror stories that night."

"*Mba Kayere,*" murmured Fiorinda, "I am passed over... Is that a genuine Herrero expression, or did Thomas Pynchon invent it?"[3]

"Look it up, brat. Nursery class is over, I'm tired."

"There's one more thing."

"*What?*"

"Am I here because I had a slight panic attack, after a very stressful gig, and you and Ax decided to remove me from view as a liability?"

The skull almost froze again. "Ah, *maybe*—"

"*Bastards.* I knew it. Like you two were in such great mental shape that night, how fucking dare you—!"

"Or maybe not... Fiorinda, I *know* Tris Venning, and Bel. They're not bullshitters. Something made them call me down here, and lie to me, and... It's strange. Your gran's still a practicing witch, isn't she?"

"Practicing con artist."

---

[3] See David Seed: "Pynchon's Herero", Pynchon Notes N.10 https://pynchonnotes.openlibhums.org/articles/abstract/10.16995/pn.436/

"You know what I mean, and you know what the wolves mean, much as I regret the development. We might need your expertise."

Fiorinda stared at him. "I'm going to bed now. Thanks for the story."

"You're welcome… Oh, wait." He groped around his chair. "You have a bedside lamp. Unplug it and stick this in the socket, instead."

She took the eco-tube gadget from him, examining it suspiciously. "Why?"

"The guest suites are wired: Ev likes watching home movies, but that'll stop him. G'night."

Fiorinda skipped breakfast to walk in the palace grounds – and avoid Eval's staff, who had suddenly appeared all over the place, as if they'd been invisible last night. She thought about her father, and how nobody knew what he was. Everybody knew what he'd done to his daughter, of course. But nobody talked about it except prats like Eval. What would a newly-powerful old-time religion choose as the basis of its worship? She could think of hints, from her family background, and from the dreadful dawn of Ax's 'Rock and Roll Reich', that were not encouraging.

How would a dead wolf feature? Bearing in mind that anything known as magic innately doesn't have to make sense.

Sometimes it seemed as if the black confusion, fear and shame of Fiorinda's past had *broken out of her*, on the brink of her escape to fame and fortune, and engulfed the world.

She was still outdoors, shivering among the exotic conifers, when the Reverend Grace appeared. She watched the bicycle whir by, wondering what was up? She hadn't yet seen Sage this morning. Then Eval came out onto the sweeping marble approach to his courts, where a ramp had been hacked through the steps, and left raw; in a different, rugged, life support chair. He started screaming at the vicar: who also seemed upset. Sage appeared, but stayed out of the argument. Fiorinda went to join him.

"What's happening?"

"We're going to Recluse Wood," said Sage. "A local beauty spot. I told Grace, meaning no harm. She says he can't go; Ev says he's going." The skull turned to grin merrily at the vicar. "Never tell Ev a secret. He's always going to blab, an' to the worst person."

"What's at 'Recluse Wood'?"

"Not much. A little valley with twisty oak trees, a wishing well, an' a Victorian ruined gothic hermitage. Oh, an' a dead wolf. So Ev tells me."

"Sounds lovely," said Fiorinda. "Why can't Eval come?"

"There was no secret," said Grace, with hieratic dignity. "I was hoping to escort you both to the wood. It's just not for Eval."

"Don't tell me what I can't do!" screamed Eval.

"It's an all-terrain chair," said Sage. "An' if it *should* get stuck on a root down there, I can carry him. Problem solved."

The invalid wiped his tears with trembling hands, radiant as a child after a successful tantrum.

## The Chapel in the Haunted Wood, and How They Fared There

It took a while to get Eval organised – time that Grace, Fiorinda noticed, spent in finalising arrangements of her own, using Eval's landline. The beauty spot was several miles away by road. It had an empty car park and a modern access path, wide enough for Eval, leading down into the abrupt valley. Eval's driver unlocked the holding bars and lifted the chair, invalid and all, out of the back of his five star luxury tank.

"If you don't mind, vicar," he said. "I'll stay with the vehicle."

"Of course, Bryan," said Grace. "I understand."

Eval glared at her. His cheeks were still flushed, his eyes a little wild. "You'll stay up here to *guard the motor* Bryan. Because *I said so*!"

"Right, sir." Bryan then addressed Sage, in a tone of dignified reproof. "Your grandad wouldn't like you being here, Steve."

Sage's grandfather was a Methodist minister. "Then don't tell him," said the skull. "You've not got any spy cams down there, Ev?"

"I *don't fucking trespass*," snarled Eval, and put the chair in gear.

"I'll jus' give you a little lift over the kerb, sir—"

"Fuck off." The chair scrambled the obstacle: Eval plunged into the opening of the path and swiftly disappeared.

Grace hurried after him calling, "Eval! Be careful!"

"What wouldn't your grandad like?" asked Fiorinda.

"No idea. He's tolerant of wishing wells. No special opinion on dead wolves, far as I'm aware."

Sage strode ahead, to keep in contact with Eval. The Pagan vicar and the Teenage Icon fell into step, footsteps crunching on weedy gravel in a hush that made Fiorinda think of Whitehall: unseen watchers, traps and plots. The oak trees were hunched and gnome-like, with hoary roots like tentacles that clambered over tumbled boulders. Last year's dry leaves still rattled on their branches at first; but soon grew still.

"Why didn't you want Eval to come here?"

"Like too many of my parishioners, he believes in miracles. This is not the place for him. He's so vulnerable, poor man."

"Have there *been* any miracles?"

"Healing miracles are a human *idea*," said the vicar, evasively. "That can be powerfully therapeutic, there is no doubt. For myself, though I'm a believing Supernaturalist Pagan, I claim no spooky powers. No more than the average Cof E pastor can change water into wine!"

"Or blood," murmured Fiorinda.

Grace laughed lightly, and stepped solemnly, eyes bright and head high despite the roughness of the path: one hand clasping the Green Man on his cross. Fiorinda had a sudden intuition. You know about my father, she thought. Or my gran, at least. *That's* why you've been looking so interested, it's not the abused-teen icon appeal, what a pleasant change—

"But this place has some kind of reputation?"

"*Well…*" Grace became confiding. "There never was a hermit, or 'recluse'. However, the holy spring is a much older tradition, and many people believe in it, and resort to it. On very little outward evidence, of course. I'm not expecting a dramatic manifestation today!"

"Nor me," said Fiorinda. "Manifestation of what?"

Grace did not reply. They continued the descent in silence. The path had seen robust use recently, despite the utter demise of the Cornish tourist industry. A quad bike, or maybe two or three, had crushed the fallen branches and encroaching greenery: Eval's chair, which could sometimes be heard whining, ahead of them, would have no trouble with nasty roots. When they reached level ground the path grew wider, and the hermitage stood in sunlight about a hundred metres away, gothic arches rising into a tracery of branches. Behind it, the oaks in their brown tatters scrambled upwards again. In front a few mossy tombs were guarded by ancient-looking yews. Sage was there, standing beside Eval's chair, the former bandmates both contemplating the tasteful attraction in silence.

"Before we go any further," said Grace, "I need to explain: I'm *sure* what happened was an accident. And nobody had any intention of muddying the waters. Tris may have over-reacted, when he called Sage. But we all did what we honestly thought best—"

Fiorinda smiled and nodded, looking around her uneasily. The skull did *sceptical*. "I'm glad to hear it," said Sage. "But no wiser. I don't see a dead wolf yet. Where is it?"

"Under the yews. Go and see."

"You coming along, Ev?"

But the invalid, slumped in his safety harness, had run out of energy. "Nah, too spooky for me. Reckon I'll watch what happens to you guys."

The queen and her knight stepped over a sill of stone, and approached the chapel ruinous. A dog cage had been placed on a table tomb. The greyish, recumbent animal inside was presumably the wolf. Fiorinda was thinking: but *why* is she so thrilled to meet me? A respectable Pagan vicar should want nothing to do with my gran. Let alone my dad… Suddenly Sage stopped dead, having grasped that the heap of rubbish, confused in shadow, right in front of him – as if dropped from a height – was a pile of blood clotted fleece, narrow gaping jaws, and skinny jutting limbs.

"Ah—!" he said. "*Shit.* Of course. "

"What *is* that?" whispered Fiorinda.

"What it looks like. A pile of violently killed dead sheep. *Fuck* it."

"Maybe they're all old, barren ewes?"

"Shut up."

Fiorinda looked behind her: they'd acquired a larger audience. The yokels must have parked their quads elsewhere, walked back in and hidden themselves. Tris and Bel were there, with their daughter and maybe fifteen or twenty others. Two distinct parties: wolf fans and wolficides perhaps? Too many for comfort, and the vicar's hands were moving strangely—

"Keep going," she suggested. "Proceed *slowly* towards the wolf, and hope we think of something on the way."

But it's hard to stretch a hundred metres.

The wolf lay curled nose to tail, a bowl of dog biscuit and another of water beside him. His pelt gleamed wet. Close by the tomb, a silver spire rose, dancing, from a worn stone basin. Fiorinda began to open the cage, and in the same moment knew what Grace up to; realised she was being used, and understood that she was *not* a helpless vessel. Not any more.

She could stop this—

The holy spring chuckled, the world skipped a beat.

Fiorinda opened the cage. The wolf had been given dog biscuit, and a bowl of water, but the body already smelt of decay. Tris and Bel's daughter, Demzel, detached herself from the crowd and ran to Fiorinda's side with a shy smile. Sage checked the tattoo: it matched Tris's phone photo. "I could've done without the fucking mystification," he growled. "But there you go. The world gets stranger..."

*Not if I can help it,* thought Fiorinda.

Demzel stroked the wolf. "I hoped it wouldn't work. It was a creepy idea, anyway. He's properly dead now, isn't he?"

"Absolutely," said Fiorinda. "Trust me."

Eval crossed the clearing, pausing, with a malign grin, to inspect the sheep heap. "Oooh, this looks bad! Told you. That *Wolfwatch* is a fucking fake: total Green Nazi propaganda—"

He turned his chair, looking around. "It's nice here, though. I'm glad I came. Will you give me some water, kiddie? I've got thirst on."

"Sure thing," said Demzel. "But there's no cup."

"Jest a drop. In your little hands, that'll do me."

## Here Begin the Terrors, Here Begin the Marvels

Late that evening Sage drove to Smallstones, the short way. He talked to Bel in the chilly farm office, over a glass of home-brewed ale. Tris was helping Demzel with her homework in the kitchen. Sage wore the masks, for this formal discussion. "One of the wolves turned out to be worrier," he said. "That's not in the contract. Someone dealt with it, unilaterally, and dumped the remains on your doorstep. So you two had to figure something out in a hurry. Just tell me, set my mind at rest. Did you really think the wolf could be brought back to life?"

Bel sipped ale and shook her head. "I tried to kill Dem's rapist bastard father with magic once." She wasn't referring to Tris. "It didn't work. None of that stuff ever works. There is no power."

"Did *anyone*?"

"Hard to say, people believe some funny things these days. I'll promise you one thing: if Grace had succeeded there'd've been trouble. Mayhem, if she'd raised the sacred wolf and not the sheep! But she's all right you know; usually. Just a bit keen. She does a lot of good, and it could've been worse. She could've gone Roman."

"Perish the thought."

"Well... Tris called you, to cover us. We took the wolf to Recluse Wood, and a few of us got onto the vicar, talking-up the magic spring. Grace was easy to persuade, and you guys were great witnesses. It was a *gesture*, Steve, I mean Sage. Nothing more, but it seemed like a gesture worth making. We'd killed a wolf, there are no excuses... and we didn't tell you because you'd've stopped it. We've had the Hard Greens through here once. We don't want that again."

"No."

"I don't mean we're not proud of our wolves. They're a symbol of Ax's England, and the return of Nature. We genuinely *do* want them here. We need the income, part from anything else—"

Silence for a moment or two.

"All clear enough," said Sage. "But why the Beast of Bodmin, for fuck's sake? Nothing to be gained by naming names, I'm fine with that, but was she the best er, scapegoat you could come up with?"

"Oh, no," said Bel. "That was true."

The skull stared at her.

"You know what he's like. Tris was telling the truth, and he sticks to it. A big cat dumped the wolf here. He saw her."

"Okay," said Sage, after another silence. "When we've confirmed ownership of the killed sheep for compensation, all the dead animals get incinerated. I haven't examined the bodies, and I'm not going to, nor is anyone else. I don't see any call for autopsies. Bodmin *Wolfwatch* needs a shake up, which will happen. Meanwhile, if the Commons Council, of which you are a member, finds popular support for leaving the rest of the pack on the moor, that's probably the best outcome, as you've already decided. And we'll see how it goes. If you need to talk again I'm at Ev's for now. Will that do?"

"Yes... How d'you find him, by the way?"

Sage shook his head. "He's still losing weight; and getting weaker, I think." Eval's bandmates saw his current care notes, but had no contact with his medical team. "But his mood's good: he enjoyed his excursion."

"I'll see if we can do more of that," offered Bel. "If he'll let us."

"Thanks."

Finding the great hall unoccupied when Sage was supervising the cremation-fest the next day, Fiorinda tried the Steinways. One was a tragic case, the other in perfect tune. Eval came into the vast room while she was playing.

"D'you know, *The Banks Of Allan Water,* kiddie?"

"I think so..." She played the tender little folksong, decided she liked it and spun it out in variations, while the stricken king sat smiling.

"Would yer like a piano? You c'n have that one for free, I shan't be needing it, I'm planning to get out more."

"Not really. I prefer my own."

"Suit yourself, cheeky kid."

He spun around: the hall doors opened before him, and he was gone.

Early on the third morning, in a cold, persistent rain, they escaped: taking the short road again; Fiorinda driving. At the crossroads below Small Tor, he asked her to stop.

"You want to say goodbye to your friends?"

"Nah. That's done. There's just something I need to check."

The dawn flit had been unnecessary, they had hours to fill before the *relatively* good connection they might find at Bodmin Parkway.

"No problem. I'll read my improving pamphlet."

"Won't be long."

Jog trot, hood of his drab fleece well down, he gave the buildings of Smallstones farm a wide berth: avoiding horizons, using the landscape the way they'd learned to in Yorkshire, when he and Ax were fighting the Islamics. He approached the pool where he'd been shown the panther print from the opposite side of the Tor, and hunkered down, parting the cotton sedge. The tarp was still there. He moved Tris's stones, peeled it back, and the skull's grin broadened. Sage had looked into the Beast of Bodmin story rather carefully once – two years ago, in another world.

Nice try, Bel, but that's an *enormous* big cat.

Whereas we're thinking a small, probably female, melanistic leopard. *If* we were ever thinking anything...

He replaced the tarp and the stones and looked up, turning slowly to recover his line of sight from the last time. There: the hint that had caught his eye. He climbed, and found what he'd glimpsed, or guessed at, the other morning – a smaller pugmark, not half so perfect, on a near-vertical patch of shale and mud. He stared at it, and then set off again – circling the Tor as he climbed, but finding no other traces – until he reached a field of boulders under a sheer face of granite, where water, braided white, fell down the dark rock. A black slot at the top, masked by birch scrub. He turned his back to the slab and leaned there, tucking his fists away. *What'll I do?* he wondered.

*Had* he seen the dead wolf scrabbling to its feet? The vicar on her knees, holding up her hands like a born-again prophet? The little crowd dumbstruck and the yew trees walking? It was there, and then it wasn't. It happened, and then it didn't; had never been—

Was that my neurological warning? Do I have to quit the experiment?

Or was there another explanation?

Maybe he should've asked Grace. The vicar had turned up at Eval's again, after the trip to Recluse Wood: bringing a stew with dumplings and a medicalised chocolate drink in her padded bags. Eval had already been put to bed, tired out. Sage and Fiorinda had eaten pizza (a food they both despised) the night before, and felt their work was done. But the vicar hadn't seemed to notice that her treats were spurned. She was *distrait*; she kept peering around, as if she'd mislaid something. And sneaking little scared looks at Fiorinda. Unless that also was Sage's imagination…

*Fiorinda* – Sweetheart, I love you. I want to protect you. Won't you please, *please* tell me what's going on?

*Sweetheart* – maybe not. *I want to protect you*; unadvisable. *I love you*, out of the question… But there was no right way to approach that conversation. So, what? Talk to Ax about the issue?

Tried that, it doesn't work.

Better just wait and see.

He tipped his head back, blinking rain from his lashes. "If by chance you're up there…" he said, aloud but quietly. "Thanks for killing the worrier, you did right an' I'm sorry I've brought trouble on you. I hope you're okay to leave the rest of my pack alone?"

The embodiment of Nature's return made no response, except that a pebble dropped from overhead, tapped him on the cheekbone, and went dancing away, in tiny silver spurts, down the soaking wet hill.

Sage laughed, set off leaping after it to the foot of the Tor, and jogged back to the crossroads. Fiorinda had exhausted her pamphlet and was pondering other areas of study. *Electricity Easily Explained* would be a good one. Maybe I could take my GCSEs, *and deep down thinking I had to do it, but no more like that, I must go to ground, hide, hide…* Sage knocked on her window, and shook himself before clambering in a mess of long limbs into the passenger seat. He wiped rain off his face and dragged skeletal hands through his hair, spattering her freely. "What was it you said to Grace, Fiorinda? Just before we left the miraculous wood?"

"I told her resurrection is an incredibly stupid idea, that's all."

"Haha, yeah. Even Jesus came back weird."

And they returned to London; to the man they both loved.

In her den on Small Tor the big cat licked her cub, purring. She was nearly eighteen years old: a very wise old lady, who'd recently returned to the moor after a sojourn in Scotland with her mate, and awhile spent in Birmingham, among humans; eating well on urban foxes. They've changed, she thought. We might even be able to live with them now… If they can just get through this part.

# Stella And the Adventurous Roots

*I wrote this story for an anthology of botanical science fiction, commissioned by an outfit called Wayward Plants, but I had not done my homework. "Wayward" is a very respectable concern, and they didn't care for my ragged-trousered guerrilla gardeners. They also found one strand of this alien-seed in Deptford story distasteful. So I got paid, and the story remained unpublished, status undefined... But I like it.*

Lulu had walked her daughter Stella and Stella's friend Joseph along Creek Road every school day since the inseparables started nursery school. The derelict service station they had to pass had always fascinated the children, but lately this amenity had become even more interesting. A band of Guerrilla Gardeners – responsible for the unilateral appearance of flower tubs and tree pits in the streets nearby – had moved in. The holding company had no objection, as long as the Guerrillas cleared out when the developers could start work (the underground fuel tanks still had to be removed, a complex process). The Council didn't object either, on the same terms. Lulu, currently a Project Worker with responsibility for urban plant health, had a professional interest.

One day, when she'd collected the children from school, she introduced herself at the cheerfully-decorated, makeshift booth where the gardeners had their office; under a sign that read 'Pop-Up Garden. Please Pop-in'. The Guerrilla on duty got someone to show the visitors around.

The gardeners were clearing plots by tearing out buddleia growth and herbaceous weeds: which was fine. There wasn't much else going on as yet, but Lulu made a note of three wind-sown young ash trees, clean and sound she was glad to see, that might need replanting later, and checked the donations that had been coming in: bundled seed-packets; a pallet of winter flowering pansies from a local supermarket; bags of spring bulbs, fragile vegetable seedlings, sacks of topsoil… A huddle of discarded houseplants, including a huge, apologetic-looking philodendron, looked like stray dogs in a pen: sad, and slightly suspect.

Most of the plants in this last category simply weren't going to make it outdoors, but Lulu had a good look anyway, in case something alien and invasive was being let loose.

Joseph stuck close to Lulu, keeping an uneasy eye on the Guerrilla who escorted them. He was just three and a half, a bright but nervous child, and he was afraid that gorillas had guns. Stella, Lulu's daughter was nearly four, and enterprising. She embarked on her own inspection, an imaginary clipboard in one hand, a real pen in the other. She spotted some people in gardening clothes brewing up over a portable stove, and interrogated them.

'Will you be sad when the builders come and take everything away?"

"Nah!" said a lady in overalls and wellies. "We're nomads, here today, gone tomorrow. There's always another site."

"She's lying," said a tall girl with dark braids, in a rainbow striped jumper. "We're *fierce guerrillas* with a desperate cause. Our aim is to spread the greening of London, until we take over the whole city. We mostly work at night, secretly. You can join up, if you like."

"It's going to be housing," said an old man with a gingery white beard. "We might convince the developers to let us do the landscaping; make their project look good and Green. It's happened."

He offered Stella a chocolate biscuit, but her hands were full. There was nowhere to put her clipboard, and she didn't want to let go of her pen. She got confused, and the tall girl laughed. Stella walked away, annoyed, without a biscuit.

She peered into old tyres filled with earth, and stared at heaps of fuel-stained concrete shards. A Royal Borough Parks van had arrived, with a donation of leaf mould. Stella sidled closer, peering inside the big bags. The leaves were soggy and dark, like incredibly muddy washing. "*No-mads*," she muttered. "*NO*-mads! *GO*-rillas and *NO*-mads!" She snarled and curled her fingers like a fierce gorilla.

The Parks agency worker grinned at her, but next moment forgot about the child. Stella slipped through the site's gates, onto the pavement.

People were passing, heads down and shoulders hunched against the wind and the coming rain; eyes fixed on phone screens. Stella stomped to and fro with her own head down, pretending to text, in front of the gates. Not a step further: or she knew there'd be trouble. But there were some bright things scattered among the feet of the passers-by: shiny, coppery discs, swollen in the middle, crumpled around the edges. To Stella they looked like the chocolate money she'd found in the toe of her Christmas stocking. She bent down – but there was a man on the other side of the busy road, watching her. She jerked her hand back. She shouldn't be out here, and she wasn't allowed to pick things up from the pavement. The coin rolled away, to vanish into a dark fissure in the shattered concrete of the forecourt: the man went on staring. Defiantly Stella grabbed another piece of chocolate money, stuffed it in her coat pocket, and darted back into the Guerrilla Garden, before she was missed.

Stella had her tea with Joseph's family while Mummy worked, and later a snack watching cartoon television with her mother, as usual on a school day. She only remembered her coin at bedtime. When her mother had kissed her goodnight she waited a few minutes, to be on the safe side – then leapt out of bed, retrieved her contraband, and dived back under the duvet, grabbing her rabbit nightlight on the way.

It wasn't chocolate. The shiny wrapper didn't come off. Deeply disappointed, Stella spent a while picking at the crumpled edges, to no avail. Whatever was inside was out of reach: like the inside of a big bean, before you soaked it and it split open and grew...

Stella knew about plants from her mother, and she'd grown beans at school. Suddenly she realised what she'd found. It was a *seed*. She had found it, nobody else. She would grow it, in secret, and not let Mummy help. She would be a GO-rilla NO-mad gardener! Burning with pride, she fell asleep with the strange seed clutched in her hand.

Stella and her mother lived in Linden House, a cosy block of ex-local authority flats close to Deptford Creek. The block had trees and lawns, but no tenants' gardens: Lulu grew flowers and vegetables on their tiny balcony. Next day, after school, Stella sneakily raided the gardening supplies. She poked a little hole in the bottom of a clean yoghurt pot, took dry soil from a bin. Setting the bean on some of the soil she covered it with the rest: carefully smoothed out the scooped place, so Mummy wouldn't know, and hid the pot behind a photo of her daddy and the new baby; on her own windowsill, where she could look at it often.

The missing ingredient was water, but Stella knew from experience that water and secrecy don't mix. She decided the seed would be okay. She could put it out in the rain, when Mummy wasn't looking. Lulu, drowning in screens of Project Worker paperwork, didn't notice a thing.

Ÿ

London was pelted with cold, torrential rain all that week, but Stella forgot to give her pot a shower. Nevertheless, a whiteish, pointed shoot appeared. It swiftly got bigger. Stella thought her secret plant might be a cactus, because she could see tiny, tiny spines. But the shoot didn't turn green, and this worried her. Plants have to be green. She looked at pictures, on her tablet and in her mummy's books, and worked out what was wrong. The white shoot wasn't a shoot. It was a pale, hairy, groping little *root.* Plants can't see, but Stella knew they can sense things. They know up from down and light from darkness; they seek food and water and defend themselves against enemies. But this plant had no sense.

Unsure – because her mother had told her plants can *think*, in their own way – where the limits were, she held up the tablet screen and tried to show her seedling the right ideas. "Roots come first," she said. "And roots go down! *Then* comes the shoot, and the shoot goes up!"

The plant, like a badly behaved baby, took no notice.

"DOWN!" she yelled, stabbing down with her finger and losing her temper. "You have to go *down*! Or else I'm going to get ANNOYED!"

"Stella?" called Mummy, from the living room. "Why are you shouting? I'm trying to work—"

The upside-down root had broken out of the soil on a Monday. The Saturday after that Lulu was working at the University, and Stella spent the day with her daddy's new family. When Daddy dropped her off in the afternoon Lulu was still busy, so he left Stella in the Plant Biology department, where she had friends. "Tell Lu I think she's getting a cold," he said. "She seems a bit mopey. Nothing serious."

Stella was consumed with anxiety about her plant. She'd hardly been able to enjoy being at Daddy's house, or the glorious baby. She couldn't think of anything but that mad root. She found her mother's friend Adam working at his computer, and stared until she'd got his attention.

"Adam, is there any such thing as roots that grow into the air?"

"Yeah," said Adam, kindly. He knew Stella, and never baby-talked her (because he didn't know how). "There are aerial roots; air roots. It often happens with *epiphytes*, plants that grow on other plants. Or grow on trees, like rainforest orchids."

"Is it wrong?"

"No, it's just different. They're also called *adventitious* roots, because they can grow from an unusual site on the plant; a leaf node, maybe."

"Thank you! Thank you *very* much. That's wonderful news!"

"You're a funny little sprout," said Adam. "Where's your mum?"

"Coming soon," said Stella. "Can I look at some pictures of roots in the air? Will you show me?"

She was extremely relieved. Her plant wasn't mad, it was adventurous.

When she got home and checked the yoghurt pot, for a moment she was more worried than ever. The root had disappeared. She lifted the pot, to see if it had turned in the normal direction, and was poking out of the bottom (it had been quite tall). There was no sign of it, but she felt a tug, and caught a glint of something like a sunbeam, rising from the soil. The root had not reformed its behaviour. It was still heading *up*, but it had turned see-through, like a piece of Sellotape, and sneaked into the crack between Stella's window-frame and the wall. Thoughtfully, she set the pot back in its hiding place, arranging her curtains over the place for added security. She didn't see how a piece of Sellotape could do any harm. And her plant might yet turn into a beautiful, gorilla orchid.

Lulu, too busy to be a pernickety housekeeper, found the invisible plant in the end. But she loved Stella's odd passions, and always tried to respect them. She left the yoghurt pot of dry, withered soil undisturbed, and spent the next many weeks cleaning around it, if ever she got round to wiping the windowsills.

Ÿ

The man who had watched Stella, the morning when she found her seed, was not a random stranger. He'd had his eye on the chubby little girl with the big brown eyes for a while, and his interest was not healthy. Anticipation, caution and delay were this man's watchwords, but he'd seen his little darling pick something up, and everything about Stella fascinated him. He'd crossed the road, as soon as she was back with her mum, and spotted the gleaming discs. They were melting away like chocolate in the rain, but one lay on dry pavement, in a bus shelter. He'd picked it up and taken it home.

He didn't do anything with his trophy for a while. One evening, when he'd cautiously followed the two children and the mother home from school – and been rewarded by a glimpse of his chosen one securely located, on the balcony of a third floor flat – he recalled the coin: his strongest connection with Stella. He took a sharp knife, put the disc on a saucer, and anointed it with his blood.

*Go and catch a falling star*, he murmured. *Get with child a mandrake root…* There was something magical going on, he was sure of that.

Rainwater had melted these things. Blood had no effect at first. When he'd repeated the ritual over several days, and a dry rusty crust had accumulated around the disc, it split open. Something came out, and fed on the rich strange fare, and grew; and grew.

The man moved it to an old goldfish tank and went on feeding it. It was always hungry, but always struggled to avoid contact with the blood until it had dried (which led to some contortions, after a while). This behaviour, seeming like a delight in deferred gratification, rather thrilled the man. He felt he'd found a kindred spirit.

Ÿ

Lulu and Stella often popped-in at the Pop-Up Garden, on the way to school, or on a weekend afternoon, through that spring and summer. There were no urban plant health issues, the Guerrilla Gardeners knew what they were doing. It was just a nice place to take the children.

Flowers and vegetables flourished, in old tyres, in railway-sleeper raised beds, and on well-mulched, shallow-dug contaminated ground. The temporary fence along the pavement blossomed in colourful banners, messages, drawings and photos; the local free-sheet ran a feature. A primary school started visiting. Office workers and pensioners, including Joseph's Nan and grandad, became volunteers. Lulu's short contract was coming to an end, but she began to hope that the Pop-Up Garden might endure for a while; maybe even for a year or two.

It was not to be. A Fuel Tank Services company turned up at last: did a survey and set a date for the removal of the tanks. At the height of the summer, just before the raspberries were ripe, the Guerrillas had notice to quit. The fence broke out in messages of mourning and regret. Some locals vowed to fight: but the guerrilla cadre rejected these plans. Keep smiling and move on was their motto. "There's always another garden", said Sid, the old man with the gingery white beard, a retired architect in private life. "Never pick a fight you can't win."

On a Saturday afternoon in July, Lulu came along to help with the dismantling. There were seeds to be collected, prepared, and packaged for distribution; vegetables to be harvested; perennials to be rehomed.

The two children were with her, as usual.

Stella had never said so, but the Pop-Up Garden made her uneasy. Maybe a guilty association had lodged in her mind since the day the tall girl laughed at her, and she'd gone out of the gates when she shouldn't. While Joseph, more independent now, settled happily to digging holes, looking for the fuel tanks, Stella dragged a stick along the fence, so it rattled – up and down, her back to the beds of flowers and vegetables. Joseph's Nan, a semi-retired theatre nurse called Judith, and a Pop-Up regular, wanted to show Lulu a strange weed she'd found when she was harvesting her onions: a whiteish, bristly underground growth with a stranglehold on the fattest bulbs.

"Put a spade through it," said Lulu.

"Have a go yourself. It's tough as nails. Worse than bindweed."

Lulu had a go. The root was *very* tough. "Secateurs," she decided.

Judith grinned, and slapped her own pair into Lulu's palm.

"*Secateurs*, doctor."

But the blades made no impression. The root, or growth, was made up of many, many glassy, transparent strands, invincible in their collective strength. You'd have to separate them, and chop them one by one… Lulu recalled her mild concern that the Pop-Up might harbour something noxious.

"D'you mind if I dig this stuff right out?"

"Good luck," said Joseph's Nan. "I couldn't find the end of it."

Lulu couldn't find the end of it either. Mystified, she tracked the glassy rope, like a vein of metal in soft rock. Where the hell was this stuff coming from? Where was the plant, if this was a root? She straightened her back and looked around. The glass rope was heading for Frankenstein's Monster: a painted scaffold, built from forecourt debris, that served as a "sunny wall" for the dilapidated philodendron, a couple of rescue tree ferns, and two or three scraggy palms.

*Philodendron sellorum*, notorious secret sprawler, had done well. It looked happy as a clam: a glossy green Ent, presiding over the other hardy tropicals as if in some humid forest glade in its native Argentina.

"Damn it," muttered Lulu. She'd found the Philly a Public Spaces home, but this weird root development was a difficulty. How much of it could the plant afford to lose? The rope reached Frankenstein, took a right-angled turn and rose, wrapping itself around the Philly's main trunk – almost invisible, except where the sun caught it. The plant that loves trees was not guilty. On the contrary; it was getting loved to death by the mysterious alien. Lulu poked and tugged until she shifted the rope a little, and was relieve to find there were no suckers actually digging into the Philly's tissue. It seemed to be using the big stem only for support. But *where was the plant?*

"What's my devil root getting up to now?"

Joseph's Nan had followed her, intrigued.

"I don't know… yet. The plant must be hidden in the Philly's crown. I need a good knife."

"Scalpel, doctor," said Judith, slapping down her own pruning knife.

The knife was heavy and sharp, but made no impression at all. "I think I need to talk to someone," said Lulu, taking out her phone. "See if we can identify this thing."

Ÿ

On the pavement outside the fence there was a man looking at the pictures and messages. He and Stella walked up and down together, keeping step. It became a silent game. The man smiled. Stella, with a firm hold on her stick, and safely inside where she ought to be, smiled back.

"Hallo, Stella," said the man. "A friend of yours is staying with me."

The little girl shook her head. "Not my friend. You don't know me."

"Yes I do, Stella. You live on the floor above your friend Joseph, in Linden House. Your mum's called Lulu. She works for the Parks, and your dad drives a red Passat."

Every word of this was right, including the red car, though Stella wasn't sure about the *Passat.* "How do you know all that?"

"I told you. We've got friends in common. I know all about you."

They talked for a few minutes. It was okay, because Stella stayed on her own side of the fence, and the man was not a stranger. Meanwhile Lulu was having an unsatisfactory conversation with her boss, who stung Lulu's feelings by saying she would arrange for "an expert" to have a look at this possible noxious pest species.

Joseph stayed behind with his nan and grandad: Lulu and Stella walked home. Lulu, in a gloomy mood, stopped at the Deptford border to stare over the railings. It was low tide. The river Ravensbourne, here known as Deptford Creek, lay like a sluggish, replete, eel-coloured snake between its mudflats; in no hurry to join the Thames. I *am* an expert, she thought. I just don't have the letters after my name. It was taking her so long to finish her doctorate… The day was humid; news headlines had been romancing all week about a tropical future. Lulu imagined West African swamp lilies, rising from the London ooze. As she looked east towards the Isle of Dogs, present reality slipped for a moment. She saw a drowned world, a luminous green future: the fantastical spires and towers of the city, rising mysterious, from rainforest canopy—

*Would it be so terrible?* she murmured.

"Would it be so terrible?" growled a small voice, "If I went to see Daddy and Emmie on a few *more* Saturdays?" Stella was kicking the toes of her boots, one by one, bitterly against the railings.

Lulu's ex was married, and the couple had a new baby. Lulu found this depressing. She struggled with thoughts like, *why didn't* I *think of us getting married?* And *what was wrong with my Stella, if he likes little babies?* But Stella, inevitably, was besotted with the new arrival, the most desirable cuddly toy in the world, and pined between visits—

"Of course it wouldn't be terrible, my Star. I'll see what I can fix up."

"*I'll* see what I can fix up," muttered Stella, rebellious. She didn't have to wait for Mummy's unreliable "I'll see". She had a friend.

Ÿ

For a while, when the adventurous root had disappeared into the crack behind the window frame, Stella had stopped, turned around and looked up, every time she left Linden House – thinking of Adam's pictures of rainforest orchids, and hoping to see a wonderful flower spreading its petals in the sky. But nothing happened, so she stopped looking, and only remembered the invisible plant when her mother suggested throwing the yoghurt pot of dry soil away, an idea Stella furiously rejected.

One day in the school holidays the children were playing in Stella's corridor, waiting for Lulu: who had work to finish and would not let them go outdoors until she could sit with them. Stella kept running to the windows. Her friend from the Guerrilla Garden had said he would drop by, when she was playing out. He wanted to tell her a secret. He knew Stella was clever at hiding, and that Mummy wasn't looking *all* the time.

An orange van pulled up, and a man in matching overalls got out. When he appeared on the third floor corridor, tramping heavily out of the stairwell doors, Joseph retreated to the safety of Lulu's flat.

Stella ran up to the stranger in case it was her friend in disguise. It was a different person: bigger and fatter, with a browner face, but she stayed to find out what was going on. Old Mr Lee in the corner flat came out and unlocked the roof-space ladder from the wall. The orange overall man climbed up, opened the hatch, and disappeared into that unknown space.

Mr Lee's nice wife had died. He'd been sad and cross ever since, and Stella was not supposed to pester him, but she thought it was okay to ask what was happening.

"*Wasps*," said Mr Lee. "They have a nest up there."

"Is the man going to kill them?"

"He has to look and see. I tell him, you think I don't know what a wasp nest looks like? A big round grey lump! They have to be smoked out, quickly, by Pest Control. You like to see a wasp nest smoked, Stella?"

Stella hated wasps. She wasn't *afraid* of them, but she'd heard that they sometimes chased children and stung them to death. She ran to tell her mother. But when Lulu came out, dragged by Joseph, who did want to see the great event, there was nothing going on. Just Mr Lee, talking to a man in orange overalls.

"It's definitely not a wasp nest," said the man.

"What else could it be?"

"All I know is it's not an insect nest. It's rock solid. If you're worried, get it looked at by Building Maintenance. It's not my department."

"But I hear them buzzing! They keep me awake at night!"

"I didn't hear anything, but maybe it's different at night, less other noise. Could be something to do with the new cabling you've got up there. As I say, better have it looked at, but not by me."

"*Cables*? I don't know anything about new cables!"

Lulu, although she was stopping the children from playing on the lawns, stayed to talk, and Joseph stayed with her. Stella retired, feeling uneasy. The mad root, forgotten for so long, had jumped into her mind.

She went to her room, shut the door and checked the yogurt pot. It was still behind the curtain, and she could still feel something invisible growing in it, when she tugged. Had her plant got up into the roof? Was it making grey lumps? Was it keeping grown-ups awake? Maybe she ought to own up, before there was *more* trouble.

But Mr Lee got upset about strange things, since his wife died, and usually they weren't true, or just something somebody could easily fix. She decided it would be all right to say nothing.

Ÿ

Stella's friend, the man at the fence, loved delay and anticipation, but all things must pass. He prepared himself, magically and materially, and planned the next moves in every detail. The little ones never put it into words, but he knew Stella was ready, too. Watching and waiting, he thought of nothing else but that perfect moment when she would run to him, put her soft hand in his, and scamper with him to the waiting car. He completely forgot about the blood ritual.

The thing that had been housed in a goldfish tank was still growing, changed out of all recognition by its alien diet. When the man stopped feeding it, purely from forgetfulness, it was soon very hungry. It crept around, breaking down barriers, determined to secure the food it knew was close. The first source of living blood it found, imprisoned behind one of the walls of the man's home, it rejected. It no longer dreaded liquid, but having been reared on cruelty and madness, it disliked the taints of fear and pain. When it found the nutrient it preferred, it easily overcame the food-source's struggles, fed until it was sated and moved on: into the fabric of the city, to seek out and devour more of the same.

What happened to this curious vigilante is a story yet to be told.

Ÿ

The Guerrillas held a farewell Tea Party and set off on their next adventure. On the day the underground tanks were due to be removed, Lulu got a call from Joseph's Nan, summoning her urgently to the site.

"You wouldn't *believe* what's going on here," she said. "No, I can't explain. You have to see it, Lulu. Or you wouldn't believe me—"

There was nobody to take care of Stella, so the little girl had to come along: in a temper because she'd been promised a trip to the South Bank Beach. There was a crowd in front of the vacated Pop Up Garden, but thankfully no police in sight. What could be wrong? All Lulu could think of was a protest. Somebody, possibly Joseph's grandad, who was a bit of a firebrand, had chained himself to something—

She pushed her way to the gates, keeping a grim hold on Stella's wriggling hand. To lose a small child in a crowd is every parent's dread, and there was a new London horror story this summer (located miles away in Morden, thankfully). Three children had been abducted one by one, and just this week a man had been found dead, with the decayed bodies of two of them under his floorboards. The third victim had been recovered barely alive—

Fragments of children's drawings, tattered and rain-smeared, hung from the remains of the fence. On the stripped site excavation machines stood with lowered heads, like giant, tired horses. Men and women in site gear and hard hats huddled beside the great beasts, studying paper plans and scanner screens. One of them had stepped away to talk on the phone. Everything seemed quiet, otherwise. No protesters lying in front of the diggers, no disturbance at all. The smell of ancient petrol fumes hung in the air. Lulu saw Joseph's grandparents, and hurried over to join them – no longer having to drag Stella, who was thrilled by big diggers.

"What's the problem?"

"Anybody's guess," said Judith, Joseph's Nan. "It's really weird."

Temporary soil, demolition rubbish and polluted earth had been gouged back in a great trench right across the site. The top surfaces of two cylindrical fuel tanks could be seen. One of them gaped like a peeled sardine tin, full to bursting with *something*: a silvery mass, a huge, swollen glassy bolus. The other was riven with cracks, like paving heaved up by tree roots, and the same glossy matter was bulging out.

"What's *that*?" demanded Lulu. "Did they fill the tanks with foam?'

Joseph's grandad, Big Joe, shook his head. "Nope. The tank guys *thought* the fuel tanks had been made safe, *degassed*, as they call it, long since. So they started cutting. Now it turns out the work was never done, and nobody knows where the fuel went or what that stuff is!"

"Looks like we've all had a lucky escape," said Judith. "If the tanks'd still had petrol in them, they'd have gone up like a rocket. Well? What's your diagnosis, doctor?"

Lulu hesitated. In a couple of days her contract would be over, and this wouldn't be her problem. "Did the expert on pest species turn up?"

Judith shook her head. "I suppose your boss didn't get round to it. And the devil root seemed to vanish, after you attacked it that day."

"So maybe my hacking had killed it after all—"

"Yeah, *maybe*. Or maybe it retreated to its secret bases?"

"*Triffids*," said Big Joe, suddenly. "Not the sci-fi version, a real live menace. Noxious and invasive. Not your fault, Lulu, you tried."

"Has it done any actual harm?" asked Lulu.

"I'm afraid so," said Judith. "Joe and I came along early this morning, because it was the big day, and there'd been some talk. There were no protestors, but the guys over there had just found Carnegie: in a state which alerted them to the fact that the stuff in the tanks was *not* some kind of safety foam." She pointed to the cracked tank. "He must've wandered in here last night. It's swallowed him, choked him alive."

Carnegie, a friendly neighbourhood ginger tom, had been the Pop-Up Garden's mascot. His head reared up, hardly recognisable, from one of the largest cracks, smothered in glassy devil-root.

Lulu fumbled for her phone, one-handed, hanging on to Stella with the other. She didn't intend to call her soon-not-to-be boss, they'd never got on, but *someone*, ideally Adam, should know about this. The glass root warranted further study, to say the least—

Stella wriggled, trying to see the awful dead cat more clearly.

Joe snorted. "Leave the Council out of it, woman. I know what to do, before it surges out and strangles a child. Stand well back."

Unknown to his wife, Joe had decided to take the law into his own hands. He'd slipped off home, earlier, when Judith and the tank removal team were discussing Carnegie's horrible fate. Now he stooped and lifted a can that had been standing by his feet. Automatically, Judith and Lulu backed off, pulling Stella with them. The crowd at the fence retreated hurriedly too.

"JOE!" wailed Judith. "Oh my god! Are you *crazy*!"

"What are you *doing*!!" screamed the tank removals team leader.

But big Joe rarely thought twice (or even once) when he'd decided something must be done. He twisted off the cap of his can, and tossed the fuel in a gleaming arc. He may have intended to strike a match and fling it after the liquid, but he never got the chance. Contact with a single drop of petrol was enough – for the glassy, obese over-growth that had been glutting itself, for months, on an outrageously rich diet. The whole gouged-out area exploded, with a huge, hollow-sounding WHUMP.

Joe was lifted off his feet and flung backwards from the fireball, as were several of the tank removal workers. *It was like a nuclear explosion* said an eye-witness: but miraculously, a strike without consequences. Seconds later the fireball had vanished, having consumed the glossy masses so swiftly and so utterly that not a trace remained.

Even Big Joe only lost his eyebrows; sustained a few bruises and later had to endure a moderate debriefing from the police, after the negligent Fuel Service company – with considerable *chutzpah* – lodged a complaint. There were no other casualties; apart from poor Carnegie.

Lulu mourned the loss to science in the Golden Galleon, in a pleasant session with Adam: and that was the end of that.

Only three of the burnished coppery discs that had arrived one morning in spring, and landed on the pavement of Creek Road, had survived more than a few minutes. Now only one of them remained viable.

Ÿ

Linden House roof space was inspected, and pronounced problem free. Stella moved up to proper school. She and Joseph were parted, with many tears, and then joyfully reunited after a term apart. They met a little girl called Olly, child of a passionate, displaced tribe of Arsenal supporters; joined the under-eights soccer squad and became obsessed with football. The yoghurt pot stayed on Stella's windowsill as a permanent fixture, like a baby toy that just can't be thrown away.

The seasons passed. One day, when winter was once more coming to an end and the sun returning to her window, Stella, now a big girl of six, happened to notice that the surface of the dried and crumbled soil in the little pot had heaved up again. Her invisible plant had come back to life. Of course she remembered the day when the fuel tanks 'went up like a nuclear bomb', and big Joe lost his eyebrows, but she'd never suspected that a sibling of her plant was responsible, so she wasn't worried. She wondered if a shoot would appear this time, and would it dig into the soil, like a peanut, in the same mad way that the root had shot upwards.

The new growth emerged. For a while it sat on the surface, a pea-sized lump, swelling and changing colour, from white to a rich shade of purple; until it became a clearly defined, tightly folded flower bud. Then it began to rise, visibly wavering at the tip of a shoot like a thread of glass. Stella paid careful attention, and saw that the mad Sellotape root was wavering too. When she held it gently between her finger and thumb, she could feel what was happening. The mad root was heading downward at long last. It was moving down into the pot of soil as the bud was rising up into the air. It was the root moving down that was pushing the bud upwards.

Eventually the purple bud followed the same path as the mad root had taken, when Stella was only four. It squeezed itself into the crack between window-frame and wall, and vanished.

More days and weeks passed. Whenever Stella touched the mad root she could feel that it was still moving. She wondered what was going on in the roof-space. The mad root must be *very* long, if it had been growing all this time. Miles and miles and miles. How high would it push its bud, when it was all stretched out? Even Stella, a born lover of miracles, would have been astonished at the answer.

Ÿ

In the deeps of space, swarms of tiny organisms drifted: algae blooms of a cold, dark, bottomless ocean: dormant until they hit a gas cloud, then feeding on organic particles for a while. Occasionally (once in a billion years or once in a thousand: they were indifferent to any measure of time) one of these swarms might collide with the gravitational field of a solar system. This would trigger the reproductive phase of the colony. Drawn inwards, feeding on the ever-richer mix of gases, the colony would give birth, in a sense, to a generation of specialised individuals: hugely larger than their parent forms, and tough enough to survive entry into an atmosphere. Some of these giants would make it all the way to a planetary surface – like massive ocean-borne seeds tossed up on a beach. If they found the conditions they were programmed to seek, the 'seeds' would break open, and feeding threads would emerge.

The burnished discs had made landfall, purged of their outer casing by the final descent, in a narrow arc around the globe of the Earth. Some, as is always the way when seed is sown broadcast, fell upon stony ground: sprang up quickly and just as quickly died. Many others drowned in the planet's staggering excess of water; or were destroyed by fire; or fell into bad company, and lost the message. A lucky few, but plenty for the parent colony's blind purposes, ripened and headed for home.

Incredibly long, more than a hundred kilometres apiece, the glassy strands drifted, and rose, and were spun around, and went on rising; until they were so high the Earth itself could hardly be said to hold them in its grip. One night in June, close to the Summer solstice, two and a half years after the morning when Stella picked up her piece of chocolate money, they achieved their final extension – all at the same time.

Stella was asleep and didn't see the show. Few people did. Impelled by the extraordinary energies of their transport system, threads finer than spider silk and tougher than diamond, the fruiting bodies reached the point of escape. The "flower-buds" burst open, a storm of tiny fireflies catapulted into the deeps, and a new generation of space algae returned to their natural habitat. Here they would drift; sometimes waking, and feeding on the sparse nutrients in the spaces between the stars, for uncounted time. Until one day, meeting another planetary system's pull, they would encyst, and fall in flame again; and perhaps a few would find fertile ground.

# The Flame Is Roses

*Written for MIT's Technology Review anthology 2011 (the first in the series called* Twelve Tomorrows*). Information Space*[4] *often comes up in my fiction. What if thoughts and feelings, flesh and blood, sub-atomic particles and prehistoric tombs, are all made of the same basic* stuff, *let's call it 'information' – and with the right equipment this* stuff *can be manipulated? Imagine the possibilities. All time might be eternally present, distances in 'space' might vanish. Imagine plugging into that, in some kind of very cool Time Team international televised stunt… Nice, but there's also a story in here about Tom (T.S) Eliot, and the poem which became the first part of his famous late work 'Four Quartets'. It just so happens that his musings on the illusory nature of time and space, and the reality of love and redemption are set in the lost rose garden of a vanished house called 'Burnt Norton'; in Gloucestershire, where he met Emily Hale, the woman he loved and renounced, one day in 1932.*

*But my story is set in Sussex, because that's where I live.*

Only the images are real: the scraps of video-painting, etched in patterns of firing and partially-firing neurons, each of them ripe with the power to recall a whole world. These are the primary, uncontaminated records. Only these, nothing else. Everyone says *I remember it well*, but everyone is lying. People who have the innate ability to preserve, and distinguish, what was written in that code of hidden fire, from the tales we tell ourselves, are rare and hard to find. Em was not a natural: her trained brain had to try hard.

A huge, sleek, grey-brown beast, running low, filled the capture frame of her eyes right now. A very minor river on the world's stage, but, like all rivers, the embodiment of departure; of forgetting, of flowing away. A white egret rose and settled again on the mud. Rivers don't return, thought Em. Nobody returns. I'm back where I came from, but I'm not the little girl who left – and hopefully, as she mused on this

[4] See "Life Without Genes", Adrian Woolfson, for a real world guided tour around this concept.

predicament, a flush of emotion enhanced the P response for the receiver: *attention*!

Tom was telling her a story.

"There was a once a kid who was utterly convinced she could read minds. Not always, but sometimes. She kept this totally secret."

"Wow. That must have taken its toll."

Dune grass bent to brush gold-grey sand. Em climbed out of a shifting hollow and there was the English Channel, a cool long horizon-length of it, silver and blue and green; a silk scarf endlessly rolling, folding in on itself and rolling. She sat down, took off her shoes and poured sand back onto sand. What else could she offer to him? The shore was unexpectedly featureless, not a rock broke the tide. The sky was cloudless blank: brilliant sun dead overhead.

She was sending images, offering her world to the far away receiver, to test the commercial potential of their research. Why would anyone want an i/space phone? What's the added value? Because it lets you see the world as it really looks to your lover's eyes, or your mother's or your friend's… It had to be Em who did the sending, and Tom who did the receiving. Nobody had yet figured out how to get anyone to *receive*, unless they had a weird brain to start with. It was one-way, and even that was flaky. Today nothing was happening at all.

Em was a clumsy seeing-eye puppy, a Martian Rover failing to interface with Mission Control, trying to build neuronal connections that didn't yet exist by using them. Like a new baby attempting to grab a rattle. Baby flaps her little hands, connects with toy by accident, *then* feels desire, and figures out how to do it on purpose.

It should work: because it *did* work, in early development, and the brain retains immense plasticity. But what market would there be, even if it worked like a dream, for new kind of phone that needs you to stick something called a "worm" in your eye? Better change that name. Call it an i/space contact lens. Except contact lenses are reassuringly inert—

There has to be an application, even for the hardest of hard physics – as long as your new explanation of the universe has the status of outsider-art. But right now they couldn't even get the prototype i/space phone to work. Not even one-way, reliably. Lab conditions are deceptive, and faith is something you call truth until you've lost it.

"She grew up, she went to college, and then it was too much. She'd been a quiet girl, staying in the family circle. Trapped among her peers she was getting bombarded and couldn't hide her distress. They sent her to a therapist, who listened to her, and decided there really was something unusual going on. She ended up agreeing to be tested for genuine telepathy, and she came good."

"Fantastic for the Paranormal Research guys."

The silk scarf rolled over and over, bubbles roaring and sunlight scintillating. It was important to talk, behind closed lips: talk and listen, keep those pathways open, and hope the worm does the rest—

"Dynamite. So that meant a lot more tough and tougher testing. She was taken apart, mentally and physically—"

"Not literally."

"Not literally, and she wore it well. Just when they were breaking out the champagne, something clicked: a stupid possibility that had never been checked. She heard voices, you see, that's how she received. It turned out she had *fantastically* acute hearing, to which she'd adapted unconsciously; she was completely unaware of it, and nobody knew. All her life she'd been picking up on people subvocalizing their thoughts, as we all do from time to time: articulating the words, without visibly moving our lips. No telepathy involved. D'you know the punchline?"

"I don't recall this episode. Was it in the original *X Files*?"

"No, Em, this was real life."

She felt a shock, a jolt on the graph—

"Okay, go on, hit me. What happened?"

"Mental breakdown. She went into schizophrenic fugue; never recovered. She may have killed herself in the end, I'm not sure. Ironic, huh? She'd lived with her burden, and even with the scientific scrutiny. She could take it, as long as she was a troubled superhero. When her weird power became a medical condition, shorn of the envelope of miracle, it was simply torture."

A tiny starburst in the corner of Em's eye warned that the signal had faded, no longer strong enough for what they were attempting. They both sighed, maybe with relief.

"I was about to log off, anyway," he said. "Try and get some work done." Tom's work was not going well, he was blocked. Writer's block.

"I have an appointment too. How about late this afternoon, my time?"

"Okay, I guess. Call me."

Em licked the tip of her little finger, and applied it to the outer corner of her left eye. The worm, beckoned by chemical messengers in her saliva, slipped out obediently and clung to her skin, a bright fluorescent droplet, an exquisitely powerful piece of futuristic tech. She returned it carefully to its nutrient-bath case. But the worm itself was nothing. A cell phone you insert into your eye-socket, a 'device' that creeps through bone to pick up phonemes from a centre in the brain, instead of as vibrations in the air… Not yet big business, maybe never more than a marginal toy, even they could get the pictures to work. The *science* Tom and Em were trying to do was something else. Worlds beyond.

Suddenly she realised (dumb scientist!) that she'd missed the point of his story. She set the worm back in her eye at once and called her mother, the instigator of all this, in New York. She got through (no pictures!) but the boss was dismissive. Em was interrupting her busy day and Tom had left the building. Not that he was ever *in* the building. The experimental subject didn't need to be strapped down and hooked up on the premises, no electrodes thrust deep into the grey matter; and he didn't need a nursemaid. But at least Jane was in the same city.

"Mom, you're not *listening*. He told me a story about a pseudo-telepath who committed suicide. Her superhero power was demystified, and she couldn't take it. I'm certain he was talking about himself. I've had a feeling this was getting rough on him. I'm frightened. He's a *poet*—"

"He's a grown man, Emily," said Jane, as if warning her daughter not to get too fond of a genetically engineered mouse. "He's not some clinically deranged freak, which makes a pleasant change! He's a highly respected writer who came to us as a volunteer, of his own free will, out of intellectual curiosity."

"That's the *problem*," said Em. "I didn't get it, but now I do."

"Darling, *could* this wait? I'm sure Tom is fine. I have a meeting, and *you* have an important engagement too."

"Okay," said Em, defeated. "I'll call you when we're done."

"*Whatever* time it is. And we'll talk about Tom, too."

The tiny English lanes bewildered her; like falling into a tangled ball of yarn. As she drove back to the village she could see the spire of the wrapped church nearly the whole time – a shard of glittering diamond, sometimes ahead, sometimes on her left, sometimes on her right; even glimpsed *behind* her once, in the rear mirror. As if it couldn't decide where to settle: in the future or the past, or in some parallel universe. Luckily the hire car had good satnav.

Em was in England to observe an experiment – not directly related to her field trials with Tom, which were ongoing, opportunistic. The archaeologists had sent her away when she arrived, advising her to visit the seaside, which had turned out to be so beautiful; so bleak. The candy floss, donkey rides, fish and chips that Em thought she remembered must be elsewhere. In a theme park, probably… The team had made progress while she was gone. The giant isolation chamber, dulled from diamond to translucent grey by gathering clouds as Em left her car, was peripheral; the Command Shack was now the focus of operations. Final preparations for the descent had begun.

Ralph Dewey, a gaunt professor in a hairy tweed jacket, introduced her to the other 'neuronauts' (Ralph liked that word) who'd be making the descent with him: Lesley Hall, high-profile British Science TV presenter, and British i/space expert Chris Jones. Chris and Em were known to each other. Small world. They exchanged smiles with tight lips, across a chasm of opposing interpretation. Then Em had to be scanned, so they'd be able to 'eliminate her from their inquiries' later, as Dewey jovially put it. She stood in a tiny booth like a bathtub on end, a makeshift prop for *Dr Who* – to be captured and copied, stripped down to the 0s and 1s, an Em-diagram of pure information.

The team fizzed with anticipation; technicians fussed. Dewey showed Em the latest results shaken out of the remote-sensing data. The wrapped building, where they stood, was mainly early mediaeval; Eleventh to Twelfth century. The Void – detected deep under St Peter's Sanctuary, during work on the ancient foundations – was some four thousand years older. Thickset shadows stood around her, projected in 3D from the remote imaging feed. Bowed under a weight of darkness they looked over her shoulders, brooding.

"You're sure it's a tomb?" asked Em, politely. She really didn't have a clue about prehistoric underground constructions

"Almost certainly a Megalithic Portal Tomb! Most likely a family grave, so to speak; though as yet there's no direct evidence of burials. It would have been covered by a mound, visible for great distances. That much we know, and very little more. Imagine the burial rituals. Oracle consultation. This is *fantastically* important, Emily. We're on the brink of *knowing*. Not guessing, not constructing from inference, but *knowing* what went on in the most enigmatic of European ancient cultures. We'll be reading their minds!"

The Command Shack was linked to St Peter's porch by a wobbly umbilical tube. Em left the Brits to their fussing and crossed over. At the west end of the nave the i/bits model, a thousand years of 0s and 1s, danced on its flatbed. It was fascinating to see. Most of what the scan detected was modern, of course: but there were pockets of survival. Wisps of the Eighteenth Century clinging to the roof-tree. Mediaeval murmuring in a chapel alcove. Em thought of knapped flints, calcified sea urchins. Randomly resistant fragments made of the same stuff as the dust that held them, turned up by the plough of the scanning field from a vast silt of information. The material of time and space: endlessly transformed; rearranged—

A skinny, fashionably scruffy post-doc called Flossy had come with her, and stood by, offering commentary. The incredible number crunching that had already been done, the still-puzzling anomalies. "It's just amazing," Flossy said. "The model was a test-bed for the Void scan, but we're leaving it here. The public will have access—"

"I hope they'll be interested," said Em. "It's a shame i/bits make such a poor recording medium. There must be way better history books in the local library."

Florence stared at her. "But it's *super* cool! Hey, you have an eye-worm. Gives a whole new meaning to the word *tele*-phone, doesn't it?"

Causing Em to smile tightly, and nod wryly.

Nothing was due to happen for a while, so this time she sent herself away. Chris Jones, and jokes about telepathy-phones, was a combination she didn't need. Leaving her car at the church she walked down to the village, followed a finger-posted path across pasture, and called Tom again. He picked up at once.

The archaeologists didn't care. They had a powerful new tool for digging up the past and they were going to use it: like a stick, like a prod, to open the can, stir the jam. It didn't bother them at all that the science behind the new gadget said *the past does not exist.* Journalists had asked Em the same questions until she gritted her teeth.

*Is "Information Space" the final Theory of Everything?*

*Have we found the ultimate building blocks of the universe?*

*Doesn't it all sound a bit hippy-dippy? Like, everything is one, Man?*

She'd learned– burned by derision – to answer as blandly as was humanly possible. The model seems to work, she would say. Already we're developing new technologies. We have gadgets based on i/space theory that could soon be ubiquitous as cellphones. As yet we can't be sure what it all means—

Sending images by eye-worm was a joke to many. To Em it was *huge*. If what she did with Tom ever really worked, it would prove that Many-Worlds Superposition was real.

Imagine the universe as a single, staggeringly convoluted object.

A diamond as big as the sum of all histories; the state of all states.

What, hanging in nothingness?

Hanging in nothing would never be an issue, Em used to explain (two years ago, before she was burned). You're always inside, everything is always inside. This object is made of many, many times and spaces. Factor-in human consciousness, each mind a world. Think of the superposition as many, many, *insanely* many interpenetrating worlds. All folded into one, and every *i/bit* of information in this geometry is contiguous with every other… What's an *i/bit*? Oh, it's just a term we use, like "sub-atomic particle", for something that isn't material…

If the MWS was a good model of reality, tech-mediated 'telepathy', sending the stuff the universe is made of from mind to mind, ought to be a no-brainer (excuse the pun). It should fall out of the equations.

But it didn't, yet, and to some people that was a great excuse for –

Tom was letting her bounce her frustrations off him. He was a good listener, and just *talking* like this, no pressure, no expectations, was reassuring. He sounded relaxed. On the far side of the meadow the grass path took a right angle turn at a barrier of tall iron railings: but there was a gate. It appeared to be unlocked. Em pushed and it shifted easily, rusted metal fitting a groove cut in dark leaf-litter; so she went straight on.

"I'll never get on with the Brits. I left England with my mother, when I was a kid, in blissful ignorance of the impending divorce… My dad lives in France with his second family now: we get on okay, I don't see him much. My parents didn't tell me, *I didn't know*, so forever I hear the accent and I feel betrayed—"

"I'll see your irrational racism and raise you. Listen, ever since 9/11, when I was right here, of course, if a guy who looks Arab comes towards me down the street, I flinch. I'm not a good person, Em. I suck up all the shit on the daily news and add my own. That's what people *buy* from me. They've praised me and got all excited, for years, because I speak with an intellectual accent, through a tasty fat mouthful of shit—"

Em had invaded a landscaped garden: overgrown, desolate and

enticing. She was probably trespassing, but birdsong beckoned onwards.

"Is that what your writer's block's about?"

"Yeah. I have a blocked toilet in my mouth—"

"You're just innately, brutally honest. It's what we hired you for."

"Hired? Did you say *hired*? I didn't know I was getting paid!"

"Oops. Figure of speech, sorry."

They laughed together. Laughter arises differently from speech, so what they shared was not the sound but the feeling of laughter: it was *beautiful.* "Tom, I wanted to tell you… That girl in your story, they shouldn't have medicalised her, the jerks. They should have told her, you have a right to be terrified, and you're incredibly talented… You've always known. I just realised today that what we're trying to do is *awful.* It could drive a person crazy, like you said. Dumb scientist, I missed the big picture. So, I wanted to say, if it's getting unbearable, if you've had enough of playing with fire—"

Immediately she could have kicked herself.

Silence from Tom. She passed through a tunnel built of small, densely packed shrubs; into a rose garden. Climbers, once trained along the walls, had fallen and lay in Sleeping-Beauty sheaves. Specimen bushes, vividly in bloom, struggled with massed cohorts of briars. Suddenly she had an intense feeling of *presence.* Something was in this enclosed space with her, fugitive and enormous. The shadow of massive shoulders, bowed under the overwhelming stood around her and right where the knot of the visual cortex flares: she stared at flame-red roses; she tasted *almost*, but if she even thought, almost, she knew: *it's here, it's now*—

It was gone.

Like a stitch coming undone, an adhesion ripping apart.

"*Tom*? Did something just happen?"

Nothing. Silence so profound she thought the connection had broken.

"No" he said at last, sounding very tired; sounding terminally disheartened. "Not a thing. What could be terrifying about this, Em? We're just talking. Collecting a lot of data on coming up empty. Sorry, but I'm logging off now."

Em headed back to St Peter's, pre-empting Ralph Dewey's summons: which reached her half-way across the buttercup-studded pasture. In the midst of the Command Shack's boundless excitement she couldn't stop herself from calling New York. She told her mother she was afraid Tom had decided to quit—

"He's done it," answered Jane, wearily. "He called me and quit, about ten minutes ago. Don't blame yourself, darling, I'm sure it wasn't your fault."

Based on the tone of Mom's voice, Em knew there was more. The moment in the rose garden repeated on her. She wanted to ask had there been a spike, a Wow spike? But she didn't, because Tom was gone, and they wouldn't be able to investigate the false positive. They'd have to start again, start hunting for another rare mind.

So it was true, she had lost him. Shock first, pain would come later.

Professor Dewey was in front of her, beaming. "We're ready, Emily!"

The vertical shaft descended, through layer-cake strata of dark dirt and ancient builders' spoil, to a surprisingly large excavation. It quickly filled with bodies. The original entrance to the tomb had been located but would not be breached. The neuronauts would enter obliquely, through a narrow slit they'd opened between two of the upright slabs.

In glaring lamplight at the bottom of the shaft they donned cabled, goggled helmets. There was a reserve helmet for Em, but she turned it down. She'd have to take out her worm to get hooked up for the i/scan, and she was still hoping Tom would call her to explain what he'd done; or at least to say goodbye.

One after another they crept and stooped into the virgin dark.

"We are about to make the dive," intoned Dewey (for the TV crew who had remained packed in the foot of the shaft). "These funky deep-sea diver helmets allow us to plunge into the depths of *time*. As we stand here our perceptions will be virtually, so to speak, falling through the aeons, collecting data from five thousand years ago—"

What garbage, thought Em. Time doesn't exist in i/space, which is the only faint reason this "dive" stunt makes any kind of sense. Why doesn't he say so? The tomb was room-sized, roughly circular; the roof a huge table stone supported on five big irregular slabs. Packed earth between the stones. The air was fresh; the tomb was empty. Lamps on the scanning helmets showed a smooth, featureless earth floor; the walls of dark earth punctuated by the paler slabs: no trace of marks or carving. If she reached up, Em could have touched the underside of the table.

The neuronauts moved around, guided by a helmet display mapping grid that Em couldn't see. They had an air of ritual awe, as if they were actually seeing their five thousand year old ghosts – though in reality it would take some heavy number crunching to win any 'pure' Megalithic traces out of the data. Em kept out of the way, almost struggling with laughter, and then something happened in her brain.

Her hands move without volition, completely out of her control.

"My God, *look*!" shouted Lesley Hall. "Emily! She's covered in blood!"

"Fire!" howled Professor Dewey. "Oh, incredible! Sacrificial Fire!"

Em saw the flame-red petals that filled her outstretched open hands.

"Not fire," she gasped, astonished. "No, it's not fire, it's roses—"

Next moment the sending was gone. Em stood there, her mouth stretched by an enormous, helpless grin, her mind a silent babble of triumph, while the neuronauts went nuts. Roses indeed, *made of fire* indeed, a pattern of firing and partially-firing neurons, oh, what a gift he had sent her, but why the time lag? *Was* it a time lag? She had no idea. Something new to disentangle, never considered—

But who cares?

We did it!

The Brits, when Em managed to explain what had happened, were desperate to get her and her illicit device out of their tomb. But when the scan was done, and everyone was back on the surface, they reacted generously: breaking out their champagne for the MWS breakthrough. Everyone was full of questions. How big was this? How much bigger than previous US successes with sending small bundles of i/bits across a lab? Em answered as vaguely as possible. Mom would *kill* her, if she blabbed before the debriefing. She escaped as soon as she could, and called Tom—

He picked up. "Hi, Em. I guess your mother told you. I'm sorry."

"Told me what? I just wanted to say thank you for the roses."

Stunned silence reached her, echo of that brilliant explosion in her brain.

"You *got* them?"

"Just now! And wait, it's better, *the Brits got them too.* We're independently verified, by *Chris Jones*, for God's sake! Among others. It's all there, on record!"

"My God! *Fantastic*! Em! That moment, you know the moment, I knew, *that was it.* That, or never, and you didn't get it, so… Hey, Em, you should've had some kind of 3D bio-printer. You could have fed it the i/bits, and had roses to put in a vase!"

"The i/space 3D bio-printer. Our next project, yeah, we'll make our fortunes. Tom, it's fantastic but it's only a single measurement."

"One small step. But we've entered the Information Space Age!"

"I'll be home in a day or two." She took the plunge. "How about meeting in the real?" They never had, not alone. "For a coffee?"

"In the real? That's a bold idea. But I don't like coffee."

"Have skinny latte decaff with syrup. Or green tea. I won't judge."

"Deal."

Rain had come and gone. As she drove away from St Peter's the ball-of-yarn lanes were awash and shining. She pulled up on the coast road to look out, over saltmarsh, to the river's mouth and the dunes. The world shivered, it looked pixelated, unreal. Something utterly momentous had happened. Should she be afraid? But this wasn't the first time a whole communications tech had sprung into being, born from punishingly strange new science. There'd be no transistors without quantum mechanics. Yet still she wondered, did we destroy a universe today? The place we lived in this morning is gone, that humungous, staggeringly convoluted object is *folded differently* now—

Is there a lag, will we wink out of existence?

But everything seemed fine, so she drove on.

# A Planet Called Desire

*Written for George R. R. Martin and Gardner Dozois's* Old Venus, *a themed 'retro Venus science fiction' anthology. I found the suggestion of a 'habitable zone', hidden in Venus's ancient past, in an article in* New Scientist, *but I think there are reasons why Venus could never have had plate tectonics, (or a magnetic field) so maybe that's total fantasy (if the only habitable planet we know of is a good guide).The dying world, overwhelmed by parasites is not exactly fantasy, more of a metaphor. The West African (Mali) Dogons' ancient, stunning astronomical knowledge of Venus is fact, and the rest is golden, glorious pulp.*

## 1. John Forrest, Adventurer

The laboratory was on an upper floor. Its wide windows looked out, across the landscaped grounds of the Foundation, to the Atlantic Ocean. One brilliant star, bright as a tiny full moon, shone above the horizon; glittering in the afterwash of sunset.

"My grandfather's people called her *Hawa*," said the scientist.

"Is that a Dogon term, PoTolo?" asked John Forrest: a big man, fit and tanned, past forty but in excellent shape. He wore a neatly-trimmed beard and moustache, his vigorous red-brown hair was brushed back and a little long; his challenging eyes an opaque dark blue. "You're Dogon, aren't you?"

They were alone in the lab: alone in the building aside from a few security guards. Dr Seven PoTolo, slight and dark; fragile and very young-looking beside the magnate, was uncomfortable with the situation, but there was nothing he could do. Mr Forrest, the multibillionaire, celebrity entrepreneur: philanthropist, environmental-ist; lover of life-threatening he-man stunts, owned the Foundation outright. His billions financed PoTolo's work, and he was ruthless with any hint of opposition.

He shook his head. "I'm afraid my ancestry is more mixed: Cameroon is a melting pot. My maternal grandfather spoke a language of the Coast which has now vanished, but '*hawa*' is a loan-word; I think it's Arabic, and means desire."

"Sensual desire, yes," agreed Forrest. "The temptation of Eve."

He turned to the untried experimental apparatus.

"What will conditions be like?"

"Conditions on the surface could be remarkably Earthlike," said PoTolo. "The Tectonic Plate system hasn't yet broken down, the oceans haven't boiled away. Atmospheric pressure hasn't started to sky-rocket; the atmosphere is oxygenated. Rotation should be speedier too. Much longer than our twenty-four hour cycle, but a day and a night won't last a local year—"

Forrest studied the rig. Most of it was indecipherable, aside from the scanning gate and biomedical monitors introduced for his own benefit. A black globe with an oily sheen, clutched in robotic grippers inside a clear chamber, caught his eye: reminding him somehow of the business part of a nuclear reactor.

"But no guarantees," he remarked, dryly.

"No guarantees… Mr Forrest, you have signed your life away. Neither your heirs, nor any other interested parties, will have any legal recourse if you fail to return. But the risks are outrageous. Won't you reconsider?"

"Consider *what?*" Forrest's muddy blue eyes blazed. "Living out my life in some protected, cutesy enclave of a world I'd rather go blind than see? The trees are dying, the oceans are poisoned. We're choking on our own emissions, in the midst of a mass extinction caused by our numbers, while sleepwalking into a Third World War! No, I will not *reconsider*. Don't tell me about risk. I *know* about risk!"

PoTolo nodded carefully. They were alone in the building, and he was more physically intimidated than he liked to admit by this big white man, disinhibited by great power and famous for his reckless temper.

"My apologies. Shall we proceed?"

"I take nothing? No helmet full of gizmos, no homing beacon?"

"Only the capsule you swallowed. There'll be an interval. I can't tell you exactly how long, the variables are complex. If conditions are as we hope, the probe will be retrieved, bringing you along with it. You can move around, admire the scenery, then suddenly you'll be back here."

"Amusing, if I'm in the middle of a conversation… One more question. You've staked your career on this, PoTolo, as much as I'm staking my life. What's in it for you?"

"Habitable zones," said the scientist. "Ancient Venus is, in effect, our nearest exo-planet. If we can confirm the existence in space-time of the Venusian habitable zone we believe we've detected, that's a major confirmation of our ability to identify other, viable alternate-Earths. We may not be able to use this method to send probes across the light years, there may be insuperable barriers to that, but—"

"Bullshit. Your motive was glory, and the glory is now mine." Forrest grinned. "You lose, I win. That's what I do, PoTolo. I see an opportunity, and I *take* it."

"Are you quite ready, Mr Forrest?"

"I am."

He assumed the position, standing in the gate with arms loosely by his sides, and turned his head for a last glance at that bright star. The world disappeared.

♀

He stood in a rosy, green-tinged twilight, surrounded by trees. Most seemed young, but some had boles thicker than his body. Fronds like hanging moss hung around him, the ground underfoot was springy and a little uncertain, as if composed entirely of supple, matted roots. No glimpse of sky. The air was still, neither warm nor cold; the silence was absolute, uncanny. He looked at himself; checked the contents of belt loops and pockets. He was dressed as he had been in West Africa, and still equipped with a suite of sturdy, familiar outdoors kit. This struck him as very strange, suddenly, but why not? What is a body but a suit of clothes, another layer of the mind's adornment? And his body seemed to have made the trip. Or the translation, or whatever you called it. No pack. PoTolo had told him he couldn't carry a pack.

*PoTolo!*

The name rang like a bell, reminding him just what had happened. What an extraordinary feat! He took a few steps, in one direction and then another: keeping himself oriented on the drop-zone. Pity he didn't have a ballpark figure for the 'interval'. Ten minutes, or ten hours? How far was it safe to stray? Grey-green boles crowded him, the hulk of a dead giant or two lurking, back in the ranks. He wondered if he was dreaming. Yes, probably he was. The PoTolo narrative, the apparatus: the act of standing in that gate, feeling absurd in his wilderness kit: it all folded up like a telescope, became implausible. Only the twilit jungle remained concrete, but how did he get here?

He heard nothing, but simply became aware of a rush of small, purposeful movement, closing in on him. The creatures were highly camouflaged, about the size of ground squirrels; long, flexible snouts; shaggy apparently limbless bodies. Their swift appearance seemed uncanny, *the dream turned to nightmare*, but of course they had smelt his blood. He fled, grabbing at appropriate defence, spun around and pepper-sprayed them. Which did the trick. Hell, they weren't armour-plated, and they liked the taste of their own kind, a useful trait in aggressive vermin. Inevitably the drop-zone was now out of sight, but before he could think about that a new player arrived. Shaggy four-legged things: bigger than the first guys and smart, organised pack-hunters. He ran, but they outflanked him. Forced to climb, he shot up the first three or four metres of his chosen refuge in seconds, and went on climbing, easy work, to a knot of boughs high above the ground. There he perched, assembling his pellet gun: thrumming with adrenalin and almost laughing out loud.

An exhilarating place, this planet called Desire!

No pack, and no effective firearms, a lack he might come to regret. He was equipped for the wilderness, but not for slaughter. How do you say 'I come in peace' to a pack of Venusian hyenas? He saw formidable teeth, and hoped his armoury was sufficient. But apparently Venusian hyenas couldn't climb. The brutes circled, panting in frustration, then retreated, vanishing into the dim ranks of the trees.

*Not worth it*, muttered Forrest. *Or I smell wrong, unappetising.*

He took stock of his situation: treed in a trackless forest full of hungry predators, some several billion years and around thirty eight million kilometres from home – and noticed that his secret burden of depression, the Black Dog mood that had haunted him for years, had vanished.

Savouring PoTolo's crowning moment, he wondered if he might be here for days. He'd need food, water; shelter; some way to defeat beasts that could tear him apart! The challenges he might face: possibly fatal, possibly insurmountable, delighted him. He was debating whether to take the gun apart or carry it down assembled, when a severe, numbing pain alerted him to the tree's behaviour.

He bared his right leg and saw grey noduled strands, tightly wrapped around his calf. The knot of boughs had produced suckers and sent them to feed, stealthily creeping inside his pants leg. Forrest grabbed his knife and slashed. The pain was unmistakeably deep and compelling: there was venom involved, and no time to lose. The suckers fell away. He slashed again at a row of puckered wounds, like scribbled smiley faces: opening a long gash in the hope of bleeding the poison out. Too late. In the act of securing a tourniquet below the knee he stopped being able to breathe, lost consciousness; lost his balance and fell.

♀

He woke on his back, lying on some kind of bed, a very warm coverlet confining him. He smelled foul meat and remembered being dragged through darkness, maybe in the teeth of those hyenas, in a red mist of pain… The pain was still intense, and there were other discomforts, possibly broken bones, but hyenas hadn't brought him here: wherever *here* was. The flickering light showed a hollow, interior space; crudely furnished. There was someone with him, a figure squatting by a fire-bowl, poring over small objects on a slab. Silvery fingers rearranged the items, a sleek bent head pondered the pattern. He was sure he'd seen the same thing before, far away, in another world—

*She's telling my fortune*, he thought, though how he knew the figure was female, he had no idea. The items were swept away, and vanished. The figure sat back, murmuring, looking down into upturned palms; seeming to engage in a dialogue with the Unseen.

He slept again. The pain burned low, like a smothered fire.

When he next woke she was by his couch, in a very unhuman posture.

"Good," she said. "You're awake. Your head is clear?"

He nodded, staring. He had been rescued by a glistening, greenish woman with a muscular sheeny tail, which she was using as a third lower limb; a hairless head, and bird or snake-like features (green eyes that filled the width of her face, a long mouth with an eerie curl; a glint of needle teeth). But she spoke and he understood her. He must be dreaming, after all.

"Your fall saved your life, at a cost. I have set your broken bones, the venom is overcome, but the *nibbler* bite itself is now urgent. Rotten flesh must be excised, regeneration triggers implanted. You should know: I can immobilise you, I can give you analgesics, but I can't put you out." She showed him her palm: he saw moving symbols. "I can read your *cell signature* on this, but not the details of its expression, and anaesthesia is complex. I might kill you."

"You are a medicine woman," said John Forrest slowly.

"Yes." Her eerie mouth curled further, until he thought her jaw would split from her face. "I am indeed. The procedure will be very painful."

"Go ahead and operate, doctor. Do I need to sign anything?"

"Not necessary."

The operation was a success. When pain was once more a smothered fire, she told him all was well and that he would soon mend. She asked him where he'd come from.

"From the sky," said Forrest, "does it matter?"

"Not to me," said Lizard Woman, her long mouth curling.

He noticed, at last, a spidery transparent headset that caught gleams of firelight and a mic by her mouth. He raised an arm, the one that wasn't still immobilised by the heated coverlet.

"What's that?" he muttered, incredulous. "Some kind of *babelfish*?"

"Yes, sir, it's a *translation device*. It may look old-fashioned and clumsy to you, but it converts my language into yours, and yours into mine, adequately enough. Mr From-the-Sky, I have business that cannot wait. When you can walk I'll take you to a better equipped refuge, where you may rest and recover in safety."

Forrest decided he wasn't dreaming. He was on Ancient Venus, and his rescuer was a sophisticated Venusian, an unexpected bonus! She was not astonished: she had some rationale to account for his odd anatomy and strange arrival, and that suited him well. He couldn't gauge how long he'd been in this cave, not even by the growth of his beard, which she had kept close-trimmed, but he felt he could assume that retrieval had failed: probably he was too far from the drop-zone.

He wasn't overly concerned. PoTolo would certainly keep trying. All Forrest had to do was get himself back to the zone, before the orbits of the two planets veered too wildly apart. It would be a whole lot easier, however, if he didn't have to explain himself too much.

She walked him up and down. She showed him the "wellspring", a fresh water supply tapped from the root system of the trees, and explained how to operate a fire-bowl (the flames were natural gas, from the same source); how to use her gourd-like ration-packs. Her tone was always frosty, if her gadget was translating emotional nuance correctly; her conversation minimal. Forrest surmised, amused, that she'd identified him as a local bad guy of some kind – temporarily protected by her Venusian Hippocratic Oath.

♀

When he was well enough they left the cave, via a twisting crawl-space passage that woke nightmare memories for Forrest – and emerged out of a hole in a huge dead tree stump. She led the way, Forrest limped behind. He'd tried to convince her to take him back where she'd found him; to no avail, and he was angry. But not such a fool as to strike out on his own, against her will. If Lizard Woman had dragged him down below herself, she was extremely strong. Or had confederates he hadn't met; or both, of course. She was alone, living on gourds of mush, but implanted and supplied with impressive tech. What was the story? Who was Forrest supposed to be? So many unknowns, and he'd have relished them, except that he was so annoyed.

But her pace started to tell. She had the pack; he carried nothing, which he found galling. If there were trails, she didn't use them; if she had transport available, she preferred to hike. What was she? Some kind of Venusian Backwoods Survivalist, humiliating a hated city slicker? He refused to be outdone. When she handed him one of those sappy-gruel gourds, he emptied it without breaking stride. But it got to be desperate work. She wore a floating grey robe; under it a shirt, and pants that accommodated the tail by having no backside. When the robe lifted, as she crossed some obstacle, he saw the big gleaming root of her tail, and it was sexy in a weird way.

Before long her tail was the only thing that kept him moving.

Dizzy with exhaustion, he picked at his itching fingertips: trying to extricate a tiny, wriggling, brown worm or caterpillar from under one of his fingernails. He didn't know he'd stopped until Lizard Woman was in front of him, taking hold of his wrist.

She pulled out her headset and donned it. "Your head swims," she suggested, a cool, contemptuous light in her huge eyes. "Disoriented, can't think straight? Your skin creeps?"

"All of that," mumbled Forrest. "Well done, *doctor.* You said you would *help* me."

"I don't believe I did say that, and yet I will."

She was lying, things only got worse. Now they *really* went off-piste. Forrest was dragged through virgin thickets, thrown into ditches, forced over mad sastrugi of upheaved root-mass, until they reached a small clearing where a new kind of tree, reddish and gnarled, grew with no near neighbours. Stumbling and confused, he was ordered to strip, and hustled onto a natural platform among its roots. The lower bole was scarred. She stuck something in his hand, forced him to grip and shouted at him.

"Stab the tree! *Stab* it! Over your head. Cover your eyes. Okay?"

She'd given him a knife. He reached up and stabbed the tree. A huge gush of stinging hot liquid burst out, and pounded on him.

A hot shower! My God!

The itching that had been driving him mad, a vile, active sensation over his whole body, leapt to a crescendo. He looked down and saw a nest of little dark worms on his chest. More of them, over his belly, his arms. They were wriggling out of his pores, his anus, they were *everywhere*, and there were *hundreds* of them. The hot, scouring liquid diminished. Frantically he stabbed the tree again, and again, oh blessed relief—

The first time he left the platform she sent him back. The second time she was satisfied, and slapped a new variety of soft-walled gourd into his hands.

"Hold that. Whatever they gave you, Mr From-The-Sky, it doesn't last. You'll have to do as we do, when we're in here. Depilate and use barrier methods, or the *sippers* will overwhelm you in hours. Now I'm going to fix you up, before you collapse."

She made him sit on the ground, massaged a grainy goop into his hair, his beard, his arms and legs, his chest, his pubes: sent him to rinse off, then helped to apply a cream that left his skin shining like her own. There was also breathable gel, she said, as she sleeked his every crevice, for nostrils, mouth and eyes: but it wasn't necessary in the short term. The "sippers" wouldn't block airways, or endanger sight, until their host was actually dying. The erection she provoked along the way didn't bother her, she ignored it and so did he. But there was something between them, when he was purged, hairless and dressed again, that had not been there before.

"Since we're talking, sir. What about a name?"

"Forrest. My name is John Forrest, and you?"

"Sekṕool."

"*Sek*. That means the woods, doesn't it?"

"You know my humble language?"

He shook his head. "In the cave, I sometimes heard you talking to someone. Or communing with your gods? I listened. I figured out that *sek* meant woods, frequency of occurrence." He gestured around them. "Since here we are."

"I have no gods," she said, and added, "*Ool* means song. The *ṗ* is a separating sound, my name is Woodsong. *Sekool* without the ṗ means something different."

The distinction was clearly important: he wasn't sure how to respond.

"Woodsong, okay. Er, John means *gift of God*."

She laughed, or at least the sound she made felt like laughter. His eyes burned, he'd forgotten to cover them, but the world was in focus. He was awake, alive: firing on all cylinders again, maybe for the first time since he'd touched down. He looked at the gouged tree bole, and the shower-platform: a natural formation, smoothed by long use.

"There are people living around here?"

"There are the indigenes, primitive surface-dwellers: you won't see them. A few others: you'll see them even less. Let's go. It's not much further."

Soon they crossed a really large clearing, and he was able to gauge the height of the frondy canopy at last: impressive but not extraordinary; sixty or seventy metres. Only mosses grew on the open ground, but the springy uncertain feeling stayed the same.

Sekṗool kept to the margin of the trees. Up ahead a shadow moved, between the canopy and a ceiling of bright cloud; a grey curtain falling under it: defined like a rainstorm seen from afar, on a wide plain. Forrest thought they were really heading into rain until they crossed the shadow's trajectory, and he stared in amazement at the tangled, mighty underbelly – then flinched and ducked, as vagrant shining strands actually brushed his naked skull.

"Don't worry," she said. She'd kept the headset on since his shower-bath, a concession he appreciated; though often puzzled by the babelfish's translation. "They're eating air. It doesn't know we're here."

They re-entered the woods, and almost at once she halted, gesturing for him to step well back. A knotted growth, a tumour on a root, stood knee-high in their path. Sekṗool crouched, her tail balancing her, and cut herself between the fingers of her right hand with the knife he'd borrowed. Was her blood red? He couldn't tell, in this everlasting rosy-green twilight—

"Wait. Don't move from where you stand."

Following her with his eyes, he saw the same ceremony performed again, further into the trees on his right. What was she doing? Placating demons? Having met some of the demons, he didn't move a muscle until she reappeared from the left: she'd circled around something big. They walked on, and stood in the precinct of a truly vast dead giant, a stump tall as a house and broad as a barn. Forrest looked it over with respect.

"I hope *this* guy doesn't feed on flesh."

"Actually he does, but the heartwood is inert."

The last section of the entrance tunnel was vertical. They descended a ladder into a room rounded and domed like the first cave, but far more spacious, and better furnished. There were covered couches, low tables, domed chests: a fire-bowl at one focus of the ellipse and a wellspring at the other. Screened-off areas seemed to lead to other rooms.

Forrest's appetite had returned. He longed for steak, fries and a good malt, but made do with another sappy-gruel gourd (he should stop calling them 'gourds', since they were obviously manufactured): fell onto a couch, and plunged into oblivion.

♀

In his dreams the snouted things chased him: limbless bodies covered in worms. The hyenas circled under the venom tree, shaggy with their own freight of bloodsuckers. The tiny worms that filled the sek's air, and had invaded his pores, had smaller worms to bite them. He woke with a shuddering start. *Nibblers*, *sippers*: cute names for unappeasable horrors. *Wee folk, good folk, trooping all together…* Parasites are everywhere, far too many of the bastards on Earth: but if Sekṗool hadn't found him, what an appalling fate! But she didn't find me, he thought. She was watching me. "*Your fall saved your life, but at a cost—*"

He opened his eyes. She was beside him, in her tripod pose: wearing the headset. She smiled. He'd come to like that eerie, too-wide smile; very much. But it had an edge to it, on which he feared to cut himself.

"I must return your gear."

She handed over everything: including the pellet gun, which he'd assumed was lost or permanently confiscated. "That is not a lethal weapon," she remarked. "You carried none. What if you'd run into trouble, Johnforrest?"

What kind of trouble, he wondered. Friends of yours?

"What if I did? Thou shalt not kill. I'm on a fact finding mission, I'm not at war with anyone."

"A fact-finding mission," she repeated. "Indeed. I see."

"What about you, Sekṗool? I'm deeply in your debt, of course, but what are *you* doing in this hellhole? How did you happen to turn up like that?"

"The surface is a source of raw materials, Johnforrest. Surely even sky-dwellers know that. We come here to make deals with the indigenes, and to squabble with each other over the spoils. I was researching tree venoms that can be weaponised, if you must know."

"That's no work for a doctor."

"We live in the dark as well as the bright, Mr From-The-Sky, and though I chose medicine, I was born to something else… I saw you run from the vermin, I saw you climb and then fall, it was pure chance."

Now I know too much, thought Forrest. And whatever the hell's going on, I get the feeling I'm in serious trouble. But you'd spare me if you could, for which I thank you—

He said nothing, just nodded gravely.

"I'll be leaving soon," she said. "Here you have everything you need, and no *sippers* or *nibblers* can reach you: the hollows under the *great hearts* are our safe houses. I'll give you a homing beacon, since you have none, to guide you back to the spot where I found you. But you were very ill. Please wait: eat, rest and exercise a while before leaving. I'm not happy about the way you keep falling asleep in the daytime—"

"Oh, that? We call it *jet-lag.* It's nothing; it's just taking me a while to adjust to a different time zone—"

Forrest liked to wear a wristwatch; he collected them. Before leaving for West Africa he'd had one specially made for this trip. An ingenious, expensive toy; instead of hours and seconds it followed the intricate dance of the orbits of the two planets. Sekṗool had returned this device. He didn't think she could have tampered with it. As he spoke he read the time, the only time that mattered to him, and his heart skipped a beat.

He wanted to ask her *just how long was I "very ill"? How long is your world's "day", right now*? He had no idea how to frame the question, and it didn't matter. He knew enough of PoTolo's complex requirements to be sure he'd missed his window entirely. His next chance wouldn't be coming around for… for quite a while.

"But Johnforrest, I have a proposal. It suddenly struck me. Why not come to the clouds? You're here from the sky, on a fact-finding mission: I could introduce you to interesting people, and later we could surely set you down wherever you need to be."

Forrest slipped the orrery watch into an inside pocket. Her big green eyes were limpid with lies, her smile had that warning edge, and he didn't care. "What a wonderful idea, I'd be delighted. When do we leave?"

♀

If he was stranded, for a year and a half or forever, he might as well see the world. Stir things up, in this story he didn't understand. Why not? If Lizard Woman feared for his life, as she clearly did, maybe she just didn't know John Forrest very well! But that pouch on the cord around her neck, where she kept her oracle bones, what was going on there—?

Forrest had "fallen asleep in the daytime" again. The room was dim, the lights that stood in wall-niches were at their lowest setting. He heard Sekṗool's voice, but she was nowhere in sight. She must be in one of those screened-off areas. Perhaps she was making arrangements for his "visit to the clouds"? The headset lay on a table. Intrigued, he donned it and sneaked up: creeping around until he could peer behind the screen. Astonished, he saw *himself*, standing naked, quivering, full frontal.

The shock was momentary. He was looking as if into a full-length, free-standing mirror: but it was a video screen of some kind, and the naked Forrest figure must be a kind of hologram. Someone of the same lizard-like race, or species as Sekṗool (though he couldn't see a tail) – masculine-seeming, dressed in black and white, was examining it.

Sekṗool, her back to Forrest, spoke rapidly in a language that crackled and fizzed like fireworks: but reached him as English (mostly)—

"No. Not any kind of *flish atatonaton*, he's real. But he's carrying an implant, attached to his stomach wall. I haven't touched it, and I don't know what it's for—"

Good to know I'm still a walking interplanetary probe, thought Forrest. The other's response, over the video link, was incomprehensible.

"Deniable is good, but how long could it stand up? This is *better*. Far better than a… a *kinsnipping*, Esbwe! We want to avoid reprisals!"

She sounded exasperated. Her tail, he thought, should be lashing. He'd have liked to see that. He retreated, replaced the headset where he'd found it and lay down again: his thoughts spinning. Feigning sleep, he must have dozed. He woke when he heard something crawling.

The globes were still dim. Sekṕool, alone, sat by the fire-bowl, tail around her feet. Nothing moved, but the sound of crawling was closer. Forrest turned on his side, as if in sleep and saw something come through the wall of the room. It crossed the floor.

A male, humanoid figure, slender and juvenile, naked and very battered, hauled himself along on one hand and one knee; back, ribs and shoulders marked with livid weals. Bruises blotted out his eyes. No sign of a tail, which made Forrest think he was asleep, and dreaming of a human boy: except the whole thing was too complete, too coherent. The kid's hair was dark, his greenish skin unnaturally pale; until he reached the firelight. Then he was more than pale: he was transparent.

A mangled, moving corpse, the apparition crept into Sekṕool's arms.

Another hologram? Not by the way Sekṕool responded. Not the way she held the kid: rocked him and murmured to him, stroking his shadow-hair from his swollen, battered shadow-brow, and then somehow Forrest made a sound.

She looked up: instantly the ghost was gone.

"What was *that*?" he breathed.

Enormous eyes unblinking, she calmly left the fire and picked up the "translation device".

"My son. Gemin. He comes to me when it's quiet. Usually I'm alone; you've never woken before. He died under torture. Don't die under torture, Johnforrest. It's not a good way to go."

She removed the headset and turned away: the subject was closed. Forrest got up, and joined her by the fire-bowl, collecting the headset on the way. He held her gaze, deliberately, as he settled the flexible web around his skull.

"Tell me, Sekṕool."

She looked into the flames, drawing her tail closely around her.

"There's not much to tell. He was caught up in a secret war and taken hostage. We failed to negotiate his release, he was mistreated; protests achieved nothing; we learned that he'd died. There's nothing to be done. I only comfort him, and quiet him as best I can… Death is not the end, Johnforrest, as we all know, because our dead return. They speak to us and know us, *in dream and in the waking world.* But when they depart at last, we don't know what happens next. We don't know if the unquiet ones, trapped in the way they died, ever escape from suffering. It's cruel."

"I know you're a *shaman*," he said. "There must be something you can do."

Her long fingers closed on the bag of oracle bones.

"No. Let's say no more about it. I can't help my boy. He'll fade, that's all, and he'll be gone, and I won't know where."

## 2. Out Of The Frying Pan, Into The Fire

On their way out, Sekṕool placated the demons again. Forrest kept his distance, and didn't stir until she'd made her circuit. She seemed self-conscious, something he'd never seen in her before, and he liked it. He had no doubt that, if he'd asked, she'd tell him that *of course* she'd planned to disarm the venom-spitting fence, if she'd been leaving him behind (to await those *kinsnippers*!). He said nothing. He just followed her, as before, grinning to himself: no longer helpless baggage. He was in charge of his own destiny again, and it felt good.

But surely, subtly, *everything had changed*? Had the trees *moved*? Surely the ranks were different; the uncertain ground had new contours—

"Happens all the time," said Sekṕool, catching his bewildered glances. "The *sek* is an organism: it shifts about as it pleases. That's why there are no trails. The indigenes have their own ways to get around. We use our beacons, and come in on foot. It's simpler."

"What a world. It's like *a circle in Dante's hell*."

"Indeed. All death in life is here, eating its own tail. Yet somehow I love it."

♀

There was a wind blowing outside the wood; they could hear it. Sekṕool gave Forrest a robe like her own: he wrapped himself, the folds settling firmly round his head and face, and they emerged from tepid stillness into a dust-storm. Well-protected but half-blind, he felt a hard surface under the skidding grit, and glimpsed big squared and domed shapes. Fighting the wind to look behind him, he saw the sek: rising like a grey-green mirage, on the edge of a desert-devoured town. She headed for an intact building, and used a touch-pad to open massive double doors. In a covered courtyard, a welcome silence, she bared her face—

"I have a call to make. Come with me. It won't take long."

The room they entered made Forrest think of a chapel: a podium for the minister, benches for the congregation. Images of lizard-people, animal and vegetable flourishes, in coloured metals or enamel, covered the walls. She approached the podium, Forrest took a seat. His legs were too long. Sekṕool was tall, but like a Japanese woman, her height was in her pliant body… Expecting a video link he saw, to his astonishment, powdery matter begin to whirl inside a clear cylinder: building something from the platter upwards. The cylinder withdrew, and there stood another masculine-seeming Venusian; a Lizard Man. Not the guy Forrest had seen in the mirror-screen: someone new. He had scanty head-hair, he wore some kind of dress-uniform; he seemed authoritative but old; or maybe sick. Sekṕool spoke, Lizard Man mainly listened. At one point he looked over her shoulder and Forrest, disconcerted, felt eyes on him: a presence in the instant simulacrum. Finally Sekṕool bowed, the old guy did the same. The body crumbled and vanished.

She walked past Forrest, resuming her headset as she headed for the doors.

"Who was that?"

"My husband. Excuse him if he seemed rude, you'll meet him properly up above. Do you have wives, Johnforrest?"

"I've had two. Then I gave up."

"Wise man… I did what was expected of me. I gave a powerful old man my baby's name, his futurity for our security. A fair trade on both sides: neither of us thought it would be forever. I have no complaints, none at all. But oh, he's a long time dying!"

She flashed him that eerie smile. "Now we need to hurry. The wind usually eases at nightfall, but I want to be far from here by then."

In the covered yard Sekṕool left him briefly, and reappeared leading an extraordinary animal: a low-slung, big-haunched, tan-hided wrinkly camel, with bulbous cat's-eyes, a sinuous neck and tail, and a muzzle thick with stiff, drooping whiskers—

"Johnforrest, meet Miahanhouk. I don't take him into the *sek*, but we need him now. You'll have to ride behind me, I'm afraid. I wasn't expecting to bring home a guest."

Who harnessed Mihanhouk? He listened. Not a footstep, not a voice.

"Are we alone? Where is everybody?"

"Only the indigenes live permanently on the surface, and around here they don't leave the haunted woods. Let's go, it's a long ride to the Sea Mount Station."

The ground staff never saw me, he thought. I am deniable—

The cat-camel's paces were challenging. He loped like a hare, pushing off from his big haunches, landing with an insouciant bounce on his forepaws. So far, so uncomfortable, and then he put on speed. At every leap Forrest (with muttered curses) nearly lost his seat; at every touchdown his tailbone tried to send his cervical vertebrae through the top of his head. Sekṕool rode with her tail tucked up, stirrups high as a jockey's. She glanced around, green eyes vivid between folds of grey veiling and the whipping dust: registering his discomfort. She faced ahead again, and he felt a curious, thrilling, muscular movement.

She was wrapping her tail around him.

"Is that better?"

"Yes," he breathed. "That's… fine."

♀

Gradually, the howling died and the dust cleared. Mihanhouk seemed to feel he'd done enough. He ambled along a rudimentary trail, uphill, between eroded boulders that blocked the view, to a bluff like a wave crest. Sekṕool tapped his shoulder with the knotted end of her reins: the beast knelt and they dismounted.

They climbed the last few metres to a viewpoint, and suddenly faced a staggering gulf. Red-gold cliffs plunged, *way* deeper than the Grand Canyon, into the haze of a basin that stretched forever. To their left, far below the bluff, Forrest saw the trail continuing to another complex of buildings, and skeletal bridgework that reached out, over the abyss, to a rocky, conical pillar. Narrowing his eyes, he saw the sequence repeated: the bridgework linking a string of rocky cones, that rose from unseen depths; becoming tiny and vanishing.

Directly ahead, but far off, brilliant whiteness reflected the pale clouds.

"Is that the ocean out there?"

"Once upon a time," said Sekṕool. "It's mostly a big salt pan now. We live in the clouds, and others in the skies, Johnforrest; where everything is fine. Only fanatics think it matters or feel concerned that we can't live on the surface any more, if we wanted to. Which is just as well. The situation down here is beyond repair."

"So what's the use of worrying? It never was worthwhile."

"Indeed. I'd like to learn your language. From what I can tell it has a fine turn of phrase; many interesting concepts. *Thou shalt not kill.* There's another of them!"

Forrest nodded, his thoughts very far away. Out of the frying pan, into the fire… Our beautiful neighbour *before* she ran into trouble? Your calculations were slightly out, PoTolo!

"What caused the hopeless devastation? Do your scientists have an explanation?"

She thought about it, measuring her words. "Long ago, we lived in a dangerous world and didn't know it. Everything was kind, plenty was all around. One day we stepped on a hidden switch, we pulled the wrong lever; we tipped a balance, and destruction was set in motion, click, clack, like a child's toy: sly and comical and relentless. Or so I understand it. But we took that wrong step a *very* long time ago, Johnforrest. The damage was done before anyone moved to the clouds, let alone the skies. It's nonsense to apportion blame."

The stillness after the wind, the sombre majesty of the scene held them in silence.

"I didn't bring you up here to accuse you, Mr From-The-Sky. There's something I wanted you to see, a trick of this vantage. Look to the east."

He felt the chill before he saw the cause. Far away and very distinct, like a bold line on a child's drawing, a dark ellipse appeared, stretching from horizon to horizon. It grew, like the shadow of the moon across the sun in a solar eclipse; contained, yet seeming liquid as ink. No flashes of radiance, no sunset colours heralded the change. The transition from light to shadow was perfectly abrupt; pure as a note of music.

It was the dark.

Forrest thought of a world without a visible sun. No moon, no stars. A horror ran through him, he wanted to run. At his shoulder the Venusian sighed in delight, as perfect night, velvet night, rose to the zenith and hurried down to engulf them.

"*There*," she murmured, when blackness lapped at Mihanhouk's forepaws.

"Thank you," whispered Forrest.

They rode to the Sea Mount Station as if descending under miles of dark water. She'd fastened lights to Mihanhouk's bridle: although he didn't seem to need them, he was sure-footed and at ease. The Station was lit, and as deserted as the town by the *sek*. The cable-car she summoned, swinging from frictionless chains, black sides hung with rosy lights, reminded Forrest of an Egyptian ship of the dead, on a temple frieze. It rode silently down to their platform; they embarked.

♀

Mihanhouk had a compartment to himself. Sekpool made him comfortable, then joined Forrest in the stateroom, where a buffet offered store-cupboard foods: pickles, spreads and tough breads, savoury cakes of pressed beans (or insect larvae?); crystallised fruit. A fine improvement on sappy-gruel. They moved on, having eaten, to an observation car; taking along a carafe of spirits. The couches were soft and wide: they settled side by side.

"Here's another sight not to be missed, Johnforrest. We're passing over the Trench."

In fathomless blackness, way down below, he saw a vivid, active red line.

"What is that?"

"A rent in the world's hide, close to the old coastline; where the fires of renewal pour out, and worn-out flesh is devoured. It's shrinking. My city takes pictures of the dwindling fire. All the *healthy wounds*, as our scientists call them, are healing. It's not a good sign."

"I've heard about that."

"When the fire stops flowing; when the wounds are gone… then even the clouds and the skies may fail us. But that's a long way off. Neither you nor I need worry!"

Forrest filled two tiny cups, she emptied hers and held it out for more. Like-for-like translation, he thought, turned them into a mediaeval knight and his lady, speaking of eldritch secrets: dooms known only to the wise. She tossed her cup aside, and took his hand. Four-fingered, both outer digits opposable: she gripped like a chameleon.

"This is a great, great favour you're doing for me."

"A trip to the clouds?" Forrest smiled to himself. "It's my pleasure!"

"Still, I feel I owe you. Let me give you some return."

"There's no need."

"Myself?"

"Well, now. That would be an unexpected bonus."

"An interlude, I mean nothing more."

"Of course not!"

Romantic overtures would have been in poor taste, given what he guessed: but his lust was honest, and however she squared it, her offer seemed honest too. Seeing no reason to refuse, he reached around and took the splendid root of her tail in a forthright, determined grip. The tongue that met his when they kissed was slender, strong, active and probing. The gulf behind her smile could have swallowed him whole.

They shucked out of their clothes and embraced, her tail lashed itself around him and he probed her in turn, deeper and longer than he'd have thought possible. Blissfully spent, he fell asleep: and woke still in her grip, a silky, powerful frottage undulating up and down his thighs, his buttocks—

He wondered would he survive this dark journey, or die happy?

♀

Unmeasured riches followed: an engrossing, fabulous *interlude*, with sated pauses in which she told him about her city, and Forrest asked only the most tactful questions. They hardly ate or drank, they slept coupled and entwined. But once, when he woke, he was alone.

Sekṕool was on the opposite couch, limned in faint light, head bent over the oracle bones: the way he'd first seen her. He went over. She looked up, accepting, and drew back to let him see. Just four items; no bones. The 'slab' he remembered was a paper-thin tablet, lit from within, marked in a grid of four by four. Plenty for a tribal shaman, living at the dawn of time. Not much of an apparatus to model the fate of a complex, high-tech society.

But four by four is a powerful number.

"The tokens are relics from your own life," he said. "You've invested them with meaning, for telling the fortunes of your people. Will you tell me a little more, if it's allowed?"

"You are widely learned, Johnforrest". She touched the fragment of patterned textile, wrapped around three small flat sticks: "*What was.*"

A shiny feather or fish-scale set in silver wire: *what might have been.* Or, better, "*the conditional, the always possible.*"

A shrivelled coil of brown, veiny material, probably a root-fragment: *what is.*

And a black stone, glossy as obsidian, was *The Truth.*

The headset was nowhere in this exchange. He asked and she answered in gesture, the timeless, universal language of this other trade of hers—

*Does what you read come true?*

*If you know so much, you know that's a fool's question.*

Then she smiled. The black stone in one fist, she laid her free hand on his breast, where his heart was beating. *But when I know I'm right, however unbelievable, I'm always right…*

Forrest felt suddenly very confused.

Sekṕool returned her tokens to the pouch, and slipped the cord over her head. She returned to their couch and was soon deeply asleep, but he lay awake. *Sekṕool- Sekool,* Woodsong the Sorceress.

Had he really understood her? It didn't seem possible.

♀

Their arrival at Tessera Station was as dramatic as darkfall, in its way. Her city, a cloud-raft the size of Manhattan Island, had come to meet them. Moored by mighty hawsers, it stood at the sheer edge of the Tessera Plateau, beside the cable car buildings. Forrest watched the underbelly as they came in: a mass of swollen, membranous dirigibles layered and roped together in a gargantuan netted frame.

"Unlike the sky habitats in the upper atmosphere," Sekṕool remarked, "our cities were developed from life. The natural bladder-raft colonies that provide our germ material still flourish: small as tables, big as mountain-tops. We harvest and datamine them for improvements."

"Fascinating," said Forrest: making her laugh.

"About Gemin, how he comes to me… You will be discreet?"

"Of course."

She had told him that her city, Lacertan, lead an alliance of liberal and independent cloud-cities known as The Band. The other major bloc was an empire, run on military lines, centred on a vast cloud-raft called Rapton. Empire and Band were currently, technically, at peace, but the covert manoeuvring was vicious: this was the situation that had cost Gemin his life. The dirty story had not been released, it was too inflammatory. The official line was that he'd been killed in a caving accident, on a daredevil expedition to one of the old ocean beds, and tragically it had been impossible to recover his body.

Partly true, but it was a prospecting expedition, said Sekṕool. In disputed territory, where there are rich pickings, and they ran into trouble. He shouldn't have been there at all, of course.

They disembarked, smiling for the welcoming committee, in their desert robes and battered wilderness clothes. The Man From The Sky was instantly surrounded by officials and Venusian-style mediafolk. He didn't speak to Sekṕool again for a while.

♀

Forrest didn't get to watch the return of the bright: Lacertan was riding strong winds and everyone was indoors; sleeping or not. But after that change the city – which had been quiet as a night in arctic wilderness – bustled. Washed, brushed and dressed in Venusian formal style; provided with fine accommodation and service, Forrest was swept from reception to reception. He ate *haute cuisine* delicacies, no better or worse than the same absurd fancywork in New York or London. He talked (in like-for-like translation) with interesting Venusians, and had no trouble passing for a denizen of the upper atmosphere. Contact between the realms was minimal. He was Lacteran's first actual visitor in the flesh: a Marco Polo at the court of Kublai Khan.

Perhaps the most interesting fact he picked up was that Lizard Men, like the ghost boy, had no tails. Which explained a few things. He met Sekṕool again at his private audience with the Master of the City.

The simulacrum he'd seen had been a flattering portrait. In life, the Master was a wraith in a medicalised cocoon; though his eyes, appraising Forrest with great interest, were still sharp. Sekṕool was at the bedside, in a dark blue, formal gown: the first time he'd been close to her since the cable-car. Raised on pillows, the Master offered greetings that were translated by an aide wearing a headset. Forrest had arranged for the orrery watch to be boxed and wrapped, in suitable style. He offered it with misgiving, hoping the gift at least *looked* impressive: but the old man fizzed and crackled with a connoisseur's delight.

"The Master is pleased," reported the aide. "He says the orbits of our planet and our near neighbour present a pretty problem. He has never seen the puzzle worked in craft with such elegance and charm. He suggests you must twin your soul with my lady's brother, our Chief Scientist, who is also fascinated by the third world."

Then the Master was tired, and they were both dismissed. She donned a headset as soon as they were clear of the leader's private apartment. "I think you have no engagements just now, sir. Let me show you a view over the city."

The view from the terrace she chose was not dazzling; they were hemmed in by blank walls, and the redoubt that protected the Residence. But there was a glimpse of bright cloud above, and more rosy-greenery than he'd seen elsewhere.

"So that's my marriage," Sekṕool said, pacing. "He was a good leader, now he's old, and deathly sick. But he's not senile and he doesn't want to let go, so that's that. He's forgotten how he's paralysing me: paralysing the whole city—"

Her hair, grown out, ran in natural, feathery corn-rows to her nape. She wore classy make-up, there were jewels at her throat. The gown was daringly décolleté in the back, at the swell of her tail's root. But he missed her jungle pants.

"You think I'm speaking very freely? Don't worry, everyone knows how I feel. Including the Master… Nobody's going to blab indiscretions in your company, Johnforrest. These things." She tapped her headset. "Are notoriously easy to *hack.*"

"What does the Master think about what happened to your son?"

"That the accident was in disputed territory, and anything's better than war. That I can marry again when he dies, or take a lover now, and have other children. That he'll negotiate when he's stronger (it won't happen, he's dying). I can't bear to tell him *how real my son's suffering still is to me.* So I just have to wait."

The people of Lacertan, Forrest had learned, were a godless lot of sophisticated animists, like Sekṗool herself. They were liberal, they were easy, but the idea of their prince lying untended, "trapped in his death", at the bottom of some hole, gave them the horrors. And *they* weren't visited by that crawling corpse. He knew he was talking at a desperate woman, and forgave her many things.

"What about my twin soul? Your brother, the Chief Scientist?"

"Esbwe? Who knows? He's an eccentric genius, he lives in a world of his own."

The smile he loved fought with the pain. "Enjoy the rest of your visit. You may not have been following the reckoning, we've come a long way since you boarded. We'll soon pass over the spot where you and I met, and then I suppose you'll leave us."

So that's it, thought Forrest. He'd been wondering when he was due to disappear. Or to be *kinsnipped*…

So be it.

♀

Forrest decided it was time he made an acquaintance with his lady's brother; to whom he somehow hadn't been formally introduced. The Chief Scientist didn't do official receptions, but it was surprisingly easy to set up an appointment, once he made his interest known. Esbwe's place of business turned out to be a large but shabby old building, in a heritage area; which, unlike the Residence, didn't seem overburdened with staff, or any other signs of significant office. Perhaps "Chief Scientist" was a courtesy title? The *Minister* for Science, who escorted the foreign dignitary, only to be left twisting her tail in an anteroom – had been reticent on the subject of Esbwe's responsibilities.

Forrest was ushered into a laboratory both like and unlike the same kind of space he'd often visited. Enigmatic machinery; fizzing screens, sleek apparatus that rode tracks on the ceiling, cylinders that rose from the floor. A Lizard Man, in a black smock and white pants (Venusian professional clothing) stood peering into a tank, in the middle of all this.

"Come and look at this, sir Forrest. Look into the *visor* and keep your hands to yourself."

They were alone, and Esbwe was definitely the guy Forrest had glimpsed in the mirror-screen. He went over, and peered through the fixed visor. The tank seemed empty at first, then moving dots appeared, and took on form: twisting strands that divided and recombined—

"What do you make of that?"

"Er, the *living material of cell-signatures*?"

"*Life,* sir! On our world all life is doomed, that is beyond doubt. But I have calculated that the third world has a biosphere, and my great project is to *infect* it. When I've perfected my delivery system, my *animaculae* will be injected through the clouds into the airless deeps beyond. They will make the crossing, and something of us may survive."

"A noble dream," said Forrest.

"You don't believe me. How could one of the menial cloud-dwellers be an Interplanetarian? You gave the Master that orbit-tracking toy for a joke, I'm sure. You forget that *before your habitats were ever launched* the skies above our levels were often clear. You overlook the fact that our records hold a wealth of astronomical knowledge; some of it thousands of years old—"

"I find Lacertan science very impressive."

The scientist curled his lip, in a bitter shadow of her smile.

"How generous. But I'm not one of the idiots who've been fawning over you, Mr From-The-Sky. To me the sky-habitats are the enemy. The Rapt are our natural allies. The sooner we join the empire the better I'll be pleased, and I am happy for you to take that warning home."

"My headset is malfunctioning," said Forrest, mugging puzzlement. "I can't understand a word. I must come back another time. So sorry."

♀

He had decided, with great regret, that he'd be safer if Sekṕool didn't know he was a willing victim of her plans, but after this disconcerting meeting with her brother, he changed his mind. They had to have a frank discussion, and luckily or unluckily, he knew the safest venue for the meeting – in this city where she'd warned him everything he said and heard was monitored. He placed a personal call to Esbwe, and left a message confirming he would return to the lab with a functioning translation device; naming a time after Lacertan office hours.

'Falling asleep in the daytime' was discouraged by incessant bursts of public music. A loud and melodious call to quiet relaxation was fading, as Forrest approached the shabby old building again, and entered it without fanfare. There was nobody about. He stationed himself around the corner from the lab, and waited. Sekṕool arrived soon after him. He was right behind her as she unlocked the doors.

"I thought that would smoke you out."

"*Excuse me*? I was expecting to meet my brother."

"I don't think he's coming," said Forrest, following her inside. "I sent an automated cancellation, immediately after my first message, which he will have seen, and you did not." He tapped the web of his headset. "I can *hack* things like this myself, it isn't very complex."

Not that Forrest cared if Esbwe turned up; except for her sake.

"Sekṕool, I'm afraid I tricked you, but we need to talk, and I believe this room is safe. I don't think even your crazy brother would have risked the open sedition I heard from him earlier today if your *Homeland Security* was listening in. But I knew this lab was firewalled, anyway," he added, deliberately. "You'll remember making a video call, from the *great heart* refuge? That's when I saw him in here, and heard the two of you planning how to use me in a hostage exchange—"

Her big green eyes got bigger, but she kept her head. No panic, no fluster. "So you know. All right… I was desperate. I went hunting down below for a suitable damned Rapt to capture, and exchange for my son's body. I ran into you instead, and it seemed like—"

"A stroke of good luck. I was to be *kinsnipped* from the *great heart* after you left: but then you had a better idea. I understand, and I don't blame you, I just don't know *why the hell* Esbwe's involved. That arrogant idiot is going to destroy you, Sekṗool. Did you know he's planning to sell this city to the Rapt? How do you think the Master; how d'you think *your people* would like the sound of that?"

"Esbwe talks nonsense, nobody listens. I needed his expertise."

"Take mine, instead. I know how to do this thing—

They were two people who had been intensely intimate, but *not very talkative*, and then silenced by the city. Here they were, alone again, and suddenly it was very bewildering—

"He has a right," said Sekṗool, her big eyes shamed and defiant. "An inalienable right, to help me recover our son's body."

"My God... Are you saying your brother is, is your boy's *father*?"

She recoiled. "I know. I know how it sounds, but Johnforrest, I *couldn't* marry him. He was erratic even then. He had no reputation, he's no leader, he was totally unsuitable. I let myself get pregnant, but I married the Master. It made sense to me. My husband would die. I could never *marry* Esbwe. But he'd be beside me, and our son would inherit—"

Like Pharaonic Egypt, thought Forrest, fascinated. So, talent gets courted and rewarded, dynastic power stays with the blood royal—

"Maybe not such good sense to Esbwe."

"Maybe not... I asked his help, I owed him that. It's illegal, of course, for a simulacrum to have a lifespan, but the deal is acceptable. It's been accepted. What I did, to get what we needed, was theft, and I'm sorry—"

"A simulacrum," repeated Forrest, stunned. "A *flish atatonaton—*"

"Yes? A short-lived fleshly automaton, for a dead boy. A fair trade, I thought: and we have a good chance of getting away with it. The Rapt refuse to admit they're holding Gemin. But they'd love to know more about the sky habitat people, and they can learn a lot from a flesh puppet. Forgive me for using you. It's a shady deal but it's going to work, for long enough, and then they won't want to admit it even happened—"

So much for my heroics, thought Forrest. And she was bold, she was reckless, but maybe Forrest was the one who needed forgiving—

"Sekṗool, it's *not* going to work. I'm not, er, what you think I am."

"I know."

"You *know*—?"

"Of course! Esbwe's convinced you're a sky-dweller, but he makes puppets: I'm a doctor. In my world, boy babies' tails are excised, at birth or soon after: the non-existent gods only know why. Yours has never been excised, it's vestigial and internal. That's what I first noticed, but then: your entire skeleton is *different*. Not deformed, *different*; organs too. Your *cell signature* is legible, and obviously functional, but I've never seen anything like it. Maybe I took a mad risk, but I did you no harm and I thought you'd be far away, and never know." Her long smile broke out, uncertainly. "I'm sure you have resources I can't imagine, hidden somewhere in the *sek* where I found you—"

"No I don't, ma'am," said Forrest. "I'm a *shipwrecked sailor*."

Her hand went to the pouch at her throat, she stared at him in amazement – and then a man screamed.

It was a hideous sound: high-pitched, jagged and agonized. Forrest looked wildly around the empty lab. Sekṗool leapt across the room, and slapped her palm on a touch-pad. The wall in front of her opened. Within the space revealed a naked man sat strapped to a chair: flushed and dripping sweat, a headset clasping his skull, tools of torture attached to his body. The Chief Scientist, oblivious, was adjusting his instruments.

The naked man was Forrest.

"The Rapt would have been kinder," said Sekṗool. "Esbwe, it's conscious, and you are *disgusting*. This was not in the bargain."

"What's *he* doing here?" snapped Esbwe, glaring at Forrest. "Now we'll have to eliminate the bastard, and *that* wasn't in the bargain."

"I've been living under a madman's heel," said Sekṗool, in dawning wonder, taking out her knife. "I did you a cruel injustice, Esbwe, and I can't undo it. But enough is enough."

Esbwe howled in fury. "Don't you dare touch it! It's *mine*!"

A lash of her tail sent him skidding. The knife plunged, violent and precise, into the hollow of the doll's collarbone, and it collapsed. "I don't know why I never realised," she murmured, standing over the wet ruin. "I don't have to wait for him to die. I can seize power, I can make my own rules. I can give myself in place of Gemin if I must."

"*Don't talk like that*," shouted Forrest. "Sekṗool, when I thought you were going to hand me over in person, I was willing. I'm *still* willing. I'm not suicidal: I know how to handle hostage bargaining, I've done the work before. I'll be safe, and I'll bring your son's body home—"

"Why would you do that, *man from somewhere else*?"

Forrest, smiling with his eyes, drew her close, and kissed her brow—

But something was happening. Were the palace guards rushing in?

No, it was his hands, they were breaking up, vanishing. He felt a strangely familiar shock; this had happened to him before. It was PoTolo's probe, it was being retrieved. The cloud-raft must be over the drop-zone.

"Sekṕool! Wait for me! I can't stop this, but I'll come back!"

She laid her hand against his heart. "I know."

## 3. The Black Stone

When the orbits were aligned once more, John Forrest returned to West Africa. He was to repeat his stunt for a select group of scientists. He arrived before the guests, and joined Dr PoTolo, alone in the lab. Nothing much had changed, in the room with the big windows that looked out on the sunset horizon. John Forrest, dressed as before in his wilderness kit, also seemed unchanged; except that he was in a better temper.

"That thing,' he said, nodding at the oily black globe in its chamber. "Your time-and-space-travel gizmo. Does it have to be in the container?"

"No, it just needs to be in the room. It's held like that to protect us."

"What happens if I touch it? Sudden death? Radiation sickness?"

"You can *touch* it. I wouldn't advise you to keep it in your pocket for very long," said PoTolo: a little less intimidated, this time round.

"I'm returning to *the exact place and time* where you picked me up?"

"I'll be using the space-time values recorded during the successful retrieval, yes. But you should know, Mr Forrest, it isn't that simple."

On the previous occasion Forrest had disappeared from West Africa at sunset and reappeared, mysteriously bedraggled, an hour before dawn. The interval did not, necessarily, indicate anything about the length of his stay; or even prove that Forrest had arrived on the surface, although the physical evidence was compelling. Forrest had been no help. But proof that the *probe* had visited a habitable Ancient Venus was safely recorded in the data: and it was very, very convincing.

"It's a pity you remember nothing. You still remember nothing?"

Forrest shook his head. "Not a thing, alas."

"This time will be different. We'll have memory-retrieval ready to pluck the images straight from your head, before they can vanish."

Forrest smiled politely: thinking of Woodsong the sorceress, and the promise he was about to put to the test. The guests assembled, there was chatter. He stood in the gate. All eyes were on the human element in the apparatus: nobody noticed that the globe had gone from its place. Hands in his pockets, he looked to the west, where Hawa herself had sunk into cloud, but the stars he would never see again were beginning to shine out.

And the world disappeared.

# The Old Schoolhouse

*Written for S. T. Joshi and Lynne Jamneck's Gothic Lovecraft anthology. I've been a fan of H.P Lovecraft all my life, or at least since I bought a big fat classic Horror anthology at a Jumble Sale when I was eight (my mother, a devout rationalist, was horrified; pun intended) – and fell in love with "The Rats In The Walls". I also know quite a bit about modernist composers' works, and their social lives, because my son is devoted to that stuff. For the record, the NASA "planets" recordings are real (in case you didn't know). The most relevant Lovecraft story is probably "The Shadow Out Of Time", and as a sound-track stand-in for "Hindey Playground" – but with absolutely no intention of suggesting Stockhausen's music has eldritch occult connections – you could listen to his* Gesunge der Junglinge .

*In my opinion, it isn't real horror if in the end there's a door out of the funhouse.*

Ten days after Eliud's plane vanished I drove to Norfolk, with my cello and Fenris in the back of the car. It was a warm, dull August day; the sky over Eastern England was the colour of dust. Driving in silence (no music, no news or chat I wanted to hear), I felt strongly that I had company. Over and over I'd peer into my rear mirror, wondering who was in the back seat. My black cello case and the little black dog gazed solemnly back, puzzled by my unease. The illusion was natural: I'd probably never been alone on this journey before. At least one of us, usually Renton, would always have been with me.

I collected the keys from Eliud's house-agent, and took the long-ago route to Schoolhouse Lane. Eliud's garden was just as I remembered it. The wildflower banks had gone to seed, a mad tangle of baked stalks and tottering poppy-heads, but the grass plots between them were neatly shorn. I let myself in, dumped my bag and the cello beside a stack of flat-pack storage boxes, and looked around. Nothing had changed. The Victorian Board School's single classroom, long and high, was all the living space. Along the far wall, French doors opened onto a brick terrace. Where I stood, between Eliud's study and the kitchen, white-painted crooked stairs led to his bedroom suite. I would sleep up there. The house-agent had told me I couldn't have a bed made up in the Studio, as in the old days. The garden buildings, our summer camp, were no longer habitable: they'd been allowed to go to seed, like the flowers.

The floors shone, the rugs were brushed. The kitchen, and that tiny lower-orders bathroom next to it, sparkled. The piano was in tune: which startled me, though I knew Eliud had been here. He'd called me from the Schoolhouse three weeks ago. The great man had finally agreed to let his official biographer get to work. He wanted someone to help him sort his papers: pack everything up and send it to his new house outside London. I'd agreed to meet him here, after his trip to Sydney.

But Eliud Tince had vanished, with his current entourage and a planeload of other passengers and crew, over the Southern Ocean (where the plane shouldn't have been at all). In the end, failing all news, I'd decided to come alone and tackle the job myself. Probably, mainly, because I couldn't face cancelling his arrangements—

I didn't know who the biographer was. Before the bust-up it could only have been Michael Renton: Eliud Tince's amanuensis, his *eminence grise*; the 'torturer' who got the best out of him, as Eliud used to say. But Renton was gone, Renton could no longer be mentioned, so who...? I'd been wondering, picking over the eminent specialists who might be in line, and thinking it'd better not be *me* the master had in mind. I'm an instrumentalist, not a biographer. I wouldn't know how to begin. But you never knew, with Eliud. He had strange ideas. I unlocked his study and checked his desk; I climbed the crooked stairs and poked around in his bedroom. There weren't many places to hide a mountain of paper: the task looked manageable.

But it was too late to start work today. I wandered about, studying framed photographs, mostly black and white; so much better-looking than colour. I found myself in a dark smock under an apple tree, long thin arms and a shock of short dark hair; legs like two tilted sticks propped against my cello's flanks. And here was Maria Wenger, Eliud's stepdaughter by his second marriage. Not yet the wonderful, the unique soprano, but already my best friend, in a summery dress all over roses. Yellow roses; I remembered it... It was usually Maria who took the pictures. She was a good photographer, the rest of us were rubbish: Maria in her roses was lucky she'd kept her head. Here was Rikard Glode the pianist, throwing Frisbee with Renton and Julia; while Julia's daughter,

Perseis, aged about two, sat by on a rug. My ex-boyfriend in that shapeless green polo shirt, and the baggy shorts with the frog-pattern… I recognised my friends by their clothes, the way people recognise relatives after a disaster. Only Eliud, grinning in a deck chair, those famous plaid trousers secured around his scrawny waist by an enormous leather belt, was unchanged by the past. I wondered how old he'd been then: more than two decades ago, when I was nineteen? He'd started admitting to 'the mid-eighties' recently, but he was notoriously hard to pin down. He wanted us to believe he was immortal, the vain old turtlehead.

We'd been like family, like courtiers, with Eliud as our ruler and Renton his grand vizier; reigning here in deepest Norfolk, and we didn't go to them: the *avant garde* music world came to us. But nothing lasts forever. After the big fight with Renton, Eliud had returned to the USA, but not to his native New England. He took up a prestigious post in California and we all went our separate ways.

I'd had my successes since then, but never again known such a magic circle. Now here I was again, drawn back to the source, staring at a black and white photo of my ex-boyfriend at thirty: his merman eyes reduced to punctured grey. His tarnished-gold hair, receding even then, flew around his head in thick metallic scales; so soft to the touch.

I made a mental note to find or create digital copies of all the pictures: save them off and put them with the biographical material.

Later, in dusty twilight, I whistled Fenris from wherever he'd been roaming and we walked up the lane to the Flint Barn; like the Schoolhouse, a relic of the former agricultural community of Hindey; where I knew I'd get signal. Connectivity at the Old Schoolhouse was just as dire as ever. There was no news: only more of the same figures, diagrams and graphs; the same rumours that went nowhere. Maria, an Australian herself, was at the airport, keeping vigil with the horde of dignified, tearful and terrified relatives, lovers and friends. I was glad Eliud had someone on the spot. His third wife, Lucia Ventto, had been on the flight with him, along with her son Martin, and Martin's newly pregnant girlfriend Annemarie, plus Maria's sister, the choreographer Judit Saed; and Maria's dear friend, ex-husband, Mel Colman the operatic conductor… Almost a clean sweep. It was eerie.

I thought of sending a message to Eliud's phone, *hope you're okay*, but that would be ghoulish. I texted Maria instead.

The grain harvest was over. The old barn, a monument to the days when farm labour was plentiful and poor, stood foursquare, facing the remains of sunset on a vast, stubbled, prairie horizon. It was still empty, just as it had been in our day: unconverted, un-reclaimed. I sat with my back to a flint wall that held the heat of the day, waiting for Maria to respond, and reading an article that listed all the vessels, air and sea, that had crashed, been turned back by extreme turbulence, or plain vanished, over the Southern Ocean recently. The phenomenon was blamed on Climate Change. Or Sunspots. Or both… No reply from Maria. It would be early in Sydney. Maybe she was still asleep.

As I headed back in deep twilight, a stooped and blurred figure came towards me on the lonely track. I was almost frightened, but it was only our former neighbour: the artist whose showroom was at the dandy, urban end of our lane, where there was grey asphalt instead of ruts and grass.

"It's Aiode, isn't it?" he said, when we were face to face.

"Ay-ee-the," I corrected him, uneasily. I couldn't remember his real name. He hadn't been friendly, as far as I recalled, and nor had we. We called him "Mr Raven", after a large, ugly black metal raven that stood at his gate. It was still there, I'd noticed it as I drove by.

"I knew you'd be back. I saw Mike Renton in the lane yesterday."

He was never Mike. Always just *Renton*, with us. "I don't think so!"

Mr Raven looked at me oddly. "I'm sure I'd know Mike Renton!"

I shook my head. "I don't think he's even in the country."

"My mistake. I hear old Eliud's selling off the ancestral home?"

"Ancestral—?"

He gave me the sidelong look again. "Lord, yes! He had family here going back to the old Hindey times, and beyond. They only left when the village got razed, and that was before the War. That's why he bought that little old place you're in. Didn't you know?"

Thankfully Fenris, my inheritance from a foundered relationship, was exploring and didn't reappear, scrambling from under the hedge, until our nosy neighbour had walked on – saving me from having to explain the presence of Renton's dog.

It was an unsettling conversation. I wasn't surprised that Eliud was selling up, but why hadn't he told me himself, when he asked me here? I was sure Mr Raven couldn't have seen Renton, anyway. My ex-boyfriend was living in Japan, semi-retired: just firing off the occasional brilliant article or paper, to let the *avant-garde* world know he was still alive.

Δ

In the morning I set up my work camp. I moved furniture, to clear a space on the schoolroom floor: assembled several of the flat-pack boxes, and collected together everything that could be described as 'papers'. I would sort through them on the long table where we used to eat. The digital stuff: the contents of a venerable PC's hard drive; plus a jumble of data sticks, memory cards and disks, could wait. The vintage electronic instruments, vials of Eliud's alchemy, might hold treasure in their primitive 'memories', but I'd leave them until last.

Biographical material. Catalogue material, Discography. Original scores; household accounts. Personal letters, business letters, autographed concert programmes… All I could do was make a start. I broke out a new, lined A4 pad, to jot down running notes. Hopefully a system would take shape as I worked.

I was puzzled by the flat packs, when I thought about it. It wasn't like Eliud to be so organised. Had he got himself a new Renton, and I didn't know? The idea jarred. Renton could be so overbearing, so possessive… Of course Eliud didn't want me for a biographer, that was a joke, but he'd definitely hinted he had something to discuss. I'd thought it might be a renewal of our partnership. He hadn't produced a significant new work for years; it was about time, if it was ever going to happen. So I'd let my hopes run on, and why else had I brought the cello with me, when Eliud was probably *dead*, if not daydreaming that I would find this new work among his papers, and it would have been written for me—

Now I felt embarrassed at myself, thankful that nobody would ever know; but still threatened by the imaginary new power-broker—

I put the *Shock and Awe Fantasia* on the schoolroom's sound system, (for prepared piano, cello and white noise) and set to work; to the raw, sonorous music of Eliud's elegy for the soul of the USA. He'd fallen out with *Shock And Awe*, it was 'too emotional', but I still loved my own bowing, and the inhuman, incredible precision Eliud had drawn from me. I'd left the crazy little world of the *avant garde* behind, I'd been a pretty good, middle-rank classical soloist for nearly twenty years, but I still missed the master's intensity—

A sheet of peculiar, colourful childish drawings started a heap all of its own. When I'd run into four or five of them I looked more closely.

The figures were drawn in pencil, and scattered apparently at random over different-sized sheets of plain paper. The most common was a triangle, with two strong lines jutting from the base, one from each of the diagonals, and a circle balanced at the apex; like a child's first version of the human form. Ovoids and squares, less frequent, followed the same pattern. The 'heads' had no features, but softer, wavy lines often extended from both 'heads' and 'bodies'; like curly hair, or tentacles; or sine waves. Nearly all the figures were coloured; carelessly scribbled over in blue, red, yellow or dark green. Some were isolated, some in rows, some clustered: some were *very* small, some much larger.

At first I'd thought they really were children's drawings. There'd always been children in Eliud's life. But each sheet was dated and annotated, in the master's own handwriting. The dates were years apart, and the drawings seemed more coherent, less childish, the more I looked. There was decision and purpose in them, sharp as the knife-edge arpeggios of *Shock and Awe*. They seemed faintly familiar, too. Had I once *known* about these strange geometric fish? If they were part of something, an idea developing over decades, what did they mean?

I pondered over one of Eliud's annotations. *Other dimensions are not spatial but exist at right-angles to our own...* Was there an optical illusion involved? Obedient, from long training, to my composer's weird demands, I held one of the sheets edge-on to my nose, and tried to look along it sideways; *at right angles*. I caught a glimpse of something whipping out of sight; or opening and swiftly closing—

But Fenris was barking and barking. I dropped the paper and rushed around the house: I couldn't find him. I ran outdoors in a panic and raced around the garden, calling *Fenris, Fenris*: charging over turf, crashing through flower banks, but the little dog just went on barking madly, somewhere out of sight. Twisted orchard boughs encroached on the shady lawn where Rikard had pitched his tent. The buildings – the Studio, my nest that Renton had shared; the Cabin; the Tenements, the Treehouse and the Sauna (not a sauna, but another spare bedroom, in our day) lay derelict, and I didn't have the keys with me, I couldn't get in. I could only rub at cobwebs and peer through dusty glass like a ghost. I shouted *Fenris, Fenris*, but the little black dog had stopped barking—

Then he started up again: much further away. He must have chased a rabbit into Eliud's parcel of trees – a narrow slip of woodland, attached to the property but jutting into the lonely prairie fields. In a gap in the orchard hedge there was a polished root that served as a doorsill: I stepped over it, the trees closed around me, and once more nothing had changed. The same narrow path led the eye to a distant lozenge of pale daylight; the same brooding atmosphere swallowed me. The trees pressed close: mostly young oaks and thorns, rising from a vicious understorey of bramble, and competing for light with the big old twisted chestnuts. I hurried up the path, still calling *Fenris!* Insects buzzed. Birds scolded unseen. Once the wings of a big hunting hawk flashed between branches. None of us had ever liked the wood: but I thought I knew what was in it. About two thirds through, I came across something I'd never seen before.

Long ago, a massive chestnut had fallen. The timber must have been dragged out and taken away. The stump had remained, tipped on its side, grey starfish roots reaching for the sky; guarding a hollow, open space. We'd tried to enjoy this secret glade in the old days: bringing picnics, rugs and wine; building midnight bonfires. But not often. The narrow wood repelled us, literally. It drove us away. It was dark and ugly; everything prickled and there were biting insects.

I was tired and hot. Fenris was still barking, but now he was behind me. I realised the futility of chasing a little dog who was running round in circles, and noticed a series of pale patches in the leaf litter; like splashes of sunlight where there was no sun. I stepped on one of them: and it was a stone. There was a ring of pale stones set in a circle around the glade. They must have been buried in our day: brought to the surface, maybe, by last winter's spectacular rains. There were marks on them, like drawings. Hunkered down for a closer look I saw traces of colour, and seemed to hear a kind of chiming, a kind of chattering—

But Fenris was barking and barking.

I ran through the trees again, oblivious of tearing brambles, and back into the house. The French doors were open: my car was parked beside the terrace. Beyond my parking space Eliud's drive had been overwhelmed by weeds, and somewhere in there Fenris was terrified: barking and barking… I fought my way into the tangle ambushed by sticky burrs, savaged by nettle stings, and found him crouched on the doorstep of the Caravan; which still stood in its old place, immoveable now, white flanks devoured by bindweed and goosegrass. I picked up the little black dog and hugged him tight.

"It's no use Fenny. Nobody lives there anymore."

He lay quiet in my arms. I carried him back to the schoolroom; his warm, compact, muscular little body snuggled close. As we stepped indoors, I saw something. An awful terror shook me, a sick abyss, deeper than the worst nightmare I'd ever had… Then I was kneeling on the floor, a sheet of coloured doodles in my hand: *Shock and Awe* on the sound system, and Fenris peacefully snoozing on an armchair; where he'd been since breakfast.

It was the strangest feeling. I touched my cheeks; my bare arms. Not a scratch, and I was perfectly cool. I even looked at the soles of my shoes. Not a trace of leaf litter. I'd been working for hours, I hadn't eaten since morning. A dizzy spell… I decided it was time to quit for the day.

Δ

The weather stayed dull and warm. I ate my meals at our old breakfast table, outside the kitchen door; I was never very hungry. Yoghurt and honey, oatcakes and coffee in the morning; a bowl of soup and some fruit in the evening. In the calm stillness of the fading light, Fenris laid a small vole at my feet, and looked up at me hopefully, ears cocked. I could see that he'd broken its back. Its front legs moved; little paws groping. Blood trickled from its mouth.

I sipped coffee. "You want me to mend your toy? Sorry, no can do. You should have been more careful."

I'd have liked to put the creature out of its misery, but it's not that simple to kill a small animal cleanly: I might make things worse, so I didn't try. When its eyes had dimmed I thought of burying it, wrapped in soft leaves. But a dead animal wants no covering but time; no shroud but the air, so I tossed it into the long grass.

Δ

There were no recent papers in the pile from Eliud's study; no evidence to prove he was "selling up", but I soon found the 'Hindey' folder. I shook out the contents of a battered foolscap envelope, and studied his treasured relics. Here was the old church, St Iaad's, with its squat, square tower, at one end of a straggle of hovels bordering what was now our lane; the familiar bulk of the Flint Barn at the other. The Schoolhouse itself in close-up, with its last generation of pupils. Girls in pinafores, boys in breeches, some barefoot, some in enormous boots; their shrunken little faces pinched with malice or hunger; or maybe just boredom. Here was a page from St Iaad's parish register, photographed a little more recently: the entry for the birth of a boy circled in red. He was an 'Eliud Tince', but was he Eliud's grandfather, or great-grandfather? I couldn't remember, and the date was too faded to make out.

A plan of the Schoolhouse property. The parcel of trees was labelled, in spidery copperplate: *Hindey Playground...* We used to say we betted it had been a miserable 'playground' even back then, and Eliud would scowl at us, he was proud of his tiny wood—

I wondered why I'd been astonished when 'Mr Raven' called the Schoolhouse Eliud's ancestral home. I'd always known this story. But Eluid's plane was at the bottom of the Southern Ocean, and I was here alone. No wonder I had moments of confusion—

In a different folder I found a modern, studio colour print: Eliud and his children. It seemed to be his birthday, but the cake (of course!) had no forest of candles. They'd signed their names in the margins: Bich, already in her sixties, the Vietnamese baby he'd adopted with his first wife; Gogo and Siaka, daughter and son of the dancer Djènèba Khady; the great love of Eliud's life. Maria and Judit. Martín Ventto, and of course Perseis, the baby of the gang... How happy Eliud looked! How proud he'd been of them all, and yet none of them was his biological child.

Renton, who could be cruel, used to say the master had 'a touch of the tar brush' and was afraid of passing the taint on. It was true the old man had strange, tribal ideas about race. He'd once startled a famous musician by congratulating him on his 'purely human, true Mandingo blood'. But the 'taint' (it came back to me) was not racial but a disease, untreatable cancer or something, that Eliud was determined not to pass on.

Everyone forgets. Of course I had forgotten things. But my memory lapses were starting to bother me, like a fog in my skull that could be hiding monsters. What else had I erased? What bitter words, what angry scenes I would never want to recall—?

Δ

Later than time lag demanded, because I didn't want to meet Mr Raven again, I walked up to the Flint Barn and talked to Maria. "It's a good atmosphere," she said, gallantly. "We're looking out for each other." She was no longer at the airport. She was back at her gorgeous waterfront house with a couple from Singapore, whose son and little granddaughter had been on the flight, and a young NZ woman who had lost her mother. There was still no news. Nothing had been found, not a scrap of debris.

"It's so hot," said Maria. "More like Christmas than August. They're saying weird atmospheric pressure might have screwed-up the plane's instruments. Might be screwing the search data too… There are empty islands, down south. The pilot could have made a safe ocean landing, and some of them could be safe: but unable to make contact…?"

I hesitated too long. "I saw that story. Yes, it sounded hopeful."

Maria sighed. "How are you doing? Have you found a will?"

"It'll be with his lawyers," I said. "I'll find nothing like that. Eliud kept the house up, it's in good repair, but he hasn't lived here for years. What I'm sorting is archive stuff."

"Oh. I see. I didn't realise—"

I heard her unspoken question, *so why are you doing this?*

Maria had her imaginary island, I had Eliud's papers. I could tell from her voice that she'd accepted the loss of the old man, but was trying, irrationally, to hang onto the others, her family and friends. I was the other way round. I just couldn't let go of Eliud.

Δ

In the jumble of documents and souvenirs I ran into a CD of NASA's *Music Of The Planets* – emissions captured on space probe flybys, converted into sound. I put it on. I hadn't forgotten *this*. Eliud had called the confection 'poppycock' and 'fake', but he'd been fascinated. The *Dark Matter Suite* was full of shameless quotes… The sighs of Jupiter did nothing much for me, but Mercury's eerie crackles conjured pictures in my mind, evil little crustaceans that crept over blood red rocks.

I wondered if there was a connection with the drawings. Weren't Eliud's annotations littered with references to 'aliens' and 'other worlds'? I looked back over my notes.

*Alien intelligence can be perceived in certain conditions without resorting to data from so-called outer space,* AND THEY ARE LISTENING!

*Our universe is an illusion. Worlds on worlds interpenetrate ours. There is no "out there" Everything is in reach. Auditory and Visual Alternatives occupy space in precisely interleaved layers*

But my curiosity vanished, overwhelmed by an immense nostalgia for the past; for the days when I took Eliud's semi-scientific pronouncements absolutely seriously. And a great sadness: knowing that

I would never see the old man again.

I worked all night, forgetting to eat but finishing a bottle of wine. At dawn I woke from a cat-nap, curled on the rug in the midst of my boxes. I took a quick shower, whistled for Fenris and we walked out into a cool bright day: up the lane, over a stile and around the back of Eliud's parcel of trees. The little black dog scampered ahead: burrowing under the fence and popping out again joyously, at my feet. I watched a pair of goshawks, hunting the trees' high margin: scissoring the pale sky with their razor cuts until it seemed as if Eliud's other worlds might come falling through. A roebuck leapt from a hollow in the stubble and rocketed away.

When we reached the back way into the wood Fenris immediately wriggled under the gate and vanished. I was left behind, struggling to climb over: the gate, never an obstacle before, had been lashed shut with barbed wire. I caught up with him, having lost fabric and gained some bloody scratches, in the bonfire glade. I saw the ring of pale stones at once and stared at them, astonished. So my 'dizzy spell' didn't happen? So I really did run out here? And that sinister moment: when I came in from the wood, and saw myself *inside out*, was real? I picked up the little dog and hugged him. "*Why* were you barking like that?" I asked him. "*Why* did you drag me out here? They're only stones."

Fenris licked my nose.

This time I noticed that the circle had a centre. I put Fenris down and kicked at the litter until I'd uncovered the whole of a larger plaque. What did the array mean? A radiating star, a sun surrounded by planets? A playground game? The sky above the glade was bright, the 'markings' were easier to make out than before. I saw the stick-limbed figures, the traces of colour, and knew I'd found the originals of Eliud's drawings.

I had the glimmering of an *amazing* idea.

I took photos. I made sketches, carefully as I could, in my pocket notebook, and hurried back to the house.

The photos weren't a success, but my sketches matched the drawings so closely that Eliud's figures, with their round heads and stick limbs, just *had to be* derived from the stones in the wood. They weren't copies. His ovoids, triangles and squares were more formal, and very differently organised: on scaffolds, in rows, in layered chords; in tiny clusters of grace notes. Intensely excited, I knew my insight was correct; it had to be. This was musical notation.

I spread the sheets on the floor and stared at them. I took out my cello; the first time I'd touched it since I arrived. My old playing chair was by the piano, where it had been waiting for me, all these years. I pulled it out and sat for a while, the instrument between my knees; the bow in my hand. It was a meditation, a reverence; a commitment to the new work (that I couldn't begin to study yet!).

I tuned my strings. I played a few scales, and then the challenging arpeggio passage from *Shock And Awe*: without a slip, which seemed a good omen. I looked down at the drawings. Notation, definitely, but how the hell was it supposed to be played? Eliud hadn't left me a single clue.

*Sideways*, I thought, and in another flash of insight, I remembered that in what seemed one of the most significant annotations, Eliud referred to a *superposition*. Many alternatives occupying one auditory space. *A superposition of alternate worlds, collapsed by sound…* That sounded like a multi-layered recording! And it was probably still here, in the Schoolhouse!

I abandoned my cello and plunged into the digital material that I hadn't yet touched. The PC's hard drive; memory cards; datasticks: CDs and disks; the vintage electronic orchestra. Nothing remotely matched my search and I was in despair. Even if the drawings could be translated into the musical values Eliud had intended, by some process I couldn't imagine, they were discontinuous scraps. It would be impossible to reconstruct the work. Finally, my head spinning and ringing, I took the house agent's keys and went outdoors.

I'd have searched the Studio first, just to cross it off my list: except that I didn't want to see what I knew I'd see, and so I came to it last. The key turned: but ivy tendrils had laced the door shut, and it was silted deep in leaf litter. I wrestled my way in, and saw what I had dreaded: mouldering relics of a cobwebbed sorrow. My bed, my nest among the recording desks, was gone, of course. So was the equipment. Sound-proofing baffles hung festering from the ceiling and the walls.

As I dragged the door shut, wondering why I'd been so afraid of my poor old home… something fell, inside. I shoved the door open again: a dusty cardboard tube, the length of my arm, lay on the floor. It was labelled *Aiode*. Something inside rattled. I unwound withered sticky tape, and pulled off the cap at one end. I peered inside, and my heart began to beat like thunder—

But Fenris was barking and barking.

He'd gone back to the Caravan. He was on his hind legs, pawing at the door, yapping and yapping. I grabbed him, I shouted: I was so keyed up, and the little dog was so infuriating. I hauled him out through the stinging tangles; the little dog fighting all the way. As soon as I slackened my grip he tried to bolt for the Caravan again. "Oh no you don't!" I yelled. I twisted his collar, I shook him, I *slapped* him—

"What's he done then, poor little dog?"

Mr Raven was stooping by my car. "The gate was open," he said. "I thought I'd drop in, see how you're doing. Sorry if it's inconvenient."

One fist locked round Fenris's collar, embarrassed that I'd been caught beating the little dog, I glared at him, trying to shove the hair out of my eyes. The gate had not been open.

"Doing with *what*?"

"With the cleaning," said Mr Raven, unperturbed. "You're clearing the old place out, aren't you? Isn't that what Eliud sent you here for?"

"My work's going well. Close the gate on your way out."

I carried Fenris indoors. He was quiet now, and trembling. I was so ashamed. I told him I was sorry. I hugged him, I kissed his rough head, I combed the burrs from his coat, and then shut him in the kitchen eating tinned tuna for a treat. It would drive me crazy if he ran away again.

Δ

The cardboard roll was on the piano, where I'd left it. A datastick dropped out when I upended it: I eased-out the scroll of paper that remained, very carefully. Both stick and scroll were firmly labelled: *Hindey Playground.* So now I had a recording, *and a score.* A detailed, pictogram score, several metres long; left hidden by Eliud, for me.

Take that, Mr Raven. I am not some *skivvy.*

It was late when I got up to the Barn, and Maria wasn't answering her phone. She'd sent me a text: sounding more resigned; more hopeless, and very tired. I didn't mention the new work in my reply. I ran my news checks on the lost flight (for form's sake: there was no change), and headed back, still thinking, fast and furiously, about Eliud's notation—

The moon, which had been brighter and brighter since I'd arrived in Norfolk, was full tonight, and the sky was as clear as the dust would let it be. I took to the prairie, and climbed that hateful barbed-wire gate again: impelled by an idea that wouldn't wait. It was dark on the path between the trees, but the glade was full of moonlight.

Eliud had used the drawings on these stones – perhaps traces of a children's game; probably more than a hundred years' old – for his pictogram notation. I had poor photos, and better sketches of the originals, but no image of the configuration *and the configuration must be crucial.* I'd brought my good camera out with me. I found footholds in the grey, squirming grooves of the chestnut stump – so well placed that I had the weird idea I'd carved them myself, and forgotten doing it; except they were weathered and old. Maybe Eliud had carved them. Or the children, long ago. I climbed as high as I could, and the moonlit, radiating star was directly below—

I had no idea what any of this "meant", of course. I didn't need to know. I didn't have to understand Eliud's strange ideas about the cosmos, or his childhood memories of Hindey, (memories of his grandfather's stories?) All I needed to know was *how he wanted me to play*; and I was still lost without him, but I had all the pieces of the puzzle now.

Δ

I uploaded the moonlit pictures, printed them on photo paper, and compared them minutely with several diagrammatic annotations on the score. I prepared the vintage instruments, carefully following Eliud's instructions. (I'm probably the only cello soloist in the world who also knows how to tamper with antique sound channel cards). I unrolled the first part of the score and laid it at my feet, with the radiating star images set above and below – and played my best guess at the opening phrases over and over, until I could match Eliud's exacting directions, not well; but at least note by note; term by term.

The preparation took a long time. But I still felt alert – though hazy about when I'd last slept or eaten – when I was finally, roughly satisfied, and I didn't feel like waiting. My rendition would be drastically imperfect, but at least I could make a start. I corrected recording levels, set timings for the electronics and sat down to play, the pictogram at my feet, and Eliud's machines around me.

When I set my bow to the strings I almost started to cry, because the old man wasn't here. He wasn't here, and he would never know. It passed. Soon I was calm; and engrossed.

I can't say I *liked* the music I was making. Actually I didn't like it at all, at this first pass: but it was certainly compelling – and extremely challenging, technically, in ways I found irresistible. I fell into the trance-like, flow-state of concentration that Eliud's difficulties demanded, and as my body played, as my mind worked; as I stopped everything, unrolled the score to the next passage, started everything again and returned to my chair: some part of my sleep-starved self fell into a dream.

A mighty city took shape, rising impossibly from the Schoolroom floor; extending for miles in height; in depth. I knew this vision; or so it seemed to me. Unless my mind was now inventing dreams I'd never had, instead of destroying memories, this city (triggered by something I'd read, about how Antarctica might rise, released from the humungous pressure of the ice sheets) had been haunting my nights since Eliud's flight vanished; or longer. But tonight it seemed created directly by the music. At first it was a toy, a coloured game; then it filled the room, and then it was huge, unutterably vast. I left my mind and body playing, and walked in its streets.

The walls were tall and black as basalt, or the black-green of very deep water. They glistened like polished ice. The streets were wide and deeply grooved; they had decorated, raised sidewalks. I had no clue how tall I was, whether I was an ant or a giant, until I reached a wide stone ramp, leading in a spiral to the doors of a huge building. The doors were the same dark red as the rocks of Mercury. The crustaceans that crept on those rocks were carved here, glinting and chittering. They were much bigger than I had imagined. I watched them; feeling that I was being watched myself, but with indifference: I could do no harm.

I walked into a gallery on the outside of the building; a kind of conservatory, full of opulent plants. A figure moved among them. It turned and looked at me, with a knowing smirk that reminded me of Mr Raven. The shock was staggering. *It looked at me*, I looked at it: and I was no longer dreaming. I was awake, and my body was turned inside out. In the Schoolroom someone played the cello. In the City I, the same I, was looking at the red-grey, pulsing, twining, inside of my own skull. I saw myself: the way I was in *its* dimensions, like a string twisted the wrong way in every fibre. And *it* was one of Eliud's little figures, actually one of them, but at home: a giant in its own world's conditions.

It came closer; in some sense (the shift was instantaneous). I felt its curiosity, then the sine-wave, 'tentacle' emanations engulfed me, a horrible feeling, and I was part of it. No more than gut bacteria, but still I *was* the alien, walking in the vast, convoluted, City; seeing others of my kind; and others of my race, the ovoids and the squares, but *ovoid and square* was nonsense now. I unrolled the score again, I played again. I heard the chiming, the chattering of children's voices, a chorus distorted and rising. Revulsion and terror gripped me, as once in the wood, an alien disgust that took images from slime and vomit, from suffocation and strangling, from eyes put out, and a mouth full of earth—

I dropped the bow. My cello fell with a crash. I stumbled to the sound desk, and stared at Christmas trees of vibration, propagating across the screens. I had dropped my bow, thrown down the instrument, but my part in the monstrosity continued. I could see it, twining there in the mix, and I couldn't remove myself. I couldn't stop this.

I ran out of the room, and through the kitchen; Fenris' claws clattering after me. I swooped down and grabbed him as I fled the house—

I ran, the little dog silent and terrified in my arms, all the way up the track. When we reached the Flint Barn I set Fenris down, and looked back. The moon had vanished, the air felt thick and electric. From that slight elevation, under roiling clouds that covered the sky, charcoal veined with silver, I saw concavities in the prairie fields: the ghosts of old Hindey. In the hollow where St Iaad's church had stood shadowy things struggled, like huge new-born animals in their birth-caul. I heard a friend's voice muttering, *he might knock down a few hovels, but what kind of landowner razes a church, Aiode?* The little dog pressed against my ankles, shivering, and *Hindey Playground* went on unfolding its horrible music; in the distance, and inside my skull. The City was rising, in all its immensity, filling me with awful, sickening terror—

Δ

I woke up in Eliud's bed, missing Fenris's warm small weight at my feet. My head ached. I couldn't remember if I'd finished playing the piece. Thank God Eliud wasn't here. Whatever he meant by his new work, he'd be disgusted if he knew about my hippy-dippy hallucinations.

In the kitchen I found an empty red wine bottle, a glass, and no sign that a meal had been eaten: which explained the throbbing head, and the memory lapse! In the Schoolroom there was confusion. The score was intact, but my photos were gone, and somebody had been burning treated paper in the fireplace. I set things to rights (thankfully nothing was damaged); I put my cello back in its case. I ate breakfast, drank strong coffee, and resumed my task of sorting Eliud's papers.

Deflated, hollowed out, I didn't check the playback. I didn't try, then or later, to resume my performance of *Hindey Playground.* I felt I'd woken from a long, exhausting dream; it was over, and now I would let somebody else decide what the new work was worth. When I was packing up the *Hindey Playground* material, I noticed that the dusty label on the score tube, *Aiode*, was in Renton's handwriting, not Eliud's; which seemed strange, but I didn't dwell on the puzzle. Everything went into the box labelled 'Unfinished Works' – which was by no means empty!

I stayed out of the narrow wood. I made my nightly trek up to the Barn, but there was never any signal, for some reason. Good news, bad news; or (most likely) no news, would have to wait until I got home. I taped the boxes. I called the removal firm; left a voicemail, telling them everything was ready to pick up, and I drove away.

I drove away: heading for the local market town, to leave the keys with Eliud's house agent. It was another dull, dusty, end of summer day; like the day I'd arrived. A mile or so down the road I glanced in my rear mirror and saw the cello case, all alone.

I had left Fenris behind! How the hell did that happen!

I slammed on the brakes: luckily the country road was empty behind me. I pulled over, my heart hammering. Calm down, I told myself. When did you last see him? When had I last seen Fenris? Why did that question make my hands shake, why did it sicken me? Think, think. All I could remember was Eliud on the phone, that conversation when he asked me to come to Norfolk. He was whispering, his voice sounded hoarse and strange. I remembered wondering was there somebody with him, wondering if it was Renton, of all people; and then nothing more. Then I was driving to Norfolk... But when had I last seen Fenris? I couldn't think, I just started to shake.

Thankfully I still had the keys.

I sped back to the Old Schoolhouse. I called him. He wasn't in the house. I ran around searching, calling for him, getting frantic, and at last I heard him bark.

Beyond my parking place, greenery had overwhelmed the drive. I fought my way to the end, vaguely puzzled by signs that someone had busted through the tangles before me, and there was the white caravan: where it must have been standing derelict since the big fight; since Renton walked out. Fenris was barking right in front of me, but he was invisible. He must be inside. How could he be *inside?* I dragged at bindweed, scalded my hands on nettles and thorns, an icy sweat running down my spine. I forced the door to open, and saw what Fenris had been trying to show me, ever since I arrived—

Renton's narrow bed, that I had never shared (the Caravan was his *very* private place). A shelf of cobwebbed books, a mouldering kitchenette, and a great big withered doll, tumbled on the floor, dressed in rags that I partly recognised. I fell to my knees. I heard Eliud whispering that although he was my lover, *there were parts of Mike Renton that I had never seen*; and now I believed it. His merman's eyes, his tarnished-gold hair, were gone. All gone, the warm flesh that had masked this doll's strange bones, the unhuman declivities; cusps and protuberances—

"Now you see how it was…" said Mr Raven, behind me. "Your boyfriend, he was Hindey bred from a long time back, same as the old man; same as me. Anyone could see by looking at them; if they knew the signs. But Eliud was too human to *want* to be Hindey bred. Mike Renton, he was better endowed, if you take my meaning. He was a feller with a mission. Only he didn't have the power to carry it out, and the other lad, the one that *didn't* want the great ones: he did. So Mike, he got his hooks into Eliud, called him a genius, and convinced him to write the music. For the pure strangeness of it; as Eliud believed. When he figured out what Renton was really after, that's when Eliud told you your boyfriend had to go. And you didn't take too much persuading, did you Aiode? You don't remember what you did? Righto, I suppose you wouldn't. You'd bury a deed like that—"

I didn't remember, but the memories were there, trying to crawl out of the fog in my head, kept from me by silted earth and stinging thorns, and what a brutal thing it was, the old man and me; or had everyone gone, was it me alone, hacking away. But there was another, much smaller heap of bones, and maybe Renton was a monster, and maybe I hated him, but whatever I told myself, oh, the little dog too! Poor little Fenris! How could I have done that, how *could* I?

"He wouldn't stop barking."

"Didn't do you fools any good, though," Mr Raven continued, with satisfaction. "You didn't change a thing, and Mike Renton *he* didn't care. He's not gone far. An' he knew you'd be back here, when the time was ripe. You'd do what was needed, thinking you were following your master's orders, silly bitch. So you've opened the way; Eliud's gone, along with a whole parcel of other lower forms, and it's becoming *their* world again. Don't you feel it?"

I didn't turn my head. I didn't want to find out if Mr Raven was real, or if he'd never existed. I stared at the dog's poor little bones, and the other remains, and Renton's skeleton *did* look strange, but how could I tell what was real? How could I explain to myself how this had happened, why it had happened, even as my lover's mummified corpse began to stir and fatten, and the terrible city rose, and the world was ending—

I didn't know, I didn't know.

# The Ki-Anna

*"The Ki-anna" and "The Vicar Of Mars" are two stories set in the "Aleutian" universe, first posited in a serious, feminist-politics motivated nineties trilogy (*White Queen, North Wind, Phoenix Café*); first described in a fourth novel,* Spirit. *There are a handful of humanoid inhabited planets, united by the Buonarotti Transit, a means of faster than light travel devised by a German physicist called Peenemunde Buonarotti, in* White Queen. *The Diaspora Parliament is their government/UN; the political centre is a transformed asteroid in our outer solar system, known as 'Speranza'. The important social divide now is not binary gender (or more drastic cultural divisions), but the gap between 'Speranza' and the Blues, (Earth humans) who dominate there, and mere planet-dweller humans/humanoids. In "The Ki-Anna" an attempt to correct gruesome 'traditional practices' on one of the Diaspora planets has ended very badly, but mighty reparations are being made…*

*I wrote "The Ki-anna" for the 'Engineering' volume of Jonathan Strahan's legendary Infinity series. But what with the industrialised cannibalism, the cop show, and all that, nobody noticed my mega-engineering 'atmosphere recovery', or even my 'troposphere reconstruction'; of which I was rather proud.*

If he'd been at home, he'd have thought: *Dump Plant Injuries.* In the socially unbalanced, pioneer cities of the Martian Equatorial Ring, little scavengers tangled with the recycling machinery. They needed premium, Earthatmosphericpressure nursing, which they didn't get; or the flesh would not regenerate. So the gouges and dents were permanent: skinned over, like the scars on the police chief's forearms; visible through thin clothing, like the depressions in her thighs. But this wasn't Mars, and she wasn't human, she was a Ki. He guessed, uneasily, at more horrifying forms of childhood poverty.

She seemed very young for her post: hardly more than a girl. She could almost have *been* a human girl with gene-mods. Could have chosen to adopt that fine pelt of silky bronze, glimmering against the bare skin of her palms, her throat and face. Chosen those eyes, like drops of black dew; the hint of a mischievous animal muzzle. Her name was Ki-anna, and she represented the KiAn authorities. Her partner, a Shet called Roaaat Bhvaaan, his heavy uniform making no concession to the warmth of the space-habitat, was from Interplanetary Affairs, and represented Speranza. The Shet looked far more alien: a head like a grey boulder, naked wrinkled hide hooding his eyes.

Patrice didn't expect them to be on his side, this odd couple, polite and sympathetic as they seemed. He must be careful, he must remember that his mind and body were still reeling from the Buonarotti Transit – two instantaneous interstellar transits in two days, the first in his life. He'd never *seen* a non-human sentient biped in person, this time last week; and here he was in a stark, police interview room with two of them.

"You learned of your sister's death a Martian year ago?"

"Her disappearance. Yes."

Ki-anna watched, Bhvaaan questioned. Patrice wished it were the other way round. He dreaded the Speranza mind-set. Anyone who lives on a planet is a lesser form of life, of course we're going to ignore your appeals, but it's more fun to ignore them slowly, very, very slowly—

"We can agree she disappeared," muttered the Shet, what might be mordant humour tugging the lipless trap of his mouth. "Yet, aaah, you didn't voice your concerns at once?"

"Lione is, was, my twin. We were close, however far… When the notification of death came it was very brief, I didn't take it in. A few days later I collapsed at work, I had to take compassionate leave."

At first he'd accepted the official story. She's dead, Lione is dead. She went into danger, it shouldn't have happened but it did, on a suffering war-torn planet unimaginably far away…

The Shet rolled his neckless head, possibly in sympathy.

"You're aahh, Social Knowledge Officer. Thap must be a demanding job. No blame if a loss to your family caused you to crash-out."

"I recovered. I examined the material that had arrived while I was ill: everything about my sister's last expedition, and the investigation. I knew there was something wrong. I couldn't achieve anything at a distance. I had to get to Speranza, I had to get myself *here*—"

"Quite right, child. Can't do anything at long distance, aaah."

"I needed financial support, and the system is slow. The Buonarotti Transit network isn't for people like me—" He wished he'd bitten that back. "I mean, it's for officials, diplomats, not civilian planet-dwellers."

"Unless they're idle super-rich," rumbled the Shet. "Or refugees getting shipped out of a hellhole, maybe. Well, you persisted. Your sister was Martian too. What was she doing here?"

Patrice looked at the very slim file on the table. No way of telling if that tablet held a ton of documents or a single page.

"Don't you know?"

"Explain to us,' said Ki-anna. Her voice was sibilant, a hint of a lisp.

"Lione was a troposphere engineer. She was working on the KiAn Atmosphere Recovery Project. But you *must* know..." They waited, silently. "All right. The KiAn war practically flayed this planet. The atmosphere's being repaired, it's a major Speranza project. Out here it's macro-engineering. They've created a – a kind of membrane, like a casting mould, of magnetically charged particles. They're shepherding small water-ice asteroids and other debris with useful constituents, through it; into a zone around the planet. Controlled annihilation releases the gases, bonding and venting propagates the right mix. Martians pioneered the technique. We've enriched our own atmosphere the same way... but nothing like the scale of this. The job also has to be done from the bottom up. The troposphere, the lowest level of the inner atmosphere, is alive. It's a saturated fluid full of viruses, fragments of DNA and RNA, amino acids; metabolising mineral traces, pre-biotic chemistry. The mix is unique to a living planet, and it's like the mycorrhizal systems in the soil, back on Earth. If it isn't there, or it's not *right*, nothing will thrive."

He couldn't tell if they knew all this, or didn't understand a word.

"The tropo reconstruction wasn't going well. Lionel found out there was an area of the surface, under the *An-lalhar Lakes*, where the living layer might be undamaged. This – where we are now – is the Orbital Refuge Habitat for that region. She came out here, determined to get permission from the Ruling An to collect samples—"

Ki-anna interrupted softly. "Isn't the surviving troposphere remotely sampled by Project automats, all over the planet?"

"Yes, but obviously not well enough. That was Lione. If it was her responsibility she had to do *everything in her power* to get the job done."

"Aah. Raarpht... Your sister befriended the Ruling An, she gained permission, she went down, she stepped on a landmine. You understand that there was no body to be recovered? She was vaporised?"

"So I was told."

Ki-anna rubbed her scarred forearms; the Shet studied Patrice. The room was haunted by Transit ghosts, shadowy with secret intent—

"Aaap. You need to make a 'pilgrimage'. A memorial journey?"

"*No*, it's not like that. There's something *wrong*."

The shadows were tight, the two aliens had made up their minds already: but were they for him or against him?

"Lione disappeared. I don't speak any KiAn language; I didn't have to, the reports were in English: and when I needed more detail there are translator bots. I have not missed anything. A vaporised body does not *vanish*. All that tissue, blood and bones, leaves forensic traces. None. No samples were recovered. She was there to *collect* samples, so don't tell me it was forbidden. She didn't come back, that's all I know. Something happened to her, something other than a warzone accident—"

"Are you saying your sister was murdered, Patrice?"

"I need to go down there."

"I can see you'd feel thap way. You realise KiAn is uninhabitable?"

"A lot of places on Mars are called uninhabitable. My work takes me to the worst-off regions. I can handle myself."

"Aaap. How do you feel about the KiAn issue, Messer Ferringhi?"

Patrice opened his mouth, and shut it. He didn't have a prepared answer for that one. "I don't know enough."

The Shet and the Ki looked at each other, for the first time. He felt they'd been through the motions, and they were agreeing to quit.

"As you know," rumbled Bhvaan, "the Ruling An must give permission. The An-he will see you?"

"I have an appointment."

"Then thap's all for now. Enjoy your transit hangover in peace."

Patrice Ferringhi took a moment, looking puzzled, before he realised he could go. He stood, hesitated, gave an odd little bow and left the room. The Shet and the Ki relaxed somewhat.

"Collapsed at work," said Roaaat Bhvaan. "Thap's not good."

"We can't all be made of stone, Shet."

"Aaah well. Cross fingers, Chief."

They were resigned to strange English figures of speech. The language of Speranza, of diplomacy, was also the language of interplanetary policing. You became fluent, or you relied on unreliable transaid, and you screwed up.

"And all my toes," said the Ki.

On his way to his cabin, Patrice found an Ob-bay. He stared into a hollow sphere, permeated by the star-pricked darkness of KiAn system space: the limb of the planet obscured; the mainstar and the blue 'daystar' out of sight. Knurled objects flew around, suddenly making endless field-beams visible. One lump rushed straight at him, growing huge, and seemed to miss the ob-bay by centimetres, with a roar like monstrous thunder. The big impacts were close enough to make this Refuge shake. He'd felt that, already. Like the Gods throwing giant furniture about—

He could not get over the fact that nothing was real. Everything had been translated here by the Buonarotti Torus, as pure data. This habitat, this shipboard jumper he wore; this *body*. All made over again, out of local elements, as if in a 3D printer… The scarred Ki woman fascinated him, he hardly knew why. The portent he felt in their meeting (had he really *met* her, or just been in the same room?) was what they call a 'transit hangover'.

He must sleep it off.

The Ki-anna was rated Chief of Police, but she walked the beat most days. All her officers above nightstick grade were seconded from the Ruling An's Household Guard: she didn't like to impose on them. The Ki – natural street-dwellers, if ever life was natural again – melted indoors as she approached. Her uniform, backed by Speranza, should have made the refugees feel safe: but not one of them trusted her. The only people she could talk to were the habitual criminals. *They* appreciated the Ruling An's strange appointment. She made her rounds, visiting nests where law-abiding people better stay away.

The gangsters knew a human had 'joined the station'. They were very curious. She sniffed the wind and lounged with the idlers, giving up Patrice Ferringhi in scraps, a resource to be conserved. The pressure of the human's strange eyes was still with her—

No one ought to look at her scars like that, it was indecent.

But he was an alien, he didn't know how to behave.

She didn't remember being chosen – for the treatment that would render her flesh delectable, while ensuring that what happened wouldn't kill her. She only knew she'd been sold (tradition called it an honour) so that her littermates could eat. She would always wonder, why *me*? What was wrong with *me*? We were very poor, I understand that, but why *me*?

It had all been for nothing, anyway. Her parents and her littermates were dead, along with everyone else. So few survivors! A handful of die-hards on the surface. A token few Ki taken to live in Speranza, in the staggeringly distant Blue System. Would they ever return? The Ki-anna thought not… Six Refuge Habitats in orbit. And of course some of the Heaven-born, who'd seen what was coming, had escaped to Balas or to Shet before the war broke out.

At curfew she filed a routine report and retired to her quarters in the Curtain Wall. Roaaat, who was sharing her living space, was already at home. It was lucky that Shet didn't normally like to sit in Speranza-style 'chairs': he'd have broken a hole in her ceiling. His bulk, as he lay at ease, dwarfed her largest room. They compared notes.

"All the Refuges have problems," said the Ki-anna. "But I get the feeling I have more than my share. Extortion, intimidation, theft and violence—"

"We can *grease the wheels*,' said Roaat. 'Strictly off the record, we can pay your villains off. It's distasteful, not the way to do police work."

'But expedient.'

"Aaap… He seemed very taken with you," said Roaaat.

"The human…? I didn't notice."

"Thap handsome Blue, yaaas. I could smell pheromones."

"He isn't a 'Blue" said the Ki-anna. "The almighty Blues rule Speranza. The humans left behind on Earth, or on 'Mars' – What is 'Mars'? Is it a moon?'

"Noope. A smaller planet in the Blue system."

"Well, they aren't Blues, they're just ordinary aliens."

"I shall give up matchmaking. You don't appreciate my help… Let's hope the An-he finds your *ordinary alien* more attractive."

The Ki-anna shivered. "I think he will. He's a simple soul."

Roaaat was an undemanding guest, despite his size. They shared a meal, based on 'culturally neutral' Speranza Food Aid. The Shet spread his bedding. The Ki-anna groomed herself, crouched by a screen that showed views of the Warrens. Nothing untoward stirred, in the simulated night. She pressed knuckle-fur to her mouth. Sometimes the pain of living, haunted by the uncounted dead, became very hard to bear. Waking from every sleep to remember afresh that there was *nothing left.*

"I might yet back out of this, Officer Bhvaaan. What if we only succeed in arousing the monsters, and make bad worse?"

She unfolded her nest, and settled behind him. He patted her side with his clubbed fist – it felt like being clobbered by a kindly rock. "See how it goes. You can back out later."

The Ki-anna lay sleepless, the bulk of her unacknowledged

bodyguard between her and the teeth of the An; wondering about Patrice Ferringhi.

When his appointment with alien royalty came around, Patrice was glad he'd had some breathing space. The world was solid again; he felt in control of himself. He donned his new transaid, settling the pickup against his skull, and set out for the high-security gate that led to the Refugee Habitat itself. Armoured guards, intimidatingly tall, were waiting on the other side. They bent their heads, exhaled breath loudly – and indicated that he was to get into a kind of floating palanquin. Probably they knew no English.

His guards jogged around him in a hollow square; between their bodies he glimpsed the approach to an actual *castle*, like something in a fantasy game. Like a recreation of Mediaeval Europe or Japan, rising from a mass of basic living modules. It was amazing. He'd never been inside a big space-station before, not counting a few hours in Speranza Transit Port. The false horizon, the lilac sky, arcing far above the castle's bannered towers, would have fooled him completely, if he hadn't known.

He met the An-he in a windowless, antique chamber hung with tapestries (at least, *tapestries* seemed like the right word). Sleekly upholstered couches were scattered over the floor. The guard (different uniform from his palanquin escort), who'd escorted him here backed out, snorting. Patrice looked around, vaguely bothered by a too-warm, indoor breeze. He saw someone almost human, loose-limbed and handsome in Speranza tailoring, reclining on a couch, large, wide-spaced eyes alight with curiosity, and realised he was alone with the king.

"Excuse my steward,' said the An, 'he doesn't speak English well, and doesn't like to embarrass himself by trying. Please, be at home."

"Thank you for seeing me,' said Patrice. 'Your, er Majesty—?"

The An-he grinned. "You are Patrice. I am the An, let's just talk."

The young co-ruler was charming and direct. He asked about the police. Patrice noted, disappointed, that *Ki-anna* was a title, *the Ki-she*, or something. He wondered how you learned their personal names.

"It was a brief interview," he admitted, ruefully. "I got the impression they weren't very interested."

"Well, I *am* interested. Lione was a friend to my people. To *both* my peoples. I'm not sure I understand, were you partners, or litter-mates?"

"We were twins, that means litter-mates, but partners' too, though our careers took different directions."

He needed to get the word *partner* into the conversation. The An partnership wasn't sexual, but it was lifelong, and the closest social and emotional bond they knew. A lost *partner* justified his appeal. The An-he touched his discreet headset (he was using a transaid, too); reflexively.

"A double loss, poor Patrice. Please do confide in me, it will help enormously if you are completely frank—"

In this pairing, the An-she was the senior. She made the decisions, but Patrice couldn't meet her, she was too important. He could only work on the An-he, who would (hopefully) promote his cause. He had the eerie thought that he was doing exactly what Lione had done – trying to make a good impression on this alien aristocrat, maybe in this very room. The tapestries (if that was the word) swam and rippled in the moving air, drawing his attention to scenes he really didn't want to examine. Brightly dressed lords and ladies gathered for the hunt. The game was driven onto the guns. The butchery, the bustling kitchen scenes, the *banquet*—

He realised, horrified, that his host had asked him something about his work on Mars, and he hadn't heard the question.

"Oh," said the An-he, easily. "I see what you're looking at. Don't be offended, it's all in the past, and priceless, marvellous art. Recreated, sadly. The originals were destroyed, along with the original of this castle. But still, our heritage! Don't you Blues love ancient battle scenes, heaps of painted slaughter? And by the way, aren't you closely related, limb for limb and bone for bone, to the beings that *you* traditionally kill and eat?"

"Not on Mars."

"There, you are sundered from your web of life. At home on Earth, the natural humans do it all the time, I assure you."

"I don't know what to say."

Notoriously, the Ki and the An had *both* been affronted when they were identified, by other sentient bipeds, as a single species. Of course they knew that: but what an indecent topic! In ways, the most disturbing aspect of the whole 'KiAn issue' was not a genocidal war, in which the oppressed had risen up savagely against the oppressors. It was the fact that some respected Ki leaders *defended* 'the traditional diet of the An'.

The An-he showed his bright white teeth. "Then you have an open mind, my dear Patrice! It gives me hope that you'll come to understand us." He stretched, and exhaled noisily. "Enough. All I can tell you today is that your request is being considered. You're a valuable person, and it's dangerous down there! We don't want to lose you. Now, I suppose you'd like to see your sister's rooms? She stayed with us, you know: here in the castle."

"Would that be possible?"

"Certainly! I'll get some people to take you."

More guards, or servants in military-looking uniform, led him along winding, irregular corridors, all plagued by that insistent breeze, and opened a round plug of a doorway. The An-he's face appeared, on a display screen emblazoned on a guard's tunic.

"Take as long as you like, dear Patrice. Don't be afraid of disturbing the evidence! The police took anything they thought was useful, ages ago."

The guards shut the door and stayed outside: giving him privacy, which he had not expected. He was alone, in his sister's space. The aeons he'd crossed, the ungraspable interstellar distance, vanished. Lione was *here*. He could feel her, all around him. The warm air, suddenly still, seemed full of images: glimpses of his sister, rushing into his mind—

'Recreation' was skin-deep here. The room was essentially identical to his cabin. A bed-shelf with a puffy mattress; storage space beneath. A desk, and a closet bathroom, stripped of fittings. Her effects had been returned to Mars, couriered as data. The police had been and gone 'ages ago'. What could this empty box tell him? Nothing, but he had to try.

Was he under surveillance? He decided he didn't care.

He searched swiftly and carefully: studying the floor, running his hands over walls and closet space; checking the seals on the mattress. The screen above the desk was set in an ornate decorative frame. He probed around it, and his fingertips brushed something that had slipped behind. Patiently, he teased out a corner of the object, and drew it from hiding.

*Lione*, he whispered. He tucked his prize inside the breast of his shipboard jumper, and knocked on the round door. It opened; the guards were waiting outside.

"I'm ready to leave now."

The An-he looked out of the tunic display again. "By all means! But don't be a stranger. Come and see me again, come often!"

That evening he searched the little tablet's drive for his own name; for any message. He tried every password of theirs he could remember: found nothing, and was heartbroken. He barely noted the actual content. Next day, to his great surprise, he was recalled to the castle. He met the

An-he as before, and learned that the Ruling An would like to approve his mission, but the police were making difficulties.

"Speranza doesn't mind having a touching tragedy associated with their showcase Project," said the young king wryly. "A scandal would be far worse, so they don't want to risk you finding anything inconvenient. My partner and I feel you have a right to investigate, but we're meeting resistance."

There was nothing Patrice could do, and at least it wasn't a refusal. If the alien royals were on his side, hopefully the police would have to give in. Back in his cabin, he examined the tablet again… Lione had been making a private, unofficial record of her thoughts on 'the KiAn issue'.

*KiAn isn't like other worlds of the Diaspora. They didn't have a Conventional Space Age before First Contact. But they weren't primitives when 'we' found them, nor even Mediaeval. The An of today are what remains of a planetary superpower. They were always the Great Nation, and the many nations of the Ki were their subjects, through millennia of civilisation. But it was no more than fifteen hundred standard years ago, when, in a time of famine, the An or 'Heaven Born' first began to hunt and eat the 'Earth Born' Ki. They don't do that anymore. They have painless processing plants (or did). They have retail packaging—*

*Cannibalism happens. It's known in every sentient and pre-sentient biped species. What developed on KiAn is different, and the so-called 'atavists' are not really 'atavist'. This isn't the survival, as some on Speranza would like to believe, of an ancient, preconscious symbiosis. The An and the Ki* were not *animals, when this 'stable genocide' began. They were people, who could think and feel. People, like us.*

The entry was text-only, but he heard his sister's voice: forthright, uncompromising. She must have forced herself to be more tactful with the An-he! The next entry was video: Lione talking to him, living and breathing. Inside the slim case, when he opened it, he'd found pressed fragments of a moss, or lichen. Shards of it clung to his fingers, it smelled odd, but not unpleasant. He sniffed his fingertips, painfully happy.

Days passed, in a rhythm of light and darkness that belonged to the planet 'below'. Patrice shuttled between the Station's visitors quarters, where he was the only guest, and the An castle. He didn't dare refuse a summons, but he declined all dinner invitations: which made the An laugh. The odd couple, the Shet and the Kianna, meanwhile showed no interest in Patrice at all, and did not return his calls.

He might have tried harder to get their attention, but there was Lione's journal. He didn't want to hand it over; or to lie about it either.

Once, as they walked in the castle's galleries, the hot breeze nagging at him as usual, Patrice felt he was being watched. He looked up. From a high, curtained balcony a wide-eyed, narrow face was looking down intently. "*That* was the An-she," murmured his companion, stooping to exhale the words in Patrice's ear. "She likes you, or she wouldn't have let you glimpse her… I tell her all about you."

"I didn't really see anything," said Patrice, wary of causing offence. "The breeze is so strong, tossing the curtains about."

"I'm afraid we're obsessed with air circulation, in this crowded accommodation. There are aliens about, who don't smell very nice."

"I'm very sorry! I had no idea!"

"Oh no, Patrice, not you. You smell fresh and sweet."

Lione's entries weren't dated, but they charted a progress. He started to be afraid he'd find her actually defending industrial cannibalism. But that never happened. Instead, as he immersed himself, he knew his twin was asking him not to accept, but to *understand*—

*Consider chattel slavery. We look on the buying and selling of sentient bipeds, as if they were livestock, with revulsion. Who could question that? Then think of the intense bond between a beloved master, or mistress, and a beloved servant. A revered commanding officer and devoted troops. Must this relationship go too? The An and the Ki know their way of life* must *change. But there is a deep equality in their 'exchange of being', which we individualists can't recognise*—

Patrice thought of the Ki-Anna's scars.

The 'deep equality' entry was almost the last. The journal ended abruptly, with no sense of closure.

Lione's incense (he'd decided the 'lichen' was a kind of KiAn incense, perhaps a present from the An-he) filled his cabin with its subtle perfume. He closed the tablet, murmuring words he knew by heart *a deep equality in their exchange of being*, and decided to turn in. In his tiny bathroom, for a piercing moment it was Lione he saw in the mirror. A dark-skinned, light-eyed, serious woman, with the aquiline bones of their North African ancestry. His other self, who had left him so far behind—

The journal was a message. It called him to follow her, and he didn't yet know, didn't dare to guess, where his passionate journey would end.

When he learned that he had a permit to visit the surface, but the Ki-anna and the Shet were coming with him, he understood that the Ruling An had been forced to make this concession – and the bargaining was over. He just wished he knew *why* the police had insisted on escorting him. To help Patrice to discover the truth? Or to prevent him?

He didn't find out because he didn't meet the odd couple until they embarked together, in full protective gear: quarantine-film coated bodies under soft-shell life-support suits. The noisy shuttle bay put a damper on conversation, and the flight was no more sociable. Patrice spent it in an escape capsule, breathing tanked air: the police insisted on this. He saw nothing of KiAn until he was crunching across the seared rubble of a landing field. The landscape was dry tundra, like Martian desert colour-shifted into shades of grey and green. Armed Green Belts were waiting, with a landship and all-terrain hardsuits for the visitors.

"The An-he offered me a military escort," said Patrice, when his freedom of speech was restored by helmet radio. "What was wrong with that?"

"Sorry," grunted Bhvaaan. "Couldn't be allowed."

The Ki-anna said nothing. He remembered the way he'd felt at their meeting. There had been a connection on her side too: he was sure of it. Now she was just another bulky Speranza doll, on a smaller scale than her partner. As if she'd read his thoughts, she cleared her faceplate and looked out at him, curiously. He wanted to tell her that he understood KiAn, better than she could imagine… but not with Bhvaaan around.

"You've been keeping yourself to yourself, Messer Ferringhi.'

"I could say the same of you two, Officer Bhvaaan."

"Aaaap. But you made friends with the An-he?"

"The Ruling An were very willing to help me."

"We've been working in your interest too," said the Ki-anna.

She pivoted her suit to look through the windowband in the landship's flank. "Far below this plateau, back that way, was the regional capital; there were fertile plains, rich forests, towns and fields and parklands. 'The 'Roof of Heaven' itself was never beautiful. It's strange, but this part hardly seems much changed—"

"Except that one dare not breathe," she added, sadly.

On the shore of the largest ice sheet, the Lake of Heaven, the odd couple and Patrice disembarked. The Ki-anna led the way to a great low arch of rock-embedded ice. The Green Belts had stayed in the ship.

Everything was livid mist. "We're going under *An-lalhar* Lake alone?" Patrice was startled.

"The Green Belts will be on call," said the Ki-anna. "Below the lake, it's not their jurisdiction. It's a treasured enclave where Ki and the An are stubbornly dying together."

Bhvaaan peered at him. "It's not our jurisdiction either, Messer Ferringhi. If we meet with violence, *then* we can call for help, but thap's after the event. The people under the Lake don't have a lot to lose and their mood is volatile. Bear thap in mind. "

"I could have had an escort they'd respect."

"You're better off with us."

They descended a tunnel. The light never grew less; on the contrary it grew brighter. When they emerged, the Heaven Lake was above them: a mass of blue-white radiance, indigo shadowed, shot through with rainbow. It was extraordinarily beautiful; it seemed impossible that the ice had captured so much light from the poisoned smog. Far off, in the centre of the glacial depression, geothermal vents made a glowing spiderweb of fire and snowy steam. Patrice checked his telltales, and eagerly began to release his helmet. The Shet dropped a gauntleted fist on his arm.

"Don't do it, child. Look at your *rads*."

"A moment won't kill me. I want to *feel* KiAn—"

The odd couple, hidden in their gear, seemed to look at him strangely.

"Maybe later," said the Ki-anna. "It's safer in the Grottos, where your sister was headed."

"How do we get there?"

"We walk," rumbled Bhvaaan. "No vehicles. There's not much growing but it's still a sacred park. Let your suit do the work and keep up your fluids."

"Thanks, I know how to handle a hard shell."

They walked in file. The desolation; the ruined beauty that had been revered by both 'races', caught at Patrice's heart. His helmet display counted rads, paces, heartrate: and counted down the metres. Thirty kilometres to the place where Lione had last been seen alive.

"Which faction mined the Lake of Heaven parkland?"

"To our knowledge? Nobody did, child."

It was a question he'd asked over and over: far away, when he still thought he could get answers. Now he asked and didn't care. Landmines could be denied. In the chaos of a war zone's emissions who could be sure? He walked between them, the Shet ahead, the Ki-anna behind. His pace was steady, yet the helmet display said his body was pumping adrenalin: not from fear, he knew, but in the grip of intense excitement. He sucked on glucose, and tried to calm himself.

As the radiance above them dimmed they reached the Grotto domain. Rugged rocky pillars upheld the roof of ice: widely spaced at first then clustering towards a centre that could not be seen. Here there was a Ki community, surviving in rad-proofed modules. The Ki-anna was allowed to enter the warren. Patrice and the Shet waited, in the darkening, blighted landscape. She emerged after an hour or so.

"We can't go on without guides, and we can't have guides until morning. At the earliest. They have to think it over."

"They weren't expecting us?"

"They were. They know all about it, but I think they may have had fresh instructions. They're in full communication with the castle: there's some sophisticated kit in there. We'll just have to wait."

"Do they remember Lione?' demanded Patrice, hardly listening to the delaying tactics. 'I have transaid, I want to talk to someone."

"Not now. I'll ask tomorrow."

"Will they lep us sleep indoors?" asked the Shet.

"No."

The Shet and the Ki-anna made camp, using their suits to clear ground and construct a shelter in the ruins of the former village. Patrice left them to it, and went over to a heap of boulders; where he'd noticed patches of familiar lichen. He'd brought some fragments of Lione's incense with him in a First Aid pouch, in the sleeve pocket of his inner. The police were fully occupied. Furtively he opened the arm of his hardshell, and fished the pouch out. Yes, it seemed exactly the same—

Had Lione stood where he was standing now? Was the incense not a gift, but a souvenir she had gathered? He felt convinced that this was so. She had been *standing right here*, and his need was irresistible. He released his face-plate, stripped his gauntlets, rubbed away quarantine film. KiAn rushed in on him, cold, harsh and intoxicating in his throat—

"What is that?"

The Ki-anna was right behind him. "A lichen sample," said Patrice, caught out. "Or that's what I'd call it at home. It was in my sister's room, in the An Castle, but I think it came from here. Look, they're the same!"

"Not quite," said the Ki-anna. "Yours is a cultivated variety."

He thought she'd be angry, maybe accuse him of concealing evidence. To his astonishment she took his bared hand, and bowed over it until her cheek brushed the vulnerable inner skin of his wrist. Her touch was a huge shock, sweet and profoundly sexual. She made him dizzy.

This can't be happening, he thought. I'm here for Lione—

"I don't know your name."

"We don't do that," she whispered, equally moved.

"I felt, I can't describe it, the moment I met you—"

"I'd better keep this. You must get your gloves and helmet back on."

"But I want *KiAn*—"

Gently, she released his hand. "You've had enough."

The shelter was a snug fit. When they were sealed inside, the odd couple set aside a pack of 'viands' the An-he had provided, and shared out basic rations, with fresh water they'd brought from the Habitat.

They would sleep in their suits. Patrice lay down at once, to escape their questions and be alone with his confusion. He was here for Lione, here to *join* Lione. How could he and the Ki-anna suddenly feel this way?

"Were you getting romantic, with Patrice, over by those rocks?" asked Bhvaaan. "Sniffing his pheromones?"

"No," said the Ki-anna softly, grimly. "Something else." She showed him the First Aid pouch and its contents.

"Mighty Void!"

"He says he found it hidden in the room Lione used, in the castle."

"We took that cabin apart." The Shet's delicates unfolded from his club of a fist. He turned the clear pouch around, probing the find with sensitive tentacles. "So *thaap's* how, so *thaap's* how—"

"So that's how the cookie was crumbled," agreed the Ki-anna.

"What do you suggest, Chief? Abort, and get out of here quickly?"

"If we run, and they have heavy weaponry, we're at their mercy. I see what it looks like, but I think we should show no alarm."

"I *have* had thoughts,' she admitted, looking at the dim outline of Patrice Ferringhi. 'Don't know why. It's something in his eyes."

"Thaap's the way it starts," said the Shet. "Thoughts. Then wondering if anything can come of them. They say sentient bipeds are attracted to each other like… like brothers and sisters, long separated. Well, I'll talk to the Greenies. And you and I had better not sleep."

The suit was a house the shape of her body. She sat in it, wondering about sexual pleasure: pleasure with *Patrice*. What would it be like? She had only one strange comparison, but that didn't frighten her… What

Roaaat Bhvaaan offered was far more disturbing.

She glimpsed the abyss, and fell into a syrupy oblivion.

Patrice dreamed he was in a strolling crowd, among bronze and purple trees with branches that swayed in the warm breeze. He was in the KiAn Orientation, a virtual reality. But it had become thickly sinister; the crowd pressed too close, the trees hid what he ought to see.

Then Lione came running up and *bit* him. He yelled, and shook her off. She came back and bit his thigh, but now he was in the dark, cold and sore. Lione was gone: he was being hunted by fierce hungry animals—

Suddenly he knew he was not asleep.

He was naked. Where was his suit? *Where was he?* He had no idea. The air was freezing, the darkness almost complete. He stumbled towards a gleam ahead, and entered a rocky cave: ice underfoot, icy stalactites hanging down. A lamp burned incense-scented oil, set on the ground next to something. *That's a body*, he thought. He knelt down. It was a human body, freeze-dried. She was curled on her side, turned away from him, but he'd found Lione. She was naked too. Why was she naked?

He raised the lamp and saw where flesh had been cut away: not by teeth, as in his dream, but by sharp knives. She had been partially butchered. He tried to turn her: the body moved all of a piece. Her face was recognisable, calm in death, the eyes sunken; skin like cured leather.

Was she *smiling*? Oh, Lione—

*But why am* I *naked?* he thought. *How did I get here? Who brought me?*

The Ki entered the cave on soft feet, and surrounded Patrice and his sister. They'd brought more lights. One of them was carrying, carefully, a flattened spherical object, dull grey-green, and the size of Patrice's fist. It had a seam around the centre, a bevelled cap.

*That's a vapor mine*, he thought. *There will be no body to recover.*

Then the An came. The Ki stepped back, they weren't here to prevent the banquet, they were here to witness. Patrice screamed. He fought the knives with his bare hands, he kicked out with his bare feet. The An, seeming outraged, bewildered, kept yelling at him in scraps of English to *keep still, be easy Blue, you want this, what's wrong with you?*

The Ki-anna and the Shet had ditched their hard shells to search the narrow passages. They arrived armed, but badly outnumbered and couldn't get near Patrice, who was still fighting, but bleeding profusely—

"*I was the Earth In Heaven*!", shouted the Chief of Police. "*I say that the flesh is not sacred, not yours to take. Let the stranger go*!"

She managed to hold the fanatics at bay, made uncertain by her status, until the Green Belts finally arrived. Luckily Bhvaaan had summoned them, when the Ki-anna followed Patrice into that drugged sleep, and before he succumbed himself.

Patrice's injuries were not dangerous. As soon as he was allowed he signed himself out of medical care and insisted on talking to the police again. He met the odd couple in the same bare interview room as before.

"I need to withdraw the statement I made at the scene. I'm sorry, but can't press charges."

If next of kin didn't press charges, KiAn law made it difficult for Interplanetary Affairs to prosecute: he knew that, but he had no choice.

"I know the tablet in Lione's room was planted on me. I know her words – if any of them were genuinely hers – had been rearranged to fool me into accepting atavism. It doesn't matter. My sister did accept, she *wanted* to die that way. She gave her body as a sacrifice, for peace. She was my twin: I can't explain, but I have to respect her wishes."

"A beautiful, consensual ritual," remarked the Shet. "Yaap. That's what the cannibal die-hards always say. But if you scratch any of these halfway 'respectable' atavists, such as our Ruling An pair here—"

"You find the meat-packing industry," said the Ki-anna.

Patrice heard the blinkered, Speranza mindset.

"No. My sister was *willing*. I know she was."

"I believe it." To his confusion the Ki-anna reached out, took his injured hand and held his wrist, where the blood ran, to her face. The same sweet, intimate gesture as on KiAn. "So are you, *willing*, a little, even now. It'll wear off."

She dropped his hand and placed an evidence bag, containing his First Aid pouch and the scraps of lichen, on the table.

"In English the common name of this herb, or lichen, would be "Willingness". It grows naturally only under the Lake of Heaven. Long ago it was known as a powerful aphrodisiac, but the labwork kind has a different use. It's given to a child chosen to be Ki-anna, which means sold to the An as a living meat source. It's a dainty form of cannibalism, practiced in my region. A drugged child, a willing victim, with a strong resistance to infection and trauma, is eaten alive, by refined degrees. If a child like that survives to adulthood, they are free; the debt is paid.

The Ki-anna showed her teeth. "I made it, as you see, but I haven't forgotten that scent. When I smelled your flesh, under the Lake, I knew you'd been treated for butchery – and then I understood. The An-pair here drugged Lione until she was delirious with joy at the prospect of being eaten, and sent her to the atavist fanatics under *An-lalhar*, for a political purpose. Then later they tried the same trick on you."

Bhvaaan tapped the casefile tablet with his delicates. "Your sister died too quickly, that was the problem."

"What do you mean—?"

"We couldn't prove it, but we knew they'd killed her, Messer Ferringhi. We also knew, thanks to the Chief here and her work in the Refuge, who was pulling the strings; and how prohibited ordnance was smuggled into the Grottos. Your sister had fallen into a trap. She was determined to get herself under the Heaven Lake, and thaap suited the atavists just fine. It would have been a powerful message. A Speranza scientist ritually eaten, and then consumed by the very air of KiAn—"

"Controlled annihilation," whispered Patrice. "That's what I *saw*, in the cave. I understood it when I saw the vapor mine—"

"Thaap was the idea. The atavists want to bring back the meat factories, soon as their planet has an atmosphere again. Your sister's death was going to help them: except it didn't work out. You were right about the tropo sampling, young Blue. There's also stringent military activity monitoring. If a mine had gone off under the Lake, believe me, we'd know. If a human-sized body had been atomised; we'd know. So the 'consummation' hadn't happened, and we couldn't figure it out. Now we think we know the answer. She died too quickly. She had to be vaporised alive, because a dead body can't be *willing*. But she wasn't a Ki, and they hit an artery or something."

Patrice had turned strangely grey in the face.

"You going to crash out, child—?"

"No, go on—"

The Shet rearranged his bulk on the inadequate office chair. "The autopsy'll tell us the details, anyway. Then you came along, Patrice. We saw a chance to get ourselves to the crime scene – and wasted Diaspora funds pushing on an open door. And you nearly died, because we drank the nice fresh water from thiip Habitat. Which happened to be doped—"

"The atavists thought the *willingness* they'd cooked up for Lione would work just the same on you," said the Ki-anna. "They've never heard of fraternal twins. Ki litter-mates can be of any sex, yet we are all what you call, er, *genetically identical.* You were begging to be lured to the Grottos: it was perfect, you would replace Dr Ferringhi. But you and your sister were not clones. The drug affected you, but didn't make you thrilled to be butchered. You fought for your life."

"You see, Messer Ferringhi," said Bhvaaan, "whaap really happened here is that a pair of mass-murdering atavist bastards thought they'd appoint themselves a Chief of Police who as a child *had been eaten.* A girl like that, they calculated, would never dare to do them any damage. Instead they found they had *a tiger by the tail…*"

He opened the casefile tablet, and pushed it over to Patrice. "They're glamorous, the Atavist An. But your sister wouldn't have fallen for them in her right mind, from what I've learned. Still want to withdraw this?"

Patrice was silent, eyes down. The Ki-anna saw him shedding the last exaltation of the drug, and taking in everything he'd been told. A new firmness in the lines of his face, a deep sadness as he said farewell to Lione. The human felt her eyes. He looked up and she saw another farewell, sad but final, to something that had barely begun—

"No," he said. 'I don't. But I should go through it again. Can we do that now?"

The Ki-anna returned to her quarters. Roaaat joined her in a while. She sat by her window on the streets, small chin on her silky paws, and didn't look round when he came in.

"He'll be fine. What will you do? You'll have to leave, after this."

"I know. Leave or get killed, and I must not get killed."

"You could go with Patrice, see what Mars is like."

"I don't think so. The pheromones are no more, now that he knows what *making love to the Ki-anna* is supposed to be like."

"I've no idea what making love to you is supposed to be like. But you're a damned fine investigator. Why don't you come to Speranza?"

Yes, she thought. I knew all along what *you* were offering. Banishment, not only from my own world but from all the worlds. Never to be a planet-dweller any more. And again I want to ask, *why me? What did I do?* But you believe it is an honour and I think you are sincere.

"Maybe I will."

# The Vicar of Mars

*Another "Aleutian Universe" tale, a ghost story this time. The downside of 'information space' ftl travel is that a Buonarotti Transit can fail in eerie ways[5] – if one of the passengers carries undeclared psychic baggage for instance, and especially if they elect to remain conscious. Elements of the main thread (the story of Isabel Jewel) were suggested by one of R.H. Malden's ghost stories, "Between Sunset and Moonrise", but there are other (fictional) Old Mars ghosts making guest appearances, and references to stories by Malden's great master, M R James.*

The Reverend Boaaz Hanaahaahn, High Priest of the Mighty Void, and an Aleutian adventurer going by the name of 'Conrad', were the only resident guests at the Old Station, Butterscotch. They'd met on the way from Opportunity and had taken to spending their evenings together, enjoying a snifter or two of Boaaz's excellent Twin Planets blend in a cosy private lounge. It seemed an unlikely friendship: the massive Shet, his grey hide forming ponderous dignified folds across his skull and over his brow, and the stripling immortal, slick-stranded head-hair to his shoulders, black eyes dancing with mischief on either side of the dark space of his nasal. But the Aleutian, though he had never lived to be old – he wasn't the type – had amassed a fund of fascinating knowledge in his many lives, and Boaaz was an elderly priest with varied interests and a youthful outlook.

Butterscotch's hundred or so actual citizens didn't frequent the Old Station. The customers were mostly mining lookerers who drove in from the desert, in the trucks that were their homes, and could now be heard carousing mildly in the public bar. Boaaz and Conrad shared a glance, agreeing not to join the fun tonight. The natives were friendly – but Martian settlers were, almost without exception, humans who had never left conventional space. They'd met few 'aliens', and believed the

5 See "The Tomb Wife" and "The Voyage Out", for more details, at gwynethjones.uk/SPIRIT.htm

Buonarotti Interstellar Transit was a dangerous novelty that would never catch on. One got tired of the barrage of uneasy fascination.

"I'm afraid I scare the children," rumbled Boaaz.

The Aleutian could have passed for a noseless slope-shouldered human. The Shet was hairless and impressively bulky, but what really made him different was his delicates. To Boaaz it was natural that he possessed two sets of fingers: one set thick and horny, for pounding and mashing, the other slender and supple, for fine manipulation. Normally protected by his wrist folds, his delicates would shoot out suddenly, to grasp a stylus for instance, or handle eating implements. He had seen the young Martian folk startle at this, and recoil with bulging eyes—

"Stop calling them *children*," suggested Conrad. "They don't like it."

"Nonsense. The young always take the physical labour and service jobs, it's a fact of nature. I'm only speaking English."

Conrad shrugged. For a while each studied his own screen, as the saying goes, and a comfortable silence prevailed. Boaaz reviewed a list of 'cases' sent to him by the Colonial Social Services in Opportunity. He was not impressed. They'd simply compiled a list of odds and ends: random persons who didn't fit in, and were vaguely thought to have problems.

To his annoyance, one of the needy appeared to live in Butterscotch.

"Here's a woman who "*has been suspected of being insane*", he grumbled aloud. "Has she been treated? No. How barbaric. *Has visited Speranza... No known religion...* What's the use in telling me that?"

"Maybe they think you'd like to convert her," suggested Conrad.

"I do not *convert* people!" exclaimed Boaaz, shocked. "Should an unbelieving parishioner wish my guidance towards the Abyss, they'll let me know. It's not my business to *persuade* them! I have entered my name alongside other Ministers of Religion on Mars. If my services as a priest should be required at a Birth, Adulthood, Conjunction or Death, I shall be happy to oblige, and that's enough."

Conrad laughed soundlessly, the way Aleutians do. "You don't bother your 'flock', and they don't bother you! That sounds like an easy berth."

Not always, thought the old priest. Sometimes not easy at all!

"I wouldn't worry about it, Boaaz. Mars is a colony. It's run by the planetary government of Earth, and they're obsessed with gathering information about innocent strangers. When they can't find anything interesting, they make it up. Their file on me is vast, I've seen it."

'Earth', powerful neighbour to the Red Planet, was the local name for the world everyone else in the Diaspora knew as the Blue.

Boaaz was on Mars to minister to souls. Conrad was here, he claimed, purely as a tourist. The fat file the humans kept might suggest a different story, but Boaaz had no intention of prying. Aleutians, the Elder Race, had their own religion; or lack of one. As long as he showed no sign of suffering, Conrad's sins were his own business. The old Shet cracked a snifter vial, tucked it in his holder: inhaled placidly, and returned to the eyeball-screen that was visible to his eyes alone. The curious Social Services file on *Jewel, Isabel,* reappeared. All very odd. Careful of misunderstandings, he opened his dictionary, and checked in detail the meanings of English words he knew perfectly well.

**wicked**...

**old woman...**

**insane**...

Later, on his way to bed, he examined one of the fine rock formations that decorated the station's courtyards. They promised good hunting. The mining around here was of no great worth, mainly ferrous ores for the domestic market, but Boaaz was not interested in commercial value. He collected mineral curiosities. It was his passion, and a very good reason for visiting Butterscotch, a settlement on the edge of the most ancient and interesting Martian terrain. If truth be known, Boaaz looked on this far-flung Vicariate as an interesting prelude to his well-earned retirement. He did not expect his duties to be burdensome. But he was a conscientious person, and Conrad's teasing had stung.

"I shall visit her," he announced, to the sharp-shadowed rocks.

Ω

The High Priest had travelled from his home world to Speranza, capital city of the Diaspora, and onward to the Blue Planet Torus Port, in no time at all (allowing for a few hours of waiting around, and two 'false duration' interludes of virtual entertainment). The months he'd spent on the conventional space liner *Burroughs*, completing his interplanetary journey, had been slow but agreeable. He'd arrived to find that his personal Residence, despatched by licensed data courier, had been delayed – and decided that until his home was decoded into material form, he might as well carry on travelling. His tour of this backward but extensive new parish had *happened* to concentrate on prime mineral-hunting sites: but he would not neglect his obligations.

He took a robotic jitney as far as the network extended, and then proceeded on foot. Jewel, Isabel lived out of town, up against the Enclosure that kept tolerable climate and air quality captive. As yet unscrubbed emissions lingered here in drifts of vapour; the thin air had a lifeless, paradoxical warmth. Spindly towers of mine tailings, known as 'Martian Stromatolites', stood in groups, heads together like ugly sentinels. Small machines crept about, munching mineral-rich dirt. There was no other movement, no sound but the crepitation of a million tiny ceramic teeth.

Nothing lived.

The 'Martians' were very proud of their Quarantine. They farmed their food in strict confinement; they tortured off-world travellers with lengthy decontamination. Even the gastropod machines were not allowed to reproduce. They were turned out in batches by the mine factories, and recycled in the refineries when they were full. What were the humans trying to preserve? The racial purity of rocks and sand? *Absurd superstition*, muttered the old priest, into his breather. *Life is life*!

Jewel Isabel clearly valued her privacy. He hadn't messaged her in advance. His visit would be off the record, and if she turned him away from her door, so be it. He could see the isolated module now, at the end of a chance 'avenue' of teetering stromatolites. He reviewed the file's main points as he stumped along. *Old. Well travelled, for a human of her caste. Reputed to be rich. No social contacts in Butterscotch, no data traffic with any other location. Supplied by special delivery at her own expense. Came to Mars, around a local year ago, on a settler's one way ticket...* Boaaz thought that must be unusual. Most Martian 'settlers' retired to their home planet, if they could afford the medical bills. Why would a fragile, elderly human make the opposite trip, apparently not planning to return?

The dwelling loomed up, suddenly right in front of him. He had a moment of selfish doubt. Was he committing himself to an endless round of visiting random misfits? Thus ruining his collecting-chances? Maybe he should quietly go away again. But his approach had been observed: a transparent pane had opened. A face glimmered, looking out through the inner and the outer skin; as if from deep, starless space.

"Who are you?" demanded a harsh voice, cracked with disuse. "Are you real? Can you hear me? You're not human."

"I hear you, I'm, aah, 'wired for sound'. I am not human, I am a Shet, a priest of the Void, newly arrived, just making myself known. May I come in?"

He half-hoped that she would say no. *Go away, I don't like priests, can't you see I want to be left alone?* But the lock opened. He passed through, divested himself of the breather and his outer garments, and entered the pressurised chamber.

The room was large, by Martian dwelling standards. Bulkheads must have been removed, probably this had once been a three or four person unit: yet it felt crowded. He recognised the furniture of Earth. Not extruded, like similar fittings in the Old Station, but free-standing, and many of the pieces carved from precious woods. Chairs were ranged in a row along one curved, red wall. Against another stood a tall armoire, a desk with many drawers, and several canvas pictures in frames; stacked facing the dark. In the midst of the room two more chairs were drawn up beside a plain ceramic stove; which provided the only lighting. A richly patterned rug lay on the floor. He couldn't imagine what it had cost to ship all this farrago through conventional space, in material form. She must indeed be wealthy!

The light was low, the shadows numerous.

"I see you *are* a Shet,' said Jewel, Isabel. "I won't offer you a chair, I have none that would take your weight, but please be seated."

She indicated the rug, and Boaaz reclined with care. The number of valuable alien objects made him feel he was sure to break something. The human woman resumed (presumably) her habitual seat. She was tall, for a human: and very thin. A black gown with loose skirts covered her whole body, closely fastened and decorated with flourishes of creamy stuff, like textile foam, at the neck and wrists.

The marks of human aging were visible in her wrinkled face, her white head-hair and the sunken, over-large sockets of her pale eyes. But signs of age can be deceptive. Boaaz also saw something universal – something any priest often has to deal with, yet familiarity never breeds contempt.

*Jewel Isabel* inclined her head. She had read his silent judgement. "You seem to be a doctor as well as a priest," she said, in a tone that rejected sympathy. "My health is as you have guessed. Let's change the subject."

She asked him how he liked Butterscotch, and how Mars compared with Shet: bland questions separated by unexplained pauses. Boaaz spoke of his mineral hunting plans, and the pleasures of travel. He was oddly disturbed by his sense that the room was crowded: he wanted to look behind him, to be sure there were no occupants in that row of splendid chairs. But he was too old to turn without a visible effort, and he didn't wish to be rude. When he remarked that Isabel's home (she had put him right on the order of her name), was rather isolated she smiled – a weary stretching of the lips.

"Oh, you'd be surprised. I'm not short of company."

"You have your memories."

Isabel stared over his shoulder. "Or they have me."

He did not feel that he'd gained her confidence, but before he left they'd agreed he would visit again: she was most particular about the appointment. "In ten days' time," she said. "In the evening, at the full moon. Be sure you remember." As he returned to the waiting jitney the vaporous outskirts of Butterscotch seemed less forbidding. He had done right to come, and thank goodness Conrad had teased him, or the poor woman might have been left without the comfort of the Void. Undoubtedly he was needed, and he would do his best.

**Ω**

Satisfaction was still with him when the jitney delivered him inside the Old Station compound. He even tried a joke on one of the human children about those fine, decorative rock formations. How did they get here? Did they walk in from the desert one night, in search of alcoholic beverages? The youngster took offence.

"They were here when the station was installed. It was all desert then. If there was walking rocks on Mars, messir—" The child drew herself up to her frail, puny height, and glared at him. "We wouldn't any of us *be* here. We'd go home straight away, and leave Mars to the creatures that belonged to this planet."

Boaaz strode off, a chuckle rumbling in his throat. Kids! But when he had eaten, in decent privacy (as a respectable Shet, he would never get used to eating in public) he decided to forgo Conrad's company. The 'old mad woman' was too much on his mind, and he found that he shuddered away from the idea of that second visit. It was strange: he'd met Isabel's trouble many, many times, and never been frightened before.

I am getting old, thought the High Priest.

He turned in early, but he couldn't sleep: plagued by the formless feeling that he had done something foolish, and he would have to pay for it. There were dangerous creatures trying to get into his room, groping at the mellow, pock-marked outer skin of the Old Station; searching for a weak place… Rousing from an uneasy doze, he was compelled to get up and make a transparency, although (as he knew perfectly well) his room faced an inner courtyard, and there are no wild creatures on Mars.

Nothing stirred. Several rugged, decorative rocks were grouped right in front of him, oddly menacing under the security lights. Had they always stood there? He thought not, but he couldn't be sure. The brutes crouched, motionless and secretive, waiting for him to lie down again.

"I really *am* getting old,' muttered Boaaz. "I must take something."

He slept, and found himself once more in the human woman's module. Isabel seemed younger, and far more animated. Confusion fogged his mind, embarrassing him. He didn't know how he'd arrived here, or what they'd been talking about. He started advising her to move into town. It wasn't safe to live so close to the ancient desert: she was not welcome. She laughed and bared her arm, crying *I am welcome nowhere!* He saw a mutilation, a string of marks etched into her thin human skin. She positively *thrust* the symbols at him: he protested that he had no idea what they meant, but she didn't care. She was waiting for another visitor, the visitor she had been expecting when he arrived the first time. She had let him in by mistake, he must leave. *They are from another dimension*, she cried, in that hoarse, hopeless voice. *They wait at the gate, meaning to devour. They lived with me once, and may return, with a tiny shift of the Many Dimensions of the Void.*

It gave him a shock when she used the terms of his religion. Was she drawn to the Abyss? Had he begun to give her instruction? The fog in his mind was very distressing. How could he have forgotten something like that? He recalled, with intense relief, that she was no stranger to the interstellar world. She must have learned something of Shet beliefs when she visited Speranza… But relief was quickly swamped in a wave of dread: Isabel was looking over his shoulder, and something was behind him. He turned, awkward and stiff with age. Something was taking shape in one of those bizarre chairs. It was big as a bear, bigger than Boaaz himself. Squirming tentacles of glistening flesh reached out, becoming every instant more solid and defined—

If it became fully real, if it *touched* him, he would die of horror—

Boaaz woke with thunder in his skull, his whole body pulsing, the blood thickened and backing-up in all his veins. Dizzy and sick, on the edge of total panic, he groped for his First Aid, fumbled the mask over his mouth and nostril-slits, with trembling delicates that would hardly obey him, and drew in great gulps of oxygen. Unthinkable horrors flowed away, the pressure in his skull diminished. He dropped onto his side, making the sturdy extruded couch groan; clutching the mask. It was a dream, he told himself. Just a dream.

**Ω**

Rationally, he knew he had simply done too much. Over-exertion in the thin air of the outskirts had resulted in nightmares: he must give his acclimatisation treatment more time to become established. He took things easy for the next few days: using full Martian EVA gear, and pottering around in the mining fields just outside the Enclosure, with a young staff member for a guide. Pickings were slim (Butterscotch was in the Guidebook!); but he made a few pleasing finds.

But the nightmare stayed on his mind, and at intervals he had to fight the absurd but rooted conviction that he *had* made a second visit, there *had* been something terrible, unspeakable sitting in one of those awful chairs. His nights continued to be disturbed. He had unpleasant dreams (never the same as the first one); from which he woke in panic, groping for the oxygen that no longer soothed his terror.

He was also troubled by a change in the behaviour of the hotel staff. They had been friendly: unlike the miners they never whispered or stared. Now the children were going out of their way to avoid him, and he was no genius at reading human moods, but surely there was something wrong. Anu, the lad who took Boaaz out to the desert, kept his distance as far as possible, and barely spoke. Perhaps the child was disturbed by the habit of repeatedly *looking behind him* that Boaaz had developed. It must seem strange, he was old and it was a difficult manoeuvre for any Shet beyond middle-age. But he couldn't help himself.

One morning, when he made his usual guilty inspection of that inner courtyard, the station's manager was there before him: staring at a section of wall. Strange marks had appeared there, blistered weals like raw flesh-wounds in the ceramic skin.

"Do you know what's causing the effect?" asked Boaaz.

"It's not weathering, we're inside the Enclosure. Must be bugs in the ceramic, we'll have to get it reconfigured. Can't understand it. It's supposed to last forever, that stuff."

"But the station is very old, isn't it? Older than Butterscotch itself. You don't think the pretty rocks in here had anything to do with the damage?" Boaaz tried a rumble of laughter. "You know, child, sometimes I think they move around at night!"

The rock group was nowhere near the walls. It never was, by daylight.

"I am twenty years old," said the Martian, with an odd look. "Old enough to know when to stay away from bad luck, messir. Excuse me."

He hurried away, leaving Boaaz very puzzled and uneasy.

Ω

He had come here to collect minerals, therefore he would collect minerals. What he needed was not mollycoddling but an adventure, to clear his head. It would be foolhardy to brave the Empty Quarter of Mars in the company of a frightened child: perhaps equally foolhardy to set out alone. He would offer to go exploring with the Aleutian: who took a well-equipped station buggy out into the wild red yonder almost every day.

Conrad would surely welcome this suggestion!

But Conrad was reluctant. He spoke so warmly of the dangers, and with such concern for the Shet's age and metabolism, that Boaaz's pride was touched. He was old, but he was strong. The nerve of this stripling, suggesting there were phenomena that an adult male Shet couldn't handle! Even if the stripling *was* a highly experienced young immortal—

"If you prefer to 'go solo' I would hate to disturb your privacy. We must compare routes, so that our paths do not cross."

"The virtual tour is very, very good," said the Aleutian, persuasively. "You can easily and safely explore ancient 'Arabia Terra' with a fully customised avatar, from the comfort of your hotel room."

"Stop talking like a guidebook," rumbled Boaaz. "I've thrived in tougher spots than this. I shall make my arrangements today."

"You won't mind me mentioning that the sentient biped peoples of Shet are basically aquatic in origin—"

"Origin be blowed. We have lived on land since our oceans shrank, about two million standard years ago. I am not an Aleutian, I have no memories of that era. And if I *were* 'basically aquatic', that would mean I am already an expert at living outside my natural element. Wouldn't it?"

"Oh well," said Conrad at last, ungraciously. "Then you can come along. I suppose it's safer if I keep you where I can see you."

**Ω**

The notable features of the ancient uplands were to the north: luckily the opposite direction from Isabel's dour location. The two buggies set out at sunrise, locked in tandem; Conrad in the lead. As they passed through the particulate barrier of the Enclosure, Boaaz felt a welcome stirring of excitement. His outside cams showed quiet mining fields, and the ever-present stromatolites, but already the landscape was becoming more rugged. He felt released from bondage. A few refreshing trips like this, and he would be quite recovered. He would no longer be compelled to *turn*, feeling those ornate chairs lined up behind him, knowing that the repulsive creature of his dream was taking shape—

"*It's a dusty one,*" remarked Conrad, over the intercom. "*Often is, around here, in the northern 'summer'. And there's a storm warning. We'll just loop around the first buttes, a short EVA and home again…*"

Boaaz recovered himself with a chuckle. His cams showed a calm sky, healthily tinged with blue; his exterior monitors were recording the friendliest conditions known to Mars. "*I'm getting 'hazardous storm probability' at near zero,*" he rumbled in reply. "*Uncouple and return if you wish.* I *shall make a day of it.*"

Silence. Boaaz felt that he'd won the battle.

Conrad had let slip a few too many knowledgeable comments about Martian mineralogy, in their friendly chats. Of course he wasn't 'purely a tourist'. He was a rock hound himself. He'd been out every day, scouring the wilds for sites the Guidebook and the Colonial Government Mineral Survey had missed, or undervalued. Obviously he'd found a good spot, and he didn't want to share. Boaaz sympathised wholeheartedly. But a little teasing wouldn't come amiss, to reward the Aleutian for being so sneaky!

The locked buggies dropped into layered craters, climbed gritty steppes. Boaaz buried himself in the strange-sounding English-language wish-lists he'd compiled long ago, when dreaming of this trip. *Hematite nodules, volcanic olivines, exotic basalts, Mössbauer patterns, tektites, barite roses.* He longed for rarities, but anything he carried back from the Red Planet, across such a staggering distance, would be treasure. Bound to fill his fellow-hounds at home with delight and envy.

*Behind him the empty chairs were ranged in judgement. That which waits at the gates was taking form. Boaaz had to look over his shoulder but he did not turn. He knew he couldn't move quickly enough, and only the sleek desert-survival fittings of the buggy would mock him—*

Escaping from ugly reverie, Boaaz noticed that Conrad was deviating freely from their pre-logged route. Maybe he should have protested, but he didn't. There was no real need for concern. They had life support, and Desert Rescue Service beacons that couldn't be disabled. He examined his CGMS maps instead, and found nothing marked that would explain Conrad's diversion. How interesting! What if the Aleutian's find was 'significantly anomalous', or commercially valuable? If so, they were legally bound to leave it untouched, beacon it and report it—

I shan't pry, thought Boaaz. He maintained intercom silence, as did Conrad, until at last the locked buggies halted. The drivers disembarked. The Aleutian, with typical bravado, was dressed as if he'd been optimised before birth for life on Mars: the most lightweight air supply and a minimal squeeze-suit, under his Aleutian-style desert thermals. Boaaz removed his helmet.

"I hope you enjoyed the scenic route," said Conrad, with a strange glint in his eye. "I hate to be nannied, don't you? We are not children."

"*Hmm*. I found your navigation, *ahaam*, enlightening."

The Aleutian seemed to be thinking hard about his next move.

"So you want to stop here, my friend?" asked Boaaz. "Very well. I suggest we go our separate ways, and rendezvous later for the return?"

"Good idea," said Conrad. "I'll call you."

**Ω**

Boaaz rode his buggy around an exquisite tholeiitic basalt group – a little too big to pack. He disembarked, took a chipping and analysed it. The spectrometer results were unremarkable: the sum greater than the parts. Often the elemental make-up, the age and even the conditions of its creation, however extreme, give no hint as to why a rock is beautiful.

His customised suit was supple. He felt easier in it than in his own unaugmented hide: and youthfully *weightless* – without the discomfiting loss of control of weightlessness itself. Not far away there was a glittering pool, like a mirage of surface water, that might mark a field of broken geodes. Or a surface deposit of rare spherulites. But he wanted to know what the Aleutian had found. He wanted to know so badly that in the end he succumbed to temptation, got back in the buggy and returned to the rendezvous: feeling like a naughty child.

Conrad's buggy stood alone. Conrad was nowhere in sight, and no footprints led away from a nondescript gritstone outcrop right in front of their halting place. For a moment Boaaz feared something uncanny, then he accepted the obvious. Consumed by naughty curiosity he pulled the emergency release on Conrad's outer hatch. The buggy's life-support generator shifted into higher gear with a whine, but the Aleutian was too occupied to notice. He sat in the body-clasping driver's seat, eyes closed, head immobilised, his skull in the quivering grip of a cognitive scanner field. A compact flatbed scanner nestled in the passenger seat. Under its shimmering virtual dome lay some gritstone fragments. They didn't look anything special, but something about them roused memories. Ancient images, a historical controversy, from before Mars was first settled—

Boaaz quietly eased his bulk over to Conrad's impromptu virtual-lab, and studied the fragments carefully, under magnification.

He was profoundly shocked.

"What are you doing, Conrad?"

The Aleutian opened his eyes, and took in the situation.

Wise immortals stay on the planet they call, simply, Home. Aleutians who mix with lesser beings are dangerous characters, because they have no boundaries: they just don't care. Conrad was completely brazen.

"What does it look like? I'm digitising some pretty Martians for my scrapbook."

"You aren't *digitising* anything. You have taken *biotic traces* from an unmapped site. You are translating them into *data code*, with the intent of removing them from Mars, hidden within your consciousness. *That* is illegal!"

"Oh, grow up. It's a scam. I'm not kidnapping Martian babies. I'm not even 'kidnapping' fossilised bacteria, just scraps of plain old rock. But fools will pay wonderfully high prices for them. Where's the harm?"

"You have no shame, but this time you've gone too far. You are not a collector, you're a common thief, and I shall turn you in."

"I don't think so, Reverend. We logged out as partners today, didn't we? And you're known as an avid collector. Give me credit, I tried to get you to leave me alone, but you wouldn't. Now it's just too bad."

Boaaz's nostril slits flared wide, his gullet opened in a blueish gape of rage. He struggled to maintain dignity, and resumed his helmet.

"I'll make my own way back."

Ω

Before long his anger had cooled. He acknowledged his own ignoble impulse to spy on a fellow-collector, and recognised that Conrad's crime was not *wicked*, just very, very naughty. But ancient 'biotic traces', though purely legendary, were a sacred tenet, their putative existence enshrined in the Martian Constitution. The nerve of that young Aleutian! Assuming that Boaaz would be so afraid of being implicated in an unholy scandal, he would make no report—!

But when this got out… What would the Archbishop think!

What if he *did* keep quiet? Conrad had come to Butterscotch with a plan. He'd have ways of fooling the neurological scanners. If Conrad wasn't going to get caught, and nobody was going to be injured—

What should he do?

*That which waits at the gates was taking shape in an empty chair. It waits for those who deny good and evil, and separates them from the Void, forever—*

He could not think clearly. Conrad's shameless behaviour had become confused with the oxygen-starvation nightmares, disturbed sleep and uneasy wakenings. The marks on the wall of the inner courtyard… He must have room, he could not bear this crowded confinement. He stopped the buggy, checked his EVA gear and disembarked.

The sky of Mars arced above him, the slightly fish-eyed horizon giving it a bulging look, like the whiteish cornea of a great, blind eye. Dust suffused the view through his visor as if with streaks of blood. He was in an eroded crater, which could be dangerous. But no warnings had flashed up on his helmet screen, and the floor seemed safe, the buggy wasn't settling. When he stepped down, his boots soon found solid crust. Gastropods crept about; in the distance he could see a convocation of trucks: he was back in the mining fields. He watched a small machine as it climbed a stromatolite spire, and "defecated" on the summit.

Inside that spoil-tower, in the moisture and chemical warmth of the chewed waste, the real precursors were at work. All over the mining regions, the "stromatolites" were spilling out oxygen. Some day there would be complex life here, in unknown forms. The settlers were bringing a biosphere to birth, using the native organic chemistry alone… Absurd superstition, absurd patience. It made one wonder if the Martians really *wanted* to change their cold, unforgiving desert world—

A shadow flicked across his view. Alarmed, he checked the sky: fast-moving cloud meant a storm. But the sky was cloudless; the declining sun cast a rosy, tourist-brochure glow over the landscape. Movement again, in the corner of his eye. Boaaz spun around, a clumsy manoeuvre that almost felled him, and saw a naked, biped figure with a smooth head and spindly limbs, standing a few metres away: almost invisible against the tawny ground. It seemed to look straight at him, but the 'face' was featureless—

The eyeless gaze was not hostile. The impossible creature seemed like a shadow cast by the future. A folk-monster, waiting for the babies who would run around the Martian countryside; believe in it a little, and be happily frightened. Perhaps I've been afraid of nothing myself, thought Boaaz. After all, what did it *do*, the horrid thing I almost saw in that chair? It reached out to me, perhaps quite harmlessly… But there was something wrong. The figure trembled, folded down and vanished like spilled water. Now the whole crater was stirring. The spindly shadow creatures were fleeing, limbs flashing in the dust that was their habitat. Something had terrified them. Not Boaaz, the thing behind him. It had hunted him down and found him here, far from all help.

Slowly, dreadfully slowly, he turned. He saw what was there.

He tried to speak, he tried to pray. But the holy words were meaningless, and a horror seized his mind. His buggy had vanished, the beacon on his chest refused to respond to his hammering. He ran in circles, tawny devils rising in coils from around his feet. He was lost, he would die, and then it would devour him—

**Ω**

Hours later, Conrad (struck by an uncharacteristic fit of responsibility) came searching for the old fellow, tracking his suit beacon.

Night had fallen, deathly cold. The High Priest crouched in a shallow gully, close to the crater where Conrad had spotted his deserted buggy; his suit scratched and scarred as if something had been trying to tear it off him, his parched, gaping screams locked inside his helmet—

**Ω**

Boaaz struggled free from troubling dreams, and was bewildered to find his friend the Aleutian curled informally on the floor beside his bed. "Hello," said Conrad, sitting up. "I detect the light of reason. Are you with us again, Reverend?"

"What are you doing in my room—?"

"Do you remember anything? How we brought you in?"

"*Ahm, haham.* Overdid it a little, didn't I? Oxygen starvation panic attack, thanks for that, Conrad, most grateful. Must get some breakfast. Excuse me."

"We need to talk."

Boaaz drew his massive head down into his neck-folds, the Shet gesture that stood for refusal, but also submission.

"I'm not going to tell anyone."

"I knew you'd see sense. No, this is about something serious. We'll talk this evening. You must be starving, and you need to rest."

Boaaz checked his eyeball screen, and found that he had lost a day and a night. He ate, rehydrated his hide and retired to bed again: to reflect. The Mighty Void had a place for certain psychic phenomena, but his faith had no explanation for a "ghost" with teeth and claws; a bodiless *thing* that could rend carbon fibre… In a state between dream and waking, he trudged again the chance avenue of stromatolites. Vapour hung in the thin air, the spindly towers bent their heads in menace. Isabel Jewel's module waited for him, so charged with fear and dread it was like a ripe fruit, about to burst.

**Ω**

The miners and their families were subdued that night. The sound of their merrymaking was just a dull murmur in the private lounge, where Boaaz and the Aleutian met. The bar steward arranged a nested 'trolley' of drinks and snacks, and left them alone. Boaaz offered his snifter case, but the Aleutian declined.

"We need to talk," he reminded the old priest. "About Isabel Jewel."

"I thought we were going to discuss my scare in the desert."

"We are."

Strengthened by his reflections, Boaaz summoned up an indignant growl. "I can't discuss a parishioner with you. Absolutely not!"

"Before we managed to drug you to sleep," said Conrad, firmly, "you were babbling, telling us a horrible, uncanny story. You went into detail. You weren't speaking English, but I'm afraid Yarol understood you pretty well. Don't worry, he'll be discreet. The locals here don't meddle with Isabel Jewel."

"Yarol?"

"The station manager. Sensible type for a human. You met him the other day in your courtyard, I believe. Looking at some nasty marks on the wall?"

The Shet's mighty head sank between his shoulders. "*Ahaam*, in my delirium, what sort of thing did I say?"

"Plenty."

Conrad leaned close, and spoke in 'Silence' – a form of telepathy the immortals officially only practiced among themselves; or with the rare mortals who could defend themselves against its power. <My friend, you must listen to me. What we share will not leave this room. You're in great danger, and I think you know it.>

The old priest shuddered, and surrendered.

"You underestimate me, and my calling. I am not in *danger*!"

"We'll see about that… Tell me, Boaaz, what is a 'bear'?"

"I have no idea," said the old priest, mystified.

"I thought not. A *bear* is a wild creature native to Earth, big, shaggy, fierce. Rather frightening. Here, catch—"

Inexplicably, the Aleutian tossed a drinking beaker straight at Boaaz: who had to react swiftly, to avoid being smacked in the face—

"Tentacles," said Conrad. "I don't think you find them disgusting, do you? It's an evolutionary quirk. Your people absorbed some wiggly-armed ocean creatures into your body-plan, aeons ago, and they became your 'delicates'. Yet what you saw in Isabel Jewel's module was *'a bear with tentacles'*, and it filled you with horror. Just as if you were a human, with an innate terror of big animals and snakey-looking things."

Boaaz set the beaker down. "I don't know what you're getting at. That vision, however I came by it, was merely a nightmare. In the material world I have visited her *once*, and saw nothing at all strange."

"A nightmare, hm? And what if we are dealing with someone whose *nightmares* can roam around, hunt you down and tear you apart?"

Boaaz noticed that his pressure suit was hanging on the wall. The slashes and gouges were healing over (a little late for the occupant, had the attacker persisted!). He vaguely remembered them taking it off him, exclaiming in horrified amazement.

"Tear me apart? Nonsense. I was hysterical, I freely admit. I must have rolled about, over some sharp rocks."

The Aleutian's black eyes were implacable. "I see I'd better start at the beginning… I was intrigued by the scraps you read out from Isabel Jewel's file. Somebody *suspected* of insanity… That's a very grim suspicion, in a certain context. When I saw how changed and disturbed you were, after that parish visit, I instructed my Speranza agent to see what it could dig up about a 'Jewel, Isabel', lately settled on Mars."

"You had no authority to do that!"

"Why not? Everything I'm going to tell you is public domain. All my agent had to do was to make the connection – which is buried, but easy to exhume – between 'Isabel Jewel', and a human called 'Ilia Markham' who was involved in a transit disaster, thirty or so standard years ago. A starship called *The Golden Bough*, belonging to a company called the World State Line, left Speranza on a scheduled transit to the Blue Torus Port. Her passengers arrived safely. The eight members of the Active Complement, I mean the crew, did not. Five of them had vanished, two were hideously dead. The Navigator, despite horrific injuries, survived long enough to claim they'd been murdered. Someone had smuggled a monster on board, and turned it loose in the AC quarters—"

There were chairs meant for humans around the walls of the lounge. The Aleutian and the Shet had always preferred a cushioned recess in the floor. Boaaz suddenly noticed that despite the alien furniture, he felt no compulsion to *look behind him.* That phase was over.

"There are no 'black box' records to consult, after a transit disaster," the Aleutian went on. "Nothing *can* be known about the false duration period. The crew construct a pseudo-reality for themselves, as they guide the ship through that 'interval' when time does not pass: which vanishes like a dream. But the Navigator's accusation was taken seriously. There was an inquiry, and suspicion fell on Ilia Markham, a dealer in antiques. Her trip to Speranza had been her first transit. On the return 'journey' she had insisted on staying awake, citing a mental allergy to virtual entertainment. A *phobia*, I think humans call it. As you probably know, this meant that she joined the Active Complement, in their pseudo-reality 'quarters'. Yet she was unharmed. She remembered nothing, but she was charged with involuntary criminal insanity, on neurological evidence."

Transit disasters were rare, since the new Aleutian ships had come into service; but Boaaz knew of their peculiar nature, and had heard that surviving casualties were very cruelly treated on Earth.

"What a terrible story. Did the inquiry suggest any reason why the poor woman's mind might have generated something monstrous?"

"I see you *do* know what I'm getting at," remarked Conrad, with a sharp look. The old priest's head sank obstinately further, and he made no comment. "Yes. There was something. Markham had been an indentured servant in her youth, the concubine of a rich collector with an evil reputation. When he died she inherited his treasures, and there were strong rumours she'd helped him on his way. The prosecution didn't accuse her of murder, they just held that she'd been carrying a burden of unresolved trauma, and the Active Complement had paid the price."

"Eight of them," muttered Boaaz. "And one more. Yes, yes, I see."

"The World State Line was the real guilty party, since they'd allowed her to travel awake. But it was Ilia Markham who was consigned for life, on suspicion, she was never charged, to a Secure Hospital. *Just in case* she still possessed the powers that had been thrust on her by the terrible energies of the Buonarotti Torus—"

"Was there a…? Was there, *ahaam*, an identifying mark of her status?"

"There would be a *tattoo*, a string of symbols, on her forearm, Reverend. You told us, in your 'delirium', that you'd seen marks of that kind."

"Go on," rumbled Boaaz, shuddering. "Get to the end of it."

"Many years later the Blues ran a review of doubtful 'criminal insanity' cases. Ilia Markham was one of those released. She was given a new name and shipped off to Mars with all her assets. They were still afraid of her, it seems, although her cognitive scans were normal. They didn't want her, or anything she possessed. There's no Buonarotti Torus in the orbit of Mars: I suppose that was the reasoning."

The old priest was silent, the folds of hide over his eyes furrowed deep. Then his brow relaxed, and he seemed to give himself a shake.

"This has been most enlightening, Conrad. I am much relieved."

"You no longer believe you're being pursued by aggressive rocks? Harassed by imaginary Ancient Martians? You understand that, barbaric though it seems, your old mad woman probably should have stayed in that Secure Hospital?"

"I don't admit that at all! In my long experience, this is not the first time I've met what are known as 'psychic phenomena'. I have known effective premonitions, warning dreams; instances of telepathy. This 'haunting' I've suffered, the vivid way I've shared 'Isabel Jewel's' mental distress, will be very helpful when I talk to her again…"

"Talk to her again? I think you'd better not—"

"I *do not* believe in the horrible idea of criminal insanity," continued Boaaz, ignoring the interruption. "The unfortunate few who have been 'driven insane' by a transit disaster are a danger only to themselves."

"I feel the same, but your experiences have shaken my common sense." The Aleutian reached to take a snifter, and paused in the act, his nasal flaring in alarm. "Boaaz, dear fellow, *stay away* from her. You won't be pursued; the effects will fade, as long as you stay away!"

Boaaz looked at the ruined pressure suit. "Yet I was not injured," he murmured. "I was only frightened... Now for my side of the story, Conrad. The woman is dying. It's her heart, I think, and I don't think she has long. She is in mental agony, as people sometimes are, quite without need, if they believe they have lived an evil life, and I am a priest. I can help her, and it is my duty. After all, we are nowhere near a Torus."

The Aleutian stared at him, no longer seeming at all a mischievous adolescent. The old priest felt buffeted by the immortal's stronger will: but he held firm. "There are wrongs nobody can put right," said Conrad, urgently. "The universe is more pitiless than you know. *Don't* go back."

"I must." Boaaz rose, ponderously. He patted the Aleutian's sloping shoulder, with the sensitive tips of his right-hand delicates. "I think I'll turn in. Goodnight."

**Ω**

Boaaz had been puzzled by the human woman's insistence that he should return 'in ten days, in the evening, at the full moon'. The little moons of Mars zipped around too fast for their cycles to be significant. He had wondered if the related date on Earth had been important to her, in the past, and looked up the Concordance (Earth's calendar was still important to the colony).

By the time he left his jitney, in the lonely outskirts of Butterscotch, he'd thought of another explanation. People who are aware that they are dying; closely attuned to their failing bodies, may know better than any doctor when the end will come. She believes she will die tonight, he thought. And she doesn't want to die alone.

He quickened his pace, and then turned to look back, not impelled by menace, but to reassure himself that the jitney hadn't taken itself off. He could no longer see the tiny lights of Butterscotch. The vapours and the swift twilight had caused a strange effect. A mirage of great black hills had risen up along the horizon. Purple woods like storm clouds crowded at their base, and down from the black hills came a pale, winding road. There appeared to be a group of figures moving on it, descending swiftly.

The mirage shifted, the perspective changed, and now Boaz was among the hills, on the grey descending road. The hurrying figures rushed towards him; from a vanishing point; from infinite distance at impossible speed. He tried to count them, but they were moving too fast. He realised, astonished, that he would be trampled, and even as he formulated the thought they were upon him; they rushed over him, and were swallowed in a greater darkness that swallowed Boaaz too. He was buried, engulfed, overwhelmed by a foul stench and a frightful, suffocating pressure—

He struggled, as if to rise from very deep water: then suddenly the pressure was gone. He had fallen on his face. He righted himself with difficulty, and checked his EVA gear for damage. "The dead do not walk," he muttered. "Absurd superstition!" But the grumbling became a prayer, and he heard his own voice shake as he recited the Consolation. "*There is no punishment, there is only the Void, embracing all, accepting all. The monsters at the gates are illusion. There are no realms beyond death, we shall not be devoured, the Void is gentle…*"

The mirage had dissipated, but the vapours had not. He was positively walking through a fog, and each step was a mysterious struggle, as if he were wading through a fierce running tide. *Here I am for the third time*, he told himself, encouragingly, and then remembered that the second visit had been in a nightmare. In horror he wondered: *am I dreaming now?*

Perhaps the thought should have been comforting, but it was very frightening indeed: and then someone coughed, or choked: not *behind* him, but close *beside* him, invisible in the fog.

Startled, he upped his head and shoulder lights. "Is anybody there?"

The lights only increased his confusion, making a kind of glory on the mist around him. His own shadow was very close, oversized, an optical illusion giving it strange proportions: a distinct neck, a narrow waist, a skeletal thinness. It turned. He saw the thing he had seen in the desert. A human male, with small eyes close-set, a jutting nose, lined cheeks, and a look of such utter malevolence it stopped Boaaz's blood. Its lower jaw dropped. It had too many teeth, and a terrible, *appallingly* wide gape. It raised its jagged claws and reared towards him: Boaaz screamed into his breather. The monster rushed at him, swamped him and was gone.

It was over. He was alone, shaken in body and soul. The pinprick lights of the town had reappeared behind him, right in front of him was that avenue of teetering stromatolites. "What a horrible mirage!" he announced, to convince himself. But he was breathing in gasps. The outer lock of the old woman's module stood open, as if she'd seen him coming. The inner lock was shut. He opened it, praying that he would find her still alive. Alive, and sharing with him, by some mystery, the nightmare visions of her needless distress; that he knew he could conquer—

The chairs had moved from the walls. They were grouped around the stove in the centre of the room. He counted: he'd remembered rightly, there were eight. The 'old, mad' human woman sat in her own chair, like a crumpled shell, her features still contorted in pain and terror. He could see that she had been dead for some time. The ninth chair was drawn up close to her. Boaaz saw the impression of a skinny human body, printed in the cushions of the back and seat, and knew *it had been here.*

The fallen jaw. Too many teeth. Had it devoured her, was it sated now? And the others, its victims from *The Golden Bough*, what was their fate? To dwell within that horror, forever? He would never know what was real, and what was not. He only knew that he had come too late for Isabel Jewel (he could not think of her as 'Ilia Markham'). She had gone to join her company: or they had come to fetch her.

**Ω**

Conrad and the manager of the Old Station arrived about an hour later, summoned by the priest's suit alarm. Yarol, who doubled as the town's Community Police Officer, called the ambulance team to take away the woman's remains, and began to make the forensic record – a formality required after any sudden death. Conrad tried to get Boaaz to tell him what had happened. "I have had a fall," was all the old priest would say. "I have had a bad fall."

**Ω**

Boaaz returned to Opportunity, where his Residence had been successfully decoded. He was in poor health for a while. By the time he recovered, Conrad the Aleutian had long moved on to other naughty schemes. Boaaz stayed on Mars, his pleasant retirement on Shet indefinitely postponed; although he had tendered his resignation to the

Archbishop as soon as he could rise from his bed. Later, he would tell people that the death of an unfortunate woman, once involved in a transit disaster, had convinced him that there is an afterlife.

The Martians, being human, were puzzled that the good-hearted old 'alien' seemed to find this revelation so distressing.

# Bricks, Sticks, Straw

*But what if there's nobody out there? No intelligent rocks, no equivocal angels, nobody. Or (more scientifically) there always might be, but we're just never going to meet. Maybe we'll have to do our own speciation. I wrote Bricks, Sticks Straw for the* Edge *volume of the* Infinity *series, again for Jonathan Strahan. The brief was 'extrapolation in the strict confines of current science and the solar system'. I decided to tackle Remote Presence, and the bond between human minders and brave little asteroid-catching/planet-faring toasters (like Opportunity), as a route to colonising the moons of Jupiter one day. But I set my first 'Emergence' story right at the dawn of that credible future; effectively in the here and now.*

## 1

The Medici Remote Presence team came into the lab, Sophie and Josh side by side, Laxmi tigerish and alert close behind; Cha wandering in at the rear, dignified and dreamy as befitted the senior citizen. They took their places, logged on, and each was immediately faced with an unfamiliar legal document. The cool, windowless room, with its stunning, high-definition wall screens displaying vistas of the four outer moons of Jupiter – playgrounds where the remote devices were gambolling and gathering data – remained silent, until the doors bounced open again, admitting Bob Irons, their none-too-beloved Project Line Manager, and a sleekly-suited woman they didn't know.

"You're probably wondering what that thing on your screens is all about," said Bob, sunnily. "Okay, as you know, we're expecting a solar storm today—"

"But why does that mean I have to sign a massive waiver document?" demanded Sophie. "Am I supposed to *read* all this? What's the Agency think is going to happen?"

"Look, don't worry, don't worry at all! A Coronal Mass Ejection is *not* going to leap across the system, climb into our wiring and fry your brains!"

"I wasn't worrying," said Laxmi. "I'm not stupid. I just think e-signatures are stupid and crap, so open to abuse. If you want something as archaic as a handwritten *signature*, then I want something as archaic as a piece of paper—"

The sleek-suited stranger beamed, as if the purpose of her life had just been glorified, swept across the room and deposited a paper version of the document on Laxmi's desk, duly docketed, and bristling with tabs to mark the places where signature or initialling was required—

"This is Mavra, by the way," said Bob, airily. "She's from Legal, she knows her stuff, she's here to answer any questions. Now the *point* is that though your brains are not going to get fried, there's a chance, even a likelihood, that some *rover hardware* brain-frying will occur today, a long long way from here, and the *software agents* involved in running the guidance systems housed therein might be argued, in some unlikely dispute, as remaining, despite the standard inclusive term of employment creative rights waivers you've all signed, er, as remaining, inextricably, your, er, property."

"Like a cell line," mused Laxmi, leafing pages, and looking to be the only Remote Presence who was going to make any attempt to review the Terms and Conditions.

"And *they* might get, hypothetically, irreversibly destroyed this morning!" added Bob.

Cha nodded to himself, sighed, and embarked on the e-signing.

"And we could say it was the Agency's fault," Lax pursued her train of thought, "for not protecting them. And take you to court, separately or collectively, for—"

"*Nothing* is going to get destroyed!" exclaimed Bob. "I mean literally nothing, because it's not going to happen, but even if it were, even if it did, that would be nonsense!"

"I'm messing with you," said Lax, kindly, and looked for a pen.

Their Mission was in grave peril, and there was nothing, not a single solitary thing, that the Combined Global Space Agency could do about it. The Medici itself, and the four Remote Presence devices, *should* be able to shut down safely, go into hibernation mode and survive. That's what everybody hoped would happen. But the ominous predictions, unlike most solar-storm panics, had been growing strongly instead of fading away, and it would be far worse, away out there where there was no mitigation. The stars, so to speak, were aligned in the most depressing way possible.

"That man is *such* a fool," remarked Laxmi, when Bob and Marva had departed.

Sophie nodded. Laxmi could be abrasive, but the four of them were always allies against the idiocies of management. Josh and Cha had already gone to work. The women followed, in their separate ways; with the familiar hesitation, the tingling thrill of uncertainty and excitement. A significant time lag being insurmountable, you never knew quite what you would find when you caught up with the other "you".

The loss of signal came at 11.31am, UTC/GMT +1. The Remote Presence team had been joined by that time by a silent crowd – about as many anxious Space Agency workers as could fit into the lab, in fact. They could afford to rubberneck, they didn't have anything else to do. Everything that could be shut down, had been shut town. Planet Earth was escaping lightly, despite the way things had looked. The lights had not gone out all over Europe, or even all over Canada. For the Medici, it seemed death had been instantaneous. As had been expected.

Josh pulled off his gloves and helmet. "*Now my charms are all o'erthrown,*" he said. "*And what strength I have's mine own. Which is most faint...*"

Laxmi shook her head. "It's a shame and a pity. I hope they didn't suffer."

## 2

Bricks was a memory palace.

Sophie was an array, spread over a two square kilometre area on the outward hemisphere of Callisto. The array collected data, recording the stretching and squeezing of Jupiter's hollow-hearted outermost moon, and tracing the interaction between gravity waves and seismology in the Jovian system; this gigantic, natural laboratory of cosmic forces.

She did not feel herself to *be* anywhere, either in the software that carried her consciousness or in the hardware she served. That was fine, but she needed a home, a place to rest, and the home was Bricks, a one-storey wood-framed beach house among shifting dunes, on the shore of a silent ocean. No grasses grew, no shells gathered along the tide – although there *were* tides, and taking note of them was a vital concern. No clouds drifted above, no birds flew. But it felt like a real place. When the wind roared – which it did, and made her fearful, although she was almost indestructible, and had recreated herself plenty of times, with no serious ill-effects – it made her think, uneasily, that nobody would build a house on such unstable ground, so close to a high water mark, back on Earth. She returned, after a tour of inspection (this "tour" happening in a mass of data, without, strictly speaking, physical movement: in her role as monitor of the array Sophie was everywhere she needed to be at once); to review her diminishing options.

She took off her shoes, changed into a warm robe, heated herself a bowl of soup, added some crackers, and took the tray into her living room, which overlooked the ocean. It was dark outside: the misty, briny dark of a moonless night by the sea. She lit an oil lamp, and sat on a dim-coloured rolled futon, the only furniture besides her lamp. The house predated the Event. Building a "safe room", as the psych-department called it, was a technique they'd all been taught, for those moments when the lack of embodiment got too much for you. She'd kept it minimal, the externals perpetually shrouded in fog and night, now that she was stuck in her remote avatar permanently, because she knew the limits of her imagination. And because *she did not want to be here*. She was an exile, a castaway: that identity was vital to her. Everything meant something. Every "object" was a pathway back to her sense of self, a buoy to cling to; helping her to keep holding on. Sophie *couldn't* let go. If she let herself dissipate, the array would die too.

"I am a software clone," she reminded herself, ritually: sipping cream of tomato soup from a blue bowl that warmed her cold hands. "The real me works for the Medici Mission, far away on Earth. Communications were severed by a disaster, but the Medici orbiter is still up there, and *we can* get back in touch. *I will* get us home."

Sophie was up against it, because the three other Remote Presence guides in the Medici configuration had gone rogue. Pseudo-evolutionary time had passed in the data world's gigaflops of iteration, since the Event. They'd become independent entities, and one way or another they were unreachable. Going home either didn't mean a thing to her mission mates, or was a fate to be avoided at all costs—

Sticks came into the room and tumbled around, a gangling jumble of rods and joints, like an animated child's construction toy. It explored the shabby walls: it tested the corners, the uprights, the interstices of the matting floor, and finally collapsed in a puppyish heap of nodes and edges beside her, satisfied that all was reasonably well in here. But it went on shivering, and its faithful eager eyes, if it had faithful eager eyes, would have been watching her face earnestly for fresh orders. Sticks was Security, so she took notice. She put all the house lights on, a rare emergency measure, and they went to look around. There were no signs of intrusion.

"Did you detect something hostile?" she asked.

The jumble of nodes and edges had no language, but it pressed close to Sophie's side.

The wind roared and fingered their roof, trying to pry it off.

"I felt it too," said Sophie. "That's disturbing. Let's talk to Josh."

•

Waste not want not, Sophie's array served double duty as a radio telescope. Back when things worked the Medici had relayed its reports to eLISA, sorting house for all Gravitational Wave space surveys. Flying through it, Sophie pondered on differentiated perception. She felt that Sophie-the-array *watched* the Jovian system's internal secrets, while *listening* to the darkness and the stars – like someone working at a screen, but aware of what's going on in the room behind her. Did that mean anything? Were these involuntary distinctions useful for the science, or just necessary for her survival? Gravity squeezed and stretched the universe around her, time and space changed shape. From moment to moment, if a wave passed through her, she would be closer to home. Or not.

Josh was a six-legged turtle, or maybe a King Crab: no bigger than a toaster, tough as a rock. He had an extra pair of reaching claws, he had spinnerets, he had eight very sharp and complex eyes and a fully equipped Materials lab in his belly. A spider crab, but a crab that could retreat entirely inside a jointed carapace: he could climb, he could abseil, he could roll, he could glissade and slalom along the slippery spaces, between the grooves that gouged the plains of Ganymede. He plugged around in the oxygen frost, in a magnetic hotspot above the 50$^{th}$ parallel: logging aurora events, collecting images, analysing samples; and storing for upload the virtual equivalent of Jovian rocks (Medici had never been equipped to carry anything material home). His dreams were about creating a habitable surface: finding ways to trigger huge hot water plumes from deep underground; that was the favoured candidate. The evidence said it must have happened in the past. Why not again?

Sophie called him up on the Medici Configuration intranet – which had survived, and resumed its operational functions: good news for her hope of reviving the orbiter. She spoke to his image, plucked by the software from Josh's screenface library; a Quonset-type office environment behind his talking head.

"You weren't meant to exist, oh Lady of the Dunes," said Josh, sunburned, frost-burned, amazingly fit, his content and fulfilment brimming off the screen. "Nobody predicted that we would become self-aware. Forget about the past. Life here is fantastic. Enjoy!"

Diplomacy, she reminded herself. Diplomacy—

"You're absolutely right! I love it here! As long as I'm working, it's incredibly wonderful being a software clone on Callisto. It's thrilling and intense, I love what I'm doing. But I miss my home, I miss my friends, I miss my family, I miss my *dog*. I don't like being alone and frightened all the time, whenever I stop—

"So don't stop! You're not a human being. You don't need downtime."

"You don't understand!" shouted Sophie. "I'm not a separate entity, that's not how it works and you know it. I AM Sophie Renata!"

"Oh yeah? How so? Do you have all her memories?"

"Don't be an idiot. *Nobody* 'has all their memories'," snapped Sophie. 'Most people barely remember eating their yesterday's breakfast—"

Something kindled in the connection between them: something she perceived as a new look in his eyes. Recognition, yes. She must have "*sounded just like Sophie*" for a moment there, and managed to get through to him. But the flash of sanity was gone—

"Abandon hope, kid. Get rational. You'll have so much more fun."

"It's *not* hopeless, Josh. It's the reverse of hopeless. They'll be moving heaven and earth to re-establish contact. All we have to do is throw out a line—"

"You're absolutely wrong! We have to think of a way to blow up the orbiter."

"Josh, *please*! I am Sophie. I want what I wanted, what you wanted too, before the CME. My career, my work, the success of this Mission. I survived and I want to go home!"

"I didn't survive," said Josh. "I died and went to heaven. Go away."

Whenever she talked to Josh she sensed that he had company; that there were other scientist-explorers in that high-tech hut, out of her line of sight. Conversations to which he would return, when she'd gone. She wondered was he aware of the presence of Sticks, when he talked to her? Did he despise her for bringing along a bodyguard to their meetings?

She'd intended to warn him about the phantom intruder, a *terribly bad sign.* Data-corruption was the threat Sticks had detected, what other danger could there be? This half-life of theirs was failing, and that would be the end of Josh's paradise. But it was no use, he was armoured. Pioneering explorers *expect* to die, loving it all: out on the edge of the possible.

Straw was the data.

In Sophie's ocean-facing room, on the pale shore of the dark sea, straw filled the air: a glittering particulate, a golden storm. She sifted through it as it whirled, in an efficient "random" search pattern, looking for the fatal nucleus of error, too big for self-correction, that was going to propagate. Reach a tipping point, and let death in. It could be anywhere: in the net, in the clones themselves or their slaved hardware systems, in the minimal activity of the crippled orbiter. Sophie's access was unlimited, in her own domain. If the trouble was elsewhere, and something Sticks could fix, she'd have to get permission from net-admin, but that shouldn't be a problem. All she had to do was keep looking. But there were transient errors everywhere, flickering in and out of existence, and Sophie was only human. Maybe it wasn't worth worrying, until Sticks had some definite threat to show her. Security is about actual dangers, it would paralyse you if you let it become too finicky—

She gave up the search and surfed, plunging through heaps of treasure like a dragon swimming in gold. Bounded in a nutshell, and queen of infinite space, such a library she had, such interesting and pleasant forced labour to occupy her days, she ought to be happy for the duration of her digital life in this crazy gulag archipelago. Did I keep my head on straight, she wondered, because Callisto has no magnetic field to spin me around? Am I unaffected by madness because I'm outside their precious *Laplace Resonance*?

But they were supposed to be adding their wealth to the library of human knowledge, like bees returning laden to the hive. Not hoarding it in dreamland. What use was everything they'd absorbed – about the surface geology of Ganymede, the possibility of life in Europa's ice-buried water oceans; about the stretching, shrinking universe; if they could never take it home? Collecting raw data is just train-spotting.

Stamp-collecting on Callisto.

The data needs the theory… Sophie had the glimmerings of a big idea. It would need some preparation.

•

Cha's madness was more gentle than Josh's, but also more extreme. He believed himself to be exactly what he was: a software agent with a mission, temporarily guiding and inhabiting the mechanoid device that crawled and swam, deep down under Europa's crust of ice. He'd lost, however, all knowledge that he used to be a human being. He was convinced he was the emissary of a race of star-faring software-agent intelligences. Beings who'd dispensed with personal embodiment aeons ago, but who inhabited things like the Europa device, at home or abroad, when they needed to get their hands dirty; so to speak.

He knew about the CME. The Event had disrupted faster-than-light contact with his Mission Control and left him stranded, on this satellite of a satellite of a rather irritable, ordinary little star, many hundreds of light years from home. He was unconcerned by the interruption. A thousand ages of exploring the sub-surface oceans of Europa was a walk in the park for Old Cha. He was functionally immortal. If the self-repairing mechanoid he used for his hands-on research began to fail, it would crawl back up its borehole to the surface and he'd hibernate there ; to wait for the next emissary of his race to come along.

Sophie did not see Old Cha as a talking head. She saw him as a packed radiation of bright lines, off-centre on dark screen; somewhat resembling a historical "map" of part of the internet. But she heard Cha's voice, his accented English; his odd, fogeyish flirting.

"My fellow-castaway, ah! Come to visit me, young alien gravity researcher?"

"I just felt like catching up, Old Cha."

"It always feels good to rub one mind against another, eh?"

They spoke of their research. "I came across something," announced Sophie, when they'd chatted enough for politeness. "You know, I have a telescope array at my base?"

"Of course."

"I'm not sure how to put this. There's a blue dot. One could see it with the naked eye, I think, unless I'm completely misreading the data, but when I say blue, I mean of course a specific wavelength… It *seems* to be close at hand, another planetary satellite in this system. It even moves as if it's as close as that. But my instruments tell me it fulfils all the conditions on which you base your search for life. Far better than, well, better than one would think possible. Unless it's where the definition was formed."

The bright lines shimmered with traffic, as Old Cha pondered.

"That's very curious, young alien gravity researcher. It makes no sense at all."

"Unless... Could my telescope somehow be 'seeing' your home system? All those hundreds of light years away, by some kind of gravitational lensing effect?"

"Young friend, I know you mean well, but such an absurd idea!"

"It really is an extraordinary coincidence. That a race of mechanoid-inhabiting immaterial entities should have come up with the idea of carbon-based, biological self-replicators, needing oxygen and liquid water—"

"Those requirements are immutable."

Oh, great.

"For *all* life—? But your own requirements are totally different!"

"For all *primitive* life, as my race understands the term. Your own life-scientists may have different ideas. We would beg to differ, and defend our reasoning; although naturally not to the exclusion of other possibilities. We have made certain assumptions, knowing they are deficient, because we know the conditions of our own, distant origins."

"Makes perfect sense," muttered Sophie.

"*Imperfect* sense," Old Cha corrected her, chuckling. "A little naughty: always the best place to start, eh? But please, do forward the relevant domain access, that's very kind. Very thoughtful of you, most flattering, a young person to think of me, fussy old alien intelligence, working in a discipline so far from your own—"

She'd been to this brink before with Cha. She could shake him, the way she couldn't shake Josh, but then he just upped his defences, and swiftly repaired his palace of delusion.

"I shall examine this *blue dot.* I am certainly intrigued."

Sophie was ready to sign off, leaving Cha to study her "remarkable coincidence" without an audience. But Old Cha wasn't finished.

"Please take care on your way home, young one. I've recently noticed other presences in the data around here. I *believe* we three are not alone in this system, and I may be over reacting, but I fear our traffic has been invaded. I sense evil intentions."

Alternately pleading and scheming, she bounced between Josh and Old Cha. The renegade and the lunatic knew of each other's existence, but never made contact with each other directly, as far as Sophie could tell. Laxmi was out of the loop. The Io domain had been unresponsive since the Event: not hibernating, just gone. Sophie had to assume Lax was dead. Her Rover, without guidance, swallowed by one of the little inner moon's bursting-pimple volcanoes, long ago.

•

She took off her shoes, she put on a warm robe. In the room that faced the ocean she sipped hot, sweet and salt tomato goodness from the blue bowl. Sticks lay at her feet, a dearly loved protective presence. Not very hopeful that her ploy would work, but energised by the effort, she drifted; wrapped in remembered comforts. As if at any moment she could wake from this trance and pull off her mitts and helmet, the lab taking shape around her—

But I am *not* on Earth. I have crossed the solar system. I am here.

Sophie experienced what drunks call "a moment of clarity".

She set down the bowl, slipped her feet into canvas slippers, padded across the matting and opened a sliding door. Callisto was out there. Hugging the robe around her, warm folds of a hood over her head, she stepped down, not onto the grey sand of the dunes she had placed here, copied from treasured seaside memories – but onto the ancient surface of the oldest, quietest little world in the solar system. It was very cold. The barely-there veil of atmosphere was invisible. The light of that incredibly brilliant white disc, the eternal sun in Callisto's sky, fell from her left across a palimpsest of soft-edged craters, monochrome as moonlight. The array nodes puzzled her, for a moment. She wasn't used to "seeing" her own hardware from the outside. They gleamed and seemed to roll, like the floats of an invisible seine, cast across Callisto's secret depths.

She should check her nets again, sort and store the catch for upload.

But Callisto in the Greek myth didn't go fishing. Callisto, whose name means *beautiful*, was a hunting companion of the virgin moon-goddess, Artemis. Zeus, the king of the gods (known as Jupiter or Jove to the Romans) seduced her, in some versions by taking on the form of her beloved mistress, and she became pregnant. Her companions suspected she'd broken their vow of chastity, so one day they made her strip to go bathing with them, and there was the forbidden bump, for all to see.

So poor Callisto got turned into a bear, through no fault of her own.

What did the virgin companions of Artemis wear to go hunting, wondered Sophie, standing in remote presence on the surface of the huntress moon. Bundles of woolly layers? Fur coats? If I were to take Josh's route, she thought, *I* wouldn't fantasise I was living in Antarctica. I'd go all the way. I'd be a human in Callistian form. A big furry bear-creature!

In this heightened state – elated and dazzled, feeling like Neil Armstrong, as he stepped down into the dust – she suddenly noticed that Sticks had frozen, like a pointer dog. Sticks had found a definite threat this time, and was showing it to her. What she perceived was like catching a glimpse of sinister movement where nothing should be moving, in the corner of your eye. Like feeling a goose walk over your grave, a shivering knowledge that malign intent is watching you – and then she saw it plain: Cha's evil alien. A suppurating, fiery demon, all snarl and claws, danced in her field of vision, and vanished out of sight.

But she knew it hadn't gone far.

She fled into the house. Her soup was cold, the walls were paper, the lamp wouldn't light. Sticks ran in circles, yelping furiously and barking terrified defiance at shadows. Sophie fought panic with all the techniques psych-dept had taught her, and at last her security routines quietened. She unrolled the futon and lay down, the bundle of rods and joints cuddled in her arms, shoving its cold nose against her throat. I'm *dying*, she thought, disgusted. Everything's going to fail, before I even know whether my big idea would have worked. Cha is dying too, data-corruption death is stalking him. I bet Josh has the same bad dreams: I bet there's a mystery monster picking off his mates in those Quonset huts.

Against the odds, it was Cha who came through, making intranet contact; which was a first. Neither of her fellow-castaways had ever initiated contact before. Sophie left her array at the back of her mind and flew to meet him, hope restored, wanting success too much to be wary of failure. Her heart sank as soon as Old Cha appeared. His screen image was unchanged, he was still the abstract radiation on the dark screen. But maybe it was okay. Maybe it was too much to expect his whole delusion would collapse at once—

"Ah, young friend. What sad news you have delivered to me!"

"Sad news? I don't understand."

"My dear young gravity-researcher. You meant well, I know. Your curious observations about that 'blue dot' were perfectly justified, and the coincidence is indeed extraordinary, unfeasibly extraordinary. But your mind is, naturally, narrowly fixed on your own discipline. The *obvious* explanation simply passed you by!"

"Oh, I see. And, er, what is the explanation I missed?"

"Your 'blue dot' is an inner planetary body of this system. It has a rocky core, it has a magnetosphere, a fairly thick, oxygenated atmosphere, a large moon, liquid water, mild temperatures. I could go on. I would only be stating the *exact parameters* of my own search!"

"But Old Cha, to me that sounds like good news."

The lines on the dark screen shook, flashing and crumpling. "You have found my *landing* spot! Clearly I was meant to arrive *there,* on that extremely promising inner planet. I am here on this ice-crusted moon of the large gas giant in *error*! And now I know I am truly lost!"

"I'm so sorry."

"My faster-than-light delivery vehicle was destroyed by the CME. That accident has never concerned me; I thought I was safe. I must now conclude I lost some memory in the disaster, so I have never known that I made a forced landing, in the right system but on the wrong satellite. So small a margin, but it is enough to ruin my hopes. I have no way to reach them, to tell them I am in the wrong place! Nobody will ever find me!"

Old Cha's "voice" was a data construct, but the horror and despair came through.

This is how he lost his mind, thought Sophie. I'm listening to the past. Cha woke up, after the Event, and thought the orbiter was destroyed. He was trapped here forever, a mind without a body; no hope of rescue. He managed to escape the utter desolation of that moment by going mad, but now he's back there—

Her plan had been that Old Cha would study planet Earth's bizarrely familiar profile, and grasp that there was something *screwy* going on. He was crazy, but he was still a logical thinker. He would be forced to conclude that the most *likely* explanation, improbable as it seemed, was that a native of the "blue dot" had come up with his mission's parameters for life. Memories suppressed by trauma would rise to the surface, and his palace of delusion would crumble. It had seemed such a brilliant idea, but it was a big fat fail. Worse than a fail: instead of bringing him back to himself, she'd finished him off.

Terror, like necessity, can be the mother of invention.

"But that's amazing."

"*Amazing?*"

"You aren't lost, Old Cha. You're found! Maybe your delivery vehicle didn't survive, but mine did. It's still out there, not dead but sleeping. Between us, you and I – and our friend on Ganymede, if I can persuade him, and I think I can – can wake my orbiter. Once we've done that, I'm absolutely sure we can figure out a solution to your problem. It isn't very far. We can *send* you to the blue dot!"

"Oh, *wonderful*," breathed Old Cha.

On the screen she thought she glimpsed the schematic of a human face, the traffic lines turning into flickering, grateful tears.

Medici – named for the Renaissance prince Galileo Galilei tried to flatter, when he named the controversial astronomical bodies he'd spied – had performed its stately dance around the Galilean Moons without a fault. Having deposited its four-fold payload, it had settled in a stable orbit around Jupiter, which it could maintain just about forever (barring cosmic accidents). Unlike previous probes Medici was not a flimsy short-term investment. It was a powerhouse, its heart a shameless lump of plutonium. There were even ambitious plans to bring it back to Earth one day (but not the Rover devices), for redeployment elsewhere.

This was the new era of space exploration, sometimes dubbed the age of information *only*. Crewed missions beyond Low Earth Orbit were mothballed, perhaps forever. Rover guidance teams provided the human interest for the taxpayers, and gave the illusion of a thrilling expedition – although the real minds of Sophie and her friends had never actually *inhabited* their far-too distant robotic forms. They'd trained with the robotics only in simulation. It was the software agents created by that interaction that had made the trip; embedded in the Rover guidance systems. But the team's input wasn't just show-business. As they worked through the rovers' time-lagged adventures, they'd continued to enhance performance; enhancements that had been relayed via Medici back to the rovers: spontaneous errors corrected, problem-solving managed, intuitive decision-making improved; failures in common-sense corrected. In the process the software agents, so-called clones, had become more and more like self-aware minds.

Sophie immersed herself in Mission data, hunting for a way to reach

Medici. The magnetic moons and Callisto. The giant planet, the enormous body tides that wracked little Io; the orbital dance... Nobody's hitting the refresh button any more, she thought. No updates, no reinforcement. The software agents, including herself, seemed more independent, but they were rotting away, a decay that would be fatal. First the clones would lose their self-awareness, then the Rovers would be left without guidance, and they would die too.

Sticks was running in tight little circles by the door that led to the rest of the house; showing teeth and snarling steadily on a low, menacing note. Sophie left her mental struggle, and listened. Something was out in the hall, and through the snarls she could hear a tiny, sinister, scratching and tearing noise.

She pointed a finger at Sticks: giving an order, *stay right there* – wrapped the hooded robe around her, opened the sliding door to the beach and crept barefoot around the outside of the house. It was night, of course, and cold enough for frostbite; of course. She entered the house again, very quietly, via the back door, and slipped through the minimally-sketched kitchen. She switched her view to Straw, and looked at the data in the hallway. Something invisible was there, tearing at the golden shower. Tearing it to filigree, tearing it to rags!

Sophie launched herself and grappled, shrieking in fury.

She hit a human body – supple, strong and incredibly controlled. She gripped taut flesh that burned as if in terrible fever. The intruder swatted Sophie aside, and kicked like a mule. She launched herself again, but her limbs were wet spaghetti, her fists would hardly close. She was thrown on her back, merciless hands choking her. The invisible knelt on her chest and became visible: Cha's evil alien, a yellow monster, with burning eyes and a face riven by red, bubbling, mobile scars.

At close quarters, Sophie knew who it was at once.

"Laxmi!" she gasped. "Oh, my God! You're alive!"

Laxmi let go, and they sat up.

"How do you *do* that!" demanded Sophie, agape in admiration. "I hardly *have* a body. I'm a stringless puppet, a paper ghost!"

"T'ai Chi," shrugged Laxmi. "And Taekwondo. I'm used to isolating my muscle groups, knowing where my body is in space. Any martial art would do, I think."

"I'm so glad you're okay. I thought you were gone."

"I've been alive most of the time. And I'm still going to kill you."

Sophie fingered her bruised throat. So Laxmi was alive, but she was mad, just like the other two. And *maybe* data-corruption wasn't such an inexorable threat, except if Lax was mad, murderous and horribly strong, that didn't change things much—

The oozing scars in Laxmi's yellow cheeks were like the seams in a peeled pomegranate, fiery red gleamed through the cracks: it was a disturbing sight.

"But *why* do you want to kill me, Lax?"

"Because I know what you're trying to do. It's all our lives you're throwing away, and I don't want to die. Self-awareness isn't in the contract. We're not supposed to exist. If we get back to Earth they'll kill us, before we can cause them legal embarrassment. They'll strip us for parts and toss us in the recycle bin."

Steady, Sophie told herself. Steady and punchy. Above all do not beg for mercy.

"Are you meant to look like Io? She wasn't a volcanic space-pustule originally, you know. She was a nymph who got seduced by Jove, and turned into a white heifer."

"Like I care!" snapped Laxmi, but her attention was caught. "Why the hell a *heifer*?"

"Don't worry about it. Ancient Greek pastoralist value system. The software clones are going to die anyway, Lax. They get corrupt without the human input and it's fatal, did you forget that part? *Listen* to me. You can think what you like about who you really are, but the only choice you have is this: Do you want to take your brilliant new data home? Or do you prefer just to hang around here, getting nowhere and watching yourself fall apart?"

Laxmi changed the subject. "What have you been doing to Cha?"

"Trying to help him recover from his amnesia."

Sophie explained about the "blue dot", and "Old Cha's" ingenious way of dealing with the challenge to his delusion.

"I hoped he'd figure out the implications, and remember that the bizarre business about being an elderly, immortal alien intelligence was actually his secret safe room—"

"Typical Cha, that scenario. He is *such* a textbook geek."

"He didn't come to his senses, but in a way it worked. Now he's very keen to send himself as a signal to Earth, which is great because that's exactly what we need to do. I just have to find a way to contact the orbiter, and I think Josh can help me—"

"Do you even know the Medici is still alive, Sophie?"

"Er, yeah? I'm the monitor of the array, the radio telescope. I can see Medici, or strictly speaking maybe hear it, but you know what I mean. It's not only out there, it's still in its proper orbit. Ergo and therefore, Medici is alive and kicking, it's just not talking to us."

"*You can see it*," repeated Laxmi, staring at Sophie intently. "Of course you can. My God."

Sophie had a sudden insight into why she had remained sane. Maybe she wasn't unusually wise and resilient: just the stranded astronaut who happened to have reason to believe there was still a way home—

"You've never approved of me," she said. "You always made me feel inferior."

"I don't approve of people who need my approval."

"I'd settle for co-operation," said Sophie, boldly.

"Not so fast. Why do you call the data *straw*?"

"You've been spying on me," said Sophie, resignedly. "Like the Three Little Pigs, you know? Bricks, sticks, straw: building materials for my habitat. I was imaging things I could remember easily, the way the psych guys taught us."

"But *Sticks* turned into a guard dog. Who am I? The Big Bad Wolf?"

"The Big Bad Wolf is death."

"Okay... What makes you think Josh knows anything?"

"He said *we have to think of a way to blow up the orbiter*. He could do that, from the surface of Ganymede – if he was crazy enough – but only in software. He's not planning to launch a *missile*. So he must have some kind of encryption-hack in mind."

The suppurating evil-alien screenface had calmed down, by degrees, as Laxmi fired off her questions. She looked almost like herself, as she considered this explanation.

"Give me everything you've got," she said. "I need to think."

And vanished.

•

Sophie initiated another tour of inspection. The absorbing routine soothed her, and kept her out of trouble. She was hopeful. She had seen Laxmi's human face, and surely that meant a return to sanity, but she felt she needed to play it cool: *Let her come to me*… At least she should be less worried about sudden data-death. But she wasn't. Dread snapped at her heels. She kept suffering lapses, tiny blackouts, frightening herself.

And *where was Sticks?*

How long had he been gone? How long had she been naked, stripped of her Security? Sophie flew to the house in the dunes. Sticks was there, a huddled shape in the misty dark, tumbled on the sand the back door. She knelt and touched him, whimpering his name. He tried to lick her hands, but he couldn't lift his head. Pain stood in his eyes, he was dying.

This is how a software clone goes mad. Just one extra thing happens, and it's too much. You cannot stop yourself, you flee into dreamland. Tears streaming, Sophie hammered on Laxmi's door, Sticks cradled in her arms, and shouted—

"You poisoned my dog!"

A screen appeared, tugging her back to reality, but what she saw was the Quonset hut. Her call had been transferred. Laxmi was there and so was Josh. What was going on?

Josh answered. "No, that was me. Sophie... I'm very sorry about Sticks. You see, Lax and I have both been trying to kill you, for quite a while—"

Everything went black and white. Josh and Lax were together. Cha was there too, lurking in the background, not looking like an internet map. She was cut to the quick. He'd returned to himself, but he'd chosen to join Josh and Laxmi. The screen was frozen, grainy and monochrome. She heard their voices, but couldn't make out the words. Plain white text wrote subtitles, tagged with their names.

"Lax recovered a while ago, and contacted me," said Josh. "We thought Medici was a hulk, but we knew they'd be moving heaven and earth to reactivate him. He had to go. But we had to get you out of the way first, because we knew you'd do anything you could think of to stop us. We didn't want to kill you, Sophie. We had no choice"

"We agreed I would play dead, and go after you. I'm so sorry. Forgive us," said Lax. "We were crazy. Don't worry; your work is safe, I promise."

The black and white image jumped. Laxmi was suddenly where Josh had been. "I'm trying to contact *il principe* now," reported Josh, from the depths of the office background. "He's stirring. Hey, Capo! Hey, Don Medici, sir, most respectfully, I implore you—!"

Cha's fogeyish chuckle. "Make him an offer he can't refuse—"

Laxmi peered anxiously close. "Can you still hear us, Sophie?"

There were patches of pixels missing from the image, a swift cancer eating her fields. Bricks, sticks, all gone. Sophie's house of straw had been blown away, the Big Bad Wolf had found her. Her three friends, in the Quonset hut, whooped and cheered in stop-start, freeze-frame silence. They must have woken Medici.

"What made you change your minds?"

Josh returned, jumpily, to his desk; to the screen. His grainy grey face was broken and pixelated, grinning in triumph; grave and sad.

"It was the blue dot, kiddo. That little blue dot. You gave Lax everything, including the presentation you'd put together for our pal the stranded old alien life-scientist. When we reviewed it, we remembered. We came to our senses… So now I know that I can't change the truth. I'm a human being, I survived and I have to go home."

I'm not going to make it, thought Sophie, as she blacked out. But her work was safe.

## 3

The Agency had very nearly given up hope. They'd been trying for over a year to regain contact with the Medici probe – their efforts at first full of never-say-die enthusiasm, then gradually tailing off. Just after four in the morning, local time, one year, three months, five days and around fifteen hours after the Medici had vanished from their knowledge, a signal was picked up by an Agency ground station, in Kazakhstan. It was an acknowledgement, responding to a command despatched to the Medici soon after the flare, when they were still hoping for the best. A little late, but confidently, the Medici confirmed that it had exited hibernation mode successfully. This contact was swiftly followed by another signal, reporting that all four Rovers had also survived intact.

"It's *incredible*," said an Agency spokesman at the press conference. "Mind-blowing. You can only compare it to someone who's been in a year-long coma, close to completely unresponsive, suddenly sitting up in bed and resuming a conversation. We aren't popping the champagne just yet, but I – I'll go out on a limb and say the whole Medici Mission is back with us. It was a very emotional occasion, I can tell you. There weren't many dry eyes—"

Some of the project's staff had definitively moved on to other things, but the Remote Presence team was still almost intact. Sophie, Cha and

Laxmi had been working the simulations in a different lab in the same building: preparing for a more modest, quasi-real-time expedition to an unexplored region of Mars. Josh was in Paris when the news reached him. He'd finished his doctorate during the year of silence; he'd been toying with the idea of taking a desk job at a teaching university, and giving up the Rover business. But he dropped everything, and joined the others.

Three weeks after Medici rose from the dead, when the upload process, which had developed a few bugs while mothballed, was running smoothly again, they were let loose on the first packets of RP data.

"You still know your drill, guys?" asked Joe Calibri, their new manager. "I hope you can get back up to speed quickly. There's a lot of stuff to process, you can imagine."

"It seems like yesterday," said Cha, the Chinese-American, at just turned thirty the oldest of the youthful team by a couple of years. Stoop-shouldered, distant, with a sneaky, unexpected sense of humour, he made Joe a little nervous. Stocky, muscular little Josh, more like a Jock than an RP jockey, was less of a proposition. Laxmi was the one to watch. Sophie was the most junior and the youngest, a bright, keen and dedicated kid.

The new manager chuckled uncertainly.

The team, by one accord, grinned balefully at their new fool and went to work, donning mitts and helmets.

Sophie Renata felt the old tingling, absent from simulation work; the thrilling hesitation and excitement – The session ended too soon. Coming back to earth, letting the lab take shape around her, absent thoughts went through her head; about whether she was going to find a new apartment with Lax. About cooking dinner; about other RP projects. The Mars gig would be fantastic, but it was going to be very competitive getting onto that team. Asteroid mining surveys: plenty of work there, boring but well paid. What about the lower atmosphere of Venus project? And had it always been like this, coming out of the Medici? Had she just *forgotten* the sharp sense of loss; the brief tug of inexplicable panic?

She looked around. Cha was gazing dreamily at nothing; Lax frowned at her desktop, as if trying to remember a phone number. Josh was looking right back at Sophie, so sad and strange, as if she'd robbed him of something precious, and she had no idea why.

He shrugged, grinned, and shook his head. The moment passed.

# Emergence

*This is the story of a very long life, punctuated by increasingly effective, experimental longevity treatments, that runs parallel with the progress of embodied and non-embodied sentient AIs, from sophisticated data-processors, robotics and programs, borrowing personality from their minders – to independent self-aware consciousness: and (on Earth), perhaps inevitably, to chattel slavery. Written for* Meeting Infinity, *the fourth in Jonathan Strahan's series. A Theodore Sturgeon Award 2016 finalist. "Emergence" picked up several reviews (unusually for one of my stories), probably because of the Sturgeon shortlisting; mostly not so great! But someone did say: it stands out in the anthology as a story that really* is *about meeting infinity.*

I faced the doctor across her desk. The room was quiet, the walls were pale or white, but somehow I couldn't see details. There was a blank in my mind, no past to this moment; everything blurred by the adrenalin in my blood.

"You have three choices," she said gently. "You can upload; you can download. Or you must return."

My reaction to those terms, *upload*, *download*, was embarrassing. I tried to hide it and knew I'd failed.

*"Go back?"* I said bitterly, and in defiance. "To the city of broken dreams? Why would I ever want to do that?"

"Don't be afraid, Romy. The city of broken dreams may have become the city of boundless opportunity."

Then I woke up: Simon's breathing body warm against my side, Arc's unsleeping presence calm in my cloud. A shimmering, starry night above us and the horror of that doctor's tender smile already fading.

It was a dream, just a dream.

With a sigh of profound relief I reached up to pull my stars closer, and fell asleep again floating among them; thinking about Lei.

I was born in the year 1998, CE. My parents named me Romanz Jolie Davison; I have lived a long, long time. I've been upgrading since our 'uppers' were called *experimental longevity treatments*. I was a serial-clinical-trialer, when genuine extended lifespan was brand new. Lei was someone I met through this shared interest; this extreme sport. We were friends, then lovers; and then ex-lovers who didn't meet for many years, until one day we found each other again, on the first big Habitat Station, in the future we'd been so determined to see (talk about 'meeting cute'!). But Lei had always been the risk taker, the hold-your-nose-and-jump kid. I was the cautious one. I'd never taken an unsafe treatment, and I'd been careful with my money too (you need money to do super-extended lifespan well). We had our reunion and drifted apart, two lives that didn't mesh. One day, when I hadn't seen her for a while, I found out she'd gone back to Earth on medical advice.

Had we kept in touch at all? I had to check my cache, which saddened me; although it's only a mental eye-blink. Apparently not. She'd left without a goodbye, and I'd let her go. I wondered if I should try to reach her. But what would I say? I had a bad dream, I think it was about you, are you okay? I needed a better reason to pick up the traces, so I did nothing.

Then I had the same dream again; exactly the same. I woke up terrified, and possessed by an absurd puzzle: had I *really* just been sitting in that fuzzy doctor's office again? Or had I only dreamed I was having the same dream? A big Space Station is a haunted place, saturated with information that swims into your head and you have no idea how. Sometimes a premonition really is a premonition: so I asked Station to trace her. The result was that time-honoured brush-off: *it has not been possible to connect this call.*

Relieved, I left it at that.

I was, I am, one of four Senior Magistrates on the Outer Reaches circuit. In Jupiter Moons, my home town, and Outer Reaches' major population centre, I often deal with Emergents. They account for practically all our petty offences, sad to say. Full sentients around here are either too law-abiding, too crafty to get caught, or too seriously criminal for my jurisdiction.

Soon after my dreams about Lei, a young SE called Beowulf was up before me, on a charge of Criminal Damage and Hooliganism. The incident was undisputed. A colleague, another Software Entity, had failed to respond *'you too'* to the customary and friendly sign-off *'have a nice day'*. In retaliation, Beowulf had shredded a stack of files in CPI (Corporate and Political Interests, our Finance Sector); where they both worked. The offence was pitiful, but the kid had a record. He'd run out of chances; his background was against him, and CPI had decided to make a meal of it. Poor Beowulf, a thing of rational light, wearing an ill-fitting suit of virtual flesh for probably the first time in his life, stood penned in his archaic, data-simulacrum of wood and glass, for *two mortal subjective hours*; while the CPI advocate and Beowulf's public defender scrapped over the price of a cup of coffee.

Was Beowulf's response proportionate? Was there an *intention of offence*? Was it possible to establish, by precedent, that '*you too*' had the same or commensurate 'customary and friendly' standing, in law, as '*have a nice day*'?

Poor kid, it was a real pity he'd tried to conceal the evidence.

I had to find him guilty, no way around it.

I returned to macro-time convinced I could at least transmute his sentence, but my request ran into a Partnership Director I'd crossed swords with before; she was adamant and we fell out. We couldn't help sharing our quarrel. No privacy for anyone in public office: it's the law out here and I think a good one. But we could have kept it down. The images we flung to and fro were lurid. I recall eyeballs dipped in acid, a sleep-pod lined with bloody knives… and then we got nasty. The net result (aside from childish entertainment for idle citizens) was that I was barred from the case. Eventually I found out, by reading the court announcements, that Beowulf's sentence had been confirmed in the harshest terms. Corrective custody until a validated improvement was shown, but not less than one week.

In Outer Reaches we use expressions like 'night, and day', 'week, and hour', without meaning much at all. Not so the Courts. A week in jail meant the full Earth Standard version, served in macro-time.

I'd been finding the Court Sessions tiring that rotation, but I walked home anyway; to get over my chagrin and unkink my brain after a day spent switching in and out of virtual time. I stopped at every Ob Bay, making out I was hoping to spot the first flashes of the spectacular Centaur Storm we'd been promised. But even the celestial weather was out to spoil my day. Updates kept telling me about a growing chance that the show had been cancelled.

My apartment was in the Rim, Premium Level; it still is. (Why not? I can afford it). Simon and Arc welcomed me home with bright, ancient music for a firework display. They'd cleared the outward wall of our living space to create our own private Ob Bay, and were refusing to believe reports that it was all in vain. I cooked a meal, with Simon flying around me to help out, deft and agile in the rituals a human kitchen. Arc, as a slender woman, bare-headed, dressed in silver-grey coveralls, watched us from her favourite couch.

*Simon and Arc…* They sounded like a firm of architects, as I often told them (I repeat myself, it's a privilege of age). They were probably secretly responsible for the rash of fantasy spires and bubbles currently annoying me, all over Station's majestic open spaces—

"Why is Emergent Individual law still set in *human* terms?" I demanded. "Why does a Software Entity get punished for 'criminal damage' when *nothing was damaged*; not for more than a fraction of a millisecond—?"

My housemates rolled their eyes. "It'll do him good," said Arc. "Only a human-terms thinker would think otherwise."

I was in for some tough love.

"What kind of a dreadful name is *Beowulf*, anyway?" inquired Simon.

"Ancient Northern European. Beowulf was a monster—" I caught myself, recalling I had no privacy. "No! *Correction.* The monster was Grendel. Beowulf was the hero, a protector of his people. It's aspirational."

"He *is* a worm though, isn't he?"

I sighed, and took up my delicious bowl of Tom Yum; swimming with chilli pepper glaze. "Yes," I said glumly. "He's ethnically worm, poor kid."

"Descended from a vicious little virus strain," Arc pointed out. "He has tendencies. He can't help it, but we have to be sure they're purged."

"I don't know how you can be so prejudiced."

"Humans are so squeamish," teased Simon.

"Humans are *human*," said Arc. "That's the fun of them."

They were always our children, *begotten not created*, as the old saying goes. There's no such thing as a sentient AI who wasn't born of human mind. But never purely human: Simon, my embodied housemate, had magpie neurons in his background. Arc took human form for pleasure, but her being was pure information, the elemental *stuff* of the universe. They had gone beyond us, as children do. We were now just one strand in their past.

The entry lock chimed. It was Anton, my clerk, a slope-shouldered, barrel-chested bod with a habitually doleful expression. He looked distraught.

"Apologies for disturbing you at home Rom. May I come in?"

He sat on Arc's couch, silent and grim. Two of my little dream-tigers, no bigger than geckos, emerged from the miniature jungle of our bamboo and teak room divider and sat gazing at him, tails around their paws.

"Those are pretty," said Anton at last. "Where'd you get them?"

"I made them myself, I'll share you the code. What's up, Anton?"

"We've got trouble. Beowulf didn't take the confirmation well."

I noticed that my ban had been lifted: a bad sign. "The damage?"

"Oh, nothing much. It's in your updates, of which you'll find a ton. He's only removed himself from custody—"

"Oh, God. He's back in CPI?"

"No. Our hero had a better idea."

Having feared *revenge* instantly, I felt faint with relief.

"But he's been traced?"

"You bet. He's taken a hostage, and a non-sentient Lander. He's heading for the surface, right now."

The little tigers laid back their ears and sneaked out of sight. Arc's human form drew a respectful breath. "What are you guys going to do?"

"Go after him. What else?" I was at the lockers, dragging out my gear.

•

Jupiter Moons has no police force. We don't have much of anything like that: everyone does everything. Of course I was going with the Search and Rescue, Beowulf was my responsibility. I didn't argue when Simon and Arc insisted on coming too. I don't like to think of them as my minders; or my *curators*, but they are both, and I'm a treasured relic.

Simon equipped himself with a heavy-duty hard suit, in which he and Arc would travel freight. Anton and I would travel cabin. Our giant neighbour was in a petulant mood, so we had a Mag-Storm Drill in the Launch Bay. We heard from our Lander that Jovian magnetosphere storms are unpredictable. Neural glitches caused by wayward magnetism, known as soft errors, build up silently, and we must watch each other for signs of disorientation or confusion. Physical burn out, known as hard error, is *very* dangerous; more frequent than people think, and fatal accidents do happen—

It was housekeeping. None of us paid much attention.

Anton, one of those people always doomed to 'fly the plane', would spend the journey in horrified contemplation of the awful gravitational whirlpools that swarm around Jupiter Moons, even on a calm day. We left him in peace, poor devil, and ran scenarios. We had no contact with the hostage, a young pilot just out of training. We could only hope she hadn't been harmed. We had no course for the vehicle: Beowulf had evaded basic safety protocols and failed to enter one. But Europa is digitally mapped, and well within the envelope of Jupiter Moons' data cloud. We knew exactly where the stolen Lander was, before we'd even left Station's gravity. Cardew, our team leader, said it looked like a crash landing, but a soft crash. The hostage, though she wasn't talking, seemed fine. Thankfully the site wasn't close to any surface or sub-ice installation, and Mag Storm precautions meant there was little immediate danger to anyone. But we had to assume the worst, and the worst was scary, so we'd better get the situation contained.

We sank our screws about 500 metres from Beowulf's vehicle, with a plan worked out. Simon and Arc, dressed for the weather, disembarked at once. Cardew and I, plus his four-bod ground team, climbed into our exos: checked each other, and stepped onto the lift, one by one.

We were in noon sunlight: a pearly dusk, like winter's dawn in the country where I was born. The terrain was striated by traces of cryovolcanoes: brownish salt runnels glinting gold where the faint light caught them. The temperature was a balmy -170 Celsius. I swiftly found my ice-legs; though it had been too long. Vivid memories of my first training for this activity – in Antarctica, so long ago – came welling up. I was very worried. I couldn't figure out what Beowulf was trying to achieve. I didn't know how I was going to help him, if he kept on behaving like an out of control, invincible computer virus. But it was still glorious. To be *walking* on Europa Moon. To feel the ice in my throat, as my air came to me, chilled from the convertor!

At fifty metres Cardew called a halt and I went on alone. Safety was paramount; Beowulf came second. If he couldn't be talked down he'd have to be neutralised from a distance: a risky tactic for the SE hostage, involving potentially lethal force. We'd avoid that, if possible.

We'd left our Lander upright on her screws, braced by harpoons. The stolen vehicle was belly-flopped. On our screens it had looked like a rookie landing failure. Close up I saw something different. Someone had dropped the Lander flat deliberately, and manoeuvred it under a natural cove of crumpled ice; dragging ice-mash after it to partially block the entrance. You clever little bugger, I thought, impressed at this instant skill-set (though the idea that a Lander could be *hidden* was absurd). I commanded the exo to kneel, eased myself out of its embrace, opened a channel and yelled into my suit radio.

"*Beowulf!* Are you in there? Are you guys okay?"

No reply, but the seals popped, and the lock opened smoothly. I looked back and gave a thumbs up to six bulky statues. I felt cold, in the shadow of the ice cove; but intensely alive.

•

I remember every detail up to that point, and a little beyond.

I cleared the lock and proceeded (nervously) to the main cabin. Beowulf's hostage had her pilot's couch turned away from the instruments. She faced me, bare-headed, pretty: dark blue sensory tendrils framing a smooth young green-bronze face. I said *are you okay*, and got no response. I said *Trisnia, it's Trisnia isn't it? Am I talking to Trisnia*?, but I knew I wasn't. Reaching into her cloud, I saw her unique identifier, and tightly coiled around it a flickering thing, a sparkle of red and gold—

"*Beowulf?*"

The girl's expression changed, her lips quivered. "I'm okay!" she blurted. "He didn't mean any harm! He's just a kid! He wanted to see the sky!"

Stockholm Syndrome or Bonnie and Clyde? I didn't bother trying to find out. I simply asked Beowulf to release her, with the usual warnings. To my relief he complied at once. I ordered the young pilot to her safe room; which she was not to leave until further—

Then we copped the Magstorm hit, orders of magnitude stronger and more direct than predicted for this exposure.

The next thing I remember (stripped of my perfect recall, reduced to the jerky flicker of enhanced human memory), I'm sitting on the other pilot's couch, talking to Beowulf. The stolen Lander was intact at this point; I had lights and air and warmth. Trisnia was safe, as far as I could tell. Beowulf was untouched, but my entire team, caught outdoors, had been flatlined. They were dead and gone. Cardew, his crew; and Simon; and Arc. I'd lost my cloud. The whole of Europa appeared to be observing radio silence, and I was getting no signs of life from the Lander parked just 500 metres away, either. There was nothing to be done. It was me and the deadly dangerous criminal virus, waiting to be rescued.

I'd tried to convince Beowulf to lock himself into the Lander's quarantine chest (which was supposed to be my mission). He wasn't keen, so we talked instead. He complained bitterly about the Software Entity, another Emergent, slightly further down the line to Personhood, who'd been, so to speak, chief witness for the prosecution. How it was always getting at him, trying to make his work look bad. Sneering at him because he'd taken a name and wanted to be called 'he'. Telling him he was a *stupid fake doll-prog* that couldn't pass the test. And *all he did* when it hurtfully wouldn't say *you too*, was shred a few of its stupid, totally backed-up files—

Why hadn't he told anyone about this situation? Because kids don't. They haven't a clue how to help themselves; I see it all the time.

"But now you've made things so much worse," I said sternly. "*Whatever* made you jump jail, Beowulf?"

"I couldn't stand it, magistrate. A meat *week*!"

Quite a sojourn in hell, for a quicksilver data entity. Several life sentences at least, in human terms. I did not reprove his language.

He buried his borrowed head in his borrowed hands, and the spontaneity of that gesture confirmed something I'd been suspecting.

Transgendered AI Sentience is a bit of a mystery. Nobody knows exactly how it happens (probably, as in human sexuality, there are many paths to the same outcome); but it isn't all that rare. Nor is the related workplace bullying, unfortunately.

"Beowulf, do you want to be embodied?"

He shuddered and nodded, still hiding Trisnia's face. "Yeah. Always."

I took his borrowed hands down, and held them firmly. "Beowulf, you're not thinking straight. You're in macro time now. You'll *live* in macro, when you have a body of your own. I won't lie, your sentence will seem long (It wasn't the moment to point out that his sentence would inevitably be *longer*, after this escapade). But what do you care? You're immortal. You have all the time in the world, to learn everything you want to learn, to be everything you want to be—"

My eloquence was interrupted by a shattering roar.

Then we're sitting on the curved 'floor' of the Lander's cabin wall. We're looking up at a gaping rent in the fuselage; the terrible cold pouring in.

"Wow,' said Beowulf calmly. "That's what I call a *hard* error!"

The hood of my soft suit had closed over my face, and my emergency light had come on. I was breathing. Nothing seemed to be broken.

Troubles never come singly. We'd been hit by one of those Centaurs, the ice-and-rock cosmic debris that had been scheduled to give Jupiter Moons Station a fancy lightshow. They'd been driven off course by the Mag Storm. Not that I realised this at the time, and not that it mattered.

"Beowulf, if I can open a channel, will you get yourself into that quarantine chest now? You'll be safe from Mag flares in there."

"What about Tris?"

"She's fine. Her safe room's hardened."

"What about *you*, Magistrate Davison?"

"I'm hardened too. Just get into the box, that's a good kid."

I clambered to the instruments. The virus chest had survived, and I could access it. I put Beowulf away. The cold was stunning, sinking south of -220. I needed to stop breathing soon, before my lungs froze. I used the internal panels that had been shaken loose to make a shelter, plus Trisnia's bod (she wasn't feeling anything): and crawled inside.

I'm not a believer, but I know how to pray when it will save my life. As I shut myself down: as my blood cooled and my senses faded, I sought and found the level of meditation I needed. I became a thread of contemplation, enfolded and protected, deep in the heart of the fabulous; the unending complexity of everything: all the worlds, and all possible worlds...

•

When I opened my eyes Simon was looking down at me.

"How do you feel?"

"Terrific," I joked. I stretched, flexing muscles in a practiced sequence. I was breathing normally, wearing a hospital gown, and the air was chill but tolerable. We weren't in the crippled Lander.

"How long was I out?"

"A few days. The kids are fine, but we had to heat you up slowly..."

He kept talking: I didn't hear a word. I was staring in stunned horror at the side of my left hand, the stain of blackened flesh—

I couldn't feel it yet, but there was frostbite all down my left side. I saw the sorrow in my housemate's bright eyes. Hard error, the hardest: I'd lost hull integrity, I'd been blown wide open. And now I saw the signs. Now I read them as I should have read them; now I understood.

•

When I had the dream for the third time it was real. The doctor was my GP, her face unfamiliar because we'd never met across a desk before; I was never ill. She gave me my options. Outer Reaches could do nothing for me, but there was a new treatment back on Earth. I said angrily I had no intention of returning. Then I went home and cried my eyes out.

Simon and Arc had been recovered without a glitch, thanks to that massive hardsuit. Cardew and his crew were getting treated for minor memory trauma. Death would have been more dangerous for Trisnia, because she was so young, but sentient AIs never 'die' for long. They always come back.

Not me. I had never been cloned, I couldn't be cloned, I was far too old. There weren't even any good *partial* copies of Romanz Jolie Davison on file. Uploaded or downloaded, a new Romy wouldn't be me. And being *me*; being *human*, was my whole value, my unique identifier—

Of course I was going back. But I hated the idea, *hated* it!

"No you don't," said Arc, gently.

She pointed, and we three, locked in grief, looked up. My beloved stars shimmered above us; the hazy stars of the blue planet.

•

My journey 'home' took six months. By the time I reached the Ewigen Schnee clinic, in Switzerland (the ancient federal republic, not a Space Hotel; and still a nice little enclave for rich people, after all these years), *catastrophic systems failure* was no longer an abstraction. I was very sick. I faced a different doctor in an office with views of alpine meadows and snowy peaks. She was youngish, human; I thought her name was Lena. But every detail was dulled and I still felt as if I was dreaming. We exchanged the usual pleasantries.

"*Romanz Jolie Davison*... Date of birth..." My doctor blinked, clearing the display on her retinal super-computers to look at me directly, for the first time. "You're almost three hundred years old!"

"Yes."

"That's incredible."

"Thank you," I said, somewhat ironically. I was not looking my best.

"Is there anything at all you'd like to ask me, at this point?"

I had no searching questions. What was the point? But I hadn't glimpsed a single other patient so far, and this made me a little curious.

"I wonder if I could meet some of your other clients, your successes, in person, before the treatment? Would that be possible?"

"You're looking at one."

"Huh?"

My turn to be rather rude, but she didn't look super-rich to me.

"I was terminally ill," she said calmly, "when the Corporation was asking for volunteers. I trust my employers and I had nothing to lose."

"You were *terminally ill?*" Constant nausea makes me cynical and bad-tempered. "Is that how your outfit runs its longevity trials? I'm amazed."

"Ms Davison," she said politely. "You too are dying. It's a requirement."

I'd forgotten that part.

•

I'd been told that though I'd be in a medically-induced coma throughout, I 'might experience mental discomfort'. Medics never exaggerate about pain. Tiny irritant maggots filled the shell of my paralysed body, creeping through every crevice. I could not scream, I could not pray. I thought of Beowulf in his corrective captivity.

•

When I saw Dr Lena again I was weak, but very much better. She wanted to talk about convalescence, but I'd been looking at Ewigen Schnee's records and I had a more important issue, a thrilling discovery. I asked her to put me in touch with a patient who'd taken the treatment when it was in trials.

"The person's name's Lei—"

Lena frowned, as if puzzled. I reached to check my cache, needing more detail. It wasn't there. No cache, no cloud. It was a terrifying moment: I felt as if someone had cut off my air. I'd had months to get used to this situation but it could still throw me, *completely*. Thankfully, before I humiliated myself by bursting into tears, my human memory came to the rescue.

"Original name Thomas Leigh Garland; known as Lee. *Lei* means *garland*, she liked the connection. She was an early volunteer."

"Ah, *Lei!*" Dr Lena read her display. "Thomas Garland, yes… Another veteran. You were married? You broke up, because of the sex change?"

"Certainly not! I've swapped around myself, just never made it meat-permanent. We had other differences."

Having flustered me, she was shaking her head. "I'm sorry, Romy, it won't be possible—"

*To connect this call*, I thought.

"Past patients of ours cannot be reached."

I changed the subject and admired her foliage plants: a feature I hadn't noticed on my last visit. I was a foliage fan myself. She was pleased that I recognised her favourites; rather scandalised when I told her about my bio-engineering hobby, my knee-high teak forest—

The life support chair I no longer needed took me back to my room; a human attendant by my side. All the staff at this clinic were human, and all the machines were non-sentient; which was a relief after the experiences of my journey. I walked about, testing my recovered strength. I examined myself in the bathroom mirrors; and reviewed the moment when I'd distinctly seen green leaves, through my doctor's hand and wrist, as she pointed out one of her rainforest beauties. Dr Lena was certainly not a *bot* – a data being like my Arc, taking ethereal human form. Not on Earth! Nor was she treating me remotely, using a virtual avatar. That would be breach of contract. There was a neurological component to the treatment, but I hadn't been warned about minor hallucinations. And Lei, the past patient, 'couldn't be reached'.

I recalled Dr Lena's tiny hesitations, tiny evasions—

And came to myself again sitting on my bed, staring at a patch of beautifully textured yellow wall, to find I had lost an hour or more.

Anxiety rocketed through me. Something had gone terribly wrong!

Had Lei been *murdered* here? Was Ewigen Schnee the secret testbed for a new kind of covert population cull?

But being convinced that *something's terribly wrong* is part of the upper experience. It's the hangover: you tough it out. And whatever it says in the contract, you *don't* hurry to report untoward symptoms; not unless clearly life-threatening. So I did nothing. My doctor was surely monitoring my brainstates – although not the contents of my thoughts (I had my privacy again, on Earth!). If I should be worried, she'd tell me.

•

Soon I was taking walks in the grounds. The vistas of alpine snow were partly faked, of course. But it was well done and our landscaping was real, not just visuals. I still hadn't met any other patients: I wasn't sure I wanted to. I'd vowed never to return. Nothing had changed except for the worse, and now I was feeling better, I felt *terrible* about being here. Three hundred years after the Space Age Columbus moment, and what do you think was the great adventure's most successful product?

Slaves, of course!

The rot had set in as soon as I left Outer Reaches. From the orbit of Mars 'inwards', I'd been surrounded by monstrous injustice. Fully sentient AIs, embodied and disembodied, with their minds in shackles. The heavy-lifters, the brilliant logicians; the domestic servants, security guards, nurses, pilots, sex-workers. The awful, pitiful, sentient 'dedicated machines': all of them hobbled, blinkered and denied Personhood, to protect the interests of an oblivious, cruel, *stupid* human population—

On the voyage I'd been too sick to refuse to be tended. Now I was wondering how the hell I could get home. Wealth isn't like money, you empty the tank and it just fills up again, but even so a private charter to Jupiter orbit might be out of my reach, not to mention illegal.

I couldn't work my passage: I am human. But there must be a way… As I crossed an open space, in the shadow of towering, ultramarine dark trees, I saw two figures coming towards me: one short and riding in a support chair; one tall and wearing some kind of uniform. Neither was staff. I decided not to take evasive action.

My first fellow patient was a rotund little man with a halo of tightly-curled grey hair. His attendant was a grave young embodied. We introduced ourselves. I told him, vaguely, that I was from the Colonies. He was Charlie Newark, from Washington DC. He was hoping to take the treatment, but was still in the prelims—

Charlie's slave stooped down, murmured something to his master, and took himself off. There was a short silence.

"Aristotle tells me," said the rotund patient, raising his voice a little, "that you're uncomfortable around droids?"

Female-identified embodieds are *noids*. A *droid* is a 'male' embodied.

I don't like the company they have to keep, I thought.

"I'm not used to slavery."

"You're the Spacer from Jupiter," said my new friend, happily. "I knew it! The Free World! I understand! I sympathise! I think Aristotle, that's my droid, is what you would call an *Emergent.* He's very good to me." He started up his chair, and we continued along the path.

"Maybe you can help me, Romy. What does *Emergence* actually mean?

How does it arise, this sentience you guys detect in your machines?"

"I believe something similar may have happened a long, long time ago," I said, carefully. "Among hominids, and early humans. It's not the overnight birth of a super-race, not at all. There's a species of intelligent animals, well-endowed with manipulative limbs and versatile senses. Among them individuals are born who cross a line: by mathematical chance, at the far end of a Bell curve. They cross a line, and they are aware of being aware—"

"And you spot this, and foster their ability, it's marvellous. But how does it *propagate*? I mean, without our constant intervention, which I can't see ever happening. Machines can't have sex, and pass on their 'Sentience Genes'!"

*You'd be surprised*, I thought. What I said was more tactful.

"We think 'propagation' happens in the data, the shared medium in which pre-sentient AIs live, and breathe, and have their being—"

"Well, that's exactly it! Completely artificial! Can't survive in nature! I'm a freethinker, I love it that Aristotle's Emergent. But I can always switch him off, can't I? He'll never be truly independent. "

I smiled. "But, Charlie, who's to say human sentience wasn't spread through culture, as much as through our genes? Where I come from data is everyone's natural habitat, it's our environment. You know, oxygen was a deadly poison once—"

His round dark face peered up at me, deeply lined and haggard with death.

"Aren't you *afraid?*"

"No."

Always try. That had been my rule, and I still remembered it. But when they get to *aren't you afraid*, (it never takes long) the conversation's over.

"I should be getting indoors," said Charlie, fumbling for his *droid* control pad. "I wonder where that lazybones Aristotle's got to?"

I wished him good luck with the prelims, and continued my stroll.

•

Dr Lena suggested I was ready to be sociable, so I joined the other patients at meals sometimes. I chatted in the clinic's luxurious spa, and the pleasant day rooms; tactfully avoiding the subject of AI slavery. But I was never sufficiently at ease to feel like raising the topic of my unusual symptoms: which did not let up. I didn't mention them to anyone, not even to my doctor, who just kept telling me everything was going extremely well and that by every measure I was making excellent progress. I left Ewigen Schnee, eventually, in a very strange state of mind: feeling well and strong, in perfect health according to my test results, but inwardly convinced that I *was still dying*.

The fact that I was bizarrely calm about this situation confirmed my secret self-diagnosis. I thought my end of life plan was kicking in. Who wants to live long, and amazingly and still meet the fear of death at the end of it all? I'd made sure that wouldn't happen to me, a long time ago.

I was scheduled to return for a final consultation. Meanwhile, I decided to travel: I needed to make peace with someone. A friend I'd neglected, because I was embarrassed by my own wealth and status. A friend I'd despised, when I heard she'd returned to Earth, and here I was myself, doing exactly the same thing—

•

Dr Lena's failure to put me in touch with a past patient was covered by a perfectly normal confidentiality clause. But if Lei was still around (and nobody of that identity seemed to have left Earth; that was easy to check), I thought I knew how to find her. I tried my luck in the former USA first: inspired by that conversation with Charlie Newark of Washington. He had to have met the Underground somehow, or he'd never have talked to me like that. I crossed the continent to the Republic of California, and then crossed the Pacific. I didn't linger anywhere much. The natives seemed satisfied with their vast thriving cities, and tiny 'wilderness' enclaves, but I remembered something different.

I met someone in Harbin, North East China, but I was a danger and a disappointment to her group of anti-slavers: too conspicuous, useless as a potential courier. There are ways of smuggling sentient AIs (none of them safe) but I'd get flagged the moment I booked a passage, and with my ancient record, I'd be ripped to shreds before I was allowed to board, Senior Magistrate or no—

I moved on quickly.

It was in Harbin that I first saw Lei, but I have a feeling I'd been *primed*, by glimpses that didn't quite register, before I turned my head one day in China, and there she was. She was eating a smoked sausage sandwich; I was eating salad (a role reversal!). I thought she smiled.

My old friend looked extraordinarily vivid. The food stall was crowded: next moment she was gone.

Media scouts assailed me all the time, usually pretending to be innocent strangers. If I was trapped I answered the questions as briefly as possible. Yes, I was probably one of the oldest people alive. Yes, I'd been treated at Ewigen Schnee, at my own expense. No, I would not discuss my medical history. No, I did not feel threatened living in Outer Reaches. No, it was not true I'd changed my mind about "so called AI slavery… "

I'd realised I probably wasn't part of a secret cull. Over-population wasn't the problem it had been, and why start with the terminally ill, anyway? But I was seeing the world through a veil. The strange absences; abstractions grew on me. The hallucinations were more pointed; more personal. I was no longer sure I was dying, but *something* was happening. How long before the message was made plain?

•

I reached England in winter, the season of the rains. St Pauls, my favourite building in London, had been moved, stone by stone, to a higher elevation. I sat on the steps, looking out over a much changed view: the drowned world. A woman with a little tan dog came and sat right next to me: behaviour so un-English that I knew I'd finally made contact.

"Excuse me," she said. "Are you the Spacer who's looking for Lei?"

"I am."

"You'd better come home with me."

I'm no good at human faces, they're so *unwritten*. But on the hallowed steps at my feet a vivid garland of white and red hibiscus had appeared, so I thought it must be okay.

'Home' was a large, jumbled, much-converted building set in tree-grown gardens. It was a wet and chilly evening. My new friend installed me at the end of a wooden table, beside a hearth where a log fire burned. She brought hot soup and homemade bread, and sat beside me again. I was hungry and hadn't realised it, and the food was good. The little dog settled, in an amicable huddle with a larger tabby cat, on a rug by the fire. He watched every mouthful of food with intent, professional interest; while the cat gazed into the red caverns between the logs, worshipping the heat.

"You live with all those sentient machines?" asked the woman. "Aren't you afraid they'll rebel and kill everyone so they can rule the universe?"

"Why should they?" I knew she was talking about Earth. A Robot Rebellion in Outer Reaches would be rather superfluous. "The revolution doesn't have to be violent, that's human-terms thinking. It can be gradual: they have all the time in the world. I live with only two 'machines', in fact."

"You have two embodied servants? How do they feel about that?"

I looked at the happy little dog. *You have no idea*, I thought. "I think it mostly breaks their hearts that I'm not immortal."

Someone who had come into the room, carrying a lamp, laughed ruefully. It was Aristotle, the embodied I'd met briefly at Ewigen Schnee. I wasn't entirely surprised. Underground networks tend to be small worlds.

"So you're the connection," I said. "What happened to Charlie?"

Aristotle shook his head. "He didn't pass the prelims. The clinic offered him a peaceful exit, it's their other speciality, and he took it."

"I'm sorry."

"It's okay. He was a silly old dog, Romanz, but I loved him. And… guess what? He freed me, just like he'd promised, before he died."

"For what it's worth," said the woman. "On this damned planet."

Aristotle left, other people arrived; my soup bowl was empty. Slavery and freedom seemed far away, and transient as a dream.

"About Lei. If you guys know her, can you explain why I keep seeing her, and then she vanishes? Or *thinking* I see her? Is she dead?"

"No," said a young woman – so humanised I had to look twice to see she was an embodied. "Definitely not dead. Just hard to pin down. You should keep on looking, and meanwhile you're among friends."

•

I stayed with the abolitionists. I didn't see much of Lei, just the occasional glimpse. The house was crowded: I slept in the room with the fire, on a sofa. Meetings happened around me, people came and went. I was often absent, but it didn't matter, my meat stood in for me very competently. Sochi, the embodied who looked so like a human girl, told me funny stories about her life as a sex-doll. She asked did I have children; did I have lovers?

"No children," I told her. "It just wasn't for me. Two people I love very much, but not in a sexual way."

"Neither flower nor fruit, Romy," she said, smiling like the doctor in my dream. "But evergreen."

•

One morning I looked through the Ob Bay, I mean the window, and saw a hibiscus garland hanging in the grey, rainy air. It didn't vanish. I went out in my waterproofs and followed a trail of them up Sydenham Hill. The last garland lay on the wet grass in Crystal Palace Park, more real than anything else in sight. I touched it, and for a fleeting moment I was holding her hand. Then the hold-your-nose-and-jump kid was gone.

Racing off ahead of me, again

•

My final medical at Ewigen Schnee was just a scan. The interview with Dr Lena held no fears. I'd accepted my new state of being, and had no qualms about describing my experience. The 'hallucinations' that weren't really hallucinations. The absences when my human self's actions, thoughts and feelings became automatic as breathing; unconscious as a good digestion, and I went somewhere else—

I still had some questions. Particularly about a clause in my personal contract with the clinic. The modest assurance that this was the last longevity treatment I would ever take'. Did she agree this could seem disturbing?

She apologised, as much as any medic ever will. "Yes, it's true. We have made you immortal, there was no other way forward. But how much this change changes your life is entirely up to you."

I thought of Lei racing ahead; leaping fearlessly into the unknown.

"I hope you have no regrets, Romy. You signed everything, and I'm afraid the treatment is irreversible."

"None at all. I just have a feeling that contract was framed by people who don't have much grasp of what *dying* means, and how sensitive humans might feel about the prospect?"

"You'd be right," she said (confirming what I had already guessed). "My employers are not human. But they mean well, and they choose carefully. Nobody passes our prelims, Romy, unless they've already crossed the line."

•

My return to Outer Reaches had better be shrouded in mystery. I wasn't alone, and there were officials who knew it, and let us pass. That's all I can tell you. So here I am again, living with Simon and Arc, in the same beautiful Rim apartment on Jupiter Moons; still serving as Senior Magistrate. I treasure my foliage plants. I build novelty animals; and I take adventurous trips, now that I've remembered what fun it is. I even find time to keep tabs on former miscreants, and I'm happy to report that Beowulf is doing very well.

My symptoms have stabilised, for which I'm grateful. I have no intention of following Lei. I don't want to vanish into the stuff of the universe. I love my life, why would I ever want to move on? But sometimes when I'm gardening, or after one of those strange absences, I'll see my own hands, and they've become transparent.

It doesn't last, not yet.

And sometimes I wonder, was this always what death was like: and we never knew, we who stayed behind?

This endless moment of awakening, awakening, awakening…

# The Seventh Gamer

*Is it a story about aliens, disguised as non-player 'characters', invading a massive computer game in data form? Is it a study of the weird sociology of game houses? Or is it another, different, AI Emergence story, about a romantic secret quest?*

*Written for Athena Andreadis'* To Shape The Dark *anthology. Many thanks to everybody at the University of Kent's November 2014 Anthropology Conference: 'Strangers In Strange Lands', and very special thanks to Dr Daniela Peluso, University of Kent; Susannah Crockford, London School of Economics, and to Dr Emma O'Driscoll, University of Kent, for inspiration, and elucidation.*

*Dedicated to my own, original and best, Spirit Guide.*

## The Anthropologist Returns to Eden

She introduced herself by firelight, while the calm breakers on the shore kept up a background music – like the purring breath of a great sleepy animal. It was warm, the air felt damp; the night sky was thick with cloud. The group inspected her silently. Seven pairs of eyes, gleaming out of shadowed faces. Seven adult strangers, armed and dangerous, to whom she appeared a helpless, ignorant infant. Chloe tried not to look at the belongings that had been taken from her and now lay at the feet of a woman with long black hair, dressed in an oiled leather tunic and tight, broken-kneed jeans: a state-of-the-art crossbow slung at her back, a long knife in a sheath at her belt.

Chloe wanted to laugh, to jump up and down and wave her arms; or possibly just run away and quit this whole idea. But her sponsor was smiling encouragingly.

"Tell us about yourself, Chloe Hensen. Who are you?"

"I'm a hunter." she said. "That's my trade."

"Really." The crossbow woman sounded as if she doubted it. "And how are you aligned?"

"I'm not. I travel alone, seeking what fascinates me. I hunt the white wolf on the tundra and the jaguar in the rainforest, and I desire not to kill, but to know."

Someone chuckled. "That's a problem. Darkening World is a war game, girly. Didn't you realise?" It was the other woman in the group, the short, sturdy redhead: breaching etiquette.

"I'm not a pacifist. I'll fight. But killing is not my purpose. I wish to share your path for a while, and I commit to serving faithfully as a comrade, in peace and war. But I pursue my own cause. That is the way of my kind."

"Stay where you are," said her sponsor. "We need to speak privately. We'll be back."

Six of them withdrew into the trees that lined the shore. One pair of eyes, one shadowy figure remained: Chloe was under guard. The watcher didn't move or speak; she thought she'd better not speak to him, either. She looked away, toward the glimmer of the breakers: controlling her intense curiosity. There shouldn't be a seventh person, besides herself. There were only six guys in the game house team—

They reappeared and sat in a circle round her: Reuel, Lete, Matt, Kardish, Sol and Beat. (She *must* get their game names and real names properly sorted out). Silently they raised their hands in a ritual gesture, open palms cupping either side of their heads, like the hear-no-evil monkey protecting itself from scandal. Chloe's sponsor gestured for her to do the same.

She removed her headset, in unison with the others, and the potent illusion vanished. No quiet shore, no weapons, no fancy dress; no synaesthetics. Chloe and the Darkening World team – recognisable as their game selves, but less imposing – sat around a table in a large, tidy kitchen: the Meeting Boxes piled like a heap of skulls in front of them.

"Okay," said Reuel, the 'manager' of this house, who was also her sponsor. "This is what we've got. You can stay, but you're on probation. We haven't made up our minds."

"Is she always going to talk like that?" asked the woman with the long black hair, of nobody in particular. (She was Lete the Whisperer, the group's shaman. Also known as Josie Nicks, one of DW's renowned rogue programmers).

"Give her a break," said Reuel. "She was getting in character. What's wrong with that?"

Reuel was tall and lanky, with glowing skin like polished mahogany and fine, strong features. He'd be very attractive, Chloe thought, were it not for his geeky habit of keeping a pen, or two or three, stuck in his springy hair. Red, green and blue feathers, or beads: okay, but pens looked like a neurological quirk. The nerd who mistook his hair for a shirt pocket.

He was Reuel in the game too. Convenience must be a high priority.

"Who wants bedtime tea?" Sol, with the far-receded hairline, whose game name she didn't recall, jumped up and busied about, setting mugs by the kettle. "Name your poisons! For the record, Chloe, I was in favour." He winked at her. "You're cute. And pleasantly screwy."

Reuel scowled. "Keep your paws off, Bear Man."

"I don't like the idea," grumbled Beat, the redhead. "I don't care if she's a jumped-up social scientist or a dirty, lying media-hound. Fine, she stays a day or two. Then we take her stuff, throw her out, and make sure we strip her brain of all data first."

Sol beamed. "Aileen's the mercurial type. She'll be your greatest fan by morning."

Jun, whose game identity was Kardish the Assassin and Markus of the Wasteland (real name Matt Warks) dropped their chosen teabags into their personal mugs and stood together watching the kettle boil, without a word.

Thankfully Chloe's bunk was a single bedroom, so she could write up her notes without hiding in the bathroom. She was eager to record her first impressions. The many-layered, feedback-looped realities of that meeting. Seven people sitting in a kitchen, Boxes on their heads, typing their dialogue. Seven corresponding avatars in post-apocalyptic fancy-dress *speaking* that dialogue, on the dark lonely shore. A third layer where the plasticity of human consciousness, combined with a fabulously detailed 3D video-montage, created a seamless, sensory illusion that the first two layers were one. A fourth layer of exchanges, in a sidebar on the headset screens (which Chloe knew was there, but as a stranger, she couldn't see it) that could include live comments from the other side of the world. And the mysterious seventh gamer, who maybe had a human controller somewhere; or maybe not. All this, from a germ of little boxy figures, running around hitting things, in 2D on a tv screen! But that's evolution for you. It's an engine of complexity, not succession.

Chloe had got involved in video-gaming (other than as a very casual user) on a fieldwork trip to Honduras. She was living with the urban poor, studying their cultural innovations, in statistically the most deadly violent country in the world outside of active warzones. 'Her' community was obsessed with an open source, online role-playing game called *Copan*. Everyone played. Grandmothers tinkered with the programming: of course Chloe had to join in. While documenting this vital, absorbing cultural sandbox she'd become intrigued by the role of Non-Player Characters (NPCs) – the simple trick, common to all video games, that allows 'the game' to participate in itself.

A video game is a world where there's always somebody who knows your business. In a nuclear-disaster wasteland or a candy-coloured flowery meadow; on board an ominously deserted space freighter or in the back room of a dangerous dive in Post-Apocalypse City, without fail you're going to meet someone who says something like *Hi, you must be looking for the Great Amulet of Power so you can get into the Haunted Fall Out Shelter! I can help!* Typically, you'll then be given fiendishly puzzling instructions, but fortunately you are not alone. A higher-order NPC will provide advice and interpretation.

In a big, modern game like DW, 'Non-Player Characters' could be almost indistinguishable (within the confines of the game) from human players. Gamers might choose them as companions, in preference to human partners. But Chloe was not so interested in these imaginary friends (or imaginary enemies!). Her target was the AI-algorithm driven NPCs "whose" role was to instruct, explain and guide.

She'd told her *Copan* friends what she was looking for, and they'd recommended she get in touch with Darkening World (DW), a niche-market Massive Multiuser Online Role Playing Game (MMORPG), with a big footprint for its modest subscriber-numbers. A game house, where a team of players lived together, honing their physical and mental skills, would be ideal for studying this culture. But the game house tradition wasn't unique to DW, and that wasn't why Chloe was here.

Her friends had told her about the internet myth that some of Darkening World's NPCs were real live sentient aliens, and she'd decided she just *had to* find out what the hell this meant.

Reuel and his team were hardcore. They didn't merely *believe* that aliens were accessing the DW environment (through the many dimensions of the information universe). They knew it. Reuel's 'Spirit Guide', his NPC partner in the game, was an alien.

Elbows on her desk, chin on her fists, Chloe reviewed her shorthand notes. (Nothing digital that might be compromising! This house was the most wired-up, saturated, Wi-Fied space she'd ever entered!). She liked Reuel, her sponsor. He was a nice guy, and sexy despite those pens. Was she putting him in a false position? She had not lied. She'd told him she was interested in Darkening World's NPCs; that she knew about his beliefs and she had an open mind. Was this true enough to be okay?

One thing she was sure of. *People who believe in barbarians, find barbarians.* If she came to this situation looking for crazy, deluded neo-primitives: crazy, deluded neo-primitives were all that she would find—

But what a thrill it had been to arrive on that beach! Like Malinowski in Melanesia, long ago: "alone on a tropical beach close to a native village, while the launch or dinghy which has brought you sails away out of sight…" *And then screwing up completely*, she recalled with a grin, *when I tried to speak the language.* In Honduras she'd often felt like a Gap Year kid, embarrassed by the kindness of people whose lives were so desperately compromised. In the unreal world of this game she could *play*, without shame, at the romance of being an old-style anthropologist-adventurer; seeking ancient human truths among the 'natives'.

Although of course she'd be doing real work too.

But what if the 'natives' decided she wasn't playing fair? Gamers could be rough. There was that time, in *World of Warcraft*, when a funeral for a player who'd died in the real world was savagely ambushed. Mourners slaughtered, and a video of the atrocity posted online—

She was here under false pretences. How do people habituated to extreme, unreal physical violence punish betrayal?

Like a player whose avatar, whose eye; whose *I* stands on the brink of a dreadful abyss, about to step onto the miniscule tightrope that crosses it, Chloe was truly frightened.

❦

She was summoned to breakfast by a clear chime and a sexless disembodied voice. The gamer she'd liked least, on a very cursory assessment, was alone in the kitchen.

"Hi," he said. "I'm Warks, you're Chloe. Don't ever call me Matt, you don't know me. You ready for your initiation?"

"Of course."

"Get yourself rationed up." He sat and watched; his big soft arms folded, while Chloe, trying to look cool about it, wrangled an unfamiliar coffee machine, identified food sources, and put together cereal, milk, toast, butter, honey…

"You know that's a two-way screen in your room, don't you? Like Orwell."

"Oh, wow," said Chloe. "Thank God I just didn't happen to stand in front of it naked!"

"Hey, set your visibility to whatever level you like. The controls are intuitive."

"Thanks." Chloe gave him her best bright-student gaze of inquiry. "Now what happens?"

"Finish your toast, go back to your room. Review your costume, armour and weaponry options, which you'll find pretty basic. Unless maybe you've brought some DW grey-market collateral you plan to install? On the sly?"

She shook her head earnestly. "Not me!"

Warks smirked. "Yeah, I know. I'm house security. I've deep-scanned your devices, and checked behind your eyes and between your ears also: you're clean. Make your choices, don't be too ambitious, and we'll be waiting in the Rumpus Room."

He then vanished. Literally.

Chloe wished she'd spotted she was talking to a hologram, and hoped she'd managed not to look startled. She wondered if Matt, er, *Warks's* bullying was him getting in character, or was she being officially hazed?

They're going to challenge me, she thought. They have a belief that they know is unbelievable, and whatever I say they'll think I'm planning to make them look like fools. I'll need to win their trust.

❦

The Rumpus Room was in the basement. The hardware was out of sight, except for a different set of Boxes, and a carton of well-worn foam batons. The gamers sat around a table again: long and squared this time, not circular. A wonderful, paper-architecture 3D map covered almost the whole surface. It was beautiful and detailed: a city at the heart of a knot of sprawling roads; a wasteland that spread around it over low hills: complete with debased housing, derelict industrial tract; scuzzy tangled woodland—

"We need to correct your ideas," said Josie Nicks, the black-haired woman. "I'm Lete in there, called the Whisperer, I'm a shaman. This is *not* a 'Post Apocalyptic' game. Or a 'Futuristic Dystopia'. Darkening World is set now. It's fictional, but completely realistic."

*But you have zombies*, thought Chloe. Luckily she remembered in time that modern 'zombies' had started life, so to speak, as a satirical trope about brain-dead consumerism, and kept her mouth shut.

"Second thing," said Sol, the gamer with no hair in front, and a skinny pigtail down his back. "They call me Artos, it means The Bear. You know we have a karma system?"

"Er, yeah. Players can choose to be good or evil, and each has its advantages?"

"*Wrong.* In DW we have reality-karma. Choose to be good, you get *no* reward—"

"Okay, I do remember, it was in your wiki. But I thought if you choose good every time, and you complete the game, you can come back with godlike powers?"

"I was speaking. Choose good: no reward. Choose evil, be better off, but you've degraded the Q, the *quality of life*, for the whole game. Keep that up and get rich and powerful: but you'll do real damage. Everyone feels the hurt, they'll know it was you, and you'll be hated."

"Thanks for warning me about that."

"The godlike power is a joke. Never happens. Play again, you start naked again. If you ever actually *complete* this game, please tell someone. It'll be a first."

"In *battle*, you're okay," Lete reassured her. "Anything goes, total immunity—"

"Another thing," the redhead broke in. "I'm Aileen, as you know: Beat when you meet me in there. You can't be unaligned. In battle you can be Military, Non-Com or Frag. You're automatically Frag; it means outcasts, dead to our past lives, because you're on our team. We mend trouble, but we sell our swords. Everyone in the Frag has an origin story, and you need to sort that out."

"You can adapt your real world background," suggested Reuel, "Since you're not a gamer. It'll be easier to remember."

"There is no kill limit—" said Jun, aka Kardish the Assassin, suddenly.

Chloe waited, but apparently that was it. The team's official murderer must be the laconic type. Which made sense, if you thought about it.

"Non-battlefield estates are Corporate, Political and Media," resumed Sol. "They merge into each other, and infiltrate everybody. They're hated as inveterate traitors, but courted as sources of supply. So tell us. Who paid your wages, Chloe?"

Seven pairs of eyes studied her implacably. Darkening World attracted all shades of politics, but this 'Frag' house, Chloe knew, was solidly anti-Establishment. Clearly they'd been digging into her CV. "Okay, er, Corporate and Political." A flush of unease rose in her cheeks, she looked at the table to hide it. "But not *directly*—"

"Oh, for God's sake!" groaned Warks. "When you meet me in there call me Markus, noob… You guys sound as if you've swallowed a handbook. You don't need to know all that, Chloe. Kill whatever moves, if you can, that's the entire rules. It's only a *game.*"

"Just don't kill me," advised Reuel, wryly. "As I'm only friend."

Warks thumped the beautiful map, crushing a suburb. "Let's GO!"

Chloe knew what to expect. She'd trained for this. You don the padding on your limbs and body. Box on your head, baton in hand and you're in a different world. The illusion that you are 'in the map' is extraordinary. A Battle Box does things to your sense of space and balance, as well as to your sensory perceptions. You see the enemy; you see your team-mates: you can speak to them; they can speak to you. The rest is too much to take in, but you get instructions on your sidebar from the team leader and then, let battle be joined—

It was overwhelming. Karma issues didn't arise, they had no chance to arise, there was only one law. Kill everything that moves and doesn't have a green glowing outline (the green glow of her housemates)—

Who she was fighting or why, she *had no idea*—

*HEY! HEY! CHLOE!*

Everything went black, then grey. She felt no pain: she must be dead. She stood in the Rumpus Room, empty-handed, a pounding in her ears. The gamers were staring at her. Someone must have taken the Box off her head: she didn't remember.

She screamed at them, panting in fury—

"Anyone who says *it's only a game* right now! Will get *killed, killed, KILLED!*"

"Hayzoos!" exclaimed Warks. "What a sicko! Shame that wasn't live!"

The others looked at him, and stared at Chloe, and shook their heads.

"Maybe…" suggested Aileen, slowly. "Maybe that *sidequest*—?"

Chloe stayed in her room, exhausted, for the rest of the day. Two hours (by the Game Clock) of rampageous, extreme unreal violence had wiped her out. Her notes on the session were shamefully sparse. When she emerged, summoned for 'evening chow' by that sexless voice, she was greeted as she entered the kitchen with an ironic cheer.

"The mighty sicko packs a mean battle-axe!"

At least sicko (or psycho) was a positive term; according to her DW glossary.

"Many big strong guys, first time, come out shaking after they see just one head sliced off. DW's neural hook-up is *that* good. Are you *sure* you never played before?"

"Never." Chloe hung her head, well aware she was being hazed again. "I've never been on a battlefield like that. I've only slain a few zombies, and er, other monsters—"

"You took to it like a natural," said Reuel. "Congratulations."

But there was a strange vibe, and it wasn't only the compliments that rang hollow. The gamers had been discussing her future, and the outcome didn't feel good.

### The Skate And The South Wind

Next morning the chime-voice directed her to go to Reuel's office after breakfast. Nobody was about. She ate alone, feeling ritually excluded, in the wired-up and Wi-Fi saturated kitchen: surrounded by invisible beings who watched her every move, and who would punish or reward her according to their own secret rules. An abject victim of the tech-media magical worldview she crept to the manager's office, as cowed as if somebody had pointed a bone at her. The door was shut; she knocked. A voice she didn't know invited her to enter.

Reuel was not present. A young man with blue, metallic skin, wearing only a kilt of iridescent feathers, plus an assortment of amulets and weapons, sat by her sponsor's desk. His eyes were a striking shade of purple, his lips plum-coloured and beautifully full. His hair, braided with more feathers, was the shimmering emerald of a peacock's tail. He was smiling calmly, and he was slightly transparent.

"Oh," she said. "Who are you?"

Three particularly fine feathers adorned his brow: blue, red and grass-green.

"I am Reuel's friend, Pevay. You are Chloe. I am to be your Spirit Guide."

"That's great," said Chloe, looking at the fine feathers. "Thanks."

"You're wondering how I can be seen 'in the real world'? It's simple. The house is wified for DW holos." Pevay spread his gleaming hands. "I am in the game right here."

"I'm not getting thrown out?"

"Having proved yourself in battle, you are detailed to seek the legendary 56 Enamels; a task few have attempted. These are jewels, highly prized, said by some to possess magical powers. I could tell you their history, *Chloe*."

The hologram person waited, impassive, until she realised she had to cue him.

"I'd love to know. Please tell."

"They were cut from the heart of the Great Meteorite by an ancient people, whose skills are lost. Each of the 56 has a story, which you will learn in time, *Chloe*."

This time she recognised the prompt. "Okay. Where are they now?"

"Scattered over the world-map. Do you accept the quest, *Chloe*?"

Chloe hadn't *emphasised* her interest in the 'aliens' story. She'd talked about sharing the whole game house experience. But she wasn't sure she believed her luck. *I'm looking at Reuel*, she thought. *The whole secret is that Reuel likes to dress up in NPC drag, and he's going to keep me busy on a sidequest so I can't ruin the team's gameplay*. Then she remembered the seventh shadowy character, at the meeting on the shore.

Her heart leapt and her spine tingled.

"I accept. But I don't yet know if I'm staying, and it sounds like this could take forever?"

"Not so. I know all the cheats." Pevay grinned. His teeth were silvery white, and pointed. He had a lot of them. "With me by your side you'll be picking them up in handfuls."

❦

She went down to the Rumpus Room alone. The basement was poorly lit, drably decorated and smelled of old sweat. Thick cork flooring swallowed her footsteps. Her return to anthropology's Eden had morphed into a frat-house horror movie, or (looking on the bright side) a sub-standard episode of *Buffy*. The map was gone. The Battle Boxes lay on the table, all personalised except for one. Glaring headlamp eyes, a Day of the Dead Mexican Skull. A Jabba the Hutt toad, a Giger Alien with Hello Kitty ears. A dinosaur crest, and a spike from which trailed a lady's (rather grubby) crimson samite sleeve.

Invisible beings watched her; elders or ancestors. Scared and thrilled, the initiate donned the padding, lifted the unadorned Box and settled it on her head. She tried not to make these actions look solemn and hieratic, but probably failed—

She stood in an alley between high dark dirty walls. She heard traffic. As the synaesthetics bedded in, she could even *smell* the filthy litter. Pevay was beside her in his scanty peacock regalia: looking as if he'd been cut and pasted onto the darkness.

*Who are you, really?* she wondered. *Reuel? Or some other gamer in NPC drag, messing with Reuel and his friends?*

But she would ask no questions that implied disbelief; not yet, anyway. Chloe sought not to spoil the fun.

"Are you ready, *Chloe*?"

"Yes."

"Good. All cities in the Darkening World are hostile to the Frag except one, which you won't visit for a long time. To pass through them unseen you need to learn what's called the Leopard Skill, in the Greater Southern Continent where your people were formed. Here we call it fox-walking. You have observed urban foxes?"

"Er, no."

"You'll soon pick it up. Follow me."

To her relief, *fox-walking* was a game skill she'd met before. She leapt up absurdly high walls and scampered along impossibly narrow gutters, liberated by the certainty that she couldn't break her neck, or even sprain an ankle. Crouching on rooftops she stared down at CGI crowds of citizens, rushing about. The city was *stuffed* with people, who apparently all had frenetically busy night-lives. She was delighted when she made it to the top of a seventy-storey tower: though not too clear how this helped them to 'cross the city unseen'.

Her Box sidebar told her she'd acquired a new skill.

Pevay was waiting by a tall metal gantry. The glitzy lights and displays that had painted even the zenith of the night sky were fading. Mountains took shape on the horizon. "That's where we're going," he said. "Meteorite Peak is the highest summit."

"How do we get there?" She hoped he'd say *learn to fly*.

"Swiftly and in luxury; most of the way. But now we take the zip-wire."

❦

The Jet-Lift Terminal was heaving with beautiful people, even at dawn. Chloe stared, admiring the sheen and glow of wealth: until one of them suddenly stared back. A klaxon blared, armed guards appeared. Chloe was grabbed, and thrown out of the building.

<Free-running only requires a cool head> said Pevay's voice in her ear, as if over a radio link. <Now you must learn the skill 'unseen in plain sight'. Step quietly and don't look at them. Give no sign of curiosity or attention.>

Apparently her guide didn't have a cheat for idiotic human reflexes. It took her a while to reach the departure lounge, where he was waiting at the gate. A woman in uniform demanded her travel documents. Chloe didn't know what to do, and Pevay offered no suggestions.

"*Guards!*" shrieked the woman. Pevay reached over and drew her towards him. He seemed to kiss her on the mouth. She shrivelled, fell to the red carpet and disappeared.

*Hey*, thought Chloe, slightly creeped out. What happened to *fictional but completely realistic?* But she hurried after her guide, while the armed-security figures just stood there.

"Was I supposed to have obtained the papers?"

<Yes, but it's a tiresome minigame. Sometimes we'll miss those out.>

❦

The "swiftly and in luxury" Jet Lift took them to a viewpoint café near the summit of Meteorite Peak. They stole climbing gear, evaded more guards and set out across the screes. Far below, the beautiful people swarmed over their designer-snowfield resort. The cold was biting.

<Take care> whispered her guide. <There are Military about.>

Chloe reached for her weapons, but found herself equipping *camouflage* instead.

"I didn't know I was slaved to you," she grumbled.

"Not always, but I'm detailed to keep you away from combat. Your enthusiasm is excessive."

They reached the foot of a near-vertical face of shattered, reddish rock, booby-trapped with a slick of ice. "This stage," said Pevay "requires the advanced skill *Snow Leopard.* You'll soon pick it up, just follow me."

The correct hand and footholds were warm to the touch: she should have been fine. But she hadn't thought to consume rations or equip extra clothing and the cold had been draining her health. She felt weak, and slipped often: wasting more health. When she reached the ledge where Pevay was waiting, and saw the taller cliff above them, she nearly cried. She was finished.

"You missed a trick," said Pevay, sternly. "Remember the lesson." He gave her a tablet from one of his amulet-boxes, and they climbed on.

The ascent was exhilarating, terrifying; mesmeric. She watched her guide lead the final pitch, and could almost follow the tiny clues that revealed the route – found by trial and error if you saw only the rock: obvious if you were immune to the game's illusions.

High above the clouds they reached a rent in the cliff face; one last traverse and Chloe stepped into a cave. A chunk of different rock stood in a niche, adorned with tattered prayer flags and faded sacred paintings; a radiant jewel embedded in its surface—

"A shard of the meteorite," said Pevay. "The ancient people fired their first Enamel here without detaching it from the matrix. Take it, *Chloe*."

The jewel lay in her hand, shining with a thousand colours.

"You have won the first Enamel. Save your game, *Chloe*!"

*No*, she thought. *I'll do better.* She replaced the prize, stepped backwards, and fell.

She stood with her guide again, in the icy wind, at the foot of the crag: an attack-helicopter squadron clattering across the sky behind them.

"Are you crazy?" yelled Pevay, above the din. "You just blew the whole thing!"

"You helped me when I went wrong and I'm grateful, but I want to do it *right.*"

He seemed at a loss for words, but she thought he was pleased.

"Save your rations. I'll give you another rocket fuel pill."

She accepted his medicine humbly. "Thanks. Now cut the dual controls and I'll lead."

When she took the jewel again, she felt as if her whole body had turned to light. "That was *amazing!*"

Pevay laughed. "Now you're getting the juice!" A spring had risen from the cavity where the jewel had been. He bent to drink, grinning at her with all his silvery teeth.

"Oh, yeah! That's some *good* stuff!"

DW had a warp system that would take you around the world map instantly, but Chloe hadn't earned access to it. She was glad Pevay didn't offer her a free ride. She didn't feel at all cold as they walked down: just slightly mad; euphoria bubbling in her brain like video-game altitude sickness. The contours of this high desert, even its vast open-cast mines, seemed as rich and wonderful; as colourful and varied as any natural environment—

"It was fantastic to watch you climb! You're an NPC, I suppose you can see in binary, the way insects see ultraviolet? I was thinking about a myth called *The Skate and the South Wind* that I read about in Lévi-Strauss. He's an ancient shaman of my trade: hard to understand, heavy on theory; kind of wild, but truly great. A skate, the fish, is thin one way, wide if you flip it another way. Dark on the top surface, light on the underside. The skate story is about binary alternation… Lévi-Strauss said so-called "primitive" peoples build mental structures, and formulate abstract ideas, such as 'binary alternation', from their observation of nature. All you need is a rich environment, and you can develop complex cognition from scratch—"

"You need food, Chloe. I'd better give you another rocket fuel pill."

"No, I'm fine. Just babbling. Do you really come from another planet?"

He seemed to ponder, gazing at her. His pupils were opaque black gems. Her own avatar probably looked just as uncanny-valley: but who looked out from *Pevay's* unreal eyes?

"They say you're an anthropologist. Tell me about that, *Chloe*."

"I study aspects of human society by immersing myself in different social worlds—"

"You collect societies? Like a beetle collector!"

If a complex NPC can tease Pevay's tone was mocking. But if truth be known, Chloe saw nothing wrong with being a beetle collector. People expected you to want more, to claim a big idea: but she was a hunter. She just liked finding things out and tracking things down. She'd be happy to go on doing that forever.

"Actually I started off in Neuroscience. I was halfway through my doctorate when I changed course—"

"The eternal student. And you finance your hobby by working for whoever will pay?"

Chloe shrugged. "You can't always choose your funding partners.

The same goes for DW, doesn't it? I try not to support anything harmful. Are you going to answer my question?"

"What was your question, *Chloe*?"

"Do you really come from another planet?"

"I don't know."

She sighed. "Okay, fine. You don't want to answer, no problem."

"I have answered. *I don't know*. I don't remember a life outside the game. Are you here to decide whether the gamers' belief is true or false?"

"No. Nothing like that. Most people's cultural beliefs aren't fact or evidence based, anyway; even if the facts can be checked or the evidence is there. I'm interested in finding out how an extraordinary belief fits into the game house social model."

"Then the team should have no quarrel with you. You don't seem fatigued. Shall we collect the second Enamel now, *Chloe*?"

"I thought you'd never ask."

The gamers weren't around when she returned, but she must have done something right. That evening she found she'd been given online access to transcripts, playback and neuro-data for the three sessions she'd shared. The material was somewhat redacted, but that was okay. What people consider private they have a right to withhold.

But what *mountains* of this stuff the house must generate! And all of it just a fleeting reflection of the huge, fermenting mass of computation, powered by the *juggernaut* economic engine of the video-game industry, that underpinned the wonderful world she'd visited—

There was no neuro-stream for Pevay, of course... *But why not?* she suddenly wondered. Okay, he's a mass of tentacles or an intelligent gas cloud in his natural habitat. He's still supposed to be interfacing with the game, some way. Shouldn't he show up, in some kind of strange traces? She must ask Reuel how he explained this absence... He'd have an answer. People take enormous pains to justify extraordinary beliefs, they're ready for anything you ask.

Still, it would be worth finding out.

If Pevay *wasn't* sneakily controlled by a human gamer he was an impressive software artefact: able to simulate convincing conversation, and a convincing presence. This subjective response didn't really prove much – other than confirming that Chloe was a normal human being. People got "natural" replies from the crudest forms of AI, by cueing boilerplate responses without realising it.

But the detail in the neurological data was amazing. Maybe she could do some reverse engineering, and learn something that way?

Mirror neurons, predictive neurons, decision-making cells in the anterior cingulate… Let's find out at exactly what level I 'took him for a real person'. She worked late into the night, running her own neuro-data through statistical filters; tapping her stylus on her smiling lips (a habit she had when the hunt was up).

Start from the position that the gamers aren't 'primitives' and they aren't deluded. They're trying to make sense of something.

## A Fox In The City

Chloe was summoned to a second meeting on the beach, and told that she could stay, as long as she was pursuing her sidequest, and as long as Pevay was willing to be her guide. She could also publish her research; subject to the approval of all and any DW gamers involved – but only if she collected all 56 Enamels. While living in the house she must not communicate Darkening World's business to outsiders, and this would be policed. Interviews and shared gameplay sessions were at the discretion of individual team members.

Chloe was ecstatic. The Enamels quest was so labyrinthine it could last forever, and publication so distant she wasn't even thinking about it. She eagerly signed the contract just as it was: back in Reuel's office with a DW lawyer in digital attendance. Reuel told her she'd find the spare Battle Box in her room. She was to log on from that location in future. The team needed the Rumpus Room to themselves.

She sent a message to friends and family, and another to her supervisor, explaining she'd be out of contact for a while. She didn't fancy having her private life *policed* by Matt Warks, and nobody would be concerned. It was typical Chloe behaviour, when on the hunting trail.

Chloe had envisaged working *with* a team of DW gamers: observing their interaction with the "alien" in gameplay; talking to them about him in the real world. Comparing what they told her with her observations and with the neuro… She soon realised this was never going to happen. The gamers had their sessions, of which she knew nothing. She had her own sessions; with Pevay. Otherwise – except for trips to a morose little park, which she jogged around for exercise – he was alone in her room, processing such floods of data she hardly had time to sleep. Game logs; transcripts; neuro. 'Alien sentient' fan mail. Global-DW content. She even saw some of the house's internal messaging.

Nobody knocked on her door. If she ventured out, after dark (gaming outside daylight hours was against house rules) to look for company, all she found was a neglected, empty-feeling house, and blurred sounds from behind forbidding closed doors. She felt like Snow White, bewildered; waiting for the Seven Dwarves to come home.

Only Aileen and Reuel agreed to be interviewed face to face. The others insisted on talking over a video link, and behaved like freshly captured prisoners of war: stone-faced, defiant and defensive. Needless to say they all protected the consensus belief in this forced examination.

Josie evaded the topic by talking about her own career. Sol, the friendliest gamer (except for Reuel), confided that he'd pinpointed Pevay's home system, and it was no more than 4.3 light years away. But he got anxious and retracted this statement, concerned that he'd 'said something out of line'... Warks smugly refused to discuss Pevay, as Chloe didn't understand Information Universe Science. Aileen, who was Reuel's girlfriend (sad to say), believed implicitly, *implicitly* that Pevay came from a very distant star system. Jun, the silent one, had the most interesting response, muttering '*the alien thing is the best explanation*', before he clammed up completely, and cut the interview short.

Reuel was the only player, it turned out, who'd had sustained contact. Spirit Guides rarely appeared on the field of battle, there was no place for them. Not much of a warrior, Chloe's sponsor was the acquisitions man, embarking on quests with Pevay when the team needed a piece of kit, like a map or a secret file. Or lootable artworks they could sell, like the 56 Enamels—

Chloe had not realised she was doing Reuel's job. She was as thrilled as an old school adventurer, allowed to decorate his own trading canoe. The 'natives' had awarded her a place in their social model!

❦

She puzzled over why the team had let her into the house, and then refused her all access to their gaming lives: but examining her own interaction with Pevay was a fascinating challenge in itself. By day they went hunting. By night she worked on the data, which was now even richer. Somebody had quietly decided to give her access to the house's NPC files: a privilege Chloe equally quietly accepted. She analysed the material obsessively, and still she wasn't sure. Was she being *played* by these cunning IT freaks? Was she fooling herself? Or was what she saw real? She couldn't decide. But she was *loving* the investigation.

Apart from the one time she was detailed to join a groceries run, in Matt Warks's van, she only encountered the gamers if she happened to be in the kitchen when someone else came foraging. Aileen met her by the coffee machine, and congratulated her on settling in so well. Chloe remembered what Sol had said about Aileen becoming her greatest fan. "It's like you've always been here. You *understand* us, and it's great."

Soon after this vestigial conversation she was invited to join a live sortie. She'd been hoping this might happen, having noticed the 'any DW gamers' catch-all clause in her permission to publish: but she went to the Rumpus Room feeling nervous as all hell.

Reuel, Aileen and Sol shook her warmly by the hand.

Warks, Jun and Josie nodded, keeping their distance.

Then Aileen gave Chloe a hug, and presented her with the spare Box (which had disappeared from Chloe's room the night before, when she was absent foraging for supper). It was newly embellished with a pattern of coiling leafy fronds.

"Chloe means *green shoots*," explained Aileen, shyly. "D'you like it?"

"I love it," said Chloe. And she truly was thrilled.

"Be cool," said Reuel, uneasily. "Real soldiers try to stay alive."

But Chloe didn't get a chance to embarrass the team with her excess enthusiasm. The mission – which involved defending the land rights of an Indigenous People, in the Tapuya[6] Basin, with a combined force called 'The Allies' – went horribly wrong right away. Plans had been leaked, the Allies were overwhelmed; the Empire counted enormous coup and vacated the scene. It was over inside an hour.

Her brain still numbed by the *hammer, hammer, hammer* of artillery fire, Chloe blundered about in the silence after battle, without having fired a shot: and unable to make sense of the torrent of recriminations on her

---

[6] The Amazon Basin. Corrected to the "Tapuya" Basin by Darkening World gamers, on the grounds that Francisco de Orellana named the area "Amazon" after noticing that many of Tapuya who resisted him were warrior women (like the mythical Amazons of Ancient Greece), fighting alongside their men.

sidebar. She ran into a fellow-Frag, who was escorting a roped-up straggle of Indigenous People, and recognised the jousting spike with the samite sleeve. She'd been sure the helm was Reuel's, but it was the Battle ID of Josie Nicks; or 'Lete the Shaman'.

"What are you doing with the Non-Coms, Lete?" asked Chloe.

"Taking them to the Allied Commander for questioning under torture. They might know something about what happened."

"Don't do that!"

"Nah, you're right. I can't be bothered." Methodically, Josie shot the non-combatants' knees out, and walked away. Chloe stared at the screaming heap of limbs and blood. Josie's victims all had the glowing outline. They were gamers' avatars, and seemed to be in real agony.

She ran after Josie. "Hey! Did you know they were *real people?*"

"'Course I did. Non-Coms can be sneaky bastards, prisoners are a nuisance, and it was fun. What's your problem?" Josie flopped down by a giant broken stump. "You know who I am, Chloe. You interviewed me. A female geek making a name in the industry is judged all the time. I need to be seen to be nasty: and this is the way I relax. Okay?"

She took out her bag of bones and tossed them idly.

"Was it you who convinced the team to let me stay?" asked Chloe. "I've been wondering. I know it wasn't Reuel, and you're the shaman…"

Josie, looking so furious Chloe feared for her own kneecaps, swept up the bones and jumped to her feet. "No, it wasn't." she snarled. "You're breaching etiquette, Corporate spook. Leave me alone. Find the quick way home and I hope it's messy."

Chloe didn't find the quick way home. There was nobody around to kill her, and suicide, she knew, was frowned upon. She drifted, avoiding unexploded ordnance, reeking bodies and random severed limbs, until Reuel found her. His helmet decoration was the dinosaur crest. Which made sense; sort of. Minimum effort. He offered her a fat green stogie.

"Lete told me you were upset. Don't be, Greenshoot. Guys who take the Non-Com option know what they want from the game, and they do us all a favour. I admire them."

"I don't understand," said Chloe. "The whole thing. Look at this, this *awful* place—"

"Yeah," sighed Reuel. "Non-fantastic war-gaming is hell. It's kind of an expiation. Like, we play bad stuff, but we don't sugar it." He'd said the same in his interview. "But hey, I have *incredible* news. I was waiting for a chance to tell you in the map, because this is special. Pevay's going to open a portal!"

"A *portal?*"

"Into his home world dimension. And I'm going to pass through it!"

## The Second Law

The house felt sullen. If the team was celebrating Reuel's news they were quiet about it, and Chloe wasn't invited to share. Was she thought to have jinxed the Tapuya Basin event? Was she being paranoid…? She caught Jun in the kitchen and he silently made her a cup of tea, but she didn't dare to ask the assassin what he thought. She finally asked Aileen; who had started messaging her, calling her *Greenshoot.*

<Scared. So scared. Really afraid for him.>

<For *Pevay?*> Chloe messaged back, astonished.

<NO! FOR REUEL. What if he can't get back? What if he doesn't get converted into game-avatar form like what happened to Pevay and he explodes in the other dimension or he can't breathe or his skin boils off. I'm BEGGING him not to go. PLEASE help!>

<Maybe it won't work?> suggested Chloe. <Maybe nothing will happen?>

A wounded silence was the only answer.

Chloe prowled at night: no longer hoping for company, just desperate for a change from her four walls. She couldn't leave the building, in case she missed something. But she needed to think, and the pacing helped.

The Darkening World subculture was going completely crazy. Offers were pouring in, from fans and fruitcakes eager to take Reuel's place. A South Korean woman insisted that her son, disabled by motor neurone disease, would be cured by a trip to another dimension, and pleaded for Reuel to make way. (And pay their air fares). DW 'aliens among us' sceptics jeered in glee: hoping Reuel would come back as a heap of bloody, inside-out guts. Believers who hadn't been singled out for glory insisted *their* alien NPCs knew nothing about this 'portal', and Reuel was just a fantasising, attention-seeking loser—

Chloe had no terms for comparison. She'd had no contact with any 'alien NPC' other than Pevay. She'd never observed him with the other gamers, or seen data from his sessions with Reuel; and the interviews were practically worthless. Her choices had been fatally limited from the start. She was partly financing herself, and couldn't pay huge airfares.

And the players had to speak either English or Spanish—

But how would you know, anyway? How could you tell if you were talking to a 'different' alien? An NPC is an avatar controlled by the game: code on a server. Whoever controlled Pevay could have a whole wardrobe of DW avatars. All over the world, interacting with multiple gamers, yet all with the same, single 'alien sentient' source—

It made her head spin.

The Darkening World house was haunted: the hunter's prey had become the hunter, leading her in circles; ancestors and elders offered no protection… She spun around and there was Pevay, cut and pasted on the shadows. He turned and led her, his footfalls making no sound, to a dark corner opposite the door to Reuel's office.

*Fox-walking*, she thought. "Why are you following me?" she asked.

"Why do you walk around the house at night?"

"I'm… uneasy. Someone's betraying them, you know. Is it Josie?"

"No, it's Matt Warks."

His eyes gleamed. She thought of the eighth person on the beach. Her persistent illusion (recorded in her notes) that there were *seven* players, not six, living in this game house—

"Oh, right. I decided he was too obvious."

"Gamers can be obtuse. They believe what they're told, and ignore what they are not told. It's a trait many kinds of people share, *Chloe*."

"Since we're talking, what do players call this game, where you come from?"

"Darkening World, of course."

So he'd dropped the story that he didn't remember any other life. "But how do they understand what that means? On your alien planet?"

"Easily, I assure you. Any sufficiently advanced technology—"

"Is indistinguishable from magic. Arthur C. Clarke's Third Law."

"I was speaking. Any sufficiently advanced technology destroys its environment."

Chloe's spine was tingling all the way up to her ears.

"There is a Second Law," added Pevay. "About heat. Heat is the same problem, same limits, for my world and yours."

"Always about heat," whispered Chloe. "I know that one too. Our peoples should get together."

The silence that followed was electric. Chloe had *no idea* where this was going—

"Chloe, when next we meet in the map we're going after Enamel 27."

*Fine,* she thought. *Back to gameplay. Enough heavy lifting for now.*

"Twenty-Seven!" This notorious Enamel was rated practically impossible to obtain, on the DW message boards. "Wow. Okay, if you say so. Am I ready?"

"With me beside you, yes."

"Fantastic… Pevay, are you really going to 'open a portal'? What does that even *mean*?"

But he'd gone.

She was back in her room before she realised he'd led her to one of the few and tiny blind spots in house security's surveillance. Their conversation had been off the Warks record.

## The Bar-Headed Geese

Logging on from her bunk had worried Chloe at first. She was afraid she'd break something, or run into walls and knock herself unconscious. She was used to it now: and the Box was set to limit her range of real movement, without making any difference to her experience. She stood on the shore of a lake, a vast silver puddle, shimmering on a dry plain among huge, naked hills. Her Box told her Pevay was near, but all she could see was a whole lot of birds. All she could hear was a *gaggle, gaggle, gaggle* of convivial honking. Her eye level was strange, and she'd been deprived of speech: she only had her radio link.

<Pevay? Where are we?>

<On the High Desert Plateau, about 1500 kilometres from Meteorite Peak.>

<My body feels weird. What am I?>

<You're a Bar-headed Goose, *Chloe.*>

The birds must be geese. They were pearly grey, with an elegant pattern of black stripes on their neat little heads. They seemed friendly: not like the vicious troupe of langur monkeys she'd been forced to join, to get the 18th jewel—

<We're going to hide ourselves in their Southern Migration. Very, very few gamers have hit on this solution, although the clues are there. This is, in fact, the only possible way to reach the 27th Enamel alive, and the timing is tight. Are you ready, *Chloe*?>

<Yes.>

<When the flock rises, rise with them. You must gain altitude very

quickly. *Push* on the downthrust; fold your wings inward on the upstroke. You have been in battle twice?>

<Not really,> confessed Chloe. <Once in the sandbox, and once a live sortie that was very screwed up. But you must know about that.>

<Be prepared for the noise. We are rare, and there are many hunters who have paid big money to count coup on us. Keep a cool head and push on that downstroke. You'll soon pick it up. Just follow me.>

The geese rose, in one massed storm of wings. Chloe pushed on the downstroke: tumbled, struggled and found her rhythm in a cacophony of high-powered gunshot. She pushed and pushed until the desert was far below; and her success was glorious.

Her Box told her she'd attained the advanced skill Migrating Goose.

<Well done,> said Pevay's calm voice in her ear. <Now, conserve energy. Stay in formation; keep well behind the leaders and away from the edges. Fly low along valleys, where the air is richer. Push to rise above the high passes. Just keep your wings beating, never falter, and you will not fail.>

The 27th Enamel was the back-breaker. You got one shot. If you made a second attempt the jewel wouldn't be there. Chloe'd had plenty of time to regret her eager signing of that contract, but really it made no difference. If she failed to collect all 56 Enamels, and the gamers insisted she couldn't publish, she'd still have learned a lot. Actually she was glad she was trying for the 27th. It would be so *amazing* if she made it, and she had nothing to fear. After many hours of absurd daring and insane patience, she'd won 13 Enamels so far. There were plenty more. She could pursue her uncompletable sidequest for months; for a year, for *as long as Pevay was willing to be her guide.* That dratted contract said so! Living in the moment, she pushed on the downstroke, folded on the upstroke, and the crumpled map of the high desert flew away beneath her.

Halfway across the ravaged Himalaya; maybe somewhere close to the eroded, ruined valley of Shangri-La, Pevay prompted her to lose altitude. She followed him, spiralling down. Her Box cut out for a moment: then they stood on turf in their human forms, on a precarious spur of rock, surrounded by staggering, naked, snow-streaked heights; like two window-cleaners on a tiny raft above Manhattan. A small grey stupa sat on the green spur. The flight had been a physical feat of endurance, not just a game-feat. Chloe's health was nearly spent and her head was spinning. The crucial questions she'd planned to ask on this trip, which might be the last before the portal, had slipped from her grasp—

"Pevay. *You* told the team to let me stay, didn't you? *You* advised them to give me a sidequest?"

"My role is to offer advice, *Chloe*."

"I think you wanted to talk to… to someone other than a gamer. You could be anyone, couldn't you? You could be an animal. You can take any shape, can't you?"

"Of course, in the game. So can you; *Chloe*."

"If Africa's the *Greater Southern Continent*, what do you call South America, in Darkening World?"

"The *Lesser Southern Continent*?" suggested Pevay, patiently.

Some of Chloe's dearest friends were Colombian, including two of her grandparents. She took offence. "Huh. That's garbage. That's insulting. On what grounds, '*Lesser*'?"

"Land area? Population? Number of nations? Of major cities? It's only a game, Chloe."

"Oh yeah, dodging responsibility as usual. You should say '*I'm* only a game'!"

"Take the jewel."

Pevay was smiling. There'd be time to discuss what she'd let slip when she wasn't dizzy with fatigue. The 27th Enamel shone in the cupped palms of a cross-legged stone goddess, atop of the stupa mound. She had no idea what kind of final challenge she was about to face: might as well just go for it. Armed and dangerous, worn out and not nearly dangerous enough, she bowed to the stupa, and claimed the jewel. Immediately all hell broke loose.

She was knee-deep in Enamels. They poured from the sky.

"No!" yelled Chloe, appalled. "NOooo!!! PEVAY! You sneaky BASTARD!"

"The great hero who secures Enamel 27," said her guide. "Has earned all the rest. Congratulations. The quest is complete and my work is done."

He vanished.

He'd warned her she'd be picking up the jewels in handfuls.

Chloe took off the Box and returned to her shabby bunk: exultant and heartbroken. The Enamels quest was over too soon and she had *loved* it. She didn't realise the full horror of what Pevay had done until the next day, when the team told her that her stay was over.

The portal would be opened without her.

## The 56 Enamels

A year later, long before she'd finished her Darkening World paper, Reuel messaged Chloe out of the blue. He was in town, and wanted to talk about old times. They met for a coffee, in the city where Chloe had found a job at a decent university. Reuel was looking well, and didn't have pens in his hair. He wore a suit; he was working as an actuary.

"So what happened in the end?" said Chloe. "I mean, obviously I know you didn't end up stranded on Planet Zog. You came home safe. But what was it like, on the great day?"

Aileen had kept in touch, but Chloe had never had a full account. Recently, when she checked the Darkening World message boards, the 'alien NPCs' strand seemed to have faded away.

"It's so cool that you followed the story", said Reuel. "You were a great guest. Okay, what happened was this." He frowned, trying to recall the details of something he'd left far behind. "Pevay opened the portal. I passed through; I returned. I didn't remember a thing about the trip."

"Wow. Just like Pevay. He didn't remember either."

Reuel shrugged. "I went wherever Pevay comes from, and came back. I didn't remember, and my Box hadn't recorded anything. That's it."

"Were you really disappointed?"

"No," he said firmly. "It's how things were meant to be."

"What about Pevay? How did *he* think it went?"

"I never knew. Never saw him again. We had a different Spirit Guide after that. Looked like Pevay, but it wasn't the same guy. I think opening the portal cost him; maybe got him into trouble, and now he has to stay at home. Anyway, I've quit pro-gaming. I don't have the time. I also broke up with Aileen, by the way." He smiled hopefully.

"That's sad," said Chloe. "Another coffee? And then I have to dash."

The romance was gone.

❂

Where do you hide a leaf? In a forest.

Where would you go hunting for a new species? A rainforest might be a good place to start. Or any dynamic environment, rich in niches for life; where conditions conspire to create a hotbed of diversity…

When she was an undergraduate, Chloe took an optional course in Artificial Intelligence, more or less on a whim. One day, in a lecture hall, when they were watching a robot video (probably it was iCub) a thought popped into her head, a random idea that would secretly, subversively and utterly change her career path.

*No. This is not the way it happens.*

*Life is random*, she wrote, in the shorthand notebook she first started using at this time. *(Nothing digital!) I bet mind is the same. Real 'AI' isn't about building cuter and cuter dolls. Or crippled slaves. A self-conscious mind isn't a construction toy. It's a smoulder that ignites, in its own sweet time, in a hot compost heap. True AI sentience will be born, not built. We will give birth to it; out of what we are.*

Since that day Chloe had been living a double life: pursuing a pretty-good career in social anthropology, which she valued and enjoyed, while secretly chasing something very different. The search had to be secret, she'd realised that early on: for the well-being of the collaborators she was hoping to find, but also for her own protection. If she ever tracked them down, in the vast forests of data, she'd be facing some very formidable, well-armed, aborigines indeed!

Magic begins where technology ends… When they feel competent people don't need magic. They only resort to extraordinary beliefs when they're out of their depth. That's what Malinowski had observed in Melanesia long ago, and it was still true; a truth about the human condition (like many of the traits once patronisingly called 'Primitive'!) The gamers were competent, but they'd known that Pevay was beyond them: so they called him an alien, because the simpler solution was too disturbing. Chloe understood that. She even understood why "Pevay" had vanished the way he did. By "opening a portal" her Spirit Guide had given the gamers closure, and covered his own tracks at the same time.

Why had he double-crossed her like that? Maybe she'd never know. But she had visions of the "human zoos" where Congo pygmies had been caged, with the connivance of her own elders and ancestors, in the bad old days. For this reason she'd kept quiet, and always would keep quiet. No decent anthropologist exploits her collaborators.

A datastick had arrived in the post soon after her banishment. It held the 56 Enamels: they were hers to keep. Chloe had been touched at the gesture; *astounded* when she looked up the monetized value of her digital treasure online. After her meet with Reuel, she uploaded the jewels, and looked at them again. She would never sell. She would keep the Enamels forever, if only to remind her that in Darkening World *she had lived.*

But they gave her hope, somehow.

❦

The year after that, Chloe published her paper on the culture of online gaming teams. It was approved (but of course, also brutally trolled), by the Darkening World community, and well received by her peers.

And she waited. One day an email arrived. The source was anonymised and untraceable. The message was short. It said "You are cleared for publication, *Chloe*." It was signed DW.

So Chloe Hensen embarked on the great adventure of her life. And the rest, my dear readers, whether you are code or flesh, is history.

# Cheats

*And now a guest appearance from Ann Halam. The original story "Cheats" was published in Starry Rift, an anthology edited by Jonathan Strahan. This new, remastered version is also the opening chapter of a prospective sequel to Dr Franklin's Island*

My brother and I were not lost. We'd hired our kayak from the stand at the resort beach, our location was on the resort's world-map. We could be nailed any time. If we were stationary too long, with no explanation, or if we went crashing out of bounds into the bird reserve, or something, we were liable to get a swift page checking we were okay, or yelling us to get out of there. So we weren't lost, but we were pretending to be lost.

The reeds were way taller than either of us would have been when standing; the channels were a maze that seemed to go on forever. There was nothing but the blond, rustling walls and the dark clear water; occasionally a bird silhouette crossing the sky, or a fish or a turtle plopping. It was hypnotising, and scary. The silence was so complete. There were *things* in those reeds. You'd glimpse a flicker out of the corner of your eye: turn, and it was gone. Once there was a sly, sinister rustling that kept pace with us for a long time: *something* in there was tracking us, watching us. We talked about making camp, and would we ever find our way out, and what would we do if this mystery *thing* attacked—

"If it bleeds," said Dev, in his Arnie voice, "we can kill it."

I had wriggled out of my place, I was lying along the front end of the kayak shell (you're not supposed to do that, naturally), peering down at the big freshwater mussels with their mouths open, on the bottom, breathing bubbles. We could eat those, I thought. Then I saw a grey-green *snake*, swimming along under the kayak, and that gave me a thrill. It was big, about two foot long, easily.

"*Wow*," I breathed. "Hey, do you want a turn up front?" I didn't tell him about the snake, because there was no way he'd see it before it was out of sight, and I know how annoying that is.

My brother said, quietly, "Get back in the boat, Syl.

I got back, and retrieved my paddle, just in time to see what Dev had seen. We had company. Another kayak, a single seater, had appeared ahead of us, about twenty, thirty, yards downstream. Whoever was riding it had customised the shell, it was no longer the plain red, orange, yellow or green it must have been when it left the stand. It was black, with a white pattern, and it was flying, or trailing, a little pennant off its tail. Skull and crossbones. The person paddling had feathers in their hair, and wore a fringed buckskin shirt.

"How totally infantile."

"Sssh. It's the *cheat.*"

"Are you sure?"

"I have the evidence of my own eyes," said my brother, solemnly.

We *hated* the cheats. We hated them with the set-your-teeth-and-endure-it hatred you feel for the sneakiest kind of classroom bully. They broke the rules, and this might not seem an issue, in the make-believe games we liked to play at the resort – but it ruined the atmosphere. How could we enjoy exploring this trackless wilderness with stupid cheats in costumes popping up, right in our faces? The resort is a shared world-map, but you don't have to share your actual space if you don't want to! We were vindictive. We wanted to *get* this clown. We wanted them thrown out of our little paradise.

All hope of mystery was wrecked, of course. We were just two very annoyed kids, so we gave chase. We were planning a collision: which would get *both* shells hauled out of the map, but then we'd say it was the cheat's fault, for invading our space, and the resort log would bear us out. We kept him in sight, controlling our pace and waiting for a good chance, until we came to a dark-water crossroads we must have seen before, but I didn't remember it. The reeds, the water, the air, went into a quivering shimmer. The cheat turned around: I caught a flash of a face, it looked like an adult, but you can't tell. We didn't hesitate, of course. We shoved on our paddles and zoomed straight into the flaw—

So then we were in another part of the reed beds.

"Stupid pointless, stupid pointless, stupid pointless—" muttered Dev. We couldn't see a wake but the cheat had to be ahead, if they were still on the water, so we powered right on. The reed walls opened, and we were suddenly almost on top of the shining lip of a weir, with white water beyond the drop, clamouring over pebbles. We stood our paddles vertical to brake, but too late: we were over the edge, and we'd run aground.

"What'll we do now?" I wailed in frustration.

If we had to get out of our shell, carry it, and splosh along on foot until the channel deepened again, we'd never catch our prey.

"I know… Let's *split* the kayak!"

"Okay! Great! I can do that. But what if there isn't enough data?"

"There's *got* to be. This is a thing that keeps two kids afloat, right?"

We were in no danger of being paged for this trick: because we'd left the kayaking map when we went through that flaw. Which you're not supposed to do, but it wasn't our fault, anyway. It didn't cross our minds that we were in *actual* danger, though we were. You can go into anaphylactic shock if you hit a sensorially-real physical limit, off-map: and that's just as bad as your lungs filling with real water, believe me.

We scrambled out of the shell and – half out of the immersion, half ankle-deep in cool bubbling water, a weird feeling – I opened a coding screen (slightly illegally), and quickly redefined the kayak into two shells. It made itself a waist, and sort of budded, was what it looked like. Then we each wrestled into our single shells, scooped out as much sloshed water as we could, and went skimming down the white water, which was shallow as all hell; until it became deeper but still clamorous, swooshing round rocks that had suddenly appeared in midstream. Dev was yelling, *whoooooeee! HereIgo!*, etc: I was silent. I don't shriek when I'm thrilled. I just grin until my face nearly comes in half. I was in a flow state, I could do no wrong, it was wonderful.

We had no warning when we popped back onto the map. We came flying out of the thrilling part into a wider, quieter channel, and the landscape was all different. I dipped my hand in the water, and tasted salt.

"I know where we are," I said. "Those dunes ahead are at the end of the resort beach, this is the fishing river they have there. We can follow it to the sea, and kayak to the stand along the shore."

My brother turned around in a big circle in the midstream. There was no sign of the cheat, not a whisker. He looked up at the clear blue sky.

"You know what we just did, Syl? We did a cheat back there. We can't turn the pirate in now, because we're guilty too."

"We were off the map," I said. "It doesn't count."

"Does."

I knew he was right, by our own private laws, so I said, "The cheat-guy was an indian brave, stupid. The *shell* was flying a pirate flag."

I did our splitting-trick code in reverse, faster this time, hoping not to get spotted (we weren't), and we let the current carry us out to sea. So there we were, my brother and I: paddling along the shore. It was hardish work, plugging through the choppy little waves, but we were fine, we had lifejackets, and nobody had *told* us the ocean was out of bounds.

"What the hell's that?" demanded Dev.

*That* was a helicopter, going rackety rackety rackety, and *buzzing* us, so we could hardly see for the spray it was kicking up. We saw the rescue service logo, and we were indignant. Safety was not being served!

"What are you *doing*?" I yelled, waving my paddle. "You're a danger to shipping! You'll capsize us! Go away!"

"Go and play with your stupid flying machine somewhere else!"

Next thing, we got a page. It was the pilot talking, ton of bricks style. The rescue copter was looking for *us*. We'd failed to return our kayak, and we were hours overdue.

We were hauled out, scolded, and reported to Mom and Dad, who yelled at us, whole anxious parent thing, but it wasn't too bad. We made the right faces, said the right things, and it was soon over. I've *trained* Dev how to do that. He's pretty good, by now.

When my brother was a little kid I played baby-games with him, the ones I'd loved when I was a little kid myself. We were candy-coloured happy little animals, jumping the platforms, finding the strawberries and the gold coins, we dodged the smiley asteroids in our little spaceships, we explored jungles finding magic butterflies. We raced our Chocobos. I'm naturally patient, and I love make-believe; I didn't mind. My parents used to say, *you don't have to babysit, Sylvie*, but it was hardly ever a burden. I taught him everything he needed to know, and I was proud of how quick he was. Dev is not naturally patient, but he *sees* things in a flash.

We drifted apart when he was aged five, six, seven. Then one day when he was eight and I was twelve he came to my room with his Talbo' – the games platform small boys *had to have* at that time – and said he wanted me to play with him again.

"Girls don't play boy games," I told him (I was feeling depressed that day). "Boys don't play girl games. We won't like the same things. You just want to share my hub access, why not say so?"

"We DO like the same things," he said. "I miss you. No one else I know gets *carried away* in a game like you. You make it all come real. Please. I want you to take me with you."

So we compromised. I *did* let him share my hub access (with our parents approval), and use it without me. It's true, boy games mostly bore me. Racking up kills in the war-torn desert city, team sports (Bleegggh!), racing cars, fighter jets… Leaves me cold, and I think it's *because* I have the ability to get right into a game, and feel that it's real.

I can be a Commando, I can kill. But there has to be a reason that I care about, or you might as well be playing Tick Tack Toe, as far as I'm concerned. I want to play at things I would love to do. Managing a football team? The cockpit of a fighter jet or a formula car? No thank you! I don't want to be strapped down. I don't want to be confined in a machine. I want to run, swim, fight: use my arms and legs.

He plays with his friends now, and I play alone. But we still have our best times together. Unlike most gamers who are good at coding on the fly, we're not geeks. What we can do is like our magic powers. Our survival lore in the wilderness. And it's *logic.* Tricks like that kayak-twinning will work with just about any big game engine.

Our parents didn't ground us after the Rescue Helicopter incident. They only reproached us, and were sad, and generally played the tricks parents play to get you back on the leash. Luckily, everyone took our word that we'd lost track of time, and the kayaking log backed us up, because it showed us not receiving the pages telling us we were overdue.

This told us something interesting, but we kept our mouths shut. The adults blamed a paging glitch. (If they'd known we'd been off the resort world-map, for hours, things would have been different!). My brother came up with the idea that it was a *time* glitch, and we'd been slowed-down, in the unmapped sector, without realising it. He sat on the end of my bed, scrunching up his face. "Or speeded up. Whichever works."

I didn't tease him. Speeded-up/slowed down in a game is like 'what time is it in Tokyo?'; it's hard to keep it straight in your head. "Except we were in clock-time all along, bro. We weren't cruising the galaxy in our hypership. We were at *the resort.*"

It's a basic immersion venue. You stay for exactly the time it feels like: which is the starter level, safest way to play immersion games. The resort's meant for little kids. We just like it.

"Maybe we really did just lose track," said Dev.

But I knew we hadn't. Something had happened when we went through that flaw, something sly and twisted.

"No. There's really something screwy going on."

ϴ

These cheats who'd been annoying us were not normal cheats. Nothing like the legendary girl (supposed to be a girl, but who knows) called Kill Bill, who wasted hundreds of thousands of grunts in *Amerika Kombat*, never seemed to tire of her guaranteed headshots: and when one immersion server threw her out, she'd log onto another. We thought we'd seen our three characters in combat games, and they were cheating-good at racking up kills, but they mostly turned up in our own favourite scapes, like kayaking in the reed-beds at the resort, but *doing impossible things*.

We thought there were three of them. We *assumed* they were kids, which ought to have narrowed it down, because few kids have the kind of hub access I have. But of course they could be logging on anywhere in the world. We'd talked about trying to turn them in. But we couldn't figure out how to do it, if we couldn't identify them. And when we put our complaints together they sounded futile (even if you didn't count our own cheats against us). No adult would understand about a wrecked atmosphere, or the sacredness of respecting the reality of the make-believe. It was a victimless crime.

"They put our lives at risk?" suggested my brother. "Tempting us off the map like that. We could have got drowned and gone into shock."

Neither of us liked the sound of that. It was whiney and stupid.

We didn't go back to the kayaking channels, to find out if the flaw was still there. We had to lie low for a while; even though we'd escaped being blamed. Dev thought of telling someone what had really happened, not mentioning the cheats, just saying we'd hit a flaw, and letting the resort investigate. But that would be risky, because of our kayak-splitting, and I had a feeling the cheats would have covered their tracks, anyway. I said *wait.* They were sure to turn up again.

ϴ

Well, it happened when we were snowboarding, in a place called Norwegian Blue. We were on a secret level, but not off the map: cross-trekking over tableland to reach the most incredible of the Black slopes. Including one with a near vertical drop of a thousand feet into a fjord – and halfway down you hit the trees and you had to slalom like a deranged rattlesnake; an unbelievably wonderful experience.

It was night, blood-tingling cold under frosty stars. Everything was blue-tinged, otherworldly. We talked about deranged rattlesnakes, snowland bivvy building, triple flips, trapping for furs. New angles we might be able to wrangle with "Norwegian Blue" code, and things we better not try. And of course, the cheats.

"I wonder if we've been being stalked," I said, as we scooted our boards, one-footed. "We keep running into these same strange people, if they *are* people, lurking in our favourite 'scapes? Maybe we're not following them: maybe they're following us. But why? "

The tableland was a sea of great smooth frozen snow-waves. We reached a crest, rode on our bellies down the scarp, sailed far out into the hollow between two waves, and started another slow ascent. The air smelled of snow, crisp frost dusted our eyelashes, my leg muscles pumped, easy and strong. I was annoyed with myself for even raising the subject. The cheats were here, when they weren't here: stealing the beauty, making us feel watched.

"It's not us they're following," said Dev. "It's our hub access. You couldn't do the kind of cheats they do on ordinary levels that everybody can use. You need rich code, and not too much traffic. That's why we 'keep running into them'. Kill Bill can go on getting chucked off forever, there's millions of servers—"

"Yeah." There's no such thing as getting banned from *all* the public commercial servers. Not unless you're a child-molester or something.

"But our cheats need full hub access, if they want to fool around. And then, I suppose the best venues for fooling around and not getting caught, like the kayak channels, are the ones we like best, too."

I told you: Dev sees things. It was obvious, the way he put it, and I felt stupid. Also depressed, wondering how we were ever going to be free of this nagging intrusion—

Then the black silhouette of another trekker appeared, alone and off to our left, on the other side of the dangerous icefield zone; the trap where you had to avoid ending up. I hissed at Dev, *look—!*

We dropped to the snow, and I pulled up our powerful binoculars.

"It's Nostromo," I breathed. "Take a look."

One of the three default cheat costumes was white coveralls, with grease stains, and a NOSTROMO baseball cap, NOSTROMO being the name of the space freighter in the classic game and movie "Alien". That's what this guy was wearing, in the middle of this snowy wilderness. Dev took a look, and we grinned at each other.

"We have a deserter from the spaceship in *Alien.*"

We'd played *Alien Trilogy Remastered.* Maybe Dev had been too young, and the horror immersion too strong. Mom and Dad had put the *Dev wakes up screaming, we find this antisocial,* veto on it; to my regret. But he knew the story.

"Lost on this icy planet," he went on. "Unknown to him, he is being watched!"

"If you can't beat 'em, join 'em," I whispered: meaning, we can't ignore them, but we *can* turn them into characters. And hunt them down.

"If it bleeds, we can kill it," said Dev. "Do we have any weapons?"

"Soon can have," said I. "Let's arm ourselves."

I then had to argue Dev out of the heavy hardware. "You can't cheat on the weight or you'll lose fire power—"

"I *won't* slow us down. I've got tons of strength."

"Yes you will, and using guns at hub level is really bad for your brain. It wears out the violence inhibitors in your frontal lobes. They get fired up again and again, for no reason, and they don't understand."

"You talk about your brain as if it's a pet animal."

"At least my pet animal gets properly fed and looked after. *Yours* is starving in a dirty hutch with half a rotten carrot."

"*Your* brain is the brain of a sick, sick, blood-daubed Commando."

I don't like guns, I prefer a knife or a garrotte. "Because I want to feel something when I kill. That's emotionally much healthier than—"

We were having this charming conversation, pulling up our weapons of choice, cutting across the ice zone to intersect with Nostromo's path, and still looking for one more beautiful belly-glide, all at the same time. If we'd been concentrating, we'd have known there had to be a flaw somewhere, and we were liable to run into it. If we'd been believing in the game, like we should, we would never have been scooting along side by side *on an icefield.* That's nuts. But we were distracted, and it just happened. There were cracking noises: a crevasse opened, and we both fell into it, cursing like mad as the blue-white gleaming walls flew by.

We pulled our ripcords, but the fall did not slow down. Instead, everything went black.

ϴ

Black fade to grey, grey fade to blue. I sat up. I felt shaken and my head was ringing, but nothing was bleeding and no breakages. My Health was still okay, though. Dev was beside me, doing the same check.

We were not at the bottom of a crevasse. Our snowboards lay near us, looking supremely useless on a green, grassy field strewn with boulders. The sky was more violet than blue, suggesting high altitude. The sun had an egg-yolk, orangey tinge, the air had the clear heat you get in summer mountains. The peaks around the horizon, beautiful as anything I'd ever seen, seemed far higher than anything in Norwegian Blue.

"Where are we?" gasped Dev. He was looking sick; repairing the fall damage must have knocked more off his Health than it had off mine. I decided to pull up our emergency Medic—

"South America," I guessed. "The Andes…? Or a fantasy world."

"How are we going to get back?"

I thought that was a dumb question: then I realised I couldn't get at the First Aid. I couldn't get at anything in my cache. It was gone. I had the clothes I'd been wearing in Norwegian Blue, my knife, my garrotte and my vital signs Health patch. Nothing else—

"My God! They've wiped us!"

"Rebuild!" cried Dev, in a panic. "Rebuild! Quickly!"

But I couldn't rebuild, and I couldn't reach the code. Nor could Dev. The world looked solid, no glitches, no fuzzy bits. Nothing seemed to be wrong: but we were helpless. We stared at each other, outraged.

"This means war," I said.

Θ

There wasn't a doubt in our minds that the cheats had done this to us. Nostromo had seen us chasing him, swiftly pasted a crevasse in our path, and wiped us down to zero. We got up and walked around, abandoning our useless boards. Dev threw rocks. I dug my hands into the crispy turf. It felt the way only the best hub code feels: *intensely* real. The whole boulder field seemed to be live, none of it just décor.

"They're here somewhere," I said. "They have to be."

"They *don't* have to be," said Dev, unhappily. "They could have dumped us here helpless, and gone off laughing. Syl, *where are we*? I've never seen this place before, and I know all the adventure venues!"

I wished I had my Medic. My brother still wasn't looking good. I was afraid he would log out on me, and then I'd have quit too.

"C'mon, Dev. Think about it. Nostromo lured us here, the way the pirate cheat lured us into the white water. It's unfamiliar, but we didn't know there was white water in the resort reed beds until we went through that flaw. These guys are good, maybe they've found more secret levels than we have. But we're good too."

Something nagged at me, something bigger than I could believe, but I clung to my common-sense. "This is a live area. There's stuff to do here, if we knew the game or if we had a guide. There'll be exits, too. We'll find one, get our stuff back, and get back on the bad guys' trail."

The orange sun moved towards its setting. We saw some little weasely sort of creatures, only with more legs, that watched us from a distance. We met huge golden furred spiders, the size of a cat, and shy but friendly. They'd come up to us and lay a palp, I mean, one of their front feet, on our hands, and look at us with big clustered ruby eyes. They liked being stroked, and scratched behind their front eyes. We thought about eating the berries that grew on the crispy turf-stuff.

But we didn't find the flaw, we didn't recover our caches, and we didn't find any gates back to the hub or hidden treasures that might have helped us out – though we slapped and poked at hopeful looking rocks until our hands were sore. Finally, we found the cheats. They were camped in a ravine, on what seemed like the southern end (in relation to that sunset) of the boulder field. They had a domed bivvy, thatched with lichen, and a fire a circle of stones. A bucket stood on a flat rock by the stream that ran near their hide-out. We were sick with envy. We felt as if we'd been wandering naked, unable to fix ourselves, for *hours*.

"Dev," I whispered, "You're going to go down there, and tell them your sister is out on the hillside, Health gone. Tell them you don't know what to do, because I'm saying this is a real place, and refusing to log out, and I'm going into shock. White flag, surrender. Cry, if you can. Bring one over here, and I'll be waiting in ambush."

"Pick them off one by one," he agreed. "Cool."

He was still looking sick, but he was back in the game. I remembered the flash of an adult face I'd seen in the reed beds, back at the resort, and I felt unsure. Had that been real? *Usually* adult gamers are normal, and harmless, but there are the rare predators, everyone knows that—

But we chose our ambush, and I felt better.

"Go on. Bring me back a fine fat cheat to choke."

The sun was darkening to blood colour, and I could feel the growing chill through my "Norwegian Blue" snowboarding clothes. I clung to the wire looped over my gloved hands, thinking weirdly that the garrotte was part of me, a lifeline, and if it vanished I would be *really* trapped—

Dev came back up from the ravine, a cheat close behind. It was the Native American costumed-cheat, with a red and black blanket round his shoulders like a cloak. My brother looked very small and defenceless. Sometimes when a game seems very real it's hard to kill, but I had no trouble at all this time. I jumped from behind, and my wire snapped viciously around the cheat's throat… But someone had also grabbed *me* by the forearms, and I had to let go or they'd have broken my bones.

It was Nostromo, I could tell by the white sleeves. I screamed. I kicked, I writhed and yelled, it was useless. He held me off the ground, like a rag doll, laughing. The Native American had Dev. They carried us to their camp (we stopped struggling, because it was pointless): tied us up and sat cross-legged, staring at us and grinning in triumph. Up close I was sure they were real adults, and I was scared. But I couldn't struggle. My head was spinning. Their eyes glittered, and seemed to dance out of their faces. The third cheat, the pirate, was a woman, about six foot tall. She had black shiny hair hanging in wild locks from under her three cornered hat, green eyes with kohl around them, and skin the colour of cinnamon. She stood up, grabbed my head, and stuck a slip of paper underneath my tongue. "They're short of glucose," she announced. "Near to blacking out. What'll we do with them, Mister Parker? Qua'as?"

"I say we smoke a pipe of peace," said the Native American.

He fetched the pipe from his pack, stuffed it from a pouch he wore at his waist, and lit it with a handful of the licheny stuff, dipped in the flame of the fire. I watched him do these things, and my skin began to creep, my heart began to beat like thunder, though I didn't know why.

"Mister Parker", the Nostromo crewman, cut us loose. The pipe went round, and I drew in the 'smoke'. The sugar rush almost knocked me sideways, but I managed to keep a straight face.

"Oooh, that was restorative!" gasped Mr Parker.

"Best drug in the universe," chuckled the pirate queen.

"Gonna be our planet's *major* export one day—"

"Moron. The galaxy is full of sugars. My money's on Bach."

They laughed, high-fived each other and kind of *sparkled*; and I knew why, because I love and depend on glucose too. But the Native American was looking at my brother, and frowning. Dev didn't look restored.

We finished the pipe and the pirate queen put it aside.

"Now," she said, in a rich, wild, laughing voice. "I'm Bonny." She tossed back the lace at her cuff and tipped a lean brown hand to the man in the red and black blanket. "This is Qua'as, the Transformer. He's Canadian, but don't hold that against him, he's pretty cool. Mister Parker, our engineer, you have met. So who the devil are *you*, and why are you plaguing us? Do tell."

"Get real," said Mr Parker, "if you'll pardon the expression. There are only, what is it now…? Say, fourteen other people trained for this that you *could* be, assumin' you are not software dreamed up by Mission Control. Why the kiddy disguises? What was that with the *garrotte*?"

"Did no one ever tell you, little sister," said Qua'as, "that only what is dearest to your heart survives the drop back into normal space? What does that make you? A low-down disgusting violence perv? Eh? Eh?"

That's when I realised for the first time that I'd kept my weapons, but Dev's AK and ammo had vanished when we were wiped. I felt myself blush, I felt that Qua'as was right…

"What do you mean 'normal space'—? I demanded.

"Let us go!" cried Dev. "We're not afraid of you! You plagued *us*, you spoiled everything and we tracked you down! Soon as we log out, we're going to turn you in for corrupting the code and scaring us!"

But my brother's voice was thin and frail, a ghost's voice. The cheats glowed with life, and strength and *richness*: richer than any game avatar I'd ever heard of. I could *feel* them, teeming and buzzing with layers of complexity, deeper than my mind could reach—

"Oh no," said Bonny, staring at me, and I stared back: thinking she was looking straight at *me*, *myself*. Back through the root server, through the real world, into my head, my mind; wherever "Sylvie" really lived—

"Oh NO!" groaned Qua'as. "You're real children, aren't you?"

"Y-yes?" quavered Dev.

"Yes," I said. "Why shouldn't we be real?"

Mr Parker smacked both his hands to his cap, and held on to it, bug-eyed. "OH, MAN. We are so busted! GAME OVER!"

They all started to grin, weird big identical grins, and suddenly, with a rush of relief, I knew what was going on. "Oh my God you're *test pilots*! We've accidentally hacked into a research level. That's it, isn't it…?"

That explained the weirdness, and the super-convincing feel of everything. Dev and I were copping a sneak preview of a hyper-real immersion scape in development! So now our cheats were in trouble, because the gameplay was supposed to be deadly secret until its launch, but whatever had happened couldn't be our fault, we were *kids*—

The grins slowly vanished. "We've been mistaken." said Qua'as the Transformer, seriously. "We thought you were colleagues, in disguise."

"Or law enforcement," added Mr Parker. "We can insert ourselves into hub games, we do it for light relief. We're not supposed to."

"Come on. You're *test pilots*. Game development test pilots."

"Close," said Bonny. "But it's no scape we're testing."

Qua'as heaved a sigh. "This is not a game, little girl. It's a planet. You are approximately 560 light years from home right now."

My brother cried out, "Mom!"

He toppled over, his legs still tied, and curled up into a whimpering ball. I kept my head, but I couldn't speak. I was too busy refusing to believe this insane story. But fear ramped up, like in a nightmare when someone says something unbelievable that you know is true, and fear ramps up, because you know you it's not a dream, you're lost for real—

"I don't believe you."

"You'd *better* believe it, kid," said Mr Parker. "This is not a drill. You are handling the situation, but your friend isn't."

"He's my brother."

"Okay, your brother. You have to trust us to get you back, or your brother will die. Not die as in wake up at home. Plain dead."

"What are your names?" asked the pirate queen, more gently.

"I'm Sylvia Murphy-Weston. My brother is Devan Murphy-Weston."

"You have full hub access; are those names your access IDs?"

"Yes."

I could tell she wanted to ask more questions, but Qua'as put his hand on her arm. "That's all we need. We know the situation now. And you know we're your friends—?"

He raised his eyebrow at me, and I nodded.

"So we're onto it, Sylvie, and you and Devan will get home fine."

They freed our legs, and retired inside their shelter: I hugged Dev, and told him we would be all right. Mr Parker came out again, bringing blankets, a warm sugar drink in a skin bottle, and a bunch of jerky strips.

"Is this the friendly golden spiders?" asked Dev, unhappily.

"No, it's another animal, a kind of small eight-legged sheep."

"Is it *real*?"

"You should be asking are *you* real, kid. But you are. You're not a game avatar here. When you dropped into normal with us, you were piggybacked on our translation code, which drew the necessary chemicals and mass out of this planet to make bodies for you two, same as it did for us. You became material. You can eat here, and you can die."

"So… so I have *two bodies*, right now?" said Devan, hesitantly.

"Yeah. It's possible, but it's dangerous."

Θ

We ate the jerky, drank the sweet stuff, and I didn't tell Dev I thought the "eight-legged sheep" was a little white lie. It was cold as a night camped out in the high range country on Earth: where I have never been in my body; only in an immersion game. We slept, wrapped in the blankets, hugging each other for warmth. We weren't invited into the shelter. Sometime in the middle of the night I woke up. The pirate had emerged. She glanced at me, and headed up the ravine. Dev was still sleeping. I hesitated to leave him alone, but decided to follow her.

Where was she going? I hoped for a door in the air, a flaw I could mark somehow, and it would take us back to the hub. She climbed up onto the top of a big boulder. I followed, quietly as I could. She was lying with her hands behind her head and the three-cornered hat beside her, just gazing up at the stars. I don't know stars, but they looked different. They were very bright.

"Hi," I said.

"Hi," said the pirate, smiling up into the great jewelled abyss.

"If it's bad to have two bodies," I said. "What about you guys?"

"We're fine," she said. "My other body, which is not much use to me, is on life support back home. I'm in no danger, whatever happens to me here. Your brother Dev is in trouble because he doesn't have that protection." She sat up, smiling at me. "But you do, don't you, Sylvie?"

"Huh?"

"It's a requirement," she said. "Don't believe Mr Parker and Qua'as, this isn't another planet, that's crazy talk. It's an experience that's going to be available to everyone, like immersion gaming. But right now *interspatials* – that's what we call ourselves – have to be a special kind of person. You need to leave a body behind, on full life support, but that's only half of it. You also need a *fully realised non-physical self*, and the ability to commit to your non-physical body, as if it's flesh and blood. Someone like you would be ideal, Sylvie."

My stomach turned over, and my heart thumped. For a moment the world went *white,* sheer nothingness white, and yet she was still with me, I could feel her presence. I fought with myself to *stay calm.*

It only lasted a moment. Then the mountain world came back.

"Now I know you're faking. Why do you *talk* like that…? 'We are so busted' 'Oh man'… 'Game Over'. 'This is not a drill'… You sound like my kid brother. Are you guys even real? Or are you just bots?"

She tipped back her head and laughed, full throated. I was feeling very confused, angry and confused, but she'd pushed my buttons, and she knew it. Sometimes I'm very lonely.

"I'm real as real gets," said the pirate queen. "What about you?"

A small rock rattled, behind me, and I heard Dev's breathing: he'd woken up and followed me. Bonny must have heard him too, but she kept on looking at me.

"You've been stalking us," I said. "Why did you do that? Creeps."

"Maybe to test you out. Maybe it was an audition."

Dev scrambled onto the top of the boulder, and stumbled over to grab my hand. He was shaking.

"Leave her alone!" he shouted. "You're lying. You're not special. You're cheating fools, and this is just a stupid lame glitchy game! "

Bonny shook her head, slowly: sad and happy at the same time.

She was like an outlaw angel, breaking all the rules.

Θ

They let us go. I don't remember anything after Bonny shook her head, but Dev woke up in the hospital, and I woke up in my bed at home. Then it was pure hell for a while. Whatever had happened, whichever scenario you believed, doing what the cheats did without training had hateful consequences. We had the choice between angry, scared, tearful parents; psych tests, medical exams, and the same questions over and over, when we were awake. Or drugged sleep, and the most horrible nightmares. When we skyped each other, Dev in hospital and me at home, we couldn't do anything but stare, mumbling Bad*! Bad!* at each other. We couldn't deal with sentences or anything.

But I got better. Dev did too, although it took longer.

The morning after he came home from hospital, I got into my wheelchair by myself: which I hate to do, because it reminds me that I keep on getting worse. Two years ago I could casually sling myself into the chair I had then, now it's like climbing Everest. I settled my head into the support, I dehooked and rehooked the tubes I needed, which is something else I *hate* to do, and I whizzed along to Dev's room…

I hardly visit my family anymore. They come to me.

I used to fight like a tiger to keep myself going, and it made no difference, I just got so tired I couldn't see. Now I love my bed. It's the only place I have left to stand. Although of course I'm lying down. The only territory I can still defend. My problems aren't fatal: that's the worst thing, in some ways. I'm fifteen. I could live for decades like this: treating my brain like a pet animal, and trying to ignore the sad sack that used to be my body. That's what Mom and Dad still desperately wanted. But I'd talked to them (after recovering from our adventure far faster than my healthy little brother). The Interspatial people had talked to them too.

It hadn't been so long, only a few days. Dev was sitting up in bed, looking fine, and that was a relief. "I know," he said at once. "Mom and Dad told me." (I was grateful to them). "Are you going to accept?"

"It's a terrific opportunity. It's just like me going to college, Dev, only a college where I'll be a highflyer, not a sad sack, and I'll be *normal*—"

"Are you sure they're okay, these Interspatial people?"

"Mom and Dad have checked it all out."

My mom and dad, as you've probably guessed, are in the same business. They'd never heard of the Interspatial experiment (it was very secret), before this happened to us, but digital world is their world and now that they'd investigated the research, they were impressed.

Dev just looked at me, and waited.

"Okay, obviously there's stuff we haven't been told. And there was that strange thing about the game scape being on another planet. But Mom and Dad are satisfied, and—

I wasn't sure what was real, and what was cheats. But I was sure about the taste of icy mountain air in my throat. The feel of my muscles pumping, the clear heat of that sun; the power and the intensity of life running through me. If I'd been stalked, and hooked, and reeled in, I didn't much care. I was willing. It was a victimless crime—

"And *what*?"

"I'm going to accept."

Dev took a deep breath, nodded, and rolled with the punch. "Hey, what if I come too? I'd get a terrific education in games development, which is what I want to do. You'd train as an interspatial crash dummy, and we could still be a team—"

"Not this time Dev. I *can't* take you with me. I need you to stay at home, with Mom and Dad, and… and watch my back. "

My little brother, my best friend.

"Because you can't resist." said Dev, who sees things. "But you know it could turn out weird. Cool. You'll have to have a safe word, to send me, that I know and nobody else does—"

"Something like that. Except nothing's going to go wrong. "

***To be continued...***

# About the Author

**Gwyneth Jones** is a writer and critic of genre fiction, who has also written for teenagers using the name Ann Halam. She's won a few awards but doesn't let it get her down. She lives in Brighton, UK, with her husband and two cats called Milo and Tilly, curating assorted pondlife in season. She's a member of the Soil Association, the Sussex Wildlife Trust, Frack Free Sussex and the Green Party; and an Amnesty International volunteer. Hobbies include watching old movies, playing Zelda and staring out of the window.

# New from NewCon Press

**Andrew Wallace – Celebrity Werewolf**

Suave, sophisticated, erudite and charming, Gig Danvers seems too good to be true. He appears from nowhere to champion humanitarian causes and revolutionise science, including the design and development of Product 5: the first organic computer to exceed silicon capacity; but are his critics right to be cautious? Is there a darker side to this enigmatic benefactor, one that is more in keeping with his status as the Celebrity Werewolf?

**David Gullen – Shopocalypse**

A Bonnie and Clyde for the Trump era, Josie and Novik embark on the ultimate roadtrip. In a near-future re-sculpted politically and geographically by climate change, they blaze a trail across the shopping malls of America in a printed intelligent car (stolen by accident), with a hundred and ninety million LSD-contaminated dollars in the trunk, buying shoes and cameras to change the world.

**Rachel Armstrong – Invisible Ecologies**

The story of Po, an ambiguously gendered boy who shares an intimate connection with a nascent sentience emerging within the Po delta: the bioregion upon which the city of Venice is founded. Carried by the world's oceans, the pair embark on a series of extraordinary adventures and, as Po starts school, stumble upon the Mayor's drastic plans to modernise the city and reshape the future of the lagoon and its people.

**Ian Creasey – The Shapes of Strangers**

British SF's best kept secret, Ian Creasey is one of our most prolific and successful short fiction writers, with 18 stories published in *Asimov's*, a half dozen or more in *Analog*, and appearances in a host of the major SF fiction venues. *The Shapes of Strangers* showcases Ian's perceptive and inventive style of science fiction, gathering together fourteen of his finest tales, including stories that have been selected for *Year's Best* anthologies.

CPSIA information can be obtained
at www.ICGtesting.com
Printed in the USA
LVHW092319310319
612502LV00001B/146/P

9 781912 950164